Praise for Gail Dayton's

# The Compass Rose

"With unadulterated sensuality that practically ignites the pages and a fantasy quest that is as masterfully intricate as it is entertaining, Dayton's *The Compass Rose* will absolutely blow away fans of romance-powered fantasy. In a word: wow!"
—Barnes & Noble's *Explorations* newsletter

"Gail Dayton has created a world that is so colorful and vivid readers will feel they made an adventurous visit to this enchanting realm."
—*The Best Reviews*

"*The Compass Rose* captured me from the first page.... Gail Dayton eloquently weaves a saga of unrequited love with the fear of rejection that haunts us all [and] cleverly and sagely reveals the heart and soul that unites a group of strangers into a family."
—*Fallen Angel Reviews*

"Top Pick, 4-1/2 stars: Court intrigues and romantic interludes keep the plot moving at a brisk pace."
—*Romantic Times BOOKclub*

# GAIL DAYTON

# The Barbed Rose

LUNA™

www.LUNA-Books.com

LUNA™

First edition March 2006

THE BARBED ROSE

ISBN 0-373-80225-0

www.LUNA-Books.com

**Printed in U.S.A.**

To April and Rhys.
You make me proud.
And to Jason, who does, too.

## Cast of Characters

**Kallista Varyl,** Captain in the Adaran army, naitan of the North, lightning thrower, Godstruck of the One

**Torchay Omvir,** Sergeant, Kallista's bodyguard and godmarked ilias

**Stone Varyl vo'Tsekrish,** former Tibran Warrior, godmarked ilias

**Fox Varyl vo'Tsekrish,** former Tibran Warrior, fighting partner to Stone, godmarked ilias

**Aisse Varyl vo'Haav,** Tibran woman, godmarked ilias

**Obed im-Shakiri,** Southron trader, godmarked ilias

**Lorynda Varyl,** twin infant daughter of Kallista and Torchay

**Rozite Varyl,** twin infant daughter of Kallista and Stone

**Niona Varyl,** infant daughter of Aisse and Fox

**Merinda Kyndir,** Adaran East naitan healer

**Serysta Reinine,** ruler of Adara, North naitan truthsayer

**Keldrey,** Serysta's bodyguard and reinas

**Leyja,** Serysta's bodyguard and reinas

**Ferenday,** Serysta's bodyguard and reinas

**Syr,** Serysta's bodyguard and reinas

**Gweric,** Tibran male magic hunter

**Joh Suteny,** former Adaran guard lieutenant, convict

**Viyelle Torvyll,** Prinsipella of the Adaran prinsipality (province) of Shaluine and government courier

**Karyl & Kami Varyl,** Kallista's twin sisters by blood

**Sanda Torvyll,** Prinsipas of Shaluine, Viyelle's birth mother

**Saminda Torvyll,** Prinsep of Shaluine, Viyelle's aunt by blood and Second Mother

**Kendra Torvyll,** Prinsipella of Shaluine, Viyelle's sedil and cousin by blood

**Vanis Kevyr,** Prinsipas of Shaluine, Viyelle's birth father

**Mowbray Syndir,** Prinsipella of Shaluine

**Tiray Syndir,** Prinsipella of Shaluine

**Dessa Torvyll,** Prinsipella of Shaluine

**Bella Torvyll,** Prinsipella of Shaluine

**Huyis Uskenda,** Adaran general in Ukiny

**Huryl Kovallyk,** Serysta's High Steward

**Domnia Varyl,** founder of the Varyl bloodline, West naitan and prelate

**Kallandra,** North naitan, military lightning thrower

**Miray,** Kallandra's bodyguard

**Tylle,** Adaran guard lieutenant

**Elliane,** East naitan healer

**Fenetta,** North naitain farspeaker at Adaran court

**Omunda,** Chief prelate of Arikon and Adara

**Oskina,** Rebel leader

**Ashbel,** Demon

**Ataroth,** Demon

**Untathel,** Demon

**Xibyth,** Demon

**Tchyrizel,** Demon

**Keqwith,** Demon

**Khoriseth,** Demon

**Zughralithiss,** Demon

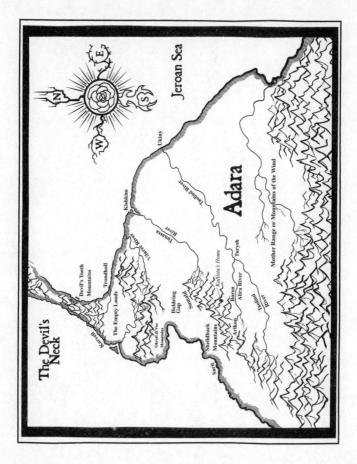

# CHAPTER ONE

"*H*alt. Stand and identify yourself and your business."

Kallista Varyl, Captain Naitan of the Reinine's Own, just recalled from extended leave, somehow managed to refrain from swearing. The guard at the Mountain Gate leading into Arikon was only doing his duty. He couldn't know the urgency riding her.

She saluted, snapped off her name and command. "I've been ordered to Arikon by the Reinine herself." She handed over a copy of her orders.

The guard's eyes widened when he saw the seals and signatures on the paper, but still he blocked her path.

Harnesses jangled as another in Kallista's party pushed her way forward and saluted. "Courier Viyelle Torvyll, Prinsipella of Shaluine." The courier began formally, then switched to a familiar, friendly tone as she addressed the guard. "You know me, Daltrey. You were standing duty here when I rode out to fetch the naitan back. This *is* Captain Varyl. These are her iliasti. I can swear to their identity. I know them all from the last time they were in the city, at court. The captain has urgent business. Do you honestly want to delay them?"

Kallista remembered the prinsipella from last year as well, and not fondly. The young woman had been a useless, annoying, mischief-making blot on Adaran society, and that was before the quarrelsome magic had got hold of her. Still, she seemed to have found something better to do with herself since then, joining the courier corps.

The prinsipella-courier had brought the Reinine's orders to Kallista along with a warning of the rebellion stirring down on the plains. Viyelle had traveled back to the capital with Kallista's party, fought through rebel ambushes with them, and at this moment, Kallista was liking the courier more and more.

"I'm sure you can, Prinsipella." The guard, who had to be nearing the end of his military service, which would make him all of twenty-two, blushed under Viyelle's attention, but he did not budge. "But rules are rules and with this rebellion on, it's worth my head if I break them. The captain must be identified by an officer she served under previously." He signaled to another footguard.

"I'll go for you," Viyelle said. "It's on my way, and I'm mounted. I'll be faster. My orders were to get the captain here, but she's not here till she's reported in, is she?" She turned to Kallista. "I'll leave your horse in the palace stables so you can find it later."

"Yes, fine, *go*." Kallista waved a hand and the courier clattered off at the best speed she could make. Perhaps she did mean to make amends for last year's calamities, as she said. Kallista decided to reserve judgment, watch and see how things unfolded. This guard, however…

Kallista glared at him, thinking hot and angry thoughts. He cleared his throat, stiffened to even more rigid attention, and didn't move.

"Don't twist yourself into a knot," Torchay murmured from beside her, trying to calm her temper when it didn't want to be calmed.

Sergeant Torchay Omvir had been doing that sort of thing for the past ten years, first as her assigned military bodyguard, and for the past year as her ilias—one of her temple-bound mates. He was an exception to the old saying that redheads have fiery tempers. Kallista's temper was many times hotter than his, but her hair was so dark a brown as to be almost black, while Torchay's hair was a deep, pure, true dark red that curled wildly when not confined ruthlessly in a military queue as it was now.

"Look around you," he said. "Have you ever seen this many people at the Mountain Gate? Something's happened."

She wanted to let her anger rage, but Torchay's murmur reached her, despite all. She looked.

Here on the north side of the city, where Arikon backed up into the sharp beginnings of the Shieldback Mountains, the walls didn't rise so high as those facing the valley to the east and south. The mountain itself gave protection to Arikon. Fewer people lived in the mountain valleys than down in the vast eastern plains, and those who lived in the mountains beyond the Shieldbacks found it easier and quicker to come through the Heldring Gap to the plains and thus to Arikon, though the distance might be greater. In all the times Kallista had been in Adara's capital city, the Mountain Gate had never seen more than a few dozen individuals seeking admittance, even on the busiest days.

Today, merchants driving carts laden with household goods were lined up behind farmers driving livestock before them, and they stood behind craftsmen bearing the looms or anvils or hammers and saws of their trade, all waiting for access to the city. Old people rested by the side of the road. Children chased each other, playing loud games with best friends just met while their parents tried to keep track of them. Kallista had been vaguely aware of the crowds as this half of their ilian approached the gate, but she hadn't truly *seen* them.

Guards searched baggage, and one by one, those wanting

into the city filed up to a table set before an army colonel with a single row of red ribbons fluttering fore-and-aft from her shoulders and a male naitan dressed in North magic blue. He looked weary, as if he'd been working magic for hours on end.

The next in line came up to the table and laid her hands flat on the rough wooden top. The naitan covered both her hands with his, and the colonel began asking her questions. A few minutes later, the naitan nodded, the woman gathered up her goods, joined the family waiting near the gate and together, they entered the city.

"Truthsayer?" Kallista spoke her thought aloud, not seeking an answer. No wonder the man looked tired, if he had to verify every person wanting to enter the city. She shivered with a sudden chill. "You're right, Torchay. Something has happened. Something bad."

And the rest of their ilian was on the road alone, traveling to the northern edges of Adara and Torchay's family, away from the rebellion disturbing the eastern plain. Her babies—twin daughters—were so small, only ninety days old. Not even three months yet. How could she have left them? What kind of mother was she, to be here, instead of there, with her children?

"Obed should have gone with them." Her voice was bitter, angry, quiet. "You should have gone with them. How can they travel safely all the way to Korbin Prinsipality with only one able-bodied fighter? We sent him alone to guard a pregnant woman, a blind man, a healer and two tiny babies."

She whirled her horse to ride north and find them, keep them safe. The two with her—the best fighters in their ilian—would never leave her.

Torchay threw himself at her reins and missed, landing hard in the lingering puddles on the rocky road. Kallista called for speed and her mount did its best, but there were too many people crowded in the road and she wasn't—quite—willing to sacrifice someone else's child to save her own. Obed caught up with her easily, wresting the reins from her hands.

Kallista fought for the reins, for control of her horse. Confused and frightened, the animal reared. Obed caught her around her waist and pulled her onto the saddle in front of him. Kallista's fear flashed into anger and she turned it on Obed, her fury rising as he accepted her blows without expression, without reaction, simply allowing her to rain them down on him.

"Damn you," she raged. "Don't you care about *anything?*" She wanted to mark him, to cut him open and see if he would bleed. Her beautiful, exotic Southron ilias with his black hair, brown skin and the tattoos of his devotion to the One God written on his face and body was beyond anything in Kallista's experience. She didn't know how to deal with him. And just now, that infuriated her.

Like the rest of their ilian, he'd been marked by the One and bound by that godstruck magic into a whole as unlike other iliani as a military troop was from the rabble of a mob. But since her daughters' birth, Obed had been pulling back, withdrawing into himself until he seemed a stone carving, rather than a man. And she didn't know why.

His behavior worried her, for more reasons than the personal. It drove cracks through their ilian, because much as she tried to hide her hurt at Obed's actions, she couldn't quite, and that made the others angry for her sake.

Torchay pushed his way into the space around the restive horses, limping slightly. Kallista refused the rising guilt, but it seeped inside her anyway. She'd caused that limp. Obed released her into Torchay's arms and he pulled her from the saddle, holding her tight when she would have turned her anger on him. He wouldn't let her strike him.

"You don't want to cause any more of a scene. Not here." He

spoke into her ear, holding her head still with one long-fingered hand planted on the back of her skull. "*Think,* Kallista. If you ride out of here, you're more likely to lead the danger to them. You're the godstruck. You're the one the rebels will watch, if they're watching any of us. You don't know for certain that there is any danger at all, do you?"

Gradually, his words sank in and made sense. She did not want to make anything worse than it already was. She stopped struggling and Torchay loosened his hold. He didn't let go of her entirely—he knew her too well for that—but he would know she was listening now.

"You have to trust in the plan." He led her back toward their place near the gate where his well-trained horse waited, calmly cropping grass. Obed followed, leading Kallista's mount.

"They're my daughters too, remember?" Torchay said. "Blood or no, Lorynda and Rozite are both mine. Don't you think I want to be there myself, watching over them, as much as you do? But this was the plan. To draw attention our way, make anyone interested come after *us.* And for that, we need Obed here.

"If we're drawing attention to you, I want our best fighters protecting you, and that's Obed and me. I won't risk you, too. We fought through rebels more than once on our way here, and more than once, it was Obed who made the difference. Trust the plan. Trust Stone and Fox and Merinda to keep them safe."

"Fox is blind, and Merinda's a healer, not a fighter."

"You know as well as I do that Fox's blindness doesn't make any difference in his ability to fight. That extra sense of *knowing* he has from your magic gives him eyes in the back of his head. You've seen it. You know it. And a healer's exactly what they need right now with Aisse so close to her time. You brought Merinda into the ilian. She'll watch over the girls and Aisse like they were her own."

The *durissas* rites weren't used much in the cities any more, but in the countryside, in the mountains and plains, they were still fairly common. During a crisis a person could be temporarily made ilias, or two iliani could bind themselves into one, swearing to guard the others—especially the children—as their own.

Merinda had come out from the capital, a cheerful, comfortable tabby cat of a woman, to help with the twins' births and wait for Aisse's baby, so she had been present and available when Courier Torvyll had brought word of the emergency. Merinda had accepted Kallista's offer, taken the bracelet from Kallista's own arm bound together with the band from Torchay's ankle, and become part of their ilian just before they'd left on their separate journeys.

Usually a *durissas* bond lasted only as long as the crisis, though sometimes it became permanent, if a child resulted or the parties agreed. In this instance, Kallista didn't care much which way it went, as long as Merinda took care of those who needed her. Kallista couldn't do it, and it was ripping her apart.

At the gate again, Torchay looped an arm around her neck for a rough hug. "They'll be all right."

"How do you know?" Kallista couldn't stop the retort, her fears eating holes in her. "You don't have any idea how they're faring."

"But you do."

*Did she?* She should. At the least, she ought to be able to find out. Kallista took a deep breath, fighting for calm. Could she do it?

Turning her back on the city, she faced North and opened herself. *There,* that was the sound of all the people dammed up before the gate, talking, laughing, complaining. She named it and set it aside, letting it fade from her consciousness. And *that* was the horses, and *those* noises belonged to the other animals—cows, chickens, dogs, cats. Kallista closed them from her mind as well.

She shut out the sound of the wind whipping the flags atop the city walls and making the trees whisper to each other. One at a time, she identified and eliminated the sounds falling on her physical ears. With everything that was in her, she listened for *more*. And she heard nothing.

No hum from the mountains. No whisper from the sun. No joyous song of magic.

She wanted to scream with frustration. Once, she had destroyed a demon with the magic she wielded. Today, she could not destroy a gnat.

Kallista pulled back inside herself and let the physical world back in. Other female naitani gradually lost their magic during pregnancy and gradually got it back after the birth. Kallista's had vanished all at once, and it had yet to reappear. At least she still had the assurance of the magical links binding her to her iliasti that the magic would return.

She wouldn't worry—hadn't worried about the magic's absence until Courier Torvyll had arrived at their mountain home, where they had retreated for the birth of their children, with news of the rebellion spreading from the plains westward into the mountains, toward Arikon. Now Kallista wanted it back. The sooner her magic returned, the sooner she could help quash the rebellion and go back home.

Needing the reassurance, Kallista reached for the place deep inside her where her magic slept, where the links with her iliasti abided, and touched them with incorporeal fingers. There was Torchay and there, Obed. And—stormwaves of panic rolled through her.

She caught Torchay's arm to keep from falling. *"They're gone."*

"What?" He put an arm around her, held her up. "Who's gone?"

"The others. Fox and Stone and Aisse. The links are gone. I can't find them." She wrapped her hand in his tunic and held on tight, shaking. "Oh Goddess, they're gone."

"Are you sure?"

"Of course I'm sure," she snapped, again taking refuge from fear in anger. "The links were there. Now they're not."

"Look again."

She already was, scarcely aware of Obed dismounting, coming to stand close, at guard. She rummaged through that hidden place. Obed, there. Torchay *there*. Fox…*not* there. Nor Stone. Nor Aisse. Frantic, she *reached,* as high and wide and far as she could. And she could not get outside her own skin.

"Oh Goddess, oh Goddess," she whispered over and over in prayer, having no other words, trusting the One to know what she prayed for.

"Kallista." Torchay shook her. He caught her face in one hand and turned it up to his. "*Captain.* Don't fall apart on us now. We need you. *They* need you. Don't assume the worst. Isn't that what you've always told me?"

"Prepare for the worst," she mumbled through numb lips.

"Prepare, yes. But don't anticipate trouble before it comes."

"Yes." She gathered up all her fear and shoved it into a mental box, sitting on it to get it closed. She stiffened her knees by sheer force of will and made herself stand on her own, away from Torchay's support. "Yes, you're right. They are a long way off, after all. A hundred leagues or more. Almost two, if they've already reached Sumald."

Goddess, if only Torchay or Obed could search on their own—but all the magic was hers to control. Without her at the center to power it, the rest had no connection to each other. Kallista took a deep breath, swallowed, blinked her eyes dry. "We've never been so far apart, have we? Not since the links formed. And with my magic the way it is…"

"Aye. I'm sure that's the only problem." Torchay still watched her with haunted eyes.

Obed took a moment from watching the crowd to look at her. Was that concern in his eyes? Who was it for?

"Are you all right, then?" Torchay called her attention back from its wandering.

"Yes." She wiped her face. She hated tears, most especially her own, but since the babies, she hadn't been able to control the stupid leaking. "I'm fine."

"Good." He tilted his head toward the gate, a spiral strand of red hair escaping from his queue to slide across one eye.

Kallista followed his direction and saw an officer striding toward them—a general by the layered fringe of red ribbons sprouting from the shoulders of her dun-brown infantry tunic. A few more paces and Kallista recognized General Huyis Uskenda. She had been in command of the garrison where Kallista was serving last year during the beginning of the Tibran invasion.

The Tibran king had sent his boats and warriors—and his cannons—to take Adara from those who lived here. He might have done it, but for the magic that struck Kallista on the city walls of Ukiny the morning the Tibran army invasion very nearly succeeded.

"General." Kallista drew herself to attention and saluted, relief ringing through her. Uskenda was one of the better commanders in Adara's army, more concerned with effectiveness than appearance or her own comfort. "Captain Naitan Kallista Varyl reporting for duty. I would like to request a troop escort for my family, General, to—"

"Wouldn't we all, Captain. You're not getting it." The general's gaze paused on Torchay, acknowledging his presence, then moved on to Obed. "Who's this?"

"My ilias, Obed im-Shakiri. You may have heard I married

after you sent me to the capital last year. There are six of us in all now. We have two babies and our other ilias is pregnant." Kallista raised her right hand to show the single bracelet from her only female ilias. "They're traveling alone to—"

"You vouch for him?" Uskenda ignored Kallista's implied plea. "You and your sergeant I know, but—"

"He's no rebel." Kallista risked interrupting the general. "He's godmarked like the rest of us. Like our other iliasti. They're carrying out a request from the—"

"We have no troops to spare," the general snapped the words out, voice hard as iron. "Do not ask again, Captain. Do not even *hint* at asking."

Kallista braced to hard attention, staring straight ahead at nothing at all. "No, General, I won't."

Uskenda didn't waste another moment, turning on her heel. Kallista fell in behind her, Obed and Torchay on guard at either side. They marched past the long lines of people waiting their turn with the truthsayer. Their frantic desperation to get behind the safety of the walls and their resentment toward those who seemed to be bypassing the system gathered thick enough to make an almost physical barrier for the small party to push through.

Something had happened. Kallista knew it, but didn't dare ask what. Not now. And sergeants didn't question generals about anything, so Torchay couldn't ask. She slid a glance toward Obed, the civilian. Would he understand what she wanted to know? And if he did, would he ask?

He met her look, flicked his eyes toward the crowd, the truthsayer, the full troop of guards at the gate, then looked back at Kallista. He somehow bowed without moving his head. "General," he said, his exotic Southron accent stronger than usual, "has something occurred that makes all this security necessary? Why a truthsayer?"

"You don't know?" Uskenda addressed her response to Kallista.

"We've been on the road almost a week and the courier took even longer coming with the Reinine's orders, so our news of Arikon is a good two weeks old." Kallista tugged at her gloves, a fresh attack of worry making her hands itch. Because the magic was returning? She stretched to keep up with the general's brisk pace.

Uskenda's face went grim, worsening Kallista's fears. "Graceday before last, twelve days ago, assassins struck all across the country, targeting naitani serving with the army. Even here in Arikon itself. Thank the One, your location was kept secret for your safety, or likely they'd have attacked you as well."

"We were already on the road coming here by then."

"They'd no' have touched her," Torchay muttered at almost the same moment.

"Yes, well—double thanks to the One. Besides military naitani, they went after high-ranking officers—colonel and above. I would have thought they were Tibrans retaliating for your…for the deaths last year, but…"

Kallista hid her reaction. It still disturbed her, some of the things her new magic had done. When she had destroyed the demon, all those who had worshipped it—all the Tibrans in the Ruler caste and many of the high-ranking Tibran Warrior caste—had died with it. It had ended the war, but left Tibre in chaos. "Are you sure they weren't Tibran?"

"They were Adaran. Adaran traitors." The general spat her contempt on the gray cobblestone paving. "The one who attacked me wore her infantry uniform. Bodyguards turned on the naitani they'd sworn to protect."

"Impossible!" Torchay burst out, shock and horror wiping out discipline.

"Not all of them turned, Sergeant." The general's eyes warmed in a faint smile. "But enough. They targeted the military naitani with the generals. I'm the highest ranking officer left. The army is in shambles, half or more of our soldiers gone over to the rebels. We've scarcely a dozen naitani still alive, and those that are—"

Uskenda paused in midstep, her foot hovering in the air while she seemed to make some decision. She pivoted, taking her step in a new direction. "The Reinine gave orders to bring you to the palace as soon as you arrived, and I am doing that, but we will take a different path."

She held Kallista's gaze as they kept moving through the crowded streets. "You need to know what we are up against."

Fox took the warm, squirmy bundle Stone handed him and tucked her inside his shirt, next to his skin. A squeak of protest told him Lorynda was not yet interested in sleeping, so he turned her around to allow her to see out while he wrapped them both in his layers of clothing. He had trouble with some elements of infant care, particularly cleanup, since his blindness kept him from seeing when the job was properly done, for which he thanked the One daily. But he was a master at keeping the babies warm and not bad at getting them to sleep.

He leaned his head against the rock wall behind him, then as the cold from the stone penetrated, he fumbled for the hood of his cape to pull up an extra layer between himself and their shelter. "Still snowing?" he asked the cave in general.

"Can't tell." Stone's soured voice came back. "It covered the cave entrance sometime last night. But it's been snowing for six days running. Why would it stop now?"

"At least we're not out there in it." Merinda spoke from near the fire.

Fox was getting heartily tired of her forced cheer, her "look on the bright side" comments. If it didn't require moving from his spot, he'd throttle her. But as it did, he supposed he would have to let her live.

"You're right." Aisse's voice so close to him would have startled him if he hadn't *known* where she was. "We could be out in the storm, but we're not. And I for one, am grateful not to be in the saddle all the hours of daylight. Fox, do you have room for Rozite, too?"

"Aye." He opened his cloak and overshirt again and loosened the lacings on his tunic more. The second twin snuggled in next to her sister and seemed to take on some of her calm, losing her restless fidgeting. They were warm and soft and smelled like contentment.

Fox rested his cheek atop their fuzzy heads a moment as he wrapped the coverings more securely about them. Then, with the babies secure in his arms, he closed his useless eyes and let his senses flow outward. Somehow, the act of shutting his eyes helped him *know* the things he couldn't see.

There was Aisse, lowering herself onto the pallet nearest the fire. Was it normal for her to sleep so much? He supposed it was, or Merinda would be jollying her awake. The healer took her responsibilities seriously, urging Aisse to eat more when she picked at her food, watching the babies with sharp eyes and with magic to see how they fared in this cold. Fox just wished she didn't have to be so bloody *cheerful* about it.

At the moment, Merinda was busying herself near the fire with something or other. And Stone knelt near the cave's entrance, his attention focused on it. Perhaps trying to measure the depth of the snow?

Fox let his *knowing* quest onward. It was how he had brought them all to this place, the day the late spring blizzard had fallen on them. Right up until the moment he "found" the opening in the rock, he'd been afraid that the odd extra sense Kallista had given him couldn't do such a thing. But it had. They had shelter from the snow and the cold.

Outside the cave, the world lay empty and silent. They might be the only souls left in existence, for all Fox could tell. He couldn't *sense* things at much of a distance. He stretched, *reaching* as far as he could, wanting desperately to feel Kallista's comforting touch against…whatever it was she touched inside him. He found only emptiness.

It had been months and months since any of them had felt that seductive brush of magic across their souls. He missed it. He wondered whether they would ever get it back. Kallista said they would, but when?

Stone was moving, doing something where he knelt, but Fox couldn't tell what it was. "Learning to dance on your knees like the horse tribes?" he asked.

"Digging a path out of this hole you've buried us in." Stone's voice sounded sharp, on edge. The women didn't seem to notice, but Fox had been partnered with Stone for almost twenty years. Since they'd entered Warrior Caste training at six. He knew the man's nuances.

Carefully, Fox rose to his feet and walked toward the cave entrance where he sat down with his back to the drifted snow. "What's wrong?"

"You're going to be sitting in snowmelt in another five ticks if you don't move."

Fox shifted a pace away and waited, wishing this *knowing* of his let him know more than mere presence or motion. He wanted to see Stone's face, his expression. "Well?" he finally had to prompt.

"We're running low on supplies." Stone kept his voice quiet as he continued digging. "There's enough for the adults for about a week yet, but milk for the babies—they're too young to be able to eat our food, Merinda says, even were it chewed for them. They could do it for a bit, in an emergency, but not for long."

Fox's arms tightened around the little bodies snuggled in against his chest. "We have to find more. A cow. Something."

"How, if the snow doesn't stop?"

"We'll find a way. I will not let our children die." The fervor in his own voice surprised Fox.

Children had little value in Tibre, until the males joined their castes at six. Women had no caste save the one that they served, so girl children were worth even less. In Tibre, children belonged to the caste, to no one. These tiny girls were *his*. His and the rest of the ilian's. That made all the difference in the world.

A gust of icy wind announced that Stone had broken through the layered snow. "Still snowing," he said.

"How thick is the snow cover?"

"Maybe two paces. Not bad." Stone moved a short distance away, then returned and laid something over the fresh opening that blocked the wind a bit. Fox touched it; a saddle blanket. Stone laid another atop the first.

Fox was about to rise and head back nearer the fire when Stone sat on the cold cave floor beside him. Apparently in the snowmelt he'd warned Fox against, for he swore and moved to Fox's other side.

"So, *is* Merinda ilias? Like the rest of us?" Stone asked in a voice quieter than any Fox had heard from him.

"I—" The question tumbled Fox's thoughts into a stinking pile. "What do you think?" Maybe if he played for time he could dredge an answer from his memory.

"I don't know. You were there when it happened, right before we left. You heard what Kallista said when she gave her the bracelet."

"*Ilian together,*" Fox quoted. "But that's not what she said—

what any of us said—the night you all married me. Was it the same before?"

As one of the original four in their ilian, Stone had been through the ceremony three times, once when the ilian was formed, once when Obed joined them and once for Fox. "Those were all the same. Not like with her. So I'm asking. Is it just to help look after Lorynda and Rozite, or is it—?"

"You want to have sex with her?"

"Khralsh." Stone swore by the warrior face of the One they all worshipped. "It's the other way round. You can't see the way she's always touching me, or the looks she gives me. She says we're ilian now, that I don't have to be—*uncomfortable,* she said. You know how long it's been, what with Kallista so soon after her time and Aisse so near hers and the magic gone besides. It wouldn't be a problem, except Merinda's always...*there.*"

"And you never were one to turn down sex." Fox grinned. "I wish I *could* see it. Stone Varyl, vo'Tsekrish, evading a woman's advances like some—some girl before her rites."

Stone clouted him openhanded on the back of his head, gently, because of the babies. Otherwise he'd have dealt him a blow hard enough to lay him flat. All in fun, of course. "You're just jealous she's not chasing you."

"Damaged goods." Fox couldn't blame her. What woman wanted a man cursed with blindness?

Stone snorted in derision. "I think she's more afraid Aisse would have her head if she tried."

"Aisse?" He went still, as one of the babies twitched in her sleep then settled again. "Not that she couldn't do it, but why would she want to?"

"Beside the fact you sired the child in her belly? She favors you. Over all of us."

Fox choked off his laugh. "Small favor. Just because she will consent on rare occasions to actually speak to me as well as point and order."

"See? Favor. So what do I do about Merinda? *Is* she ilias?"

Fox sighed. "I don't know, and there's no one to ask who does, with all of us here born Tibran."

"Except Merinda." Stone's sigh was a longer echo of Fox's. "I won't betray my ilian."

"No." His *brodir's* loyalty was never in doubt. Once given, it remained. Fox took another deep breath. "*Ilian together,* Kallista said."

"And Torchay."

"So." Fox moved a tiny hand that was digging tiny furrows in his skin with tiny fingernails. "All we can do is assume that means what it says. We are ilian together, in all ways. If you want what she offers, take it."

Stone remained where he sat. "I wish Kallista were here."

"So do I. But since she's not, we can only muddle through as best we can." He froze. "There's something outside."

Stone scrambled for weapons as Fox stretched his peculiar sense in a desperate attempt to discover what it was. Rozite squalled when Merinda plucked her from inside Fox's shirt but quieted once she was placed against Aisse's warmth.

"Not human," Fox said, relinquishing Lorynda to the healer. "Large. A deer, perhaps. We hunt."

"In the storm?" Stone asked as he handed Fox a quiver of arrows and a spear.

"I can find our way back," he said with a confidence he did not quite possess. "The babies might not like the blood, but it will feed them, will it not?"

Stone merely moved aside the blankets from the entrance and ducked through it.

## CHAPTER TWO

The new path General Uskenda took led Kallista and her men around the bulk of the palace, along the broad surrounding avenues where trees planted decades ago for beauty were being cut down to recreate the defensive space. On the downhill side east of the palace, they passed through an iron gate in a high wall. Kallista felt the tingle of barrier magic as they crossed into a quiet garden where invalids wrapped in thick dressing gowns basked in the pale spring sunlight while they sat on scattered benches. Beyond the garden rose a tall sprawling building, Arikon's main healing center.

Uskenda led them inside and cut sharply right, taking them up a wide stairway to the third floor. She strode down the long corridor that turned left, then right again before she rapped on a door and entered.

A man with bandages wrapping every visible part of him—head, arms, torso—struggled to rise from the bed where he lay.

"No, no, Sergeant. Don't get up." Uskenda motioned him back, and he subsided to a seated position, adjusting the blanket over the smallclothes that were apparently his only garment.

"How is she?"

"The same. They're keeping her under for fear of what might happen when she knows—" The injured man broke off, voice thick with emotion.

Kallista knew him, knew his face, his voice, but she couldn't place who he was.

"Miray." Torchay stepped forward, knelt and carefully took the man's hand in his. The pieces fell into place for Kallista.

This was a naitan's space, with an outer and an inner room. Miray was bodyguard to a young naitan who had served with them in the Kishkim swamp campaign five years ago. Kallandra had the same lightning magic as Kallista, so that was the only time they'd served together, but Kallista had liked the young woman. She believed they had moved beyond fellow naitani to comrades. Perhaps even friends.

Kallista glanced at the general and found her looking back, her expression even more grim. *What now?* Hadn't she suffered enough shocks today? But Uskenda showed no sign of relenting from whatever her purpose might be.

"Might we look in on her?" Uskenda paid the bodyguard the courtesy of asking permission, though in his condition he could do little to stop them, did he want to. "Just the naitan and myself, to keep from disturbing her."

Miray turned his face away, releasing Torchay's hand. "Deep as they've got her dreaming, nothing short of hell opening would disturb her. And even that might not."

"I'll wait here." Torchay moved into the chair beside the bed. Obed simply widened his stance in front of the doorway, standing guard.

Kallista did not want to go into that other room, did not want to see Kallandra lying motionless on a healer's bed, but she could not avoid it. Not only because the general insisted, but also—Kallandra was one of the Reinine's Own, a military naitan. Kallista could not turn away, could not fail to give the other woman the respect and honor that was her due.

Uskenda opened the inner door and stepped back, waiting for Kallista to pass through. The smaller room was dim, lit only by a sliver of reflected light from a high clerestory and that entering by the doorway. Kallista moved to one side to wait for her eyes to adjust to the gloom and for the general to enter.

After a few ticks, she could make out a form lying still and dark against the pale sheets. General Uskenda stood at the foot of the bed looking down at the woman in it. Then she looked up at Kallista, but remained silent. How bad were the injuries?

Kallista swallowed down her dread and crossed the small space to stand beside the narrow bed. Kallandra's face showed the years that had passed, or perhaps the strain of her injuries, but seemed otherwise unmarked. Kallista took in the rest in one swift glance, saw Kallandra's arms lying atop the sheets with bandages swathed from her hands past her elbows.

No. That wasn't right. Something was off, something *wrong* about the bandages. They were—

Kallista's right knee buckled, but her left somehow held and she did not fall when she realized what it was. The bandages did not begin at Kallandra's hands. *She had no hands.*

Her arms stopped short somewhere between elbows and wrists, the thick pads of bandage mocking the missing length.

"Oh dear, sweet Goddess," Kallista whispered. Her hand groped for support, found the wall. "What—"

"Outside." Uskenda jerked her head toward the open doorway.

Kallista nodded, tears burning her eyes again. She took a moment to whisper a blessing on the desperately damaged woman and stumbled back into the bodyguard's antechamber. Torchay jumped up and ushered Kallista to the chair he'd vacated as Uskenda closed the door gently behind them.

"What *happened?*" Kallista whispered.

"What?" Torchay demanded. "What is it?"

"They took her hands." Miray's voice was ice, cracking. "The thrice-damned murderers took all their hands—the naitani's— before they killed them."

"*Goddess.*" Torchay's hand drifted to the sword hilt locked in place over his hip, one of the twin Heldring-forged short swords he wore in the double scabbard on his back, as if he thought an assassin might lurk nearby.

"Kallandra is still alive," Uskenda said.

"But she has no hands," Miray retorted.

Kallista couldn't suppress her shudder. Obed took one step out into the hall and emptied his stomach on the tile floor, then returned to guard as if nothing had happened. Kallista steeled herself against the horror that spun her head and roiled her own stomach, tightening her focus to Torchay standing in front of her. To his hand resting on his hip.

It emerged from the leather cuff holding one of his everpresent blades, which the sleeve of his tunic didn't quite cover. Narrow, long-fingered and remarkably free of scars, his hand showed the calluses of his trade and the dirt from their rough journey to this place. His hand...

*Kallandra had no hands.*

Torchay caught Kallista's hand, clasped it tight, saying nothing. What was there to be said? Almost all naitani needed their hands to use their magic. Bakers kneaded preservation magic into bread with their hands. Weavers wove waterproofing or longwearing strength into fabric with their hands. Healers laid their hands on the sick and injured to mend their hurts. And soldier naitani aimed their magic and sent it against the enemy with their hands.

Only farspeakers and sometimes truthsayers did not use their hands. Some farspeakers had to hold an object that had belonged to the one to whom they spoke, and only a few truthsayers—the Reinine was one—did not have to touch a person to know if they lied.

This was why all military naitani were required to wear gloves in public. Any covering over the hands interfered with the use of magic, and leather blocked all but that under the most exquisite control. Because military naitani held deadly magic, the public's fear of what might happen if it escaped the naitan—and the occasional frightening incident—had brought about the glove regulation.

What would losing her hands do to Kallandra? To any naitan?

Kallista shuddered, squeezing Torchay's hand tighter.

"The Reinine is waiting," the general said. "We must go."

"Yes." Kallista let Torchay pull her to her feet. "Blessings of the One on you, Miray, and on your naitan."

Miray looked up at her, his eyes widening as he seemed to realize just who offered these blessings. "Thank you, God-struck. May it be as you say."

She left the room at a normal pace, but couldn't help feeling as if she scuttled like a bug running for the safety of darkness. Kallandra's injuries were too unsettling, too horrifying. When Obed fell in beside her, Kallista reached for his hand, too, needing the feel of a hand in both of hers, needing to know she could still do it. He gripped her tight, as if he needed the same assurance.

"You don't need your hands to do magic," Torchay said quietly as they reached the first flight of stairs.

"Not for the ilian magic, the godmarked magic, no. I don't think so." She refused to release either hand as they started down the stairs, forcing them into an angled formation. "I used my hands to direct it, shape it, but not because I had to. It was just—they gave me something to see. But for my lightning, I *need* my hands."

"They will not touch you," Obed said. "I swear my life on it."

"I swore mine ten years ago." Torchay waited while they caught up with him on the second-floor landing. "We'll keep you intact."

"But who are they?" Kallista burst out. "What do they want?"

"To change the order of the universe." Uskenda led them in the opposite direction from the entrance stairwell. "The rebellion was instigated by the Barbs, the Order of the Barbed Rose. BARINIRAB. They want—"

"They want to destroy West magic." Kallista finished the sentence for her. "And I'm the only practitioner of West magic Adara's seen in fifty years."

The Order of the Barbed Rose was an ancient and heretical conspiracy shrouded in mystery, often fading from public knowledge for decades at a time, becoming no more than a whispered tale told round hearth fires. And always it tempted the people because of its enmity toward West magic.

West magic was about endings and mysteries, things that couldn't be easily understood or explained by mortal beings. Though death's ending was as much a part of life as birth, it frightened people. So did unexplainable mysteries—such as seeing things that had yet to happen or talking to the dead. And what people feared, they often wanted to destroy. The Barbs, whose influence had been slowly growing over the past fifty years or more, seemed to think that by destroying the magic, they could destroy death itself.

Kallista hadn't been born with West magic. Her personal magic was of the North—the ability to cast lightning bolts from her hands. It had awakened just after puberty, as magic usually did in those gifted by the One. A person either had magic or they did not, and they only received one gift, which never changed.

A good half of Adara's naitani held the practical South magic of hearth and home, magic that called the hearth's fire or brewed better beer or built stronger tables. Most of the remaining naitani were divided between the East magic healers and growers, naitani who dealt with living things and beginnings, and the North naitani whose magic operated on inanimate objects and natural forces like wind or lightning. A very few were given the mysterious talents of the West.

But since that day on the walls of Ukiny a year ago, Kallista had been able to call magic from three of the four compass directions. That is, she'd been able to until the magic left her half a year later in the Tibran capital.

Merinda believed pregnant naitani lost their magic because using it was too hard on the mother. Kallista hoped that was so, and not because the magic somehow harmed the unborn child. She hadn't seen any signs that either Rozite or Lorynda was less than perfect, but she'd used so much magic in those early months…. She thrust that worry away yet again. Her babies were born and she wanted her magic back.

General Uskenda opened a heavy barred door at the end of a twisting corridor to reveal another, heavier iron-bound door behind it. She knocked a rhythm with the hilt of her dagger, received a second rhythm in return and responded with a third before the sound of keys turning in locks came to them. The door cracked open and they stepped through into a well-manned guard chamber inside the palace wall.

Kallista had known there was direct access to the main healer's hall from the palace, but had never known where it was. Now she did, and the thought disturbed her. As if she had been shown the way because she might need it in the near future.

"Whatever the Barb's goals," Uskenda said, accompanying Kallista down the stairs to the courtyards and gardens surrounding the palace buildings, "they did not make you one of their victims. A few others were spared—those who were deep in the countryside on assignment, or whose bodyguards were able to fight off the assassins until help arrived. That is our fortune and the rebels' misfortune. We will need all the fortune the One shines our way, I fear."

The general scowled. "Civil war is always an ugly thing, and they have taken much of the northern coast. They can get firearms from Tibre."

"Maybe it won't come to actual war." Kallista knew she was grasping sand, but hope was all she had just now.

"It wouldn't, if you could take out their leadership like you did before."

Kallista held her tongue. Until her magic returned, she couldn't light a candle with a spark, but no one needed to know that.

Nor did the world need to knew that she—and her ilian— had ended last year's invasion in such a spectacular fashion. She couldn't stop the rumors, but as long as no one knew for certain…

"Or if you could repeat what you did in Ukiny," the general went on when Kallista didn't respond, "that would make these rebellious idiots think twice."

True. When every enemy in a two-hundred pace radius died in the space of a breath, it did tend to make those remaining rethink their plans. Kallista shifted her shoulders against another magic-born thing she didn't like remembering. "These are Adarans. I hate to use such a weapon against our own, even if they *are* rebelling against the Reinine."

"If it comes down to it—"

"I know. If things reach that point, we'll have to use whatever we have. But we're not there yet. Are we?"

"No." Uskenda begrudged the word. "But if things don't

change, it could be soon." She turned Kallista and her iliasti over to the guardpost at the east entrance to Winterhold Palace and departed.

A guard led them through chaotic corridors. Not only was half the land in rebellion against the duly-chosen Reinine and the other half apparently in Arikon seeking refuge or assistance, but it was also nearing time for the annual move from the snug, warm chambers of Winterhold to the cool, airy Summerglen Palace in another part of the enormous royal complex here in the center of Arikon. Trunks and crates lay stacked in the halls and servants bustled everywhere, weaving their way through the throngs of military.

Kallista craned her neck as they passed through one particular section of the palace, but she couldn't see whether the courtyard where she'd first practiced her new magic—the one blown to bits by gunpowder—had been repaired. Only by the grace of the One God and Kallista's poorly controlled new magic had she been able to shield herself, Obed and Stone from the blast.

Palace windows stood open today to let in the warmish breeze. Doubtless a few days earlier, they'd been closed tight against the chill rain that had frozen the travelers on their entire journey south. Except for the overflow of soldiers and the organized chaos of the move, court looked much the same as the last time Kallista was here.

Courtiers dressed in eye-blinking color combinations milled about vying for notice and position. The younger reckless set still swaggered in their half capes with their short-cropped hair and their fancy fencing swords at their sides, putting on a show. Viyelle—prinsipella, now courier—had been one of them. Was she still?

Serysta Reinine waited in the war room behind her audience chamber. The Winterhold audience chamber was vastly different from the one in Summerglen that Kallista had passed through on her first meeting with the Reinine. This chamber was all warm dark woods and cozy tapestries meant to give at least the illusion of warmth, but the war room was much the same. Save for the extra bodies. It was crowded with dozens more army officers and prinsipi, all demanding attention at once.

One of the Reinine's bodyguards noticed Kallista and her companions and murmured a word in his charge's ear. The Reinine turned away, giving the room her back.

"Thank you for your concerns." High Steward Huryl spoke. Kallista hadn't seen him until that moment, but she instantly recognized that thin voice with its falsely humble tone. "The Reinine will take them all under advisement. Thank you."

Spreading his multicolored arms wide in their fluttering stripes of black, gold, blue, green and white, he herded the room's occupants before him. They complained, especially the prinsipi, but they went. Huryl followed them out. Kallista glanced back to be sure they were truly gone and recoiled. The High Steward was just slipping out the door, looking back into the room, his face filled with virulent hatred.

The glimpse was for but a second, before the door closed on him. Had she seen it, or only imagined it? And if she *had* seen that hatred, who was it for? Huryl's glance had raked the entire room, and Goddess knew, Kallista had not gotten on well with the man during her previous sojourn in the palace complex. Maybe his hatred was for her alone. The Reinine had promoted him to his present high position. Why would he hate her? If indeed Kallista had seen what she thought.

Torchay touched her arm. "K'lista? She's waiting."

*Right.* Kallista moved into the room, stopped well away from the bodyguards, put her right leg forward and swept into a low bow. "My Reinine, you have need of me?"

"Get up, get up." The faint chime of metal on metal accompanied Serysta Reinine's brisk movement away from the windows.

As Kallista rose from her bow, her gaze fell on the low shoes and snug black stockings of the nearest bodyguard and the slim gold bands around his ankles. Two on the left, two right. Kallista hid her surprise and speculation, but she couldn't stop her mind from spinning.

She recognized the man from her previous visit. He'd been in the Reinine's service for some time even then, and he hadn't been married. The Reinine's bodyguards did not usually marry. The other bodyguard, much younger and unfamiliar, wore no anklet. But that one did. Kallista shot a quick glance at the Reinine, at the three bangles chiming softly together on her left wrist and the one on her right.

Serysta Reinine waved the bangles, flashing them imperiously. "Yes, I married my bodyguards. Yes, I know it was of no political benefit whatsoever. No, I do not care."

Kallista bowed again, deeper this time. "Far be it from me to question, my Reinine. I married my own bodyguard. I know the…bonds that can grow over the years."

When she rose this time—was the Reinine blushing? Surely not.

"Please, be seated. All of you." Serysta gestured to the chairs set before the room's hearth as she chose a high, wingbacked seat for herself. Kallista took the chair nearest the Reinine, and the four men ranged themselves about them, standing.

Serysta glowered at all the bodyguards. "Sit down. Please."

Her ilias—the stocky man with short-cropped iron-gray hair—answered for both, shaking his head "no" without speaking. Kallista glanced at her own iliasti. "It's no use arguing. They get even more stubborn and protective once you've married them."

Serysta sighed, still glowering. "I've noticed."

Her gray-haired ilias gazed at her blandly. They spoke a whole conversation without words before Serysta jerked her eyes away to stare at her hands in her lap. She took a deep breath. "Has your magic returned, Naitan?"

Kallista's insides knotted up. "No, my Reinine, it has not." She lifted her gloved hand. "This is simply regulation. And protection from the cold. I am most heartily sorry."

"As am I, Naitan. We could use your talents now." Serysta lounged back in her chair, her gaze on the low fire, her thoughts obviously elsewhere. "Will it return, do you know?"

"I believe so." Kallista quelled a brief surge of panic, mentally stomping down the lid of the box where it had been penned and throwing a strap around it. Then another. She had to trust that the One would keep the others safe. They were needed.

"Is something wrong, Naitan?"

Kallista attempted a smile. "As you suggested, we sent the rest of our ilian to safety with the children. We've never been separated like this since we were bound together. It is an…adjustment. Especially since we are bound with magic as well as oaths." She paused to clear her throat.

"My Reinine, we sent them off before we knew of these assassinations, or of the army's defections. Two babies, two women—one of them pregnant and near her time—and two fighters, one of *them* blind. If I could beg of you a troop escort—"

"Ah, Naitan." The Reinine's eyes were filled with a sad sympathy. "There are no troops to send. None we can trust. They will be safer alone and anonymous. Truly."

Kallista wanted to ask again, wanted to beg on her knees, but she didn't want to risk the kind of reaction she'd gotten from the general. "Then may I ask a farspeaker send a message to Korbin, to family there? They can send a party to meet them."

"Yes, of course. Write out your message and I will have it sent immediately." The Reinine gestured at the table between them littered with papers, inkwells and quills.

Kallista scratched out a brief message and the Reinine's younger bodyguard passed it to a servant outside the door. The message would go by farspeaker to Korbin's capital and from there by courier to Torchay's family, but it should reach them no later than tomorrow. Weeks sooner than a message could arrive over land.

She took a ragged breath and looked up at the Reinine. Kallista had never fully answered her question. It was time she did.

"The bonds of magic are still there," she said. "But at the moment, I cannot use them. The fact that they exist makes me believe that the magic will return. When? I cannot say. Merinda Healer said that because I had twins, it could take longer for things to return to normal."

Serysta obviously bit back a curse. "Is there anything to hurry the process along? We need your particular magic rather badly. The few military naitani we have left are scattered and will take time to bring in safely. That blind Tibran you brought back seems to have some skill at foresight, but he's so afraid of his gift—"

For a moment, Kallista was confused. Fox had no magic of his own, except for that uncanny ability to sense his surroundings. Then she remembered. The boy they'd rescued, the one they'd brought with them from their trip to the Tibran capital. He'd been a casteless "witch hound," used by the Ruler caste to sniff out users of forbidden magic. They'd taken his eyes first. Fox couldn't see from his eyes. Gweric had none to see with.

"How is he?" Kallista had left him with her family in Turysh so her birth mother could work her healing on Gweric's feet, broken by his Tibran masters to keep him from running away. When he was well enough, he'd been brought to Arikon, to the naitani academies for training.

"Well enough, I suppose. Getting around better than I would have believed. What can you do to speed up the magic?" Serysta refused to be distracted.

"I don't know. I've consulted with all my sources. They don't know either." Kallista's only real source of information was the last godstruck naitan so blessed by the One. Belandra had lived a thousand years ago, but she came visiting from time to time to advise her successor. Belandra, however, had been older when the Goddess struck her. She'd already had all her children, and none of them had been twins.

Serysta Reinine's lips thinned as she pressed them tight together in an uncharacteristic show of impatience.

"What is it you need?" Kallista asked. "Perhaps there is some other way we can provide it?"

"I need to know what these rebels are doing. I need to know their goals, where they will strike, what their numbers are—everything there is to know."

"Don't you have spies?" Kallista knew she did. Uskenda would not have left so necessary a thing undone.

"I *did*. I have sent six persons to infiltrate the rebels. Somehow, they found each one and sent them back in pieces."

"Goddess," Kallista murmured, not missing the grim looks the four bodyguards exchanged. "Did your people have magic?"

"One had a small illusion gift. Otherwise, no."

"You've no magic just now either, Captain," Torchay reminded her.

"The others were all sent to infiltrate?" Kallista got the Reinine's nod of confirmation. "What about observers?"

"None sent specifically for that. We've been gathering information from the troops coming in, but that's all. So far."

"We could—"

"There are others with those skills," Torchay interrupted.

"Those who could do a better job without risking you. No one else can do what you can."

"Not even me." She *reached* for her magic, stretching as high and wide as she could. And found nothing.

"It'll come," he said. "Likely the more you fret, the longer it will take."

Kallista made a face. "Likely."

"Your sergeant is right," the Reinine said. "We're not yet at the point of desperation. Pray the One we never reach it. There is another matter to discuss, however."

"Of course, my Reinine." Kallista bowed as best she could while seated.

"Before you left here with your godmarked iliasti, I sent word across the country that anyone with a similar marking should be brought to Arikon."

"I remember." She refrained from touching the back of her neck where she and her ilian had been marked. Red and raised, something like a birthmark, her mark resembled a complete Compass Rose, the symbol of the One. The marks on the others were a rose alone, without the compass points reaching from it.

She'd once believed the godmarks in the old stories to be symbolic rather than literal, just as the stories themselves were some allegorical fable, rather than historic fact. They'd all learned otherwise.

Now, Kallista's insides tied double knots. "You're reminding me of this because another marked one has turned up."

Serysta Reinine's smile held kindness beneath the cynicism. "As it happens, yes." She lifted a hand and the younger bodyguard returned to the door, opened it and murmured to someone outside. They waited.

Kallista's knee jumped in a quick, jittery beat, until she noticed and stilled it. The silence stretched her nerves taut, as if someone should be telling her something she ought to know, but wasn't, and that lack of knowledge would blow up in their faces like the gunpowder in the practice courtyard.

Finally the door opened again. Iron shackles rattled in the audience chamber as the wearer shuffled across the polished wood floor. Guards entered first, then a wild-looking man chained hand to foot. His tangled hair fell well past his shoulders, blending with a ragged beard. It matched the dirty rags he wore. *This* was the godmarked man?

Kallista stood, wondering whether she was appalled for his sake or her own. Did she want this man in her ilian?

"Is he so mad that he must be treated like this?" Torchay moved between Kallista and the chained man.

"The mark has affected him profoundly, yes." Serysta Reinine remained seated, tips of her fingers tented together. "However, he wears chains for another reason. He has come here from Katreinet Prison."

She crossed her legs and swung her foot in a leisurely fashion. "Do you not recognize him?"

Kallista stepped forward, next to Torchay, which was as close as he would allow her to approach. Obed glided a few steps more, placing himself nearer the prisoner. She studied the man, tried to picture him with his beard shaved and his hair neat. He looked up at her, the blue of his eyes blazing bright as one of her sparks.

Then intelligence flared in those eyes, sharp and clear, and she knew. She breathed his name. "Joh."

## CHAPTER THREE

The prisoner in the Reinine's war room straightened to attention and bowed as formally as his chains would allow. "Captain."

Joh Suteny had been the lieutenant in charge of the guards escorting Stone as a prisoner of war to Arikon last year. He had stood as witness to the wedding that bound their original four together. And he had been the one to hide the gunpowder inside the broken gargoyle in the courtyard where she practiced her magic with Obed and Stone.

He had fired the sparking trail that exploded it and nearly killed them. He had confessed to his own actions but refused to lead them farther in the plot. And now he claimed to be marked by the One?

The odd rumbling Kallista had been hearing for some moments erupted from a growl into a roar, pouring out of Torchay. She jumped toward Joh—Torchay had come close to killing him the day of the explosion. But Torchay launched himself in the other direction, at Serysta Reinine.

"Torchay, no!" Kallista spun, too late to catch him. The Reinine's bodyguard grappled him, having to grab hold again and again as Torchay kept slipping free. The other guard moved to help and Obed stepped as if to prevent him.

"*Stop it.*" Kallista's hand on Obed's chest held him still. She sprang at the fighting men, inserting herself between them before blades could be drawn. She shoved hard at Torchay. He tried to push her out of the way, but the attempt disengaged him from the Reinine's man and Kallista was able to move him farther away.

"What is wrong with you?" She snarled the words, trying to keep a semblance of discretion. "Attacking the Reinine? Is madness catching?"

Torchay's eyes still failed to focus on her. He panted with his rage, fists closing, opening, closing again. "She'll no' force *that* on us. *Pentivas* or no, we'll no' be makin' that one ilias. I don't care if she's the Goddess Almighty."

Kallista glanced over her shoulder. The Reinine still sat, seemingly unconcerned, in her high-backed red velvet chair. Her bodyguards flanked her, close enough to touch, but they held their places.

"Obed," Kallista said. "Go see if he has the mark."

His eyes flashed dark fire, but he bowed obedience and strode toward the chained man who was trembling so hard now that his bonds set up a faint rattle. Obed pushed the prisoner's head forward, brushed the matted tangles away from his neck and looked to see what might be there. A moment later, he met Kallista's gaze and nodded, once, slowly.

*So.* Yet another problem to be solved. Kallista took a deep breath and let it out in a sigh.

"We will *not* have him," Torchay said through clenched teeth.

Before anyone else could speak, Joh did, startling them all. "Is that your choice to make?"

Kallista held Torchay beside her with just a touch this time. "It is all of ours, his as much as anyone's."

"Is it?" Joh said. "Who made the first choice, when you took a Tibran as ilias?"

Torchay glanced back at the Reinine, but Kallista shook her head, finally following where Joh was trying to lead her.

"It wasn't the Reinine," she said. "It was *the One* who chose to accept what we offered. The One bound us together before any ceremony was performed. Who are we to reject the gifts She brings us?"

"Do we no' also have the gift of free will? The right to *choose* where we go, what we do and who we do it with?" Torchay's expression was as closed as his mind.

Kallista sighed. She didn't yet know what she herself thought about this new situation. What with the hard riding of the past week, she hadn't truly dealt with the separation from half her family and the absence of her ten-week-old babies, much less the concept that rebel assassins wanted her death. She'd faced death before—both on the battlefield and directed particularly at her.

Which of course was the problem, since the hand that had directed it in particular belonged to the man standing before her in chains. She needed time. More than she would be given, likely, but she would take what she could get.

"My Reinine." She turned and bowed to the ruler of all Adara, remaining at a distance to keep the royal ilias and his fellow bodyguard happy. "Would you allow me time and the space for privacy? I must confer with my iliasti. While I do that, perhaps—" She paused to choose her words. "Perhaps the prisoner would benefit from a bath and a shave, more suitable clothing. Then, if you will permit, I should like a chance to speak privately with this man, to investigate his claim. I think it a thing done best without an audience."

"You'll no' be meetin' him alone." Torchay's north mountains accent was as thick as she'd ever heard it, an indication of the extreme emotion possessing him.

Kallista turned her head a fraction, addressing him quietly. "No, of course not. This is a matter for the ilian. I want you both there."

"Do I need to order guards present to protect Suteny?" the Reinine asked.

Now Kallista faced Torchay head on. "Must I order you to hold back your hand? Will you, if I do?"

He did not look happy about it, but he nodded, a single abrupt jerk of his head. "Aye. I'll no' kill him—unless he makes the first move."

"Fair enough," the Reinine said.

Kallista looked then at Obed. She knew better than to assume he would keep any promise Torchay made. "Will you swear to the same?"

His expression bland, Obed inclined his head in agreement, a lock of black hair sliding forward on his face.

"Your word, Obed," she insisted. "I want to hear you speak it."

A tiny smile curved his lips and he bowed deeper. "I will not kill this man, unless he makes the first move. This I swear to my Chosen One."

"Agreed." Serysta Reinine came to her feet and addressed the guards officer. "Have a servant direct you to the palace barbers. When your prisoner is presentable, take him to the Noonday Suite in Daybright Tower. I assume, Captain, that your previous quarters will be acceptable. Since we will all be moving to Summerglen in another few days, I see no sense in locating you here only to uproot you so soon."

Kallista swept into her best court bow. "Thank you, my Reinine. Your generosity is gratefully accepted." She bowed again, this time to the bodyguard mate of her ruler. "Thank you, Reinas, for your restraint and for the life of my ilias. I apologize for his foolish and reckless behavior."

The gray-haired man inclined his head. "It's not your apology to make. But for the thanks—you're welcome."

His face flushed red, Torchay stepped forward and bowed stiffly, head almost touching his outstretched knee. "My apologies. I was…overcome."

The older man did not respond, leaving Torchay bent in his awkward bow, until the Reinine spoke his name. "Keldrey."

He exchanged a look with her before relenting. "Apology accepted. But—" he went on as Torchay straightened "—if it happens again, I'll cut out your heart."

Torchay met the man's gaze without blinking, giving back stare for stare. Finally he tipped his head in a slight acknowledgment. Keldrey did the same. Torchay spun on his heel and urged Kallista from the room following the already departed prisoner. Obed waited until they passed him before whirling in a dancelike move to act as rear guard.

"What was that all about?" Kallista thumped Torchay on the arm when the door shut behind them. "She is the Reinine of all Adara, not some backwoods naitan with a grass-green bodyguard."

Torchay shrugged. "A bodyguard's a bodyguard, whoever the body to be guarded."

She thumped him again. "We do not have time for you to be playing 'whose is bigger?' games. And if you ever do something that stupid again, I will *let* him cut out your heart."

He gave her a look that so obviously meant "We will see whose heart is removed," and she thumped him once more.

Servants were still whisking dust covers from the elaborate white and gold furniture in the suite when they arrived. Every piece Kallista had ordered removed during their previous sojourn, clearing the first two-thirds of the long central room for a practice area, had been replaced, requiring them to thread their way through the obstacles.

"Perhaps we should have paid a visit to the palace barbers as well." Kallista stripped off her grubby overtunic, letting it lie where it fell. "I scarcely feel human." She plucked at the damp shirt beneath. She didn't think she'd been dry since they left home.

"Servants will bring baths," Obed said. "I requested it before they departed."

"Bless you." She touched his cheek, stretching up for a kiss he ducked away from. He disguised it as a bow, graceful as a dancer, but he could not disguise the truth. He did not want her kiss.

Hurt, she turned away, found Torchay there as always, and kissed him. But that was not fair to him, to give kisses because they were refused elsewhere. She rested her forehead in the curve between his neck and shoulder, taking comfort in the arms around her until the tension in him broke through her pout.

Kallista tried to move back, but Torchay's arms tightened, holding her in place. His hand moved, cupping the back of her head, and he turned his face to nuzzle her ear. "This has to end, Kallista," he murmured for her only. "We've arrived. We don't need his sword. If he hurts you again, I'll kill him."

"You can't." She kept her voice low despite her need to scream at something. Obed's behavior offended Torchay most, because he knew her best, saw better how it hurt her, cared more that it did. "He won't. He hasn't."

"Has he no'?" He softened his grip enough she could see his face, turned toward Obed with angry challenge in his eyes.

"We need him, Torchay."

"The One sent him. She can send another."

"You think She will? If we destroy Her gift?" She worked her hands free and clasped his face between them, forcing his gaze away from Obed to her. "Do not turn your anger at this…this *mess* onto one who bears no fault for it."

"I blame him only for his own faults." Torchay tried to lift his head, to glare at Obed again, but Kallista held him with a touch he could easily break.

"Your anger is out of proportion with this fault." She brought his face down to hers and kissed him.

No longer seeking comfort or offering thanks, this was a kiss of desire rekindled and passion delayed. She scuffed her hands through the week-old growth along his jaw, savoring the bristly softness against her palms. He opened his mouth over hers and she welcomed him in, needing the taste and feel of him like she needed the very air to breathe. His hand at her waist slipped lower, cupped her bottom and brought her in hard against his arousal, thick and straight and all for her.

Kallista's moan nearly drowned out the distant sound of a genteel knocking at the door. It registered only when Torchay set her away from him. "Too much demands our attention now," he said.

The quick, gasping rate of his breath eased Kallista's frustration. A bit. Most new mothers did not wait so long before welcoming their mates back to their beds. Because Kallista had borne twins, and because her magic was so strange and so strong, Merinda had advised caution. So Kallista had followed the healer's advice.

Now, caution drowned in a flood of passion and she was in no mood to resurrect it. She needed this, needed to know soul deep that what family remained to her here was indeed hers as she was theirs. And if Obed didn't want her, Torchay did. But he was right, damn it. Now was not the moment.

Her own breathing finally under control, Kallista glanced up, saw Obed following the teams of servants bearing tin hip baths and willed him to look at her. Maybe the magic was returning, for he did what she wished. Or maybe the guilt she read in his eyes the few seconds he met her gaze made him look.

Why guilt? Did he believe he should want her kisses? He had wanted them—wanted *her*—once with a fervor that pulsed so powerfully through the magic linking them it had come near driving her insane. What had changed? Could it be changed back? Did she have any right to do so?

Torchay ordered the tubs set up in three of the small private sleeping rooms off to each side of the main parlor. A wise decision. If they'd bathed together in the same room, Kallista feared little bathing would have been accomplished. On her own, she washed quickly and efficiently, using the extra can of water to rinse her hair of soap. Dressed again in fresh clothes provided by the ever efficient Torchay, she was the first to emerge, her hair spread across her shoulders to dry.

She notified the servant waiting outside the suite door that her bath was ready to be removed and returned to find Torchay, clean and freshly shaved, if a bit crumpled around the edges. She was no better. Saddlebags did not keep clothing in the best of press. He drew her like one bespelled, but the only spell was the man himself. Fortunately, Obed joined them a moment later or she might have shocked the servants. Certain things called for the privacy of the ilian.

The last tub had just been carried out when another knocking, this one far from genteel, pounded at the door. Likely the guard had been waiting for this moment. Kallista caught Torchay's gaze, then Obed's, silently reminding them one at a time of the promises they had made. Then she called out. *"Come."*

The door flew open and the guard lieutenant filled the opening, a sturdy young woman with a square jaw, taut now with disapproval. "The prisoner, as ordered, Captain. My men will remain here at the door." Obviously she disapproved of leaving her prisoner unguarded.

"Outside the door, if you please, Lieutenant." Kallista tried a smile, but when that had no effect, she put on her captain's face. "Produce your prisoner."

The lieutenant saluted and stepped back, vacating the opening. With a rattle of chains, Joh Suteny was shoved stumbling through the doorway. The ornately carved door slammed shut behind him with a noticeable "on-your-head-be-it" boom.

Kallista could only stare. Joh's rags were gone, replaced with…nothing. He wasn't quite naked, she realized once she managed to blink. He'd been given a loincloth, the sort worn by the poorest of the poor beneath their ragged tunics when summer grew too hot for trousers. It didn't cover much.

He stood motionless there at the far end of the room and let her stare. Kallista had always thought Joh a fine-looking specimen of Adaran manhood, but she'd never suspected him of hiding this sculptured perfection beneath his uniform. She took a deep breath. If the One had indeed marked him, as Obed had verified, Her appreciation of male beauty had not diminished any over the past year.

"Come." Kallista beckoned him closer.

Hobbled by his shackles, Joh did as he was bid. Kallista sensed more than saw Torchay's tension and quieted him with a touch. Joh's hair, beginning to dry from its washing, streamed from the dropped peak at his forehead back over his shoulders nearly to his waist. He'd worn it in a queue before, but one three times longer than an enlisted man's short regulation braid. The prison had obviously not required him to cut it.

His hair was brown, a rich color lighter than Kallista's own near-black, and much darker than the pale brown left behind after Stone had cut away all his gold fluff. The warm shade somehow made his eyes seem a brighter blue.

The barber had removed his beard, revealing the clean angles of Joh's face, exposing the crisp edge of the mouth that had so often before been pressed into tight disapproval. Now, his lips pressed themselves together, but with some other emotion Kallista could not read. His face was the same, but different—more lines, or perhaps the same lines carved deeper. He seemed somehow thinner, though his defined musculature mocked that thought. Still, he seemed...as if all the unessential bits had been burned away leaving behind pure Joh.

"Far enough," Torchay's voice growled out.

Joh halted, his chains rattling to rest. Kallista heaved a little sigh, resisting the urge to roll her eyes at Torchay's overprotective attitude. Joh stood a dozen paces away, too far for her to see any mark. Too far even for comfortable conversation. But she could change that when the time came.

"Sit down." She gestured at the gilded seating surrounding them.

"There." Torchay pointed to a high-backed chair upholstered all over in a pale yellow velvet. Kallista remembered it as deep and soft and well nigh impossible to get out of in a hurry. A good choice.

Joh looked at the chair and back at Torchay as if asking whether he was truly meant to sit in such luxury. Kallista nodded, smiled, turning her hand toward the chair in invitation. Slowly, hampered by his chains, hesitantly, Joh shuffled toward the chair and lowered himself into it. When he was seated, Kallista strode forward, ignoring Torchay's protest, slipping past his outstretched hand, and sat in the chair opposite. She left the two chairs on either side for her ever-vigilant bodyguards.

Neither of them sat. Almost as one, they moved the chairs back out of the way and stood, bright flame and dark, between Kallista and the bound, near-naked, oh-so-dangerous prisoner.

She waited until Joh met her eyes. "Tell me what happened."

He shuttered the bright blue of his gaze as if against pain and

drew in a breath through his fine, straight nose. With that for-
tification, he looked at her again.

"I did not know the powder would explode." His voice was
deep, intense, laden with emotion. Kallista could almost taste
it, reaching with absent magic in a vain attempt to drink it
down. His mark pulled at her. This was not what she meant him
to tell, but apparently he needed to.

"What did you think, then?" Torchay's voice held scorn, rage.
"That it would carry them off to sweet dreams of paradise?"

Joh didn't look away, focusing only on Kallista. "I was told
it would heal you."

"Of what?" Torchay spoke again, but Joh ignored him, spoke
over the interruption.

"The vapors from the powder's burning would enable an East
healer to free you of the hold West magic had on you."

Now both her men reacted with derision. Kallista ignored
them, just as Joh did.

"I was a fool," he said, voice gone bitter. "I couldn't understand then what it meant to be marked by the One. I was a child
frightened of the dark with a head full of half-truths and whispered lies, and I let myself believe them. Because I was afraid."

Kallista watched him, trying to read the flickers behind his
steady gaze, and she waited. Often, silence would bring her
more than words.

"And I was angry," Joh said so quietly she had to strain to
hear. "I—I liked you. But when you married the Tibran *di
pentivas*—"

"At the Reinine's order." Kallista spoke as softly as he.

"But back then, I felt betrayed." His mouth twisted in a tiny
smile. "Emotions seldom bow to reason. I admired you for
treating me as you would any other officer. I had thought you
free of the prejudice that sees a man as nothing but passions
and brute strength. And then—"

"I proved you wrong."

"It seemed so then. But I never wished you harm. We were officers in the same army. Sedili-in-arms. It was easier to believe that West magic had twisted you somehow. I wanted to think the powder's smoke would—would return you to the captain I admired. I burned some, earlier, to test it, and that was all it did—make sparks and smoke. I never dreamed…"

"Where did you get it? The powder?" Torchay had not softened any. Kallista would not have expected him to.

"From a Barinirab master," Joh replied without hesitation. "I never saw his face. He disguised his voice. He told me these things, that the smoke would heal and not harm."

"You are one of these Barbs?" Obed shifted, hand coming to rest on the hilt of his saber.

"I was."

Steel appeared in a tattooed hand so quickly Kallista did not see where he'd drawn it from. "Obed, you swore to me. He has not offered harm."

She knew Torchay could move and attack with that lightning speed, but she had not known it of Obed. Where had a merchant-trader needed such skills?

Kallista touched his arm and reluctantly Obed tucked the knife in the sash around his waist. It had not been there before, she knew.

"You no longer belong to the Order of the Barbed Rose?" she asked.

"I will not be part of a group that manipulates its own people into doing murder." Joh's eyes held the anger his voice did not.

"But you won't tell who gave you the powder," Torchay said.

"I do not know." Joh pushed the words through gritted teeth. "I was a Renunciate. Only Initiates and above meet the masters without masks."

"Renunciate? What is that? Tell me about the Order." Kallista needed whatever information he could give her. She'd never known anyone who admitted membership. The Order kept many secrets, not least, who they were.

"There are nine levels—BARINIRAB—beginning with a ceremony they call 'Birth.' Then Apprenticeship, Renunciation, Initiation, Naishar or service, Institution, Rejuvenation, Ascension and Birth again, to a state of unity with the One. The man I met wore the badge of a Rejuvenate on his cloak. I was only at the third level—second, really, for the first is just the ceremony."

"When did you join? How?"

He took a deep breath and let it out. "It was not long after I was promoted to lieutenant. Some of the other officers sounded me out in discussions about West magic. I was curious. I wanted to learn more, and when they offered the chance to join, I took it. What I learned did not seem…evil. And I did not learn much. That was reserved for Initiates. As a Renunciate, I did not—*do* not know enough to be a danger to them."

Joh paused before speaking again, holding Kallista's gaze. "I wish I did. I would tell you all."

She smiled and tucked her hands beneath her thighs to keep from reaching across the gap to pat his knee. "You will. Every single thing you know and some you don't realize you do."

"Brown cloaks with red linings." Obed spoke, startling Kallista. He fingered the hilt of his dagger. "Are they of this order?"

Joh frowned. "You saw them? Men—women—wearing cloaks like that?"

"In the mountains, on our way here," Kallista said.

"The middle ranks—Initiate, Naishan, Institute—wear the brown. But I never saw them in public. Why would they be now?"

"Because they're no longer hiding their goals? Perhaps they were hunting us as they hunted the other naitani." Kallista still felt the horror of knowing what they had done.

"Hunting *her*," Torchay said. "The rest of us were just in their way."

Joh looked as if hell had opened before him and devils were pouring out. Perhaps they were. A single demon had caused all the trouble from the north last year. Was there another? One causing Adarans to turn on each other? Kallista needed her magic back. Now. Possibly Joh could give it to her, but she wasn't ready to find out yet.

"Tell me how you were marked," she said.

"How is it that you can sit here calmly and talk with us?" Torchay added. "Why haven't you lost your wits?"

Last year, Stone's magic-driven urgency to reach Kallista had him half-leaping from boats or falling into convulsions. Fox had likely been much the same, for he remembered little of his journey to them.

"I don't know." Joh shifted in his too-soft chair, chains clacking together. "I believe that I did. I don't remember much of the trip here. And my hands—" He held them up, showing injuries he might have acquired trying to dig through prison walls. Stone's hands had borne similar marks when he'd been brought to Arikon and Kallista. "It could be I am rational now in her presence because I was marked not so long ago."

"When?" Kallista glowered at Torchay to keep him quiet this time. "What happened?"

"Just over a week ago. The guards put us back in the cells after breakfast instead of herding us out into the courtyard because of some disturbance in the countryside. I was reading the *Meditations of Orestes* and praying. There was—I can only call it joy, but that isn't a tenth of what I felt." His expression glowed, making Kallista shiver with its overflow.

He shook himself, recovered his thoughts. "And next I knew, I found myself clawing at the walls. It took the prison governor a few days to learn of it, and several more days to bring me here. And a few more for you to arrive."

"How long ago did it happen?" Torchay asked. "What day?"

Joh shook his head. "I lost so much time—"

"Guess."

"It—it might have been— It was a Graceday. Maybe the twenty-sixth or -seventh of Terris?"

A chill ran down her back as she met Torchay's gaze. "That disturbance in the countryside. Do you know what it was?"

"No." Joh looked from one to the other of them, fear growing in his expression. "Why?"

"The rebels struck throughout Adara on Terris twenty-seventh, assassinating naitani and military officers. The day the One marked you." Kallista took a deep breath.

She could not put it off longer. Likely should not have delayed this much. The interlude given her to enjoy simply being ilias and mother had ended. She could not stretch it longer by wishing. She was who she was and could not be other. The signs that Joh had truly been marked by the One were all there. It only required her touch to *know*.

## CHAPTER FOUR

Kallista slid from her chair to her knees. "Give me your hand."

"Captain, no." Joh struggled to rise and Torchay clapped a hand on his shoulder, holding him in place. "Do not kneel before me."

"If I fall, I'd rather be closer to the ground." She raised an eyebrow. "Surely you remember what could happen when our hands touch." He'd been there for both Stone's and Obed's first touch.

"I—yes." He sank back into his velvet prison, his whole body tense with nervous anticipation. "What—"

"I don't know what will happen. Perhaps nothing. My magic has not yet returned since the twins were born."

"Twins?" Joh whispered in shock while she went on.

"It could be this will wake it. Or not." She smiled, shifting to one side, off her knees. "I can promise, whatever happens, it won't hurt."

Joh did not seem to believe her.

"Torchay, let go of him," she said.

He looked at her, expression bland. "I'd rather not. You lost the magic the same day I was marked. I want to know what the others know."

"There's plenty of time for that."

"I'm tired of waiting."

She didn't think that was his only, or even his primary, reason for keeping his grip on the chained man, but she let it go. Arguing him down would take time she didn't think they had. "Joh, give me your hand."

With a faint rattle of the chains holding them together, Joh extended both hands and opened one out flat. He turned his head away slightly, nostrils flaring as if he faced something terrifying. Magic could terrify, she supposed, if one were not used to it. Hoping her smile looked reassuring, Kallista took his hand in hers. And nothing happened.

She wanted to scream in frustration. Her fingers tightened, squeezing his hand. She took his other hand in her empty one, silently shouting for the magic, *Wake up! Do something!*

And it slammed into her with a force that brought her high on her knees, bowing her backward in an impossible arc as she screamed with the near-forgotten pleasure of it.

The magic swept every inch of her, a storm scouring her end-to-end with delight, blasting open paths that had withered shut over the winter. Creating new ones.

Dragging her in its wake, the magic roared back into Joh. As Kallista tumbled toes to nose in the wave, there was a sort of wrenching, of something twisting aside or tearing open, and Joh cried out. Goddess, *she'd forgotten.*

She reached for him to soothe his pain and he was there, with her, riding the magic. She tasted his fear, breathed in his desperation, his need to make things right. She saw the colors of his soul, though she couldn't have matched them to any tints she knew—colors of loyalty, passion, loneliness, honesty, deep and agonizing remorse….

Kallista felt the magic swelling. Something new. She caught Joh tight, wrapping him in her unseen embrace, whispering wordless, voiceless reassurance as the magic whipped across the skin-to-skin contact into Torchay.

He cried out, knees buckling, though Kallista thought he somehow managed to stay upright. The magic lashed them with pleasure, tearing sounds from three throats, but it had not finished with them. Kallista reached out as Torchay spun past, brought him into the web and knotted him there, adding his booming strength to the harmony they made as the magic swelled yet again.

It leapt across the gap to Obed, increasing the pleasure four-fold with the addition of the fourth. His shout drowned them all out and he fell to his knees. Kallista barely had time to bind him into their knotted chorus before the magic expanded again, spinning outward until she thought she would leave pieces of her soul scattered across all Adara.

She fought to keep the men whole. They were helpless and vulnerable without magic of their own and she shielded them with layers of herself.

Then the magic crashed into yet another, and Kallista tasted Fox. He was cold, worried and falling to his knees in snow as he shoved his fist in his mouth to stifle the shout of delight, but he was alive. Was he in danger? Kallista had no time to tell, barely enough time to pull him safely into the bonds, before the magic poured out of Fox and into Stone. Who fell full length on his face in the snow and shouted loud enough to wake the dead.

Laughing, Kallista scooped him up, wove him into place with the others, ready now as the magic rolled on to find Aisse. She was sleeping, somewhere dark and smoky but safe, seeming to think she dreamed when the magic first caught her up. She woke only as it spun them tighter in the ecstasy it made.

Kallista held on fiercely, twining their separate selves into a glorious whole—Torchay's strength, Obed's truth, Fox's order, Stone's joy, Aisse's faith, Kallista's will...Joh's vision. All her marked ones were there.

The magic pushed them, pulled, whirled and tumbled them as it rose to explosive heights. Again and again, Kallista hauled it back, building the power and the pleasure with each check of its escape while it bounced again through each one of them. Her pleasure fed theirs, which fed back to her and into the magic which then spilled back through each of them to push the cycle higher still.

"Goddess!" Someone screamed it, or maybe all of them did. And the magic exploded out of Kallista's control.

It blasted through them in a seven-fold sexual climax before it erupted into a cloud of glittering fallout visible to every nai-tan in Adara who might chance to look toward Arikon. Then it drifted slowly down, folding back into its separate homes.

Kallista blinked, alone inside her body again, and found herself seated on the floor, her arms draped across Joh's naked legs, her face buried in his lap. Torchay sat slumped against her, weighing her down, and Obed lay curled on his side a short distance away. She shoved at Torchay and he shifted his weight off her, leaning bonelessly against the chair holding Joh.

"Beware of what you ask for," Torchay mumbled through lips that didn't seem to be working quite right.

"I asked for nothing." Obed sounded bitter, his voice choked with some hidden emotion. He'd told her more than once that he wanted nothing to do with sex by magic.

Kallista wanted to go to him, to bring him closer, but she couldn't move from her spot. She stretched out her leg, touched him with her bare toes, and he flinched away.

"I'll kill him." Torchay lifted a hand toward the sword hilt over his shoulder, then let it fall again. "Later. When I've rested up a bit."

"Don't kill him just yet, please." Kallista rolled her head to one side and Joh gasped. The chains rattled and she realized his hands were tangled in her hair. He started to pull them back, but Kallista managed to close a hand over his wrist and prevent it.

"I hope Fox and Stone manage to get themselves out of the snow before they get frostbite," she said, her mind not quite turning all its gears yet. They were *alive*. They were safe.

"What are they doin' in the snow anyway?" Torchay raised his hand again, and this time managed to push his half-dry curls out of his face by means of lowering his head to meet his hand.

"Hunting, I think. That was the impression I got." Her thumb made little circles on the skin inside Joh's wrist. "I imagine they scared off whatever they were hunting and everything else within hearing distance."

"Aye, likely." Torchay opened an eye, then both of them, meeting Kallista's gaze. "They seemed well, safe enough."

She settled her cheek more comfortably against Joh's thigh. "They did, didn't they?" The box full of fear had vanished from her mind.

Torchay sighed, pushing away from the chair to sit unsupported. "Might as well not have bothered with bathing. Soon as I change my trousers, I'll get the key from the lieutenant." He shook his head at her. "Do you always have to pet the new ones?"

Was she? Kallista lifted her head a fraction and saw her hand stroking over Joh's thigh, her other caressing his wrist. "I suppose I must." She slanted a look at Torchay. "Did I not pet you enough when you were first marked?"

"We were busy escaping from Tsekrish, as I recall." He leered playfully at her, a bit of Stone rubbed off on him, perhaps. "But if you want to make up for it, I won't object."

She lifted a hand weighted down with invisible rocks and pointed at the suite door. "Go get the key."

"After I change." He crawled to his hands and knees and used Joh's chair to pull himself to his feet. In silence, Obed hauled himself upright and staggered after him. Kallista bit her lip, watching him go, then put her worry out of her mind. If Obed refused to share what troubled him, she couldn't resolve it on her own.

If things didn't get better, something would have to be done. She didn't want to let him go. Besides her personal feelings, they needed the magic he carried, but if he couldn't bear to stay, she would have to do it. That could wait, for now.

Her neck scarcely seemed strong enough to connect head to body, much less actually raise her head from its very comfortable spot, but she forced it to do so anyway. "Joh?"

His cheeks were wet with tears that squeezed from beneath his tight-closed eyelids. When she whispered his name, he raised a shoulder and wiped his face across it. "Sweet Goddess—" His voice rasped like stones grinding together, its former deep richness lost. "What *was* that?"

Kallista had to laugh, though it sounded little better than Joh's croak. "The magic."

"Saints and all the holy sinners—why didn't the Tibran fall to his knees and beg you to keep him when I brought him as a prisoner to Arikon?"

"It's never been like that before." She had lazed on the floor long enough, but halfway to her feet, a wave of dizziness hit her. She managed to collapse on the arm of Joh's chair, then slid down into the seat, more on top of him than beside him. "Sorry," she mumbled, holding her head up with both hands.

"Head down." He nudged at her elbows propped on her knees. "You shouldn't have tried to stand so soon."

"*They* did." And she was the captain. Maybe she didn't have the same strength as her men, but she'd always been able to match Torchay in sheer endurance.

"They weren't holding that—that madness together. You were." Joh urged her head toward his knees, moving his chains out of the way.

"It wasn't like that before." She let him push her where he wanted, unable to argue, until the dizziness began to fade. Then it felt too nice, even if she was bent nearly in half. And she could think again.

"What was different about it?"

"Before, it was only me and the one I was touching. Well, except with Obed, when Stone got in the way. But then it was only the three of us, because we were all touching. And it only happened when the marked one wasn't with us when he was marked. Like you. It didn't happen with Aisse and Torchay at all." Kallista lifted her head again, and when the dizziness remained at bay, she sat up, resting her head against Joh's shoulder in case it returned.

Joh cleared his throat. "Never everyone at once?"

She took a deep breath. "You smell good. They didn't bring us scented soap."

"Doubtless because I had more odors to scrub away and disguise." The smile was audible in his voice.

"At the weddings," she said, finally answering his question. "When we all took hands at the end, something like that happened, but not so…intense."

"Ah."

"And of course, we were all there together and holding hands. That was before Torchay and Aisse were marked, of course, which could be the difference. That they weren't part of the magic then. But I think it happened this time because my magic has been asleep for so long. When your mark woke it, I think it needed to—to make sure we were all still together. All still bound."

"What happens next?" Joh asked.

"I get the key to those shackles of yours." Still tying up his trouser laces, Torchay came out of the far right-hand bedroom, the one he'd briefly shared with Kallista when they were here before.

Joh tensed when the red-haired bodyguard spoke, but the sergeant strode past them, paying more attention to his pants than to his naitan snuggled in the lap of the man who had almost killed her.

"What is he doing?" Joh did not understand.

"Getting the key." The captain rolled her head off his shoulder. "Look at me. Let me see your eyes. Are *you* all right?"

"Quite well." Obedient to her word, Joh looked at her, let her search his eyes with her lightning-bright gaze. "Other than feeling I've been beaten with washing paddles, wrung out and hung to dry."

She snuggled in again, her hair soft and damp on his shoulder. *Why?* He had no right to questions, had no right to anything, but his mind buzzed with them. Joh tipped his head back in the chair and closed his eyes, trying to calm the buzz. It didn't work. The captain's presence distracted him, kept the questions coming, kept his mind twirling with a thousand contradictory thoughts.

"I don't understand." Joh's words slipped out through clenched teeth. He couldn't hold them back. "Why has Sergeant Omvir left you alone with me? Why am I still alive? I almost killed you, for the One's sake."

"If She forgave you, how can we do less?" Then Kallista shook her head, her dark hair sliding across his skin in a damp caress. "But it's not that, Joh, not truly. It's more. We know you now. We *know*."

Something ran icy fingers down his spine where it pressed against the warm velvet of the chair. West magic was as much a gift from the One as East healing. He knew that. He believed it. Now, after his long study and thought in prison, even more after what just happened. But it still unnerved him when he saw it in action.

"We were all together in the magic." The captain was still speaking. It was getting difficult to think of her as *the captain,* with her half-lying in his lap like this and him wearing little beside chains and a smile, especially since the magic. But he had no right to think anything at all.

"I know you now, Joh," she went on. "*They* know you. And you know us. There's no room for lies in the magic."

He felt her face move against his skin and thought she might have smiled as she spoke again. "There *is* room for misunder-standings. Great, big, stinking enormous ones. But we do know for certain that you mean us no harm—and never did. And now, you're bound to us so tight that no one will be able to take ad-vantage of—of any confusion."

"*No.*" The guard lieutenant's voice rang through the cham-ber with such force, Joh flinched in spite of himself. Lieuten-ant Tylle had regulations written on her spine and nothing but contempt for those she guarded. Not that he deserved better.

"No, what?" The captain spoke casually, did not change her lounging posture, but the habit of command rang in her words.

Sergeant Omvir came to attention, looking decidedly unmil-itary with his hair curling loose around his face. "Captain—"

"No. I will not allow you to remove the chains from my pris-oner," the lieutenant interrupted. "This man is an inmate at Ka-treinet Prison, despite his current…relocation. As long as he is outside the walls of the prison and not in a properly secured cell, he will be kept in chains.

"Now, if you are through with your…consultation—" The

lieutenant's expression betrayed her disgust at what she assumed had been their purpose—and truthfully, she was not far wrong, given what had happened. "I will take my prisoner back into my custody and return him to his cell."

"No, Lieutenant Tylle, you will not." Captain Varyl rose to her feet, backing the lieutenant away as she did so. The captain now was powered with the energy she'd seemed drained of only moments ago. "Do you forget who is captain here? This man is now in *my* care. He is—"

"Does a quick fuck substitute for transfer orders now?"

The captain stood motionless, shocked by the lieutenant's insubordinate obscenity for only a moment. Then she backhanded the shorter woman across the face with a power that rocked her on her heels and sent her stumbling back. Omvir caught the captain around the waist and swung her back before she could follow up on the blow.

Joh struggled out of the chair to his feet, his chains setting up a furious rattle. What had just happened? Was the captain defending her own honor or—or *his*?

Surely not his. He had none. Though he had begun to hope he might be given the chance to regain some small part of it. Still he was not worth a quarrel. "I am ready to go, Lieutenant."

Tylle reached out to grab his arm and the captain blocked her. "And just how far do you think you'll get, Joh?"

What did she mean by—? *Oh.* He remembered then, how for weeks the Tibran couldn't get more than twenty paces from her without collapsing in a fit. Joh sank back down, perching this time on the edge of the chair so he could stand more quickly if need be. He was well and truly bound to her. Trapped by his own will. If he had not offered himself to the One, he would not have been accepted, and now he could go nowhere but at her side until the link between them was fully forged. And she terrified him.

Captain Varyl had pulled paper from a nearby desk and was scratching out a message with the poorly trimmed quill left on the desktop. A moment later, she thrust the message at Sergeant Omvir. "Take this to the Reinine. It's a request for transfer orders." Her eyes flicked toward the lieutenant. "Take it yourself, Torchay. Don't hand it off to a servant. Obed can stand in as bodyguard. His skills are almost the equal of yours."

"Better, in some things," the sergeant muttered, tucking away the note, then reaching up to gather back his hair. He tied it, rather than braiding it properly, but it helped make him look a bit more military. "Maybe we ought to see about getting Obed a set of blacks."

"I have my own blacks," the dark man spoke, seeming to appear from nowhere, dressed in unrelieved black; a loose, foreign-looking robe over Adaran tunic and trews.

The captain's bodyguard looked him up and down. "So you do. But there's nothing about them to show who you serve, is there?" He spun on his heel and departed, leaving Joh feeling caught in undercurrents he could not map.

"Please, Lieutenant, sit." The captain's military mien faded a bit and she gestured at the chairs, playing hostess. "Obed, ring for refreshments, if you would."

"My presence here is for duty, Captain," Lieutenant Tylle sneered. "Not pleasant diversion."

"*Sit.*" The steel in Captain Varyl's voice had the lieutenant plopping down hard on one of the spindly armed chairs.

"You think I know nothing of duty?" The captain snarled, bracing her hands on the wooden arms, her face inches from the guard lieutenant's. "There is a rebellion in Adara. These rebels threaten to destroy everything we hold dear. But rather than stay and see my family—our pregnant ilias and my children—to safety, I obeyed my Reinine's orders. I left my babies—twins, just ten weeks old.

"Ninety days, lieutenant—that's how old my little girls are. But I rode to Arikon with half our men because Serysta Reinine commanded it. Only two of the men in our ilian stayed with the babies—and one of them is blind. We did not know about the assassins' attacks on the army and its naitani until we arrived. We did not know whether our iliasti still lived. But my Reinine commands and I obey.

"We rode eight nights through the rain to get here. We have not had anything to eat since we arrived, but went straight into conference with the Reinine, then directly here to deal with Lieutenant Suteny's godmark. And you *dare* snivel at me about duty?"

"I—I—" The lieutenant gabbled, opening and closing her mouth, her face gone pale in the face of the captain's anger.

Joh glanced at the man with the tattoos on his face. Obed. Joh remembered him and the spectacle he had created with his first appearance in Arikon. Now Obed glared at the lieutenant, as angry with her as the captain was. Joh would find no help in calming the situation there. He had to do something. It would not go well for his captain if she did what she seemed to be considering. Striking the lieutenant once as she had was bad enough. Striking her again, like this, would be far worse.

He touched her arm, cringing inwardly at the rattle of chains as he did. Goddess, he hated that sound. "Captain. You're tired. Perhaps a bit—overwrought? I am sure Lieutenant Tylle didn't mean anything by her words."

"And I am sure that she did."

"I—I apologize," the lieutenant managed to stammer. "I did not know. That is, I—"

Captain Varyl glared a brief moment longer. "You see the folly of assuming what you do not know?" Then she sighed and allowed Joh's touch to move her back. "Apology accepted. Goddess knows, I'm exhausted."

She straightened, closing her eyes with another long sigh.

Now, finally, her tattooed ilias came to urge her into a chair. Then servants arrived with food and the small crisis was over.

The captain and her ilias ate. The lieutenant nibbled. Joh refused refreshment. He was a prisoner, a convicted felon who should be in prison rather than here in luxury. Besides, the chains would rattle and clash every time he brought the food to his mouth, and though he deserved it, he could not bear that humiliation.

Sergeant Omvir returned from his errand, saluted sharply, handed over the papers he held, saluted again, then collapsed gracelessly into the nearest chair. He dropped a cloth bag at his feet with a faint clank, and began stuffing himself with the food that remained. "Goddess, I'd forgotten how good the cooks were here."

"Is that a complaint about my cooking?" A fond smile curved the captain's mouth as she lounged back in her chair.

"Saints, no. It's a complaint about my own." He bit off a chunk of bread. "Mine and Obed's here. And Stone's. That lad can burn water if he's no' careful."

Joh watched their easy familiarity, greed and envy burning holes in his heart. He *wanted* that. With a desperation that made him pull back inside himself where it was safe. He couldn't have it. Not after he'd come so near to destroying it. The sergeant should have killed him when he'd had the chance.

Lieutenant Tylle stood, papers in hand, and saluted. "Captain, I am at your command."

She removed the key to Joh's chains from her belt where it hung with her service awards, and laid it on the table, sliding it across to rest in front of Captain Varyl.

The captain returned the salute from where she sat. "You'll forgive me if I don't stand. There are quarters for you and your men just outside the suite, where Lieutenant Suteny was quartered last year. And I think you won't take it amiss when I say that I desperately hope you do not return in another year's time bearing your own godmark."

"Goddess, no!" Tylle's face paled in horror and Joh hid a smile. He felt much the same, and he was marked.

"Captain," she went on, "I hope *you* won't take this amiss, but think again about removing the chains. This man is *not* an officer in the Adaran army. Do not call him 'lieutenant.' He is not. He's a convict. The only reason he was not hanged for murder is that his victims chanced to live."

The captain's gentle smile stabbed Joh to the heart. "I know, Lieutenant. We are the ones he almost killed. I have my bodyguards and my magic. All will be well."

The lieutenant did not look as if she believed it—Joh did not believe it either—but she saluted and left the room. Joh had done the exact same thing many times last year, his curiosity to know what happened behind the closed doors burning him whole.

Now, he was left behind, his curiosity about to be fed, and he remembered the sergeant's words. *Beware what you ask for.* Joh was not certain he wanted to know what would happen now that the parlor doors were closed.

## CHAPTER FIVE

Captain Varyl tossed the heavy iron key to Sergeant Omvir, who set it back on the table. He picked up the bag he'd brought with him. "Reinine sent you something else. Said if you mean to have him out of those chains, you'd better be willing to put him in these."

Omvir opened the bag and pulled out a set of *di pentivas* anklets with their delicate looped and chiming chains. The bracelets followed. Unlike a woman's ilian bangles, they were wide and close-fitting, with clips and locks that would fasten a man's wrists together and bind him closer than the chains Joh currently wore.

All four of them stared at the decorative bonds spilled across the table. They were shackles just as truly as the iron that bound him now, their delicacy deceptive due to the magic that had forged strength into them. The main difference was that his present chains marked him as felon, as prisoner. The others would declare him ilias, part of a family.

*Di pentivas* rites lingered from Adara's ancient history like the odor of some stinking mold from a forgotten closet, from the days of warlords and the battles of metal against magic. The magic—even more predominantly female then than now—had prevailed of course, and to keep the peace, many of the men on the losing side were married *di pentivas* into Adaran iliani.

The men had no choice in the matter, and could not divorce or be divorced from the ilian. However, if they settled into the marriage and accepted it, they could eventually leave off the wrist bands and exchange the anklets with their looped and chiming chains for the ordinary anklets of a married man.

Though they were still legal, no one practiced the ancient rites any longer, nor had in a hundred and a half of years. Save for Kallista and her ilian, last year.

The captain touched one of the chains. "They look like the ones Stone wore."

"They are. I don't think the Reinine will let you give them back again. She didn't seem best pleased you gave them back the once."

She stirred the chain on the table and looked up at her body-guard ilias. "So?"

The red-haired man took a deep breath and scrubbed his hands across his face. "What do you want me to say? What *can* I say? It would be stupid for me to object now. He's *already* ilias."

"What?" The word was startled out of Joh and he wanted to hide when the others turned their eyes on him. "You can't be serious."

"As a sword's bite," Obed said.

"I told you." The captain's gentle voice sliced deep. "The only time anything remotely like that seven-fold magic ever happened before was during the ilian ceremonies. When the One bound us together into an ilian. This time, She did not wait for the ceremony to bind us. Torchay is right. We are already ilian."

"Madness." Joh gripped his hands tight so their shaking wouldn't show, but he could do nothing to stop it from spreading through his entire body.

Again she smiled that sweet, cruel smile. "Isn't it? Look at the ilian you're part of. Even with you, we're as much Tibran as Adaran. You get used to the madness after a while." She pushed the iron key toward her bodyguard again and this time he took it up.

"Sergeant—" Joh sank back into the chair as if he thought he could escape the man. "You're her bodyguard. It's your duty to protect her. You said it yourself. This is impossible."

The hawk-nosed man paused in the act of unlocking the leg irons and looked up. "So was that bit of business that happened when she touched you." He turned the key and the lock fell open, the chain fell to the ground. "And my name's Torchay. You'd best be getting used to using it. The one of us you've not met face-to-face is Fox. The rest you know."

"Sergeant, *think*," Joh hissed out the words. Were these people all mad? "Where's the man who would take on the Reinine herself if she endangered your captain?"

"Oh, he's here." This time when the sergeant looked up, death rode in his eyes. "Never mistake that. He's always here."

He tossed aside the first set of iron shackles. "But you're no danger to her, now. Not physically."

The sergeant picked up one of the *di pentivas* ankle bands and fastened it around Joh's left ankle, saying the words Joh had never expected to hear, beginning the process of binding him into the family. When Omvir moved back, the captain was there, fastening on the other band, shackling Joh again in bonds forged of silver, magic and sacred vows.

He shook his head, not sure whether he was trying to deny the captain's action or the emotions snarling through him. She gave him her kiss and the dark, tattooed man moved in, fastening a gold bangle around his ankle, saying the same words.

Joh shuddered. He could not do this. He could not possibly be part of any ilian, much less one he'd almost destroyed. *"Sergeant."* He tried once more when the red-haired bodyguard took up the iron key, this time to unlock the manacles.

"Torchay," he corrected. "And now you're one of us, you'd better be calling her Kallista. She doesn't like it when we don't."

The first iron cuff dropped away. Torchay spoke matter-of-factly as he took up a wide, gold band. "You might want to wipe your face."

*Saints and sinners.* It was covered in tears. He'd never been good at handling things like this and he had been bombarded with so many conflicting emotions in the last few moments. With his liberated hand, no chains rattling, Joh swiped his face dry. *Goddess,* he hated this, hated feeling so churned up, so guilty, so grateful, so overwhelmed.

When Joh went still again, Torchay—the sergeant—fastened the *di pentivas* band around his wrist, then did the same on the other side.

"I've made no oaths in return," Joh muttered, resentful that they paid his objections no mind. "I've given no bands."

"You're *di pentivas.* You don't have to." Torchay sounded almost cheerful.

Then the dark one, Obed, slapped his hand down on the table between them. When he pulled it back, two plain slim anklets and a matching bracelet lay there gleaming. "There," he said. "Give them. Swear the vows. They are written on your heart whether you say them with your mouth."

"Where did these come from?" Kallista—no, the *captain*—asked the question in Joh's mind.

The dark man lifted a shoulder and let it drop. "You said we should keep a supply, for instances such as this, when the One adds to our number."

*This happened often?* Joh supposed it must, recalling last year's events.

"Have you been carrying them with you all this time?" Kallista reached out as if to touch the bangles, then did not.

"I had to get more, after Fox. But since then, yes." Obed turned those strange, dark brown eyes on Joh and fell silent. The other two did the same, just watching him. Waiting.

Joh let his head fall back against the high softness of the chair and shut his eyes. He should not be here. He had almost killed them, for the One's sake. And yet—

He couldn't deny the mark, couldn't deny that the magic had swept him along with the others. Nor, much as he might wish to, could he deny wanting what they offered, or the paralyzing fear of taking it.

He pressed the heels of his hands into his burning eyes. He had been praying for a chance to serve, for a way to make things right, but deep down he had never really thought the One would take him up on his prayers. Now, however, the opportunity was here. He could not turn his back on it, no matter how much it terrified him. He could only take the next step and trust to his newfound practice of faith that he would not fall off a cliff.

He moved his hands from his eyes, marveling at the silence when no chains rattled, and focused his bleary vision on the bands gleaming softly atop the inlaid wood. Taking up the smallest, the band meant for Kallista, Joh struggled to the edge of the chair and fell off it, onto his knees.

The sudden motion had the other men startling, touching hands to blades, but nothing more. Kallista shifted, as if she meant to rise, to meet him.

"No." Joh shook his head, crossing the small space between them on his knees. "I come to you. I may wear *pentivas* chains, but I come to swear my own vows."

He slid the band over the hand she held out to him, adding it to the other four bangles on her left wrist. "I come pledging myself to you. Heart to heart, my body for yours, in whatever comes our way. We, above all others, joined as one before the One who holds all that is, was and will be. So I swear with all that is in me."

The tears were back. This time he let them go, for wonder of wonders, there were tears on Kallista's face as well. She bent and touched her lips to his before wiping her tears away with a little self-conscious laugh.

One at a time, Joh took up the ankle bands and repeated the oath, first to Torchay, then Obed. And it was done. The first step was taken. Pray the One the next steps got easier.

Aisse lay on her pallet in the gloom of the cave, pretending to sleep while she waited for the warriors to return. Two babies slept tucked against their sedil still inside her who never seemed to sleep and even now thumped and turned. Aisse could feel Merinda watching her.

The healer was worried, she knew. It had to have been alarming to see Aisse come awake screaming, caught in an apparent fit. But the woman wouldn't leave her alone, endlessly pick, pick, picking, wanting to know what had happened, how she felt, was the baby moving? As if she couldn't see it moving in great waves and bulges.

Aisse sighed. Merinda went silent and still in her corner, forcing Aisse to pretend at dreaming, smacking her lips, mumbling wordlessly. Merinda would drive her mad. She might be ilias— of a sort—but she wasn't marked. She didn't know what the magic could do, hadn't been caught up in it when it swept through them. Aisse hadn't known herself it could reach so far.

Perhaps it was petty, but Aisse didn't want Merinda to know. The magic was hers. Hers and the men's. Merinda didn't have any part of it, nor did she need to. Not unless Kallista said, and Kallista wasn't here. Merinda could do sex with the men if she wanted. Aisse didn't care about that. But the magic was theirs alone.

"The mighty hunters return." Stone burst through the low cave entrance. "We come, bearing success before us."

"Actually, we come dragging a goat behind us," Fox amended, ducking inside. "And if Stone hadn't shouted loud enough to be heard back in Tibre, we'd have a deer as well. If he could have shot straight enough to kill it."

Hiding her smile, Aisse heaved herself more or less upright, patting the babies back to sleep when they stirred. Fox hauled on the rope he held, and true enough, a small goat came baa-ing into the cave. Its hooves scrabbled against the stone floor as it fought to free itself of the tether.

"It came running up to us," Fox said. "I think it wanted to be milked. Something must have happened to her kid. But it doesn't seem to like ropes." The goat kicked at him and he dodged the blow.

"It heard me shouting and came." Stone winked at Aisse as he sat beside her near the fire. "Thought I was calling it. See there? If I hadn't shouted, we wouldn't have the goat and since we were hunting food for the babies, a she-goat is better than a deer any day. I'm *frozen*."

"Why were you shouting?" Merinda brought him dry trousers from the packs across the fire.

Stone surprised Aisse by looking her way rather than Merinda's, question in his eyes. She gave him a subtle shake of her head and he answered with an equally subtle nod. He took the trousers and stood to change, delaying his response further.

"I fell," he said. "Tripped over something under the snow, slid down a bank and laid out full length." He displayed his ice-crusted frontside before stripping off the wet garments. "It was cold."

"Come and change, Fox," Merinda called. "You need to warm up, too."

"I didn't fall. I'm not as wet as Stone. Let me see to the animals." He paused, apparently observing the goat with his other sense. "Does anyone know how to milk a goat, or is this another thing we have to discover how to do?"

Merinda sighed. "I can do it. You come dry off. Warm up." Her green robe swished against her wool-clad legs as she strode across the cave to the side reserved for the animals—riding horses, pack horses and now the goat.

Fox waited for her. "Thank you, Merinda." He set his hands on her shoulders and kissed her forehead, both cheeks, then her lips, brief and almost—but not quite—chaste. He left the healer staring after him in bemusement for a moment before she turned slowly toward the goat. It baa-ed at her.

"What was that?" Stone asked when Fox reached them.

"You said she wants sex. If we give her that—as much as we can right now, more later—maybe she will not ask questions. She doesn't need to know about the magic."

"Yes, exactly," Aisse agreed. "What happened?"

"You were there." Stone pulled his dry tunic down over his stomach and turned his back to the fire, rubbing warmth into his buttocks. "You know what happened. The magic—"

"Yes, but *how?* Why?" Aisse picked up Fox's discarded trousers. "These need washing, don't they?"

"And mine as well." Stone grinned cheerfully at her.

"Someone I didn't know was there, in the magic," Fox said, dressing again quickly. "Did you sense—*him,* I think. A man. Another ilias? Another marked one?"

"I think you are right." Aisse frowned. "He seemed familiar. As if I've met him."

Fox shook his head. "I didn't know him."

"I think I did," Stone said. "Maybe someone we met in Arikon? Before Fox found us."

"Maybe." Fox gathered up the wet clothing. "At least we know they reached Arikon safely."

"What are you three discussing so seriously?" Merinda's voice, coming so unexpectedly from so close at hand, made Aisse jump and jostle the twins. Fortunately, only Rozite protested. Stone scooped his daughter up for comfort.

"When the weather might clear enough to go on," Fox said. "We need to reach Sumald sooner rather than later."

He tossed the clothes he held into the pile of soiled baby things and slung an arm over Merinda's shoulder. He took the bucket of milk from her and set it near the fire. "I can think of more interesting matters to discuss between us." He led her away toward the shadows at the back of the cave. After a moment, Merinda's giggle came floating out.

Aisse allowed herself a fleeting smile before turning her mind to the question of how exactly she might maneuver her frigate-sized self around to reach the milk bucket and prepare feeding bottles for the twins.

"Take Rozite," Stone said. "I'll make the feeders." He tipped his head toward the shadows that made such interesting rustling noises, eyes asking questions. "You don't mind? I thought—"

"Why would I mind? It's sex, not magic. And she's ilias...I think." Aisse frowned then. "Isn't she? If she is not, I will kill her. When I can get off the floor by myself."

"We talked about it, Fox and I. We decided she is."

"You just want to do sex with her."

Stone leered happily at her. "Of course. I'd rather do it with you, mind, but she'll do in a pinch."

"Me? I'm fat. A pig is smaller than I am."

"But you're *our* fat pig." Stone caught her around the middle and rolled her onto his lap, babies and all, nuzzling her neck under her short-cropped hair.

Aisse squealed, sounding far too piglike for her own comfort, and slapped at him, one-handed, clutching a squalling Rozite in the other arm. Stone just laughed and changed his nuzzling to loud, smacking kisses before he let her go. He handed her the feeder.

"I wish you would have me, Aisse," he said, voice suddenly low and far too serious. "There's only you and Kallista, and Kallista's not here. I miss the belonging."

Aisse stared at him as he prepared the second feeder against Lorynda's waking, as Rozite sucked eagerly at the warm goat's milk. She would never have thought it mattered to him other than the quick, pleasurable release of sex. She kept thinking of him as a Tibran Warrior, one of those who saw women as things, conveniences, rather than persons, one of those who had made her previous life a misery. But he wasn't. Hadn't been for more than a year. He was Adaran ilias. As was she.

And he was hers. Like Fox. And Torchay and Obed and Kallista, off away in Arikon. And Merinda too, maybe, for a time. Fox had never hurt her, had given her pleasure and a child. None of the others would hurt her either, because she was theirs. They belonged, all of them together. And if any of them wanted to do sex with her, well then…Aisse wanted it, too. She should have understood this long ago, but at least she understood it now.

"Stone." She touched his shoulder. "I will have you, if you truly wish it. But—don't forget to keep Merinda busy."

He turned, leaned toward her, holding her gaze with those blue eyes that seemed so strange in such a Tibran face. He watched her, coming closer until his lips touched hers, softly at first, then with more and more intensity until he broke off and backed away.

"You do mean it," he said, controlling his breath with effort. "I was afraid you were just—"

Then he grinned. "Good. After our little adventure in the snow, I can wait. But I have your promise."

Aisse couldn't help smiling in the face of that grin. "You have it."

What was left of the day in Arikon was spent in finding clothing for Joh, resting, eating again and more resting. Now and again, Kallista touched the links inside her with delicate fingers, the magic quiescent. She wanted to test it, to see whether it had truly returned, but after such a display, the magic seemed sluggish.

Tired, perhaps. Goddess knew, Kallista was tired. And without Fox to give the magic his order, she was a bit afraid to tap into the massive power Torchay held. Who knew what that much magic would do if it got away from her?

In the middle of her seventh yawn in as many ticks, Torchay spoke. "Why are we sitting here yawning when there are beds for sleeping just behind those doors?"

The long central parlor was lined on either side with enough small bedrooms for every member of the largest ilian, a full twelve-strong, to find privacy, and one large bedroom in case they found privacy overrated. Last year, at the ilian's beginning, they had all slept in the separate rooms. Kallista wasn't having any of it now.

She rolled to her feet and caught Obed's arm before he could escape on some pretext. "Go." She shoved him ahead of her, toward the large sleeping room. "In there."

"I need to—"

"No, you don't. Whatever it is can wait." She kept her grip on him, steering him where she wanted him to go. "Joh, you'd better catch up if you don't want a nasty surprise."

A quick jingle of silver chain behind her told her their new ilias had heeded her warning. The parlor darkened. Torchay snuffed the lamps save for the one he brought with him when he took over the lead.

The single lamp cast the big room into romantic shadows and made the enormous bed look even larger, as if it stretched past the darkness into eternity. Ivory velvet covered the vast expanse, promising a sensory treat even without the masses of gold, white and yellow silken pillows piled upon it.

"I—" Joh had to stop and clear his throat before beginning again. "I think I should sleep here." He indicated a cot near the door, intended for children or perhaps a servant.

Kallista exchanged a look with Torchay. Aisse had slept apart for several months until she became accustomed to being part of an ilian, one full of men. Due to her past, she had trouble trusting men. Still did, save for her iliasti. Kallista supposed they owed Joh the same opportunity. It would give Joh and Torchay both a chance to get used to the new situation.

And it would occupy the cot so Obed couldn't sleep there. If she forced a physical closeness, refused to let him retreat, perhaps he would eventually open up and allow a more complete intimacy. She feared for the magic if Obed kept himself so shut off from her, not to mention the heartache it caused. Why did he have to wait until she had come to love him before pulling back this way?

When she nodded, Joh sat on the cot and unwrapped one of the chains looped around his ankle bands. Kallista watched, intrigued. She hadn't known the extra chains were more than decorative. Joh threaded the chain through a painted metal eyebolt near the door and snapped it shut with the click of a lock.

"I hope we have the key." She raised an eyebrow at Torchay before looking back at Joh who was now pulling off his tunic. "Those chains are more than a century old."

Torchay hung his tunic on a hook by the bed. "It's on my dress uniform belt. I forgot it when you returned the chains to the Reinine last fall."

"Did you bring your dress uniform?" Kallista drew back the velvet coverlet, exposing silken sheets.

"We were coming to court. Of course I brought it. You brought yours, too."

Obed was standing motionless where she'd pushed him, his face shut down, eyes unfocused, seeming to stare inward. Kallista dragged his Southron robe from his shoulders, startling him to awareness.

"Get ready for bed." She held on to the robe when he would have shrugged it back on. "You're sleeping here. With us."

With great dignity, he inclined his head, expression masklike. "As you wish."

Kallista sighed, stripping down to her chemise and smalls while Obed slowly removed his weapons, then his tunic and boots. He eyed Torchay who waited bare-chested, wearing only his knee-length smallclothes. With a subtle sigh, Obed unlaced his trousers and slid them off, though he left his undershirt on. Kallista said nothing. He was Southron, after all. Likely he felt the cold more. Torchay blew out the lamp.

With a hand in the warm center between his shoulders, Kallista pushed Obed onto the bed and followed. He gave her his back. She didn't care, tucking herself around him as Torchay curled himself around her back. Pale moonlight glimmered faintly through the far windows, but Kallista was too tired to admire it. She slept.

As the moon rose higher and night deepened, Kallista's sleep grew restless. She twisted between her men while dreams battered at thick walls, trying to wake the magic within. It stirred, then tucked itself tight against disturbance.

The dreams circled, probing, teasing. The magic swirled, uneasy, but held the dreams at bay until they found a gap. A tiny chink in the wall, singing with power. The dreams bled through and followed the power, carrying their message along.

Torchay stood in the Veryas Valley before Arikon. Without having to look, he knew his family was behind him—Kallista, their children, Aisse and the others. And danger lay before him.

Why he stood alone, he did not know, but he knew that he alone stood between his loved ones and unspeakable horror.

His twin Heldring-forged short swords were in his hands without having to draw them. They would do no good against the thing that was coming, but he had no other weapons. He had no magic of his own.

He waited, praying with every breath as the darkness rolled toward him. It had no shape, no substance he could distinguish with any of his senses, but he knew it was there, coming inside the darkness. He'd seen it before, known it before, but this was different. Worse. In one small corner of his mind, he wondered if this was what Fox's *knowing* was like. Mostly, he waited. And prayed.

Then it was there, filled with hate and an evil so ancient it could almost be touched. Be smelled. Rot and blood and old burning metals, foulness so complete Torchay fought against retching in his sleep.

He slept. This was a dream. It wasn't real. He could cast the dream aside, turn it from this horror.

But the thing would not go. It slithered past, laughing at his feeble defense, reaching for the helpless ones sleeping behind him. He shouted, lunging at it. The thing did not seem to like his taste, so Torchay ran at it again, and this time, it struck back.

Pain pierced his soul, like knives in his gut but worse. Torchay screamed, falling to the ground, scrabbling on his back in the dirt as the foulness raked through him. He knew this pain, had felt it before, but— Goddess, it *hurt*.

"Kallista, wake up!" he shouted. He could not do this alone. "Wake up, all of you! Wake up!"

"*Torchay*." Strong soft arms around him, quiet voice in his ear. "Torchay, I'm awake. It's all right."

It wasn't, but he was awake now, too, sweating and gasping in Kallista's arms like he'd just fought off a thousand demons.

"Oh Goddess," he groaned. "*Demons.*"

Now he knew where he had felt this pain before—last year, when the demon Tchyrizel had got its insubstantial claws in him, in the Tibran capital, before Kallista destroyed it.

"It was just a dream." Kallista tried to pull him in, cradle his head against her, but he refused the comfort.

"Not a dream. Or not *just* a dream." He shoved his hair out of his face with both hands, wishing he could shove the dream out of his head the same way.

"What do you mean?" Obed was awake, too. Of course.

They were all awake after Torchay's shouting—probably awake clear to Winterhold. His throat burned from it.

"I'm the one with dreams that aren't just dreams," Kallista protested.

"But you're asleep. Your magic is asleep. I dreamed that."

"What did you dream? Tell me."

He wanted to tell her, but speaking the horror aloud would somehow make it real, would bring it into this room that was— or should be—their refuge. "Not here," he said. "Out there. In the parlor."

"Torchay—" Kallista began another protest, but he was already moving, heading for the room where he'd left his saddle bags and the key to Joh's chains. It was a nuisance, having to deal with another new-marked man.

He gathered all the bags from the separate rooms, keeping

his mind busy with trivial matters so he wouldn't think about things he would rather avoid. The key was quickly found and Joh unlocked from his cot cell. Then they all gathered in the parlor, shivering in their sleeping wear.

When they were situated to Kallista's satisfaction, huddled together for warmth against the spring's night chill—even Joh—she demanded the dream. Word by word, she pulled it from him, insisting on every detail, every nuance.

Finally, he had no more to give, and she sat back, frowning.

"I don't like this." Her fingers tracing lightly across Torchay's shoulder made him shiver, but he knew her attention was elsewhere.

"Nor I," Obed said.

"You think I do?" Torchay scowled across Kallista at his dark ilias. The man had used up nearly all the patience Torchay possessed, by the hurt he gave Kallista. And with the former lieutenant added to the mix, the strain would only get worse.

"You truly think this a dream of omen?" Obed shifted, as if to pull away.

Torchay clamped a hand on his wrist, holding him in place on Kallista's other side. "I do."

"So do I." Kallista's hand moved from Torchay's shoulder to his bare knee. "And for you to be dreaming my dreams means that things are not right."

"But your magic woke," Joh said. "We all felt it."

"It woke, yes, but…"

Torchay felt the faintest shiver of magic across his skin. Even before he'd been marked, he'd been able to tell when Kallista used magic, but this was different. Better. The magic quivered again and faded away.

"It's sluggish," she said. "Maybe because our ilian is separated. Maybe for other reasons. I don't know. I can't get it to rise. Not like it should."

"What—" Joh fell silent without finishing. He obviously still considered himself a prisoner. And since Torchay considered him one as well, that was good.

"Ask, Joh." Kallista leaned forward to see him past Torchay. "What does it mean?"

"Demons," Torchay said. "Felt like demons. *Smelled* like demons."

"I think so," Kallista agreed. "I wish I had dreamed it."

"*So do I.*" Torchay shuddered. "I want no more of them."

Kallista sifted through the dream details Torchay had given her, hunting meaning. Huddled between the warm bodies of her iliasti, she felt cold, a cold that she feared no amount of warm bodies could chase away. "The demon threatens Arikon," she said. "It's here in Adara, not across the sea."

"It threatens *us*." Torchay stilled her hand on his knee, pressing it flat beneath his hand. "It wasn't some mass of humanity I was defending. It was you. It was the twins. And we need your magic to stop it."

"You think I don't know that?" She would have thrown herself to her feet to pace save for Torchay's arms holding her back, Obed's arms joining them. "I don't know what else to do. I don't know how to bring it back. Belandra doesn't know. Nobody knows."

"Easy now, love." Torchay kissed her forehead, offering comfort. "We're in Arikon. Perhaps there's something in the archives."

"You don't think Serysta Reinine has had scholars scouring the shelves since the girls were born?"

"We can ask. We'll find a way. Somehow. It will happen. Your magic will return."

Kallista nestled her cheek against Torchay's chest, enjoying the feel of skin against skin, and sensed more than felt Obed's withdrawal. Physically, he was present. Emotionally and otherwise—Kallista sighed.

"I can sense all of you through the links," she said. "Before today, I couldn't. It's improved that much, at least."

"Aye." Torchay stood, lifting Kallista in his arms. "But now, you need to sleep. We all do."

"Without any more dreams." She meant to catch Obed's arm, to bring him with them, intended to, but didn't. He followed anyway as Torchay bore her back into the sleeping room. Maybe her plan was working.

Kallista sorted out the strand that hummed of Obed, barely tasting his faint exotic scent that faded as she sought it. As if he pulled away even here. Maybe the plan stunk.

They had bigger things to think of than a moody, bad-tempered ilias, but Kallista couldn't help feeling in the bottom of her gut that—despite the demons—this was important. As sleep came to claim her, she wondered whether it might be important *because* of the demons.

Kallista woke to the touch of kisses along her collarbone above her chemise, to the caress of silk-soft hair trailing over her breasts. She opened her eyes to the sunlit scarlet of Torchay's hair as he kissed his way up her throat to her mouth.

"Good morn, sweet ilias." His lips spoke against hers before opening in a deep, drugging kiss.

She felt half-asleep, lost in a sensual dream as Torchay brought her body awake with the stroking of his rough-callused hands. She'd missed this, missed *him* these last few months.

"Good morn to you." She returned the greeting as his mouth left hers to follow the path his hands had taken. "No more dreams?"

He shook his head, not bothering to disturb his focus on lips against skin as he shoved her chemise up out of his way. Kallista's whole being concentrated on the same path, but even so, she noticed the bed felt empty. "Obed?"

"Awake. Gone." Torchay licked his tongue down the slope of her breast and across her nipple, bringing her up in an involuntary arc. He smiled against her skin and made her gasp.

"Joh?" She could say that much.

"Asleep." He made her gasp again as his fingers slid between her legs into the wet, slick heat there.

"You sure?"

Torchay lifted his head, met her gaze. "Do you care?"

His thumb stroked across her sweet spot as his fingers slipped inside her, and Kallista came up off the bed onto head and heels. "No."

He smiled and moved his body over hers, into the place she made for him in the cradle of her hips. She smiled back. Oh, she had missed this, the heat and silken strength of him pushing deep inside her. Her breath sighed out as she took him in, and they fell into the familiar rhythm old as life itself.

"Call the magic." He breathed the words so quietly, she wasn't sure she heard him.

"What? Now?"

"Do it. Call magic." He drew back, holding his weight on his hands, never ceasing the deep rhythm as the lightning-bright blue of his eyes gazed into hers.

"Are you—" She locked her legs around him, trying to hold him still, but couldn't stop the motion of her own hips. "Is this no more than an attempt to wake my magic?"

She tried to fight free of him. Torchay collapsed, pinning her with his full weight, pressing her down.

"*No,*" he growled. "This is me making love to you. Nothing more. And nothing less."

He pushed deeper inside her, and she gasped. "I love you, Kallista. For ten years, I've loved you. Don't make this harder than it is."

"Then why—" She fought for breath as he stroked inside her again. "Why magic?"

"After yesterday, you have to ask?" He nuzzled her ear, licked her earlobe, brought himself out and back in. "I listened to the others wonder how much better ordinary sex might be with the magic added. I want to be the first to know. I wasn't the first one marked. I wasn't the first one you took to your bed. I want to be first at something."

"Oh, Torchay." Kallista's throat clogged with tears she refused to shed—save for the one, no, two, three—that got away. She wrapped her arms around him, holding him close with arms and legs, urging him on with an undulation of her hips. She turned, hunting through his wild red waves of hair till she found his ear. "I loved you first," she whispered. "I love you most."

He rose back onto his elbows, giving her a faintly mocking smile as he picked up his pace. "I bet you say that to all your iliasti."

She smiled, tried to shake her head, but the pleasure he gave her distracted. So she *reached* for magic instead, and found it.

Massive and sluggish, slow to rise, the magic allowed her to coax a tiny shred of it to life. Enough to make Torchay gasp as it flowed down the link between them. She played it back and forth, matching the magic to the rhythm of their increasingly frantic passion. He drove into her, harder, faster, until all three of them—Torchay, Kallista and the magic—exploded into climax together.

And Joh screamed.

# CHAPTER SIX

Torchay was on his feet, a blade in his hand, before Kallista could fight off her body's after-sex lassitude and scramble to the edge of the massive bed. Obed burst into the room, sword drawn, and Joh cried out again, thrashing on his narrow cot.

"*Joh.*" Kallista stumbled across the crowded space to bend over her new ilias. She smoothed his hair back out of his face and caught it between her hands. "Joh, wake up. It's a dream."

Behind her, Torchay had the key, was unlocking the chain from the wall. Joh shuddered, moaned, still caught by the dream. *Her* dream, she knew, one she should be dreaming. She got an arm beneath his shoulders, hauling his limp weight up into her lap where she could cuddle him against her naked body. Torchay had awakened from his dream when she held him close. Maybe it would bring Joh back.

"Wake up, soldier." She spoke into his ear. "Wake. Leave the dream behind. You're needed here."

Body racked with tremors, Joh's arms closed around her and tightened slowly, as if the dream were reluctant to let him go.

Kallista held him tighter, murmuring encouragement as he fought his way to consciousness.

She looked up once, saw Obed watching with his flat, black stare, his face devoid of all expression. Save for the tension she could see in his jaw, the flaring of his nostrils. He was not happy.

Deliberately, she turned from him, pressed a kiss to Joh's forehead and rested her cheek against his hair.

"Oh God." Joh was fully present now, his voice a frog's croak.

He held Kallista tight enough almost to hurt. She couldn't tell whether the damp against her breasts where his head was cradled was sweat or tears. It didn't matter. She stroked a hand down the long, straight sweep of his hair, past his shoulders to his waist. "Tell us your dream."

Joh let her go, sitting up, drawing himself straight as he wiped his face with both hands. "Not here. Sergeant Om—Torchay is right. This should not be spoken of in this room. It already invades our sleep. We do not need more."

Kallista pulled on the tunic Torchay handed her, but didn't take time for trousers. Obed went with her into the parlor, but waited for the others in silence, across the room from her.

"Is this how you keep your vows as ilias? Your promise to be one of us?" Kallista's question brought Obed's head around, and he stared at her.

"I ask only to serve you," he said after a moment, "and through you, the One above us all. But how can I, if I am not given the opportunity. Even the newest among us has been given—"

"Beware what you ask for, Obed." Torchay came into the room, Joh jingling behind him, both of them fully dressed. "Believe me when I tell you, you do not want these dreams. You don't." Torchay settled onto the sofa beside Kallista, touched her shoulder.

Joh sat on her other side, a careful distance away—enough room for Obed between. Kallista beckoned him closer without even glancing at her dark ilias. His choice, his problem. Joh obeyed, submitting to her arm around his shoulders with only a faint twitch.

"Before, when—" Joh hesitated, choosing words. "When Torchay told his dream, I heard him say 'demons,' but I still thought 'dreams.' I thought 'A dream is not so bad. A dream isn't real.' Demons are disturbing, perhaps even distressing, but in a dream, they aren't real. I thought Torchay…exaggerated."

He took a deep breath, hands closing blindly into fists. Kallista covered one with her hand, turning it, clasping it. After a time, he gripped her tight.

"I was wrong," he said. "It was not as real as you, here, holding my hand." He curled his other hand around hers. "But it was no dream."

"Yes," Torchay said. "What did you dream?"

Joh hesitated, eyes seeming to turn inward. Kallista used her free hand to tuck a stray strand of hair behind his ear, wondering whether she should encourage him or simply wait.

"I dreamed demons." He turned his eyes on Kallista, capturing her gaze, and held it while he spoke. As if she could keep the horror at bay. "Seven of them," he said. "The number of misfortune."

*Seven.* Kallista didn't speak aloud, not at this point. She wanted him to tell it at his own pace, without interruption, but her heart sank. *Seven demons?* Goddess help them all.

"Six were small, as if the largest, the oldest—" a sudden shudder caught him, but his eyes never left hers "—the most evil of them had pinched off bits of itself and sent them out to cause independent mischief. No—not mischief. Wickedness. Destruction. Death out of time."

"Why do you say that?" Kallista asked. "Death out of time?"

He blinked, slowly, the blue of his eyes shuttered, then shining again. "While I was away—in prison—I came to understand that death in itself is part of life. A blessing. It is death that comes out of its proper time that is an evil thing."

She tucked his words away to consider later. "Did you see all seven of the demons?"

"I could not see forms. Only darkness. Seven…darknesses. Scattered across Adara."

"Could you see where?"

"Here. At least one of them is here. Maybe two. If not here in Arikon, the second is close, I think. The others—" He grimaced. "I don't know. *Not* close, but how far away, I can't say."

Kallista struggled to wake the magic, to send it questing forth, seeking evil, but it merely turned round on its rug and lay down again. She swore. Torchay soothed her temper with a hand on her shoulder.

"Why did you shout?" he asked.

"Shout?" Joh chuckled, wry and self-mocking. "Speak truth. I screamed, friend."

"Ilias," Torchay corrected.

Joh's lips pressed tight. He didn't seem quite ready to accept the name or the role. But he clung to Kallista's hand. "It attacked me—I assume the same way it did you." He shuddered and Kallista put her arm around him again, hoping it would help. "That foulness…touched me. It was like—like the filth in the prison, but all that evil concentrated together into one touch that went *through* me."

He hunted words, chose them with desperate care. "It touched not just my skin, my outside, but *me*. It wiped that rotting filth on—on my soul. I can't—*God*." He shuddered. "I may never feel clean again."

"Now? You feel it now?" The idea worried Kallista. Could a man wear two marks?

She *reached* through her skin-to-skin link with Joh and kicked the magic awake. It had to be pushed and prodded every inch of the way, leaving Joh gasping with every shove as she hunted any sign of a lingering taint.

"You're clean." Relief had her leaning her forehead against his. "The demon left nothing behind."

"Saints and sinners." Joh shifted, turning his face away from the intimacy. "Is it like that every time?" He looked at Torchay, who shrugged.

"She lost her magic the day I was marked," he said. "After she destroyed the demon. I wouldn't know. Before yesterday, I've only been part of the magic that once."

Both men turned to look at Obed. Kallista looked, too. He wore his tattoos like a mask. "Yes," he said, voice empty. "The magic always feels good. Sometimes it feels better than other times, but always, it is good."

"You are sure the demon…left nothing?" Joh squeezed Kallista's hand, brought her attention back to him. "Why do I still feel it?"

"Memories linger." She leaned toward him, not particularly thinking of a kiss, but when he turned his face away to avoid one, she felt the loss.

Sick to death of men pulling away from her, Kallista stood and headed for the bedroom. "We need to see what this magic will do. As soon as we eat."

Through the half-closed door as she hunted clean trousers, she heard the hoarse tenor of Torchay's voice quietly pitching into Joh. *"Don't,"* he said. "Don't you ever again turn away. If she wants a kiss, you give it. Whatever she wants, you give it."

Joh's deeper voice rumbled something and Torchay came right back. "Damn right you don't deserve it. But you don't get to decide what you deserve. *She* does. She's the naitan and the captain. You're *di pentivas*. It's bad enough dealing with that one. She doesn't need two of you turning away."

Kallista sighed. She didn't need to force anyone either. That was as hard on her pride and her heart as having them back away.

"Torchay." She called his name through the door and the diatribe stopped. Or became quieter than she could hear.

After food and clothing, Kallista collected her gloves and her men and headed out into the huge palace complex, looking for enough privacy to practice her errant magic. She didn't know whether any magic would come when called, but she didn't want to take the chance that it would and then escape her control. Finding what they needed, however, seemed to be a more difficult problem than she'd anticipated.

The palace teemed with people. Kallista and her ilian already had neighbors in the suite below them and likely on the floor above, given the thumping coming through the ceiling. Likely had them on the floors above that as well. When they crossed over into Winterhold, it showed no signs of being emptied out for summer. In fact, it seemed more crowded than Summerglen.

Kallista spotted a familiar face in courier's gray and reached out to snag Viyelle before she vanished in the crowd. "Are you on assignment?"

"No, Captain." Viyelle saluted with perfect form. "What are your orders?"

"No orders. Just didn't want to delay you if you already had them." Kallista stepped into an alcove out of the jostling streams of people, drawing the younger woman with her. All three men took up posts at its entrance, playing bodyguard. Time to give the courier an opportunity to prove herself. The One was a God of second chances. Kallista could do no less. "Has every minor prinsep in Adara decided to take up residence in the palace?"

Viyelle's grin looked harassed. "It must be so. If I hadn't already taken oath as a courier, I would now, just to get a little space to breathe. As it is, I still have to share with my mother, because Courier's Quarters are filled up with displaced colonels and majors. I'm going to beg for an assignment. Any assignment. Anywhere. It's that or be taken up for matricide."

Kallista chuckled, amused by the prinsipella's irreverence. "If it gets too bad, you can come share our suite. We're only using one sleeping room. There are plenty more."

"I may. Since it didn't happen on our trip south, I know you won't kill me by accident while you sleep." She winked at Kallista.

"Brat." Kallista cuffed the back of her head, laughing. "If the rumors give us some privacy, I don't mind them. But listen, do you know of any place where we can practice our magic? Where no one will get cut if I happen to break a few windows?"

Viyelle made a face. "I'm not sure. Truly? I don't think so. The palace is overflowing. I have never in my life seen so many people crammed inside, and I've been coming here since before I can remember."

"What of the yard she used last year?" Joh turned slightly, spoke over his shoulder. "It was badly damaged in the explosion. Has it been repaired?"

Viyelle stared at him, and a slow flush rose on Joh's cheeks. "Isn't he the one—" she began.

"Yes," Kallista said. "But that's over. He's ilias now. Joh Suteny, Viyelle Torvyll."

"*Ilias?*" Viyelle's shocked expression smoothed into perfect courtier's courtesy when she glanced at Kallista. "Of course, Naitan. I am honored."

She put her right leg forward and swept into a graceful bow, flourishes and all. Joh blushed a deeper red and nodded.

"The courtyard?" Kallista prompted.

"Oh." Viyelle blinked back to awareness, out of her shock. "As he said, it was badly damaged. It may be available. Do you want me to investigate?"

"No need. We can check ourselves."

"Please, Naitan, let me see. Give me an assignment. Anything. *Please*. Do not send me back into that den of prinsipi that is my mother's chambers."

Viyelle's dramatically rolling eyes made Kallista laugh. "Go first and find out whether there might be real work for you. If there are more couriers than assignments, then come back and find me. We can discuss matters then. Oh, and Courier?"

"Yes, Captain?" She snapped to attention again.

Kallista blew out a breath. "I wish I knew whether it would be better to quash rumors or spread them."

"*Which* rumors, Naitan?" Viyelle asked carefully.

"Any rumors. About my magic. About our new ilias. Any of it." Kallista looked at Viyelle, seeing possibilities. "You've been coming to the palace since you were born. What would you recommend?"

"Spread them. They're going to talk anyway. See if you can turn them the way you want." Viyelle's eyes strayed toward Joh, her curiosity obvious. "I think—it is a good thing to have them a little afraid of you, Naitan. Taking this one as ilias shows you can forgive, that you are not totally heartless. The fact he is *di pentivas,* though—that shows you are not wholly foolish either."

"Good." Kallista squeezed Viyelle's shoulder, gratified by the good sense she showed. Maybe she had matured some. "And as we were not bosom friends the last time I was here—" she ignored Torchay's snicker "—everyone will believe you when you share this gossip."

"Yes, Captain." Viyelle saluted, face solemn, eyes dancing with mischief.

"It's not an official assignment, mind. The Reinine may have real work for you. But if you can…"

Viyelle grinned. "I like working with you much more than I thought I would. No wonder you collect men like honey draws bees."

And she was gone, leaving Kallista staring openmouthed after her and Torchay choking with laughter.

"Come along, woman." He snagged Kallista by the back of her neck, drawing her out of the alcove. "Let's go find your courtyard. Your collection is getting tired of standing about."

The courtyard was exactly where they had left it last summer. The huge slabs of broken stone that had tumbled from the walls in the gunpowder explosion had all been cleared away and the flooring swept clear of stone dust and powdered glass. But the windows lining two of the walls were still covered with boards on both the first and second floors, and the courtyard itself was abandoned.

Kallista made a circuit of the area, noting where masons and carpenters had put in posts and patches to brace the walls. The flagstone paving gleamed dully under its smooth coating. In one of her practice sessions, she'd converted the glass broken out of the windows by a ghost she'd raised into this impervious floor surface. She supposed it might have made the sweeping a bit easier, but otherwise didn't know what use it was.

"It looks safe enough," she said. "I doubt the walls will fall down on our heads."

"Not without another keg of gunpowder," Torchay agreed easily, watching Joh flush red.

Kallista slapped his arm. "Behave. And it seems quiet enough. The boards over the windows will help. No more glass to break, and it will keep the curious at bay. We may as well work here. We're not going to find any place better, not with this many people crowded in here."

"Agreed." Torchay looked to the other two, received their acknowledgment. He dropped to one knee and raised his hands palm up over his bowed head. "Naitan, I accept your gloves."

At those words, at the old, familiar ritual of a military naitan preparing for battle, Kallista felt her magic stir. Not the godstruck magic gifted by the One a short year ago, but her own. Magic given at her birth, wakened at puberty. Magic she knew better than her own heart, the lightning that had directed the course of her life.

One finger at a time, she drew off the supple, brown-leather regulation gloves that blocked all magic save for that under the most exquisite control. Once, the gloves could not block her lightning, but that had changed—along with everything else— one bright dawn on the battered walls of a city under siege. Now, Kallista could not swear to what might happen. Which was why they were here, in this protected place.

"Back away." She laid the gloves in Torchay's uplifted hands. "All of you. Joh, as far back as you can go. I'm calling my magic first, not yours."

Obedient but reluctant, the men moved away, all three of them clumped together at the end of Joh's magical tether. Kallista took a deep breath, refusing to think of the possibility that her magic might not answer her call. She'd felt it stir at Torchay's words. It was there. It would come. It had to. She wanted her babies safe.

Thrusting her fears back into the box from which they'd escaped, Kallista shook the tension from her shoulders, down her arms and out her bare fingers. Then she turned to face the direction of her magic—North—opening herself to its cold clarity, its icy precision. Its swift, ponderous, terrible face. And she *reached,* into the North, into the air around her, and called the lightning.

It was slow to build. It didn't flash into existence in a split second to blast forth and slaughter supper with a smell of burnt chicken feathers, as it had when she was barely thirteen. Tiny sparks skittered across her skin and set the loose hair at the nape of her neck to standing straight out. Kallista swept the sparks down, focusing the magic in her hands until she held a blazing, crackling ball before her.

She wanted to let it dance, send sparks pirouetting from finger to finger, but she could sense her control was precarious. The magic might simply fade away, or it might suddenly blaze with the power of a thousand natural lightnings and go blasting through the courtyard with deadly results.

So she focused carefully on what she wanted the sparks to do, compressing them between her hands until they became one, glowing almost too bright to look upon. Then with an outflung breath, she threw her hands wide and let the lightning fly. It slammed across the yard into the broken-off head of a gargoyle, scorching it black.

"So." Torchay sauntered toward her. "The lightning is back, but your control is not."

"And how would you know, Sergeant Know-It-All?" Kallista called a tiny spark, to be sure she could, and flicked it at him.

He dodged it, experience of years giving him the skill, and she snuffed it into nothing. "Because, love, if your control was all it should be, you'd still be putting on a show to impress our new ilias, rather than just blackening that poor, put-upon gargoyle."

She flicked another spark at him, catching him this time with a tiny shock on his shoulder. He simply stretched out his hand and touched her cheek, shocking her in return with the static that had built up around her. She laughed. "Not fair. I can't run or Joh will fall over."

"Then keep your sparks to yourself, woman." Torchay beckoned the others over. "What about your other magic?"

"Goddess, you are such a drill sergeant."

"I'm damn good at it, too. Can you call the other?"

Kallista let out a breath. She had her lightning back. She did not particularly want the rest of it, though she knew it was there. She'd been part of its violent reawakening, after all. However, much as she might prefer it, she couldn't ignore this god-struck magic. Truly, she wouldn't wish it away. She needed it. Torchay had seen demons. Joh had seen demons. Seven of them.

She held her naked hand out toward her newest ilias. With the link not yet fully formed between them, she needed skin-to-skin contact to call his magic. Without hesitation, Joh slid his hand into hers and closed his fingers gently. His trust felt good.

When the magic didn't rouse on its own, Kallista *reached* into Joh and nudged it. Then she hauled back and kicked it with iron-toed boots. The magic sputtered blearily into motion, and Kallista reached through the links to her other men.

The magic Torchay carried came only half-awake, but his magic held so much power that half-awake felt about right. She twined his magic together with Joh's, smacking it now and then to keep it alert, and she reached for Obed's magic.

Instead of answering her call and coming to do her bidding, the magic…turned its back on her. That wasn't exactly what it did, but that was what it felt like, like all the times Obed turned his back or walked away or looked through her. Kallista *reached* again, ready to shake it into obedience as she had been forced to do with Joh's and Torchay's magic. And it snarled at her, showing sharp, ugly teeth.

# CHAPTER SEVEN

Kallista jerked back, physically as well as magically. The braided magic in her hands fell to pieces, snapping back into its respective homes, leaving her with nothing.

Joh fell to his knees with the backlash, crying out in pain.

Torchay staggered but remained standing. "What happened?" He bent double, gasping as the reaction rebounded through him, hands braced on his knees. "What was that?"

"Backlash." Kallista tipped Joh's face up, checked him quickly—no permanent damage—and crossed to Torchay. "Sit down before you fall. Don't be such a bodyguard."

"I am a bodyguard," he rasped out as he sat on the ground. "I can't help it."

She could sense his nausea through the link, and when it settled, he would have a terrible headache. The backlash had hit him harder because his magic held so much more power. Like Fox's magic held order and Obed's held truth, Torchay's magic was power, strength. Which apparently had its price.

Kallista fought to control her anger. She had a right to it. Obed's attitude had put them all in danger. But this was not the time or place to let it out.

Blood trickled from Torchay's nose and he blotted it with a finger, surprised. Frantic, Kallista dove questing through his veins. If he bled where it could not be seen, it could kill him. But only the small vessel in his nose was broken.

Kallista held back any attempt to heal it. She knew too little of East magic, trusted too little in her control just now, and it was small enough to heal quickly on its own.

"What do you mean, backlash?" Torchay blotted his nose again and looked for something to clean his fingers. Kallista handed him her handkerchief. "What…? Was that magic?" He glared accusingly at Obed. "I thought you said the magic always felt good."

"Backlash doesn't." Kallista pushed Torchay's head forward. "Pinch your nose till it stops."

"Bud whad is—" he began.

"Backlash happens when the magic breaks. When it is interrupted for some reason, it snaps back into—usually into the naitan who is attempting to use it. Infirmaries at the academies are full of students suffering backlash. In this case, it snapped back into all of us."

"So why ab I de odly one wid a bloody dose?" Torchay sounded aggrieved.

"Because your magic is stronger than Joh's."

"Whad aboud Obed?" Torchay lifted his head, released his nose and wriggled it, testing for leaks. "He's just standing there like he wasn't touched."

"He wasn't." Kallista didn't look at her dark ilias. Not yet. She was too angry. "Obed and I are going to discuss it as soon as we get back to our chambers." She got a hand under Torchay's arm and lifted. "Up you go."

"Good idea." He swayed when he reached his feet. "I've had enough magic for today."

"Help Joh." Kallista snapped the order at Obed as she got her shoulder under Torchay and got him steadied. "And pray the One my temper calms before we get back."

The crowds they pushed through only made Kallista's temper worse. Thank the One that the crowds kept Torchay from asking the questions she knew were piling up behind his teeth. And the slow pace they were forced to take gave Torchay and Joh the time to recover most of their strength and equilibrium before they left Winterhold. By the time the door to their suite closed on the stream of people climbing the stairs to the towering heights above them, Kallista was angry enough to chew nails into bits.

"*You.* In there." She shoved Obed toward one of the small bedrooms, hard enough to make him stagger. Shoulders hunched, he went. Of course. She'd given him a direct order. "Wait until I come for you."

She turned to the others and had to make fists of her hands to stop their shaking. She had never in her life been so angry. "Joh, give me your hands."

When he held them out, his face calm and accepting, she unfastened his wristbands.

"Kallista, what are you doing?" Torchay stepped closer, then swore, blotting his nose. The bleeding had started again.

The sight of his blood showing bright red on the pale fabric of her handkerchief calmed her. The rage was still there, but it was deeper. Colder. Unaffected by petty annoyances like crowds or courtiers. Her hands no longer shook.

"I am going to deal with Obed." She gathered Joh's wristbands into one hand. "This is going to end today."

"Maybe you should wait. Let him stew in there for a while. Give yourself time to calm down."

"I am as calm as I wish to be. He needs to understand my anger."

"I don't," Torchay said. Joh let his confusion speak in his expression.

"You don't have to. Not now." Kallista looked down at the broad magic-spelled cuffs in her hand. "I won't hurt him—at least not more than he deserves. I have that much control." Her anger burned cold as she met Torchay's gaze. "This ends today, one way or another. He will overcome his difficulties and join with us, or I will have his mark."

"Can you do that?" Joh whispered.

Kallista did not pause to consider. "Today, I think I can."

She started for the door to the room where Obed waited. "Stay out, no matter what you may hear. You should rest."

"You expect us to rest after you say a thing like that?" Torchay took a step as if to accompany her, but stopped when she looked back at him. He straightened, saluted. "Yes, Captain."

"Joh, see he does it," she ordered. "Our room is close enough to this one that you shouldn't have problems."

"Yes, Captain." Joh was rubbing his wrists. The bands hadn't chafed. Maybe he felt strange with bare wrists. He had been shackled a long time.

Torchay wiped away another trickle of blood, refreshing Kallista's icy anger, and she entered the small bedroom.

Kallista did not see Obed as she closed the door behind her, and she wondered if he might have gone out the window. But the window was too narrow for his shoulders to fit, and Obed was not one to run from punishment. From Kallista and uncomfortable emotions, yes, but not punishment or duty.

Then she saw him. He lay naked on the bare wood floor at the far side of the bed, arms and legs outstretched in an *X*, his nose pressed flat against the floor. Kallista walked past the foot of the bed, staring. His lips moved, brushing the floor with every whispered word.

"Obed?"

He flinched, his whole body jerking as if she'd struck him rather than merely speaking his name.

"What are you doing?" Kallista stepped carefully over his right leg into the space next to his body, between his out-stretched arm and leg.

He did not turn his face to the side but kept it pressed straight into the polished wood as he spoke. "I have failed you and forsworn my vows. I am most abjectly sorry for my faults and I beg that you instruct me. Correct my flaws. Discipline my weaknesses so that I might not fail you again."

It sounded as if he repeated some ritual apology.

Would she never cease bumping into more of his Southron strangeness? It already had her losing her grip on her anger, though not on her determination to solve this problem.

The sight of his long powerful body stretched naked before her could also have something to do with the lessening of her anger. She had never before seen him completely nude, and not often without a shirt. He did not strip down as easily, as casually, as her other men did. Now, she could not help looking, especially since he was so well worth looking at, lean muscle beneath sleek skin in shades of brown from dark to pale to palest.

The wristbands shifted, clinked together, reminding Kallista she held them. She went down on one knee beside him, and was distracted by a silvery mark across the ivory skin of his buttocks. She touched it, and again he jumped as if struck.

Now she was close enough, she could see more of the marks, dozens of them. Scores. All across his buttocks, thighs and lower back, silvery and faint, but there. She traced her fingers across one and then another; Obed shivered, quaking under her touch.

"What are these?" She brushed the palm of her hand lightly over the webbed stripes on his thigh. She thought she knew, but asked anyway.

"Marks of discipline." Obed's voice came hoarse and rusty, choked off.

"Scars?"

"Yes."

Kallista sat, curling her legs to one side, and she sought out, touched, traced all the scars. "How did you get them?"

Obed took a shuddering breath. "When I was first sent to be a dedicat, to be trained as champion for the Shakiri line, I was unruly and without discipline. The first time—"

"No." She cut him off. She would hear his stories, all of them. She would learn what a dedicat was, what a champion did. But that was for later. "I mean, tell me what thing—what tool made these marks."

"The lash."

Kallista sighed. She did not know whether he was being deliberately obstructive or if he simply expected her to know these things. She laid her head on Obed's back where it rose toward his shoulders, watching her hand move across his marred skin. "Tell me about the lash. What is it like? What is it used for?"

"It is five long strips of soft leather bound to a short handle. It is used for discipline because it gets the attention of the rebellious without causing serious injury."

"But you have all these scars."

"I was very rebellious. And I—my skin marks easily, and holds the mark."

"These marks look as if they've been here a fair piece of time." Kallista rolled her head forward and pressed her lips to one of the scars in the small of his back. Obed jolted and she smiled. "Why is that?"

"I did, eventually, learn discipline. I have not known the lash for fifteen years."

*How young had he been when he acquired these?* She would discover this, but later. "And you expect me to use this lash on you?"

Every muscle in Obed's body went tight, almost bouncing her head from his back. "I have failed you and forsworn my vows," he said. "I am most abjectly sorry for my faults and I beg—"

"Be still." Kallista sat up and set her hand on his head to quiet him, combing her fingers through his hair.

She had come into this room filled with a cold and righteous rage, ready to cast him aside if he could not control his moods. She had found him waiting for the worst. Expecting it, as if he deserved nothing more.

Perhaps the problem here was not that Obed was out of control, but that he was *too* controlled. Perhaps if Kallista took control out of his hands so that he did not have to master himself—would he let her? Could he let himself go so far?

"Give me your hand."

Obed bent his arm at the elbow, lifting his hand in the air above his head, and Kallista closed a band around his wrist.

"Now the other." She rose onto her knees and completed her tasks. When both cuffs were on, his hands still raised in the air, she linked them together and locked them down.

Obed's trembling grew, becoming an almost continuous shudder. Kallista stroked her hand from his head, down his shoulders, across his back to his buttocks and along one thigh. Then she got to her feet.

"I have failed you and forsworn my vows," Obed began again, voice breaking. This time she let him get all the way through the ritual formula, mouthing the words with him to imprint them on her memory.

"Stand," she said.

He brought his hands down and used them to push himself off the floor, straightening slowly. He did not seem to know what to do with his locked-together hands, finally letting them hover at chest height. He stared straight ahead, as if he could see through the wall into the room they'd shared last night. And he was beautiful, just as he had been in her dreams before he ever walked into the Reinine's great hall and into her life. But this was no dream. He was here, naked, aroused and under her control.

"Oh, Obed, what am I going to do with you?" Kallista set her hands on his shoulders and rested her forehead against the warm dark skin of his back. "Are you truly abjectly sorry? Do you even know what happened?"

"I—I am *most* abjectly sorry for my faults and I beg that you instruct me." He stuttered as her arms came around his waist. "I—instruct me."

"You don't know, do you?" Her hands pressed flat over the smooth skin of his stomach and he sucked in a sharp breath.

"Instruct me." His breathing did not even out, became more ragged, though Kallista's hands did not move. "Correct my flaws. Discipline my weaknesses. *Please*." The word was a groan. "I would not fail you again."

She turned her head, resting her cheek against his back, holding him in her arms. "Your discipline is so strong. For fifteen years it has been perfect. What I would teach you is not discipline."

"Then teach me what you wish me to know." The words burst from him and he shuddered violently. "Instruct me."

But how? Kallista could feel the tension humming through him as he trembled in her embrace, as if standing motionless required all the will he possessed. She could sense nothing through the link and doubted she would, as tight as he maintained his control.

She stepped back from him. "Up." She gave him a little push. "Onto the bed. On your back."

Another shudder jolted through him as he obeyed. Did he shake with fear or arousal? Perhaps both. Obed raised his hands over his head when she touched his elbow and motioned. On the headboard, she found an opening as if made to hold the *pentivas* cuffs. Had there been so many *di pentivas* mates in those times? Or had the Reinine gathered up all the specially made furniture and sent it here? It didn't matter. Kallista fastened the cuffs in place and felt Obed's muscles lock tighter.

"This is not discipline, Obed." She smoothed her hands down his arms till they came to rest on the tattoos high on either side of his chest. "I am not going to punish you. But I will not allow you to fail me again."

He turned his face away, flushing a dull red beneath the tattoos on his tanned cheekbones.

Kallista took his face between her hands and brought it back. "Look at me, Obed. Listen to me. You are not solely to blame in this. It is as much my fault for not making you understand. For not trying to understand you. For allowing this to happen.

"I am the naitan. I am the one with mastery over the magic, and it is my task to control it, not yours. This was *my* failure."

"*No.*" A whisper of a word, almost lost in the harshness of his breathing.

"You don't even know what happened. How could it be your fault?" She smoothed the black tangle of his hair from his face and stood.

"You said backlash happens when magic is interrupted. It was my anger that—" He broke off to stare as Kallista stripped off her tunic and chemise in one awkward motion. Moments later, she was as bare as Obed, and she stretched out onto the bed beside him.

He squeezed his eyes tightly shut, pressing his head back into the pillows, and groaned. "Goddess, save me."

"I won't let it happen again." Kallista held herself back from the need for skin-to-skin contact, keeping a small distance between them. "I will not let you fail. Do you trust me to do this, to keep you from failing?"

"Kallista—" He ground out her name through clenched teeth, twisting away from her, pulling against the cuffs that confined him.

"Look at me, Obed. *Listen.*" She caught his shoulder and pushed him flat on the bed. "You can't escape me. I won't let you hide. Do you trust me?"

The struggle went out of him in an instant and he finally met her gaze. Long moments passed as he stared into her eyes, then his eyelids fluttered shut and he took and released a deep breath. "Yes," he said. "I trust you."

Kallista let go of the breath she hadn't realized she was holding. She could sense Obed through the link again, the faintest awareness of his presence. He did trust her, it seemed.

Finally, she let herself roll against him, her breasts pressed to his side, her knee sliding up over his legs. His whole body went taut.

"I cannot—my control is—" He closed his teeth on the words, hands fisting in the wide gold-and-silver cuffs. His hips rose, thrusting his erection into the air.

"You don't need control. I have it. I have you." She rose to straddle his thighs. "I remember what you said. That when we made love, it would be skin to skin, you inside me."

"Kallista, *please.*"

The instant she came down over him, he convulsed in climax with a shout, lifting her off the bed in a wild, bucking ride. She opened the link wide, let his climax sweep her into one of her own, taking care in the midst of pleasure to prop the door open so he could not shut her out again.

She was lying bonelessly over him, beginning to assemble a few random thoughts when she realized Obed was speaking. He was repeating that damned apology again, but he kept getting stuck at "I am most abjectly sorry."

Summoning up the strength to move, Kallista slid her hand up and put it over his mouth to stop the flow of words. Then, as he slipped out of her, she heaved herself up onto an elbow so she could see his face. "What in seven hells are you sorry for now?"

She took her hand from his mouth and he answered, "I have failed you and forsaken—"

She put her hand back. "I do not want to hear that again. Talk sense. How *exactly* have you failed?"

"I did not—I—" He blushed. It was adorable, but Kallista resisted kissing him. With effort. "A man ensures that his—ilias finds her pleasure before taking his own. I was…hasty. My control—"

Kallista slapped his chest, hard. "Damn your control. What do you think you are going to control lying locked to this bed? I am in control, Obed. Not you. *Me.* Besides, what makes you think I didn't 'find my pleasure'?"

He blinked at her. "Because I was so… You did?"

"The magic helped. I told you I wouldn't let you fail. Couldn't you tell?"

"I—that is—no, I haven't done this before, so I wasn't—"

"Wait." Kallista put her hand over his mouth again. "What do you mean? You haven't done this—ever?"

He shook his head, his silence reminding her to move her hand so he could answer. "Except for the times you caught me in the magic, this was the first time I have made love to a woman. To anyone."

"Well…" Kallista struggled for words. "Khralsh's bloody hells. No wonder the magic got all bollixed up. Why didn't you tell me? I mean, a year without sex is bad enough, but—you're what? Thirty-three?"

"Thirty-four."

"Oh my saints and all the holy sinners." Kallista couldn't get her mind around his news. "How? *Why?*"

His lips twitched in a self-mocking smile. "How? *Discipline*. As for why—for twenty years, I was a dedicat champion. One of the holy sinners. We refrain from many things to make up for our necessary sins. After that—I was coming to find you."

He jerked at the cuffs holding him prisoner. "Will you release me? I want to hold you."

"Not yet." Kallista lay back down on top of him, wrapping him in her arms and legs. "I'll hold you. There really are such things as holy sinners? But how can you be both? No—" She shook her head, before settling it atop one of his chest tattoos. "Never mind. You can tell me later. We need to be sure the magic is sorted now."

Obed went quiet. She sensed him pulling away from the link and she slapped it back open, but she waited for him to speak.

"Is that why you made love to me?" He wouldn't meet her eyes again. "For the sake of the magic?"

Kallista sighed. Men were so difficult. "Partly. But *only* partly."

Through the link she could sense anger, sorrow, seething jealousy, shame. Only honesty could fix this. "I wanted you from the beginning, Obed," she said, "but it didn't feel right. Not until I came to love you. Until I admitted to myself that I did. But that was when you started to pull back from me. I thought I ought to give you space to decide what you wanted, and when you were ready, you would let me know. Obviously, I was wrong."

His eyes flicked up, caught hers. An improvement. "Did you just say—you love me?"

"I should have told you." She heard his vulnerability, began to hide her own, then didn't. She couldn't demand his trust without offering hers. "I said it, but not to you, not this way, between us alone. It gets…diluted when everyone is there. But I wasn't sure you wanted to hear it."

"I want to hear it again."

She laughed, scooted up his chest to kiss him. "I do love you, Obed."

"And I you," he breathed. He jerked at the cuffs. "Let me loose."

"Not yet," she said again. She found his ear, closed her teeth on his earlobe and spoke while she held it. "Your ears are so small and close to your head at their tops and so big and loose down here. You should wear an earring."

He shuddered as she bit down a fraction harder. "That is decadent behavior."

"Be decadent for once. If I give you an earring, will you wear it?"

"Yes." He turned his head, hunting her lips. Kallista evaded him to pounce on his other ear. "You know I will do anything you ask."

She pulled back to see him. "But will you do it grudgingly? Or with joy?"

"I—"

"Joy isn't a sin, Obed. It's not something you have to deny yourself. I think perhaps you have denied yourself so many things, for so many years, you don't know how to stop. You don't know how to let go, how to be happy."

"Instruct me," he said. "Correct my flaws. Use me, Kallista. Teach me joy."

She reached for his magic and this time, it rose to her call. She could feel his body respond as well, both through the link and against her inner thigh. He groaned as he grew thick and firm, his erection lying straight along his stomach.

"I told you," she whispered. "I will not let you fail me. This magic is inside you. It is part of you, put there for me, and if matters are not right between us, it shows in the magic. Give yourself into my hands. There is nothing here you must control. Nothing you *can* control. Not even your own body. I love you. I will take care of you. Trust me."

"I do."

Kallista let the magic slide away. She didn't want it hurrying anyone along, not this time. Obed's first experience should be more than a brief explosion.

Her own initiation into the wonders of sex had been so long ago she could scarcely recall it. Behind the protection of magic, Adaran youth were permitted to explore, particularly after the young men went away at sixteen to fulfill their six years of military service. Once an Adaran joined an ilian, however, exploration was limited to the other oath-bound members. Obed deserved his opportunity to explore, to be explored. To be loved.

She began at the top, pressing a kiss to his forehead. She kissed each of his eyes closed, smoothing her thumbs over his heavy eyebrows as she outlined the tattoos on his cheekbones with her tongue.

Obed twisted, stretching toward her. She kept just out of his reach for a moment and a half before she let him kiss her. She taught him the openmouthed dance of tongues, giving what she would take, then left him before he was ready, to finish her journey.

Inch by inch, she discovered her lover's body, using hands, lips, tongue, sometimes teeth. She found his nipples hidden in the coating of black hair that covered his chest and teased them into hard peaks, then found it needful to have him do the same to her own.

The tattoos on his body called to her, intrigued her. Kallista traced the two high on his chest first with fingertips, then her tongue, following the flowing liquid shapes of Southron writing.

"What do they mean, your tattoos?"

## CHAPTER EIGHT

Kallista moved down Obed's body to the tattoo encircling his navel and began her exploration again.

Obed's stomach jerked when she touched him. "That one says that my victory comes from the One."

"Are you victorious, my Obed?"

"Am I not here with you?"

"And that constitutes victory?" She smiled though his words worried her a bit. "Who did you defeat to win this victory?"

"I did not defeat anyone. I surrendered. And I have won everything."

Perhaps he did understand. By giving himself completely into the hands of the One, just as he gave himself into her hands, he gained everything he wanted. It wasn't necessarily what he *thought* he wanted—Kallista knew that from her own experience. And from that same source, she knew that what he gained would be a thousand times more than he had ever hoped.

"What of the other marks?" Kallista touched his shoulder and the marking below it as she licked across his navel. "What do they mean?"

Obed paused to catch his breath before speaking. "On my

face, the marks show that I am a dedicat, set aside for service to the One. I received those the day I entered the skola." He choked and had to cough his way clear when Kallista settled herself between his legs.

She kissed his thigh. "Go on."

"On my hands—" His voice began rusty, then evened out. He lifted his right shoulder to indicate the imprisoned hand. "This one says 'Duty.' The other says 'Service.'"

He bent his left knee, running his foot up the back of her leg. "This foot proclaims 'Faith,' for I must stand fast in my faith to prevail, and this—" He brought his right foot up, embracing her with his legs. "This mark says 'Knowledge,' for without grounding in knowledge, all men are fools."

Obed groaned, pulling her in tighter to his body with his legs. "Kallista, I will go mad."

"Not yet, you won't." She licked along the soft, vulnerable line between his hip and leg, then blew on it, laughing gently when Obed thrashed and swore. "Finish. What do these mean?"

She slid her hand up his body, stroking across the ivory silk of his skin, noting each scarred imperfection. He had many more scars than the marks on his backside, marks from fighting, from knife and sword and other, stranger, weapons. She touched his left shoulder. "What does this one signify?"

"Sacrifice."

"And this?" She swept her hand to the other tattoo.

"Purity." He yanked at the cuffs with sudden violence, fighting hard to get free.

She backed away and let him struggle, trusting the *pentivas* magic to hold him, giving him room so he could let his frustrations go without having to fear hurting her.

He didn't fight for long, collapsing into the bedding with a shout. "Why do you torment me? Why do you keep me bound? Do you not trust *me*?"

"Shh." Kallista came back over him, sliding her body along

his, the link wide open so she could feel his pleasure as well as her own. "I trust you, my love, but you do not yet trust yourself. You fear failing me. You fear doing the wrong thing. But since the cuffs will not let you do anything, they—I hope—will allow you to let go of these fears. It doesn't matter what you do. Shout. Fight. Even sulk. You won't fail because I won't allow it."

"Even if I spill myself across the white skin of your belly because you have teased me beyond enduring?"

His words made her whole body draw tight with anticipation. "If the magic can push you to climax, don't you think it can also hold you back?" Kallista wasn't any too certain it could. She'd never tried it, but Obed needed certainty from her or he would never relax his defenses.

Even now, with the link between them wide open, he held part of himself back, clinging to his precious control. His hard-won discipline. Kallista *reached,* took hold of his magic, drawing a gasp from him. His body jerked, his penis throbbed against her stomach, but the magic proved her right.

"Let go," she whispered. "You're not in this alone. Together, we can fly." And as she sensed the last bit of Obed's resistance dissolve, Kallista lifted herself and took him inside.

His shout echoed around the little room and out the open window. Kallista laughed, delighting in his pleasure, letting it add to her own. The magic played between them, binding them closer, mingling the sensations until she scarcely knew which were her own or who it was that needed more, faster, harder.

With one hand, she released the simple latches that held Obed's cuffs to the bed, then found the catch binding them to each other. As soon as his hands were free, he threw them around her. Kallista twined her legs in his and rolled, bringing Obed on top.

Before he had a chance to think, to worry about "doing it right," Kallista bit down on one of his fat earlobes. "Now. *More.*"

She licked over his earlobe and sucked it into her mouth a moment. Then she released him and sent the magic crashing through them both.

It swept everything before it as Obed began to drive into her, as if he wanted to come out the other side. Kallista wrapped her legs higher, around his waist, and rose to meet every wild, out-of-control thrust. She was as out of control as he and she loved every frantic instant of it, bodies slamming together, cries forced from two throats, magic careening crazily through them. The magic escaped her and for a brief moment she caught a faint sense of Torchay before climax hit and obliterated everything but screaming, drowning pleasure.

Obed collapsed on top of her. Kallista held him close, kissing whatever part of him lay within reach. His shoulder, she thought, and his neck, his throat. When she believed her voice might work again, she spoke. "If you ask me, control is highly overrated."

"I felt it," he said, "felt *you.* I felt your pleasure with my own. That is not…ordinary."

"Magic. *We* are not ordinary, love." She let her arms fall to either side, releasing him, and cocked a suspicious eye at him. "That doesn't break some secret rule of yours, does it? To call magic while we—"

He chuckled, moving off her. "No. You are my only rule now."

"Oh. Well…good." Sleep lapped at the edges of her consciousness, but something nagged at her, something she needed to be sure of before she could relax. The bed felt empty.

They were an ilian. They had other mates, and she didn't think it would be good for Obed to pretend otherwise. She suspected that might have been part of his difficulty before. She wished she knew for certain.

Kallista rolled away from him when he would have gathered her close. "Come." She took his hand and pulled him from the bed. "I'm tired. Our sleep last night was interrupted too many times, but I can't sleep without all our iliasti around us."

She led him naked through the parlor into the big room next door. Torchay roused briefly when she shoved him over to make room for two more.

A knocking at the door to the suite roused Torchay who stumbled out to see what in blazing hells the interlopers wanted. He returned rubbing sleep out of his eyes and hair out of his face, staring at the piece of unfolded parchment in his hand. "How awake are you, Kallista?"

She rolled her head onto Obed's naked back and opened one eye. "Why? How awake do I have to be?"

"More awake than I am." He yawned and handed her the paper.

With a heavy sigh, she opened her other eye and crawled higher to prop her elbows on Obed. Then she looked at the parchment. The note was written in an unfamiliar scrawl. Kallista frowned, trying to focus her eyes well enough to decipher it.

"What is it?" Obed asked from his position beneath her, lying on his face.

She moved the note closer to her eyes, then farther away. Neither one seemed to help. She'd seldom seen handwriting so bad. "It's either an order to extricate swollen monkeys from beer barrels in the attics at midnight, or it's an invitation to dine with the Reinine and her ilian in their chambers tonight. I think." She handed the note back to Torchay.

"On the whole," he said, peering at it with one eye closed, "I think I'd rather deal with the monkeys."

"As would I," Obed agreed.

"You'll get no argument from me." Kallista stretched, rolling onto her back. "However—"

"Aye." Torchay sounded as disappointed as she felt. The monkeys might have been fun.

"What time is it?" She peered out the distant window, but couldn't see any of the tower clocks.

"Time to start getting ready." Torchay opened the massive wardrobe that contained their pitifully small collection of clothing.

"What is Joh going to wear?" Kallista sat up, a yawn popping her jaw. "We don't have his dress uniform."

"I'm not a lieutenant." The chain fastening Joh to the wall rattled as he sat up on his cot. "I couldn't wear it even if you had one."

"You can wear my green." Torchay pulled the garment from its hook and crossed the room, searching in his waistpocket for the key. "And I wish you'd stop fastening yourself to the wall every time I blink. It's getting damned tedious to keep *un*fastening you."

"I am still a convicted felon." Joh caught the tunic Torchay threw at him. "I am required to be confined."

"You are confined. You can't get twenty paces from her without falling down in a fit." Torchay unlocked the chain. Joh began looping it around the ankle band again.

Kallista made a mental note to ask the Reinine for another favor during the meal. She heard Obed rustling behind her and managed not to startle when he kissed her bare shoulder. She didn't need to be skittish of him now, not when she'd finally got him past his skittishness. She reached over her shoulder to touch his cheek, let him know his kiss was welcomed. It seemed to satisfy him.

"I'll need the armbands back." Joh crossed to pour more water into the basin Torchay had just emptied.

"I don't think so." Kallista shook her head. "I think Obed needs to wear them a while yet."

Torchay slanted her a quick glance as his head appeared through the top of his dress uniform tunic. He'd brought the sleeveless summer uniform, though time to change from the long-sleeved winter ones hadn't yet arrived. It doubtless would before they got home again. "That will look a bit peculiar, won't it?" he said. "With one ilias in the ankle chains and the other in the cuffs."

"Everyone thinks we're peculiar already." Kallista shrugged. "This won't make much difference."

"I don't mind." Obed tucked his arm around her waist and pulled her back into his still-naked body.

Kallista tilted her head to give him better access to her neck for more of the kisses he was laying there. Her dress tunic hit her in the face, followed quickly by her chemise.

"Get yourself dressed, woman," Torchay said, voice bland. "Or you'll have the rest of us joining you and we'll be late. You don't keep the Reinine of all Adara waiting because you're too distracting naked."

With a quick kiss on Obed's bristled cheek, Kallista escaped the bed's temptations and scrambled into her chemise. "It's you three who are too distracting. You know how mindless I get around handsome men. Given our ilian, it's a wonder I have any sense left me at all."

Pulling her tunic on for an extra layer of safety, Kallista pounced on Torchay to claim a kiss, and laughing, he gave it. "Have a care with the magic," he murmured in her ear, pretending to nuzzle. "You caught me in it for a moment there."

"Not necessarily a bad thing," Kallista murmured back. She took the leggings he shoved into her hands and wriggled into them before crossing to Joh, dressed now in Torchay's best, darkest-green tunic.

She caught his arm, turned him to face her and he stiffened, drawing himself straight, away from her. Then he seemed to catch himself, or perhaps it was that their gazes tangled. He was still filled with tension, every chiseled muscle taut, but all of that tension was focused on her. "You have a kiss for me?"

"Are you not ilias?" The words slid out on a breath and when they were gone, she touched her mouth to his.

The magic inside him shuddered and his mouth opened, his hands gripped her arms, his tongue thrust past hers. Then the magic quieted when she did not command it. Joh seemed to suddenly recognize his actions and stifled his demands, offering only acceptance.

It made it possible for Kallista to end the kiss. "I prefer your aggression," she said to him alone. "It lets me know I am wanted, rather than merely endured."

"Doesn't the magic tell you everything?" He spoke just as quietly.

Her smile was crooked. "I cannot read your mind. Cannot always tell emotions—especially if you hide them. You are still only yourself alone inside your head." She nudged him toward a chair. "Sit. I'll repair your queue for you."

His startlement showed in his eyes. "Yes. Thank you."

In the end, Kallista braided the queues of her iliasti who wore them, and Obed—who always wore his hair loose to his shoulders—braided hers. It wasn't as tight as Torchay could get it, but Obed offered first.

They were a fine-looking group, Kallista thought rather smugly as they paraded through the palace to the tower the Reinine had appropriated for her quarters this summer. Torchay positively glittered in the candlelight reflecting off the gold threads in the shield of his home prinsipality embroidered on his tunic. The red-and-gold stag almost leaped to life. Light flashed from the layered honors dangling from his chain belt, chinking against each other as he walked. Kallista's belt made as much noise and together they nearly drowned out the sound of Joh's chains.

Joh looked strange to her, wearing the plain-cut, unadorned tunic of a civilian, but the green suited him almost as well as it suited Torchay. Even Obed glittered tonight. The black of his so Southron ankle-length overrobe was thick with silver embroidery over his shoulders and at the hems of the sleeves. The ilian caught the attention of everyone they passed. It worried Kallista a bit. Last year, attention had brought gossip and gossip had brought trouble. She hoped this year would be different.

Starlight Tower was slightly farther from Daybright than the tower the Reinine had used last year. They had to walk through more of the crowded palace corridors to reach it. Unlike most other Reinines in Adara's history, Serysta Reinine chose new chambers with every move from summer to winter and back again. She was said to claim it kept her from boredom. Kallista didn't know the truth of it. She hadn't asked. She and the Reinine weren't chums. They were ruler and captain.

Kallista used the longer walk to keep her eyes and ears open, hoping to pick up a sense of the city's mood. Or at least, of the palace's mood, and its attitude toward her and hers. She saw Courier Viyelle Torvyll Prinsipella in her grays, lounging near the stairs leading up into Starlight Tower, as she gossiped with a cluster of bright-plumaged courtiers, most wearing the short-cropped hairstyle of the young, reckless bravos.

As Kallista passed with her men, Viyelle gave no sign of noticing them, until she lowered one eyelid in a slow, hidden wink. Did that mean the rumor-mongering went well?

Surely it did. Kallista had not noticed any of the sudden silences or hissing whispers they'd been surrounded with last year. She handed the note to the guard at the foot of the stairwell. He looked at it and gestured them up. Now,

Kallista could feel the envious stares stabbing between her shoulders. Nothing good could come of this favoritism showed by the Reinine. She hoped nothing too awfully bad would result.

The door to the Reinine's private suite was opened by a woman in a dress uniform identical to Torchay's—bodyguard's black, trimmed with blue, save where Torchay's bore a stag, hers was embroidered with a triad of scallop shells in silver and white. Kallista could not remember which prinsipality claimed that shield, except that it was somewhere on the long northern coast. The bracelets on both her wrists were silver to match.

The woman was older than Kallista by at least ten years, and taller. Tall as Torchay or Joh. She wore her reddish brown hair pulled back hard into a regulation queue, and freckles liberally dotted her tanned face. She stood blocking their path long enough for Kallista to observe all this as well as the fine lines radiating from the corners of her eyes and the blended green and brown of those eyes, until the Reinine spoke.

"Leyja, have our guests arrived?"

"They have, Naitan." With one last glare at Torchay, the woman stepped back and admitted them to the private chambers of the ruler of all Adara.

Kallista swept into a deep bow in unison with her men. This might be an "intimate" dinner, but the Reinine was still the Reinine.

"I bid welcome to your ilian, welcome to this house." As the highest ranking member of her ilian, the Reinine spoke the old words of formal greeting.

"I thank you for your generous hospitality." Kallista rose from her bow, speaking for her family. "Peace between us."

"Peace between us," Torchay echoed her a fraction faster than the other two. He stepped forward, offering an open hand to the Reinine's gray-haired ilias.

After a moment's hesitation, Keldrey gripped it and nodded. "Peace."

"Peace?" The woman who was bodyguard and ilias sounded outraged.

"Yes, Leyja, *peace.*" The Reinine laid a hand on her ilias's arm. "If they can forgive enough to marry one who nearly killed half their number, you can be civil to one who offended far less."

Kallista touched Joh's arm to ease his recoil at the Reinine's words. Torchay bowed again, lower. "I apologize for my offense. Peace between us."

Still Leyja scowled, until the Reinine—did she pinch her? Kallista hid her smile as Leyja stepped forward and spoke, "Peace."

She did not take Torchay's hand, but the Reinine was satisfied, so Kallista was as well.

"Let me make you known to my ilian." The Reinine gestured them farther into the elegant silver-and-blue-appointed parlor. "Keldrey you have met. These are Leyja, Syr and Ferenday."

The two other men were of an age with their iliasti, Syr tall and lean with pale brown hair behind a receding hairline and Ferenday stocky and dark. They nodded without speaking. Kallista introduced her mates to those who hadn't met them already and the Reinine led the way to a table groaning with food. Kallista's stomach reminded her that she hadn't bothered to fill it since morning.

When the food had been blessed, shared among plates and begun to enter empty stomachs, Kallista dared to move beyond trivial small talk. "I know we were isolated in our mountain home, but I wonder that we had not heard of your marriage, my Reinine."

"You should not." Serysta Reinine sounded sour. "The prinsipi's council would far rather it had not happened at all, but since they have no power to dissolve it without our agreement, they seem determined to keep it secret, or pretend it did not take place."

Kallista frowned. "Why would they do that? I admit, I know nothing of politics or diplomacy—"

"The marriage of a Reinine—indeed, of a prinsep or prinsipella—is a matter of state. Alliances are made, and sometimes broken, through bonds of ilian. There was no political advantage to marrying my bodyguards."

"Then why did you? If you don't mind my asking."

"We've asked her that ourselves," Keldrey said from the far end of the table. "Often. Especially when the council has been yapping at her again."

"Because I could not contemplate life without the four of you at my side," the Reinine snapped. She paused to eliminate her small show of temper. "Forgive me for my lapse in manners."

"No forgiveness is required, Your Majesty." Kallista did her best to bow while seated, without much success.

"When I was selected to be Reinine, I left my temple bonds. I decided that I would not marry again. I was older than you are now, my children were grown, or nearly so. I thought I could avoid problems by avoiding entanglements. There would be no appearance of partiality, none could accuse me of favoritism." She took a deep breath and let it out. "These four were named my bodyguards at that time, two on duty at every hour."

Kallista nodded. The Reinine was certainly more important than an ordinary military naitan with a single guard. In the part of her mind not paying attention, Kallista wondered why the Reinine had not been targeted with the army's naitani in the assassins' attack. Because of those bodyguards? Because the Reinine's truthsaying magic was not as dangerous as a soldier naitan's fire or lightning? Or was it that the rebels were not yet ready to make such a move? She shook off the disturbing questions to listen.

"Last year," Serysta went on, "with the Tibran invasion, the prinsipi's council began making noises about new body-guards. These four were getting old, they said. Losing steps."

"They were right," Keldrey said. "We are losing steps."

Leyja nodded agreement. The other two just watched. They seemed even more silent than the usual run of bodyguard.

"I don't care," Serysta retorted. "I want you with me. Who knows if these barely budded beginners can be trusted? There's a rebellion on."

"You know," Leyja said. "You're a truthsayer. You know."

Serysta frowned. "It's just that—" She waved a hand. "No matter. We are ilian, and that's the end of it. If I knew who would be selected as Reinine after me, I would tell her 'Bring your ilian with you.' It's not good to do this alone."

"It will be many years yet before Adara must face that choice." Cold ran down Kallista's spine at the thought of Adara's prinsipi and prelates gathering to select a new Reinine. Almost as if the magic reacted.

"Enough about personal matters." Serysta Reinine's smile was sly. "Or at least about *my* personal matters. What of yours? You seem of different minds than when you left me yesterday."

"We…worked things out." Kallista lifted her glass to her ilian. "When magic carries you through a person's soul, you know very well what sort of person he is. Joh will do very well with us, I think."

"And your magic? How did it go in the courtyard this morning?"

Kallista saw Obed's blush and couldn't hide her own. "We ran into a few more things that needed to be worked out." Her solution had worked, but she couldn't deny that tying up one's ilias for sex was decadent behavior.

"But your magic *has* returned."

"I think so." Kallista shook her head, frowned. "Control over my own magic, my lightning, is not what it should be. Control over the godstruck magic is worse. I can scarcely call it to my hand. It does not respond willingly, and I don't know whether that is because it has not completely recovered after the twins, or because three of our number are not with us. I know two of those missing hold order and eagerness in their magic, which could be the cause of the problem."

The Reinine frowned, exchanged a glance with her iliasti. "But you *can* use it, can't you?"

This third question about the magic disturbed Kallista. Even with the attacks on the generals and the naitani, Arikon itself was secure. Wasn't it?

"My Reinine." Kallista set her fork beside her plate. "I realize that I am only a captain in your service, and that there are many things I do not need to know. But is there some urgency greater than I have been told?"

She realized then that she knew things the Reinine did not know. Things that were very, very urgent.

"I have been—" Serysta began at the same time Kallista spoke again.

"You should know—"

They both broke off, and the Reinine gestured for Kallista to go on. "What is it I should know?"

"Dreams," Kallista said. "My iliasti have had dreams. This is why I do not yet trust my magic, because their dreams should have been mine."

"And what have your iliasti dreamed?" Serysta lounged in her chair as if relaxed, but the knuckles on her hand around the silver goblet were white.

Torchay leaned forward. "Demons," he said. "On the plain before Arikon."

"Seven demons," Joh said from his spot near the far end of

the table. "At least one of them inside the city. Another close by. The rest are scattered across Adara."

Serysta Reinine slowly set her goblet back on the table. "You are certain of this? That it was demons you dreamed?"

"What else could hold such evil?" Joh asked.

"I know demons," Torchay said. "I've seen one before, in the Tibran capital when Kallista destroyed it. I saw it through her eyes. I know how they appear. I felt its attack. I know their evil. *I know.* They were demons in my dream."

## CHAPTER NINE

Serysta Reinine looked up from her plate. "This could explain a problem of—"

"No, Naitan," Leyja protested as Keldrey called the Reinine by name.

"She must know." Serysta waved aside their protests. "The captain is godstruck. There is no falsehood in her, only concern for Adara. I can trust her and her ilian. You were there when they were bound. They are truly one. You know that. They are the only ones I can trust, aside from you, my ilian, in this whole deceit-riddled place."

The depth of trust displayed by the Reinine of all Adara made Kallista blink. "However I may serve, my Reinine, you know you have only to ask it."

Serysta's smile held teasing. "And then you will argue with me until I have changed my mind."

*Did she dare respond in kind?* Kallista pretended to frown. "Not so, my Reinine. I will argue until *you* have changed *mine*."

Serysta laughed, then her mood went solemn. "Your magic is not the only missing magic in the palace. Mine seems to have gone astray as well."

Alarm shot through Kallista, then echoed through the links from her marked ones. "Completely?"

The Reinine shook her head. "Erratically. The larger the group I am in, the less likely I am to be able to read truth, though sometimes in small groups, the magic is silent as well. I cannot find—I have not been able to distinguish what causes it to come and go, but…"

"The demons could explain it." Kallista tried to reason her way through. "Demons have no physical presence. They can act only through the humans they influence or possess. Have you noticed your magic failing when any particular person is present?"

"I haven't paid much attention to who was present when it failed," Serysta admitted.

"I have," Leyja said.

"And I." Syr spoke for the first time since they'd been introduced.

"What have you noticed?" Torchay asked.

"Nothing." Leyja's anger sounded in her voice. "When the magic fades, different people have been present. Not *all* different people, of course, but no one person has been there *every* time."

"How do you know?" Serysta asked, more curious than inquisitorial. "How do you know when the magic fades?"

"I can feel it." Leyja looked at Syr and got his confirming nod. The other two agreed as well. "I couldn't before we were ilian. Or maybe it's that your magic never faded before. Your magic is—it's always there. Always reading truth. Like light or warmth surrounding you. Not like—"

Leyja glanced at Kallista, raising a questioning eyebrow. "Not like other naitani who must *call* magic, correct?"

Kallista nodded. "My magic sleeps until I call it, except for the—well, even in the godmarked, it sleeps until it is called."

"But yours never sleeps," Leyja went on. "So when it fades, we feel the—the cold. And we look to see who is there."

"I can look also," Kallista said. "I should be able to see what your iliasti cannot."

"If we can afford the time for it," Serysta amended.

"I think we must take the time." Kallista tried to bow in her chair again. "All respect to the Reinine, I—*we* are Adara's only weapon against demons. I do not know what other task you might have for me, Your Majesty, but I do not think I should leave Arikon until we find this demon and…contain it. Destroy it, if I can, but without my other iliasti…"

"I will send troops to escort them here," the Reinine said. "Troops that you and I together will test for loyalty. For this, I will find troops, no matter how my new generals scream."

"Thank you, my Reinine." Kallista put all her gratitude and relief into her voice. "If they hurry, they might find them at Sumald, where they were to resupply. Of course, someone will have to be sent to carry the gold the rest of the way to Korbin, but that shouldn't be—"

"Gold?" The Reinine frowned, held up a hand. "What gold?"

"The payment for the new string of cavalry remounts due from the Korbin horse breeders." The bad feeling in the pit of Kallista's stomach got worse with every word she spoke, as the Reinine's expression failed to clear.

"Courier Torvyll brought the gold along with her summons. She said that you suggested—very strongly suggested—I send Aisse and the babies to safety in Korbin, and since they were traveling that way anyway, would they please take the gold along with them for the horse farms? She had the gold. She had all the paperwork. Was it false?"

"There is a payment sent every year when the remounts come down from the mountains and off the plains," the Reinine said, "and we do on occasion ask ordinary citizens to carry this money if they are making the trip, but always in a regular caravan, and never—why would anyone think a family with two infants and a pregnant woman a suitable transport for such a thing? Especially in a time like this?

"And I merely commented that your children might be safer elsewhere. I certainly never meant to order them as far as Korbin, or even to suggest it." She looked at her ilian. "We will look into it."

"Ilias," Keldrey spoke, "one more thing. We're the only ones who know about the demons. It should stay that way. To avoid panic."

"I agree." Kallista nodded energetically. "Not to mention the way people look at you when you talk of things they believe mere legend. Bad enough to *be* a legend come to life."

"Of course, of course. We all know the need for discretion." Then the Reinine smiled, almost forcibly. "I look forward to seeing how your daughters have grown."

Kallista couldn't help beaming in return, despite her renewed worry. "They grow stronger and more beautiful every day. Rozite already was holding her head up when we left them. We are all most anxious to be together again."

"It may not be safe for them here," the Reinine warned.

"With demons on the prowl," Kallista said, "is there anywhere in Adara that is truly safe? If they are here, *we* can protect them, rather than simply worry."

The dishes on the table held only bones and crumbs. The nine of them dining had put away the food with the outsized appetites of active warriors and magic workers. Leyja and Ferenday got up to collect the tray of pastries, cheeses and sweet cordials on the nearby sideboard. Kallista had been feeling sufficiently fed, but the sight of the delicate buns oozing cream and other delights changed her mind.

"Cha for me," she said, requesting the hot brew, "rather than a liqueur. If it's not too much trouble."

"No trouble." Ferenday pulled the cord signaling the servants. "Especially if we are through with state secrets."

"We are, mostly." Serysta poured liqueur for those requesting it. "Though there are a few other matters to be brought up."

Ferenday gave instructions to the servant at the door and returned to the table.

"This is something of a secret." Serysta Reinine took a sip of her drink. "General Uskenda wants to send you to scout the rebel camp. And while I think this is an excellent idea—your magic kept you hidden last year through all of Tibre after all—I agree that we must deal with this demon first. And I find that I do not like the thought that such a precious resource as yourself can be ordered about by any general—or major or colonel—who takes it into her head to do so."

"I *am* a captain in your army, my Reinine." Kallista did not think she liked the way this talk was going.

"That can be changed. You're overdue a promotion."

"As are many of Adara's officers. Nor would I turn one down—if it is to major. But please, Your Majesty, only to major. I do not care to deal with the repercussions or the envy if you advanced me higher."

The Reinine considered, nodded. "Done. But I will detach you from all other duty. You will report directly to me."

"Thank you, Your Majesty." Kallista's mind raced. "And if I could make another request?"

Serysta waved a hand, resignation in her face. "Why not? What is it you want?"

"Two things. Or it might be three. Send Lieutenant Tylle and her quarto back to the prison. She is not needed here, truly. Unless General Uskenda has some use for her."

"Truly?" Serysta looked at Joh.

"Truly," he said. "I am not the man I once was."

"No, you are not," Serysta mused. Kallista could almost taste her truth-magic. "You have become much more, I think. Very well, that is done. And the other thing?"

"If you could attach a courier to my—command. Viyelle Torvyll would do very well if, as I believe, your investigation finds that she only followed orders in bringing that gold. She did a good job in that and I believe she would be useful to me."

Serysta Reinine flicked a finger toward Syr who nodded. "Done, if she passes the investigation. Anything else?"

Kallista bit her lip. Did she dare ask? But nothing ever succeeded without the attempt. "I ask that you pardon my new ilias."

"What?" Joh burst out.

Torchay merely sighed. Obed watched, silent as he had been through the whole of the meal.

"I have already placed him in your custody, Major." The Reinine straightened in her chair, drew authority around her. "I do not see what benefit pardoning him would have. He did commit the offense. He tried to murder three of you."

"Isn't a person's intent taken into account?" Kallista dredged her memory for the bits of law she'd studied in the academy and officer's training. "He did not intend murder. He was told burning the powder would heal us. At most, he injured us through negligence, or recklessness."

"Is this true, Suteny Ailo?" Serysta's stare arrowed the length of the table to Joh.

He sighed. "Yes, Your Majesty."

"Why didn't you tell us this at your trial?"

"I did not think it relevant."

Serysta scowled at him. "Truth is *always* relevant." She leaned back in her chair, drumming her fingers on the glossy tabletop as she considered. "I will not pardon him, Naitan," she said finally. "He did after all hide the powder and set it off."

She held up a hand to forestall Kallista's protest. *"But,"* she said, "I will commute his sentence to the time he has already served. As of this moment, he is a free man. Syr, see the paperwork is done, will you?"

*"Thank you,* Your Majesty."

"Is there anything else you require, Naitan?" The faintest edge of sarcasm rode the Reinine's voice and Kallista flushed red with embarrassment.

"No, my Reinine. You have been far more than generous with your loyal subject."

"Oh, stop groveling." The Reinine winked. Actually *winked* at Kallista. When she stopped goggling at the idea, she had to smile.

Serysta Reinine went on. "There is something I would request of you in return."

"Anything, my Reinine."

"You might ask your iliasti before promising such a thing." Serysta's smile was wry. "I recall that they tend to have their own opinions of certain things."

Kallista glanced at her men. Only Torchay raised an eyebrow. The other two gave her blank faces, but she could sense Obed's reservations through her link. "Then I suppose we ought to hear what this request is, before we agree to it."

"The Tibran boy, the naitan you brought us. I want to...attach him to your command as well. He is a West naitan, as far as anyone here can tell. There is no one to teach him. He makes people uncomfortable with his scars and empty eyes." Serysta brooded over her tiny cordial cup. "Something tells me he is important, but...he worries me. He does not need to be so alone."

"Of course." Kallista agreed before she remembered to check

with her iliasti. Torchay and Obed both nodded agreement. Joh hesitated a moment before nodding, too. "Send him to us tonight, if you like."

"Tomorrow is soon enough. Is there anything else, Major? I can arrange for temple vows with Joh, if you like."

"I think we would rather wait until the others arrive for that." This time, she glanced at the others as she spoke, sensing approval through the two fully formed links. Then she glanced at her still-empty dessert plate. "I don't believe I require another thing—save perhaps for one of those cream pastries. And then, I doubt I *require* one." She smoothed down her snug dress uniform. "Twins seem to have had a considerable effect on the fit of my uniform."

Everyone laughed, including the Reinine. With a smile, Leyja slid two pastries onto Kallista's plate. "Have two. Heaven knows you've earned them. *Twins.*" She made a face, and over general laughter, the conversation turned to more pleasant matters than rebellions and demons.

The night passed quietly, without demons, to everyone's relief. The morning had not advanced much beyond breakfast before Courier Torvyll entered the parlor, saluted sharply, then swept into a low bow.

"Congratulations, Major, on your promotion," she said as she rose, "and thank you from the depths of my spirit for requesting I be assigned this duty." She paused for dramatic effect and slanted a teasing look toward Kallista. "It *does* require quartering here, does it not?"

Kallista laughed. Viyelle had not been nearly so amusing last year. "Yes, Courier, it does. Come. Sit. We should talk." The Reinine's investigators had obviously cleared her of any complicity in the gold shipment, or she would not be here. It was time Kallista learned more.

Joh trailed after them on his magical leash. Torchay was moving furniture out again, opening a practice/workout area in the first half of the parlor.

Obed approached. "I go to meet with our bankers. There are matters to be attended."

"You don't go alone. Torchay?"

He shook his head. "I'm not leaving you here without Obed or myself. No offense to our new ilias, but he doesn't have proper training yet to protect you."

"Then we wait till we can all go together. None of us is to be alone."

Obed gave his muted bow. "As you will it." He pulled off his Southron robe and went to help move furniture.

"Now." Kallista settled onto her favorite velvet sofa, gesturing Viyelle into the chair beside it. She tugged Joh down next to her and leaned against him, getting comfortable. "When I knew you last year, Viyelle Prinsipella, I would never have expected to see you in courier's grays. How did this come about?"

Viyelle fidgeted, looking uncomfortable. "It was the explosion, Major. Until that moment, the war was very far away. Not real. But something like that—that wasn't magic, but could shake the whole palace, could bring walls down and kill… It made the war very real."

"But why join courier service? You're a prinsipella."

"With no chance of becoming prinsep after my mother." Viyelle's flippant tone tried to cover an old bitterness.

"I thought any child of a prinsep's ilian could be named heir." Kallista had studied governance, but had no experience of the reality.

"Technically, theoretically, yes. That is the way the laws are written. Practically, however—only my sedili with magic have any chance at being chosen. I have no magic, therefore I have no purpose. Or last year, I had none." Viyelle flushed red, but kept talking. "Which is why I…did the things I did."

Those things were more mischief than wickedness, Kallista had to admit now. Viyelle had no idea Stone would collapse if she danced him too far away, and the fight she started—one with blades in the halls of the palace itself—had been caused by magic spelled to induce anger and quarrelling. Even then, Viyelle had not seemed bad. Merely…purposeless.

"The explosion—it was Tibran gunpowder, not magic," Viyelle was saying. "If it could do all that it did without magic, might not I also do something without magic? So, after much consideration, I joined the couriers. And have been listening to the objections ever since. From all three of my mothers. Especially my birth mother who manages Shaluine's concerns at court and saw me as following her path for whichever of my sedili becomes prinsep. I prefer courier's service."

"As would I." Kallista glanced at the clock on the table, a new addition to the suite. Small, tabletop clocks were the latest craze among the wealthy. Small clocks and handguns, which had been created with borrowed Tibran technology and the new gunpowder. Both were recent inventions, and the novelty had yet to pall. Kallista doubted it would. Both were quite useful in their own arenas.

"We have another joining our company," she said. "I had hoped he would be here by now so we could get the introductions out of the way and be about our business."

"If I might ask, Major, what is my business to be?"

"At this moment, more of what you have been doing. Collecting information. Giving it out. I need to know what is happening in the palace, the mood here." Kallista took a deep breath. Admitting fault was never easy. "I allowed our ilian to be isolated last year, and that was disastrous. While I would rather not involve myself in courtier's games, I cannot wander about in ignorance. None of us can. There will doubtless be other tasks for you, though I don't know what right now."

Viyelle inclined her head in acknowledgment as a knock sounded at the door.

"That will be Gweric." Kallista stood. She had not seen the boy since Fox recovered from his surgery in Kallista's home city of Turysh. Fox's leg had been severely injured and he'd lost his sight in the battle for Ukiny, where the first of them had been marked by the One. It had healed badly, but they'd been forced to wait until after their journey to Tibre and back to have the lameness corrected. They'd taken Gweric with them to have his injuries healed as well.

Gweric's feet had sustained much more damage—the bones broken and set wrong, tendons and muscles cut over months and years by the Tibran Rulers who feared his magic at the same time they sought to use it. Gweric had remained in Turysh for more surgery when Kallista and her ilian had moved to their new mountain estate to await the births of their children.

The youth entered the parlor, his limp scarcely noticeable. Kallista's mother had done wonders with her healing. Gweric stopped short, just inside the door. His face with its empty eye sockets and deep scars turned from one to the other of them.

"Naitan?" His voice was near to a whisper. "Kallista?"

"Yes." She strode the length of the room to wrap him in a hug, Joh hurrying behind her.

He looked good. Gweric was a handsome boy despite his scars. His shining gold hair fell down over his face and he stood straight and tall, well-formed. He was just seventeen now, the age an Adaran boy would be in his second year of military service. He could not serve as other young men did. The Tibrans had ruined him for that. He had only his magic.

Gweric hugged her tight, tighter than she expected, but he

did not cling when she released him. Torchay greeted him with a backslap, Obed with a bow.

"How are you?" Kallista led him back to the sitting area. "You're walking well. Very well. You look good."

"Do I?" He turned his face to her.

"You do." She patted his cheek, urged him into the chair Viyelle had vacated, submerging her guilt for leaving him behind in bustling. She sat again, next to Joh on the sofa. "What have you been doing since we saw you last?"

"Learning to walk again." Gweric seemed to look around the room. "Where is Fox? And Stone?" He frowned accusingly at Kallista. "None of your Tibrans are here."

"Aisse hasn't had her baby yet. She couldn't travel as fast as I needed to." Kallista left out unnecessary information. "Fox and Stone are with her and the twins."

Gweric's frown softened slightly. "They're coming, though?"

"Slowly, but yes. What of you? How do you like Arikon? Which academy are you attending?"

He shrugged. "North. No one else would have me. Said I curdled the milk, or disturbed the ether, or something."

"Those East folks can be delicate like that. Are you learning anything?"

"No." His face turned from Kallista to Torchay, Kallista to Obed, as if he watched something. "There's a new one. Someone I don't recognize in your dance."

"What dance?"

"Of magic. I forgot how brilliant it is. But there's a new one. Isn't there?"

"I apologize for not introducing you before. We have a new ilias, another of the godmarked. Joh Suteny, this is Gweric vo'Tsekrish."

Joh clasped Gweric's hand without hesitation. "A pleasure to meet you, son."

"You mean that, don't you?" Gweric sounded surprised.

"I do. Are you truthsayer?"

"No. At least, I don't think so. I just—your magic… sparkles. I can see it dancing between all of you and things show in the magic. The truth. Someone without magic…"

"I am honored to meet you as well, Naitan," Viyelle spoke up.

Gweric startled at the sound of her voice, jerking around to face her. "Who is that?"

"My manners have left me completely." Kallista was glad the boy could not see her blush, though everyone else could. "My only excuse is that I was so glad to see you I forgot everything else. This is Viyelle Torvyll, a courier attached to my command."

Viyelle took Gweric's hand in both of hers, bowing over it. "It is my honor and my pleasure to meet you. I look forward to furthering our acquaintance, Naitan."

Gweric shut his mouth with a snap. "I cannot read your truth. I cannot see you at all."

Viyelle's smile twisted. "I have always known I have no magic whatsoever. Less than none."

Now Gweric blushed. "I did not mean to insult you, Aila."

She patted his hand. "None taken, dearest." Now, finally, she released him with another subtle squeeze, giving a bland smile in answer to Kallista's raised eyebrow.

Kallista took back the conversation, trying to decide what, if anything, all that hand-patting and squeezing meant. "You said you are not learning at the academy?"

"I am learning some things. History, philosophy, magic theory—but I cannot do the other things. My—my magic—" He still sounded uncomfortable saying the word even after almost a year away from Tibre. "My magic doesn't *do* anything. It just…watches."

"What does it watch?"

"Everyone else's magic. I told you. I am a witch hound. I see magic."

Kallista leaned back until she found Joh behind her, turning the boy's words and the things the Reinine had told her over in her mind. "Perhaps that is your magic after all," she said. "That you see things. Things others do not see."

"And I do not see things that others do," he muttered, sounding all sullen youth.

Thinking hard, Kallista slid her gaze toward Viyelle. It came down to a matter of trust. Could Viyelle come smack up against West magic without flinching? Kallista had to decide, and did. "I have a teacher for you, Gweric."

"I thought *you* would teach me." More sullenness.

"I don't know enough to teach you. I need to learn myself, especially about West magic." Kallista spoke as matter-of-factly as she could, watching Viyelle without appearing to. "Let me call her."

Since she was sitting against Joh, Kallista touched her bare arm to his and pried up the merest whisper of magic. Slapping it awake, she sent it questing through the palace and waited for response. It was not long in coming.

"Back again, are you?"

"Hello, Grandmother." Kallista watched both Viyelle and Gweric now. The boy stared openmouthed, obviously *at* something. Viyelle peered around the room trying to see who Kallista spoke to.

"I have a pupil for you, Grandmother. Gweric is a West naitan we brought back from Tibre with us. Gweric, I make known to you Domnia Varyl, founder of my bloodline and dead these—what? Two hundred years?"

"You expect me to keep up with those things?" Domnia retorted. She bustled closer. "Well, boy? Do you want to learn?"

She didn't wait for him to respond, speaking to Kallista. "Is he lack-witted? What's wrong with him?"

"Gweric?" Kallista laid her hand on his shoulder.

"I can see her, Kallista," he whispered. "Not just the magic floating about her, or dancing like yours between your ilian, but *her*. Eyes, nose, mouth, fingers—*everything.*"

"I suppose, dear heart, that is because my many-times great-grandmother is a ghost. Her whole being is of the magical realms. Still, she does know West magic. What little I know of it I learned from her. Are you willing to learn from a ghost?" Kallista squeezed Gweric's shoulder, then risked a glance at Viyelle. She looked more fascinated than horrified. "Gweric, what say you?"

"But my magic doesn't *do* anything," he protested. "Except see other magic."

"Then I will teach you to understand what you see," Domnia said. "If you are not afraid to learn."

Kallista held her breath. The pride had been beaten out of him in Tibre. Had enough of it come back for that sort of challenge to work?

"I am not afraid." Sullen, not defiant. But he was taking up the challenge. If only to prove her wrong. "Whatever you teach me, it won't change anything."

"We will see." Domnia looked around her in disgust. "Oh, bloody Khralsh. You're going to want me to pay attention to those infernal clocks. Well, I won't. I'll be here at dawn tomorrow. Be ready." And Domnia faded out of view.

"Excellent." Kallista clapped her hands together and stood. That task was done. "Viyelle, choose a room and get settled in. Help Gweric get settled."

She looked at the furniture movers, now finished with their task. "Are we ready to visit the bankers? If we're going to stay at court a while, we ought to do some shopping as well. We all need clothes, but especially Joh."

"For ribbons," Torchay said. "You need insignia for your new rank."

Oh, yes. She had to replace the two white ribbons on each shoulder for her captain's rank with three ribbons in gold. "You have my gloves? Are we ready?"

Torchay drew her brown regulation gloves from his belt and handed them to her, then bowed, gesturing them toward the door.

"Leaving already?" Viyelle said from her place near Gweric. Very near Gweric. "Will you be gone long?"

"Long enough." Kallista walked backward across the open space, trying to decide how she felt about any dalliance between them. "Be gentle."

"I am always gentle, Naitan. No worries."

With a last niggling qualm—Gweric did not need his heart broken, too, after all he'd been through—Kallista turned her back on them and Obed opened the door to the suite.

Gweric called out. "Be careful, Naitan. Watch the heights."

All four of them stopped at the doorway to look back at the youth. "What did you say, Gweric?" Kallista asked gently.

"W-watch the heights. The high places in the city." He stammered as he repeated himself. "I do not know why—I just—"

"We'll watch," Torchay said. "We watch everything, always, to guard our naitan."

"But I will watch more carefully," Obed said as they left the room.

"We all will." Torchay fell back to his place in the rear.

Kallista took Joh's hand against separation in the crowds, and they ventured forth into the palace and on into the city.

## CHAPTER TEN

The crowds only grew thicker the farther Kallista and her ilian walked from the palace. The bank they patronized was one of the closer ones, but they still had several sections of the city to cross.

"Maybe we should have had the bank come to us." Kallista clung to Obed's belt with one hand and Joh's with the other while people jostled them on all sides.

"You should have thought of that before we got into this mess." Torchay came near to shouting to be heard from his position behind them. Kallista knew he had hold of Joh's belt because their human chain had been Torchay's suggestion at the beginning.

"I wanted to shop." She rose onto her toes, trying to see past the people surrounding them to the businesses edging the square they currently threaded their way through. "Aren't we in Tailor's Square?"

"I think so, yes."

"The shop I want is that way. Left." Kallista pushed Obed's shoulder, steering him into an abrupt left turn.

"'Ware!" Joh shouted as he jumped forward into Kallista, knocking her aside, to the ground.

A woman screamed. An arrow quivered in her thigh where she stood a few paces ahead, along the path they had been taking. She screamed again when she saw it and collapsed to the street.

Another arrow sprouted from the chest of a graybeard on Kallista's other side. He fell without making a sound save the escaping of his breath. There was a moment of eerie silence, punctured only by the cries of the injured woman and the angry hum of yet another arrow.

"Assassin!" Torchay leaped forward and the arrow pierced him rather than Kallista.

The plaza erupted in shouts and screams as the crowds of people fled. A man lifted the woman in his arms; the arrow bobbed with every step as he ran from the square with her.

"Get her out of here," Torchay wheezed. Kallista stared in horror at the arrow point coming out the front of his tunic while Joh held him upright. "*Now*, before he gets the rest of us and she has no one to shield her."

Obed lifted Kallista to her feet, shielding her with his body. She threw her gloves to the ground, scooped up magic and packed it around the arrow piercing Torchay through, her desperation making the magic's reluctance irrelevant. They didn't have time to remove the arrow now, but she would not let him bleed to death before they did.

"Joh, bring him," she ordered. "You!" She pointed at a dun-clad soldier who appeared as the crowd vanished, like a rock emerging from receding tide.

Two more arrows buzzed into the crowd, drawing more screams. Obed picked her up and carried her bodily into the dubious shelter of the fountain at the square's center. Fortunately, the soldier followed, along with Joh half-carrying Torchay. Kallista called more magic to ease his pain, then a bit more to find that damned assassin. As she sent it winging out, she noticed more soldiers gathering in the shelter of the fountain and read the ranks on their sleeves.

"Sergeant," she addressed the burly lifer first. "Take half these men and circle round to the right. Corporal, you take the rest to the left. See if you can flush this demon-lover out. He is—" The magic found what it sought and Kallista jerked it, as if hooking a fish, marking him.

"He is there. My magic has marked him, though I don't know exactly how. You will know which man he is though. I am sure of that. I'll see what I can do to get us some help."

"Yes, Captain."

Kallista didn't bother to correct him. She hadn't got her new insignia yet and the sergeant was already counting off men and readying his rush across the square.

It was empty now, save for the people huddled behind the fountain and in the shelter of the buildings. Save for the two bodies lying motionless in their own spilled blood gleaming brightest red in the sunlight: the old man who was the second to fall and a child struck when the killer fired wildly into the crowd, a boy of ten or twelve.

The assassin fired at the oncoming soldiers, striking one. Kallista threw sluggish magic at the injured man, hoping it would stop the bleeding from this distance. The others all made their destinations safely. They needed more help. Could she—?

"I'm calling magic." Kallista caught Joh's bare wrist.

"You haven't been already?" Torchay's breath was shallow, wheezy, but he seemed to rest comfortably on his side.

"I need more. I'm going to try farspeaking. We need help, more than those few searching for our would-be killer."

"He is not 'would-be'" Obed said. "He has shed innocent blood."

"But he has not killed *us*. And we are the ones he wants."

The boy in the plaza stirred, moaned. He was alive. Kallista reshaped the braid of magic she held, wrapped it around him, hoping to keep him that way. If she could touch him, she could do more. The sniper hadn't fired in some time. She rose to peer over the fountain's edge. Obed pushed her back down as an arrow whizzed past to shatter on the cobblestones.

"Do *not* put yourself at risk," he hissed. "*I* will get the boy. *You* get help."

"Obed, wait—"

But he did not, of course, flying across the square in a flutter of black Southron robes through a hail of arrows. Only five, but it seemed a veritable hailstorm to Kallista who held her breath till Obed returned.

"Call for help," Torchay said, grunting as he sat up with the arrow protruding front-and-back from his chest. "I'll check the boy."

"You have an arrow running clear through you," Kallista protested.

"But I'm not bleeding." He gestured at his near-spotless tunic. "Nor do I hurt."

The sooner she tried calling, the sooner she could stop Torchay's demented behavior. Arguing would only prolong it. Quickly she yanked up more stubborn, reluctant magic, wound it together and sent out her call, using both words and the images in her mind, hoping she would reach someone. Anyone.

"Who…is this?" A faint and tentative voice sounded in Kallista's ears. No one who was physically present. A woman's voice.

"Never mind that. Just send help. Lots of it. Tailor's Square." Kallista released the magic and turned to her injured mate. "Lie back down," she ordered. "Carefully." She helped Joh ease him back onto his side.

"The boy's lost a lot of blood," Torchay said. "But you've stopped that. His lung's perforated. It should be collapsed, whistling. But somehow you stopped that as well. He'll make it till we can get the arrow out of him."

He looked down at the arrow sticking out of his own middle. "As will I. I'll be glad to be rid of the thing. It's a bit awkward, you know. A bit disconcerting. Especially since it doesn't—exactly—hurt. Not that I mind not hurting, mind you. I'm not particularly fond of pain. But it is a bit disconcerting."

Kallista put her fingers over his mouth. "Stop talking. I'd think you were drunk, with all this babbling, save I'm not sure I've ever seen you drunk."

He kissed her fingers. "Drunk on magic."

Shouting and noises of fighting came from the building where the assassin lurked. More soldiers poured into the square from three other streets, followed by a troop of green-robed healers. Kallista turned Torchay and the boy over to them and would have stood to meet the officer in command, save that Obed refused to allow her to rise. Not until the sergeant appeared on the street escorting a bound man whose skin was the stark, colorless black of charcoal. The magic had indeed marked him.

"I don't know what you're playing at here, Captain, sending out an alarm like that." The officer in charge, an infantry major, strode to the fountain as Kallista finally got to her feet. "You made this sound like a massacre by a whole army of rebels rather than just one man."

"One man can commit a great deal of harm to the defenseless," Kallista said. "It *was* a massacre, except that only one has died so far."

"You have obviously not been in battle, Farspeaker, or you would know—"

"Excuse me, Naitan." A healer broke into the conversation. "Where is your healer? She must release her magic so that we can begin our work."

"Oh. Sorry, I didn't realize." Kallista turned from the major. "Are your healers ready?" She stroked her hand over Torchay's hair. "My ilias is precious to me—as I am sure the others are to those who love them. Of course, you are ready. You would not have—" Now she was babbling.

She drew breath and *reached,* cutting the magic and letting the threads ravel, beginning with the soldier, then the boy and finally Torchay. "Can I leave the magic easing his pain? I think I can do the same for the others, if it would help."

The healer's expression would have made Kallista laugh if she had not been so worried about Torchay. "*You* did this? But you wear blue—that is—yes. Our anesthetist would appreciate the assistance."

Kallista caught Joh's hand and called magic from him and Obed. She didn't know whether calling Torchay's magic would help or hinder his healing and wasn't willing to experiment. She touched the boy to *see* him better. He was not bound to her, so she took extra care in easing his pain to be sure she did nothing she did not intend. Then she did the same for the sweating soldier. He was scarcely older than the boy—maybe as much as nineteen. The relief in his eyes thanked her before he closed them.

When she turned back to Torchay, he lay on his back on a stretcher. The tip of the arrow's point still protruded from the front of his tunic, but the long feathered end lay cut and discarded in the street.

General Uskenda clattered into the square on a rawboned black horse, more troops behind her. "Well, Major," she said, swinging off her mount. "You certainly know how to create a stir."

"General, I—" the infantry major began.

Uskenda cut her off. "I was speaking to Major Varyl here. No time for your golds yet, I see."

"No, General." Kallista straightened and saluted. "I have—

we were—" She stopped, gestured helplessly. "My ilias is hurt." She fidgeted with the need to follow the healers bearing Torchay away.

"While saving you, no doubt. Are you certain it was only the one man?"

"As much as I can be. Only one archer, at least. Ask the men who dug him out."

"Farspeaking, healing, demon-slaying—I think blue may not be the right color for you, Naitan."

"General," Kallista pleaded, desperate in her need to follow Torchay, to know he was and would be all right.

"Yes, yes, Major. Go. We will investigate matters here." Uskenda released her with a flip of her hand and Kallista darted after Torchay, so fast she caught Joh and Obed flat-footed.

In their main hall just outside the palace, the healers had all the wounded—even the woman who'd been borne away by her ilias—in one large room divided by lightweight, movable walls. Kallista found the healers to be quite movable as well, when first one, then another tried to stop her short of Torchay's side. Several more seemed to be converging on her when the one in charge, who had been in the square, waved them off.

"I must protest, Elliane Naitan," the healer in Torchay's cell spoke as Kallista, Obed and Joh entered. Kallista ignored her, rushing to Torchay's side. The woman went on. "This is against policy. You know how family members interfere with treatment."

"Hush. She kept him alive—kept them all alive when they might have bled dry."

Torchay lay on his back on the hard narrow bed, his tunic cut in pieces and discarded on the floor. It hurt Kallista to look at him, to see the arrow point in the center of the trickles of blood painting his pale skin.

"There you are." Torchay clasped the hand she slid into his. "No more trouble? They kept you safe coming here?"

Kallista nodded, blinking back tears, swallowing down the boulders in her throat. She'd get one down and another would roll in, forcing her to swallow again. She assembled a smile from bits and pieces she found lying about—mostly in Torchay's eyes smiling back at her.

"You really must stop doing this sort of thing," she said. "How can we carry out our mission if I keep having to use all the magic to patch you back together?"

"You haven't done any patching yet that I can see." Torchay tried to grasp the arrow point, but his fingers slipped in the oozing blood. "Get this great nasty thing out of me, patch up the hole and let's go home."

"Torchay—" Kallista glanced back at the healer, still arguing with the one she'd called Elliane. What would be the best thing to do?

"Obed, pull it out." Torchay beckoned their dark ilias with a jerk of his head.

Obed approached, edging round the hissing argument of the naitani. "I would not injure you worse."

"It's got to come out, doesn't it? Pull it out. You won't hurt me. Kallista's seen to that."

Obed nodded, a sharp jerk of his head. Kallista moved out of the way, toward Torchay's head. The healer wasn't paying any attention to her charge. Kallista wanted him healed, and if they wouldn't do what was needed, she'd heal him herself. She'd done it before. But she didn't want to pull the arrow out. She didn't think she could. Not because she didn't have the physical strength, but because this was Torchay.

"I may have to—" Obed licked his bottom lip. "To work for a grip on the point."

"You can shove your fingers clear to my heart and I doubt

I'll feel it." Torchay's hold tightened on Kallista's hand, show-ing he wasn't quite sure of his statement. "Just get the damn thing out of me."

Again Obed nodded. He grasped the arrowhead.

"Wait." Kallista beckoned to Joh still hovering at the en-trance to the tiny space. She took his hand and set it on her neck, beneath her queue, over her mark. Her hands would be occupied, and she wanted all possible magic at her disposal, ready to heal Torchay. "All right. Go ahead."

With a quick glance that encompassed both Torchay and Kal-lista, Obed adjusted his grip. He set his other hand on Torchay's stomach and pressed it down, away from the metal point. More of the shaft appeared, allowing Obed to work his fingers be-hind the barbed heel of the arrowhead for a more secure hold. In one steady, swift pull, he drew the rest of the arrow's cut shaft through Torchay's flesh and out. Kallista would never, ever for-get the awful sound it made as it came.

She called magic, willing it to see, to heal. She lashed its slug-gish behavior into obedience, refusing to accept anything less than perfection. This was *Torchay*. The magic he carried—magic he couldn't touch, magic for her to use—was still more pow-erful than the other two together. It leached through Kallista's block, laying the injury clear. She had done this before, remem-bered all she had done last year, after their escape from their brief Tibran imprisonment. But it was easier this time.

Torchay was linked. The magic he held gave her access and guidance. And he was not near death. Kallista pushed torn edges back together, fused broken vessels, drove out foreign substances.

"That feels peculiar." Torchay lifted his head to look down at Kallista's hand on his bared stomach. "Tickles, almost."

"I do not need a commentary while I do this. You'll make me forget something." Kallista focused on her task, or tried to.

He let his head fall back on the cot. "We certainly don't want that, do we? I'll shut it." He paused. "But it does tickle."

"Here! What are you doing?" The healers finally noticed that something other than visiting was happening.

"Taking care of what you weren't," Torchay said.

Kallista lifted the edge of her hand and peered underneath at Torchay's middle. A new, red scar showed a few inches to the right and just above the one he'd received last year.

"All done?" Torchay rose on his elbows to look. Kallista moved her hand out of the way to let him. "Good." He sat up. "Ready to go home then?"

"More than ready." Kallista's knees felt wobbly.

"You can't just walk out of here like that," the healer protested.

"Why not?" Torchay jumped to his feet and spread his arms, displaying his just-mended torso.

"You can't be healed. Not so quickly."

Kallista leaned back into Joh, needing him to help hold her up. She was feeling a little dizzy.

"But I am."

Both healers came forward to inspect Kallista's work, despite Torchay's obvious annoyance. Elliane brushed her fingers over the new bloodstained scar. "Can you do this for the other injured?"

"I don't believe so." Kallista didn't know whether she could or couldn't, but she feared the healers would drag her all over the city to experiment, and she had neither the time nor the energy for it. She wasn't sure she had the magic. "Torchay is one of my godmarked companions. We're bound together in a way that allows me to do this for him, but I have no such connection with these others."

"It's *impossible*," the other healer was muttering for the eleventy-first time, now inspecting the entry wound scar in Torchay's back.

"Obviously not," he said, "since it's done. I'm leaving now. Where are my blades?"

Speechless, the healers gestured toward Torchay's ruined tunic, his Heldring swords and other blades scattered beneath it. Most of the belts had been cut, to his vocal disgust. He used part of his tunic to form a bag to carry them.

"Here." Obed shrugged out of his over-robe and handed it to Torchay. "The day is cool and if you do not wish to take time to wash—" He indicated the smears of blood on Torchay's stomach and chest.

"Right." Torchay handed the makeshift sack to Joh and put on the robe. "We don't want to scare the populace, do we?" He used his uniform belt to tie it closed and sighed. "I suppose I'll be going into summer uniform sooner than I wanted."

He drew one of his short swords, spun the hilt in his hand till it settled to his satisfaction, and nodded. "All right. Let's go."

Kallista motioned for Obed to take the lead and wound her arm through Torchay's unoccupied one. She needed to know he was whole. The feel of the thick Southron silk over his arm reminded her. "*My gloves.* I left my gloves in the square. I can't—"

"Here." Joh slapped them against his leg, knocking off dust and sand. "I have them."

"Thank you." Shaking, Kallista accepted his help in putting them on. Once she would never have left the square without them. Today, she'd been too upset over Torchay's injuries to think of anything else. Thank the One her out-of-kilter magic hadn't done anything fatal on the journey here. She had to get hold of herself and her emotions.

"You look after the big things," Joh murmured, as if reading her mind. "We'll take care of the little ones. It's what we're here for, after all."

With a slight bow, Obed whirled and led the way back

through the main chamber. They made a strange procession, Kallista thought. Obed stalked ahead like some dark predator. Torchay strode along swaddled in Obed's black robe with a naked sword in one hand and Kallista clinging to the other. Joh brought up the rear, carrying the bundle of Torchay's remaining blades. When Kallista stumbled over the threshold leading outside, Joh caught up in a step and took her other arm so she was supported on both sides.

"This isn't right." She tried to pull away from Joh, then from Torchay. "I'm not the one who was hurt."

"No, you're just the one throwing magic around like it was feathers when it's really sandbags. Uncooperative sandbags." Torchay held tight to her. "I'm good as new. Never better. I merely got run through with an arrow. You did much, much more. I can tell how the magic fights with you."

Obed jerked his head around to look over his shoulder at them. "Backlash?" Then he recalled his duty and scanned the crowds around them.

A few more moments and they would pass through the palace gates again. Kallista hoped the target she felt on her back would go away once they did.

"No, not backlash," she reassured Obed. "Your magic answered beautifully."

"Truth, Kallista," Torchay said.

"You heard what I told the Reinine. Without our other three, the magic requires more effort to control. It's different from before Fox joined us, when Stone was here. Then it rushed about, escaping before I could command it. Now, it's slow. Like a boulder that needs a hard push to get it moving. Especially yours, Torchay. The bigger the rock, the more effort it takes to move it. So yes, truth. His magic did all I asked of it, despite the effort required."

They finally reached Daybright Tower. Kallista did not want

to look at the stairs, much less climb them, but between Joh, Torchay and more laughter than her pride could take, they got her up them and into their suite.

"Are you well, Sergeant?" Viyelle strode across the open space to greet them. "I heard you were—well, skewered."

"I was." Torchay pulled off the robe to show his new scars. "Kallista fixed me. So she's a bit knackered at the moment. Is there water so I can get this stuff off me?"

"It was just brought up." Viyelle gestured toward the rooms. "What happened? Is there anything I can do?"

"Someone started shooting arrows at us in the middle of Tailor's Square." Torchay poured water into a basin in the big bedroom while the others filed in behind him. Kallista wanted to sit, but she was afraid of the sleep that hovered just behind her eyelids, so she leaned against the wall beside the washstand.

"That was a bit of good work, by the way, Joh ilias." Torchay wet a cloth and started scrubbing at the dried blood. "How did you know that first one was coming?"

"I saw it." Joh seemed to want to shrink inside himself as attention turned his way. "Gweric Naitan said to watch the heights, so I did. Just happened I was in the back nearest the assassin."

Torchay nodded approval. "Good eyes. Good instincts." He exchanged a glance with Obed. "I'd like you to begin advanced training this afternoon with Obed."

Both men nodded acknowledgment. Obed spoke. "Another blade in defense of the Chosen One is always welcome."

Kallista took the cloth from Torchay and turned him so she could clean the blood from his back.

"What can I do?" Viyelle's voice coming from the open doorway reminded Kallista of her presence.

"You can take a message to the blasted banker." Kallista dropped the cloth into the basin and leaned against the wall again. "We never did make it that far. Escort him back here. And ask a few merchants to drop by with some of their wares. Clothing. Belts. Boots. We need to outfit Joh pretty much from the skin out, and the rest of us need extras for court. Uniforms. Whoever has the local contract for uniforms. Send for them, too."

"And I?" Gweric spoke from behind Viyelle. Only now did Kallista notice he had his tunic on inside out.

"Suggestions?" Kallista made the question general. "As a West naitan he's vulnerable. He needs to know how to defend himself. When Fox gets here, they can work together, but—"

"I will teach him." Obed inclined his head. "His limitations are not so very limiting."

"Excellent." Kallista pushed off the wall. "Where's lunch? I'm starved."

Aisse walked stiff-legged across the meadow, hands in the small of her back to help her stretch.

"How are you faring?" Fox walked beside her, worried. "I know you couldn't rest well in the cave, and now we're traveling again. That's even harder on you." He set a hand on her shoulder and pushed his thumb gently into her aching muscle.

"More." Aisse managed to speak through her groan of pleasure.

Fox chuckled and complied, bringing both hands to bear in the massage, pleased she let him do it.

"Better now," she admitted. "This morning, I felt—"

"Unsettled." Fox finished the sentence for her. "Like something was wrong. Badly wrong."

"Exactly." Aisse turned to look at him. "You, too?"

"Yes. And Stone." He moved behind her again and went back to work. "Do you think Kallista and the others were in trouble of some kind?"

She bit her lip. "I don't know. I wish I did. I don't like this."

"Nor do I. But at least the weather's turned. If I hadn't been up to my knees in it, I wouldn't have believed this pass was too full of snow to travel just two days ago. Not as warm as it is today."

"Spring," Aisse said, as if that said it all. And it did. "Come, the babies are almost done. We can eat while we ride. We should hurry."

"As long as you take no harm from the hurrying, I agree." Fox escorted Aisse as they joined the others. There, he asked the question worrying him. "How much longer to reach Sumald?"

"At this pace?" Merinda considered. "Three more days, at least. Save for the storm, we'd have been there Graceday past, I'm sure."

The goat bleated from its tether tied to a pack horse. With a sigh, Fox grabbed the rope and started hauling the animal in, its hooves digging into the dirt in protest. Merinda had insisted that dragging the beast on its side behind the horses because it refused to walk would interfere with milk production. So it rode tied atop one of the pack animals and came down to graze every time they halted to tend the babies.

Fox was getting heartily tired of tying, untying and retying the infernal beast, and especially tired of getting kicked and bit. He gathered it up by the hooves and slung it gently into place. The babies needed it. But when they reached Korbin—goat stew.

"If we're ready, we should go," he said when the creature was secured. Kallista would worry if she came to meet them in Korbin and they weren't there. Their family needed to be together again. It was another thing he *knew* without being able to explain it.

# CHAPTER ELEVEN

The next few days in Arikon passed quietly. So quietly Kallista thought she might scream with frustration. Torchay suggested, and they all agreed, that routine would give another assassin a chance to succeed where the earlier one had failed, so they tried to avoid doing the same thing twice, even rotating bedrooms within their suite. If the palace hadn't been so crowded, Kallista was sure Torchay would have had them moving from suite to suite.

Some meals they took in their parlor, though with the palace so full the servants were running themselves to the bone trying to keep up with the demands of those who thought they had a right to demand. The ilian often ate in the various dining rooms in both palaces that had been turned over to the military: in sergeant's mess with Torchay in uniform and Kallista in plainclothes, in officer's dining with Kallista in uniform and Torchay in his blacks, even in courier's hall with Viyelle leading the way.

They trained in their suite and any other open space they could find. Of course, any time Torchay bowed to accept her gloves, whatever space they were in became vacant, or mostly so. On occasion Gweric would follow and watch the magic.

The demons haunted them all. Kallista's dreams remained

empty. Her men dreamed of ordinary things—training, sex, walking naked into the Grand Hall for a state dinner. She wanted to show Gweric how to *see* a demon, how it appeared to magical vision, but she found nothing to show. The demon—if it still lurked within the city—managed to elude any magic she sent looking for it. And since the magic still wasn't working quite properly, Kallista wasn't sure whether her magic was at fault or the demon might have departed.

Three full days had passed since the archer's sneaking attack on Kallista, but Obed was not fool enough to relax his vigilance. None of the other military naitani left to Adara had been attacked again. The rebels seemed to be focusing all their venom on Kallista. But he and her other iliasti would keep her safe. When he had trekked across the Southern desert and mountains to find the Chosen One, he had thought his wealth would be of greatest value to his beloved—and it was of value. But his skill as a fighter seemed to be valued even more, and that was a thing that felt strange to him. Strange, but good.

He prepared for sleep, removing his garments, laying his weapons where he could reach them quickly. Joh slept near the door, first defense if assassins got past the guards at the suite's entrance. Obed was second defense tonight, sleeping with Kallista behind him, with Torchay on her far side against the wall, protecting her between them.

Even after most of a year, sleeping in a bed that held another person—much less two or more others—was another thing that felt strange to Obed. Though he had married her—them—that long ago, it was not until Firstday of this same week that he had truly accepted what this binding of theirs meant. What it was. It was too strange a thing from what he'd known all his life, too difficult to understand and accept all at once, and so it had taken this long.

She loved him. She *saw* him, Obed im-Shakiri, flawed with pride—though he had little enough to be proud of—filled with stubbornness and selfishness and too many more things to name. And she loved him anyway. When his flaws pushed him into doing things that hurt her, she forgave. Because she loved him. He understood it now. He knew it. He felt it. How could he do any less?

Kallista lay in the bed next to Torchay, watching Obed, smiling. He couldn't help smiling back. The expression was beginning to feel not quite so strange on his face. Obed lay down beside her, turning so she could tuck herself into his back. This was where he belonged.

In his dreams, Obed rode along a muddy track at the back of a small caravan. Four other riders only, with four additional pack animals, two men riding as guard before and behind the two women. There was a live goat tied atop one of the pack-horses, bleating in indignant protest. It made Obed smile.

This was the rest of their ilian. Obed realized it when he saw how heavily pregnant one of the women was and matched that state with her cropped yellow hair. The path where they rode led down by a series of crookback turns along a steep mountainside to a thatch-roofed village. Obed's smile widened. Kallista would be glad to know the others were safe.

Then, when their road came down onto the level plateau where the town was built, Obed saw them. Brown-and-scarlet cloaks in the village. Rebels.

"'Ware!" he cried, spurring his horse to ride ahead. "Beware! It's a trap! The town is taken!"

In Obed's dream, Fox heard his warning and threw aside his cloak, drawing his sword. He shouted something to the others. Stone gathered the women and babies, hurrying them back up the trail. But as Obed watched, Fox fell, cut down by rebel swords. One by one, the others fell also, until only the screaming of an infant could be heard over the coarse laughter of the villains.

Obed shouted, struggled to swing his weapon, but his arms would not move. His feet were nailed to the ground. One of the rebels walked to the dead horse that had borne a now motionless Aisse. She swung her sword, and the crying ceased.

He roared his rage and grief. Obed wanted out of this dream. He needed to know it wasn't real, but he could not wake.

Then he saw it. Or felt it. Or perhaps he smelled it. Evil condensed to its purest essence. Red eyes smirked at him. "Truth," the demon whispered. "You carry truth."

"No!" Obed shouted. "Lies! All lies!"

His shout still echoed in the small room when he jerked upright and awake, bringing Kallista with him. She was wrapped around him, her hands on his face, lips to his ear, whispering reassurance. Obed wrapped his arms around her and held on tight, letting his agony go in a groan.

"Are you with us?" Torchay laid a hand on his shoulder.

Obed took a shuddering breath, hoping to clear his head. "I think so. Goddess, I must have been mad. To think I was jealous of your nightmares." His arms tightened around Kallista. "But if these are the dreams you suffered, beloved, then I am glad to take some of the burden from you. We all are." He included the others, because he could not speak less than truth. He knew they felt as he did.

"I'm not." She got to her feet and drew him with her, out of the bed. "I have more defenses than you. Come. Into the parlor. Tell us what you saw."

Obed's tale, told as he held tight to Kallista with Torchay at his back and Joh's hand on his shoulder, made her heart freeze. Frantically, Kallista searched inside her, counting up links. She couldn't access the magic of her absent iliasti, couldn't reach them through the links, but since her magic's more-or-less return, she could at least sense the presence of their links.

"When you woke, you were shouting 'lies,'" Kallista said. "And it *was* a lie, Obed. You knew it for what it was. My links with them still hold. They are alive and unharmed."

"Praise be." He relaxed against her, resting his forehead on her shoulder. "It seemed so real. I am glad to know it was not."

"Still—" Kallista stroked a hand down the unbound silk of his hair. "It wouldn't hurt to ask the Reinine to send a warning to her troop heading that way, and perhaps one to Sumald, if they've a farspeaker of their own. This dream may have come as warning, and was merely seized by the demon for torment."

"I pray the One that is so." Obed shuddered and held her tighter. "Our children..."

Kallista pulled back his hair and pressed a kiss to his bared temple. He had never before referred to them as *our children,* only *yours.* She would not call attention to it. She would simply be grateful it had happened.

"We should go back to bed," Torchay said. "Get what rest we can."

"Maybe I can get a warning through to our iliasti." She had been able to reach farspeakers in Arikon who had no links with her during the assassin archer's attack.

"All right, try." Torchay slid his hand along Kallista's arm. "But don't exhaust yourself doing it."

Kallista lifted a hand to cup Joh's face where he sat behind her and turned her head till his cheek touched hers, accessing his magic that way, though his hand rested on her shoulder. She found the three silent links deep inside where her magic lived and kissed them, willing them to wake.

"Drawing," she warned, wrapping invisible fingers in the magic she could reach and hauling it forth.

She spun it fine—it had to reach a long distance—and loaded it with warning before she sent it flying down the links, dragging out more and more magic to keep the line unbroken. On and on it sped into an endless distance, draining her energy with every immaterial league it passed. Just before it faded, she caught a faint sense of her absent iliasti, Fox, Stone and Aisse together.

Fox sent a questioning thought, but Kallista had time and strength only to give her love and the warning before the magic frayed into nothingness and she collapsed.

"Up you go." Torchay lifted her in his arms. "You're done for the night."

She looped her arms around his neck and snuggled in. "They're all right. Could you sense it?"

"No, but I'm glad you did." Torchay rolled her into the bed and crawled over her to the wall side. "No more dreams," he ordered. "From anyone. Me included."

"At least we know I can reach them if we have to," Kallista mumbled through lips that already slept.

"Good. Now sleep." Torchay pulled her back against his chest. "Where's Obed?"

"Here." He moved closer, sandwiching Kallista snugly between their two big male bodies. "Sleep."

Now she could.

Aisse woke with the dawn's breaking to find Fox sitting next to the fire, staring into its flames. She groaned upright, crossing her legs at the ankles to provide support for this enormous child of hers. "It wasn't a dream, was it?"

He turned his face to her, for all the world as if he could see her. "You felt it, too? Kallista's touch?"

"Oh, yes. She was worried." Aisse held her hands out to him in silent appeal.

"She was warning us." Fox walked over, took her hands and hauled her to her feet. "But I don't know what she was warning us against. Or what she meant for us to do."

He escorted her to the place they'd made behind a cedar bush for a privy and turned his back. She hated the necessity, but she would need his help to stand again.

"Are you sure it was a warning?" she asked when they were beside the fire again. "I know they've been worried about us."

"I'm sure." Fox brought her a satchel. He couldn't always find what he wanted by touch, and his *knowing* didn't seem to work in distinguishing things from each other. She didn't mind serving as his eyes, especially now when he served as her strength.

He frowned, waiting while Aisse searched for food supplies. "Kallista wasn't the only one I sensed," he said.

"No?" That surprised her. None of them could sense any of the others through the links except during those moments of…binding. Only Kallista. They'd discussed it on occasion.

"I felt—it seemed as if *Obed* warned me as well." Fox brought her the cookpot from another bag. "That bit seemed more like a dream—not so real as when Kallista touched us."

Now Aisse frowned. "*Two* warnings…"

"If Obed's was real."

"I'm not sure it matters. We should be very, very careful. And maybe go to another town to resupply."

"Agreed. Though I don't know the country well enough to know what would be a safe place."

They hadn't seen other travelers on this road. Given the uncertain weather and the upheaval in the political situation, Aisse wasn't surprised, but it made her even more uneasy than before. People didn't travel when there was trouble afoot. She wanted safety. "How far is it to Torchay's family?"

"A long way," Stone said quietly. He'd extricated himself from Merinda's sleeping grasp and come to join them. "Torchay showed me on the map before we left. Past the Gap, across more mountains and another stretch called The Empty Lands. A long way."

"Sounds far enough away to be safe." Aisse liked that.

"Which means it will take a long time to get there," Fox said. Aisse didn't like that.

"You heard the warning too, then." Stone looked from one to the other. "You think bandits have heard about the gold?"

Aisse gasped. She hadn't thought of that. The blasted horse payment increased the danger a hundredfold. Or more. "Sweet Goddess—can we get rid of it?"

"We agreed to transport it." Stone scowled at the fire. "I don't like failing to do something we agreed to."

"But if—" Aisse began.

"If something happens, we'll deal with it then. I have no problem handing it over to any bandits. If they think we have it and we don't..." Fox took a deep breath. "We should go around Sumald if we can. There's bound to be somewhere else we can resupply, and we've got the goat for the girls if it's far."

"Agreed," Aisse said as Stone nodded his agreement.

"What are you all whispering about?" Merinda's cheerful early morning voice bustled with her up to the fire, grating on Aisse's sensibilities. Aisse wasn't necessarily grumpy in the mornings, but she didn't see any need for too much cheer. *That* made her grumpy.

"It won't wake the babies if you talk in normal tones," Merinda was saying as she checked the oat porridge Aisse had set to cooking, and gave it a stir. Another thing that grated on Aisse. Merinda didn't seem to trust anyone else to do things as well as she could, from changing nappies to stirring oats.

Still, they couldn't have made his journey without her. Two

babies seemed to require four times as much care, and before long, there would be three. So Aisse squelched her irrational irritation and smiled as brightly as she could manage. "We were deciding to bypass Sumald."

Merinda blinked at the three of them. "Whatever for?"

"To avoid danger," Stone said.

"Oh. If you're sure…" Merinda didn't sound any too sure.

Lorynda let out a hungry wail and the goat bleated. Aisse left Merinda to the cooking and went to tend their child.

It turned out they couldn't bypass Sumald after all. The road they followed wound down through the unfamiliar pass without branching one way or the other. Fox and Stone discussed taking off cross-country, but with Aisse in her state and two infants to deal with besides, they decided there was less risk in taking their chances with Sumald. The warning had not been very specific. It could as well warn against ambush on the trail. Or nothing.

All the same, Fox and Stone rode unencumbered, leaving the babies to the women's care. Merinda knew nothing about fighting and Aisse was in no shape for any. Fox took the lead, throwing his odd *knowing* sense as wide as he could to search for danger. They could do no more.

Sumald seemed peaceful late that morning as their small party came down off the narrow mountain trail onto the flatter plateau where the town was built. The wide Heldring Gap spread out below them where it cut between the Shieldbacks and the Okreti di Vos Mountains to the north. Fox surmised that Sumald had been built here on the mountainside to make it more defensible. Or perhaps to be nearer the iron mines. They'd passed more than one abandoned mineshaft on their way down.

Fox rode ahead, widening the gap between himself and the women, all of his senses heightened. People moved about the town, mostly loitering in the streets, near buildings. Not like workers busy about their tasks. He slowed his horse, held up his hand to slow the others. Stone moved forward, in front of the women, and Fox turned his mount to ride back and join them. He did not need to face a thing to know where it was and what it did.

"What do you see?" he asked when he was close enough to be heard without shouting.

"Nothing." Stone backed his horse nearer the others. "I don't like it."

"Nor do I. Especially since there are…" Fox paused to count. "Eight people in the streets."

"Not good. Is there another way out of here?"

"Don't know. All I can sense is space. Those in the town, the buildings, and space—the mountain falling away. If there's another way down, it's going to take eyes to find it."

"I have eyes," Aisse said. "I'll look."

"Carefully," Fox warned her. He turned his horse again to face the village. "They're moving around. Getting restless. I don't think they like us stopping out here."

"Too bad." Stone controlled his nervous mount.

"We don't want them attacking before we've found a way out." Fox started toward the village again at a slow amble. "Let them think we're still coming on."

After a moment, the others followed. Aisse and Stone rode nearer the drop-off than made Fox comfortable, but then the sense of *nothing* was so great as to be almost overwhelming. Perhaps true sight made it easier.

Motion in the village caught his attention. They were coming, rushing to the attack. Fox drew his sword, the magic-forged blade that had been matched to him. "Find the way down. I'll hold them off."

Stone spurred his horse forward. "No, Fox. Let me—"

"No!" Fox cut him off. "I can do this. You know the way.

They need *you*." He shouldered his horse into Stone's, urging him back toward the others.

With a last, brief pause, Stone went. "Find the way down," Stone ordered. "A goat track. Anything. Let's go."

Fox clucked to his mount and trotted toward the troop of rebels forming ranks on the edge of the town. They would not harm his family. Not while he had breath in his body. He kicked up the pace slightly, charging the rabble. Except they didn't behave like rabble.

The enemy lined up two deep. Did they have pikes? Fox couldn't tell. Then he caught the faint aroma of gunpowder. Dear Goddess, they had *muskets*. He angled his approach, turning his attention back to "see" Merinda disappear over the edge of the plateau. They'd found an escape. Too close to the rebels for his comfort, but it would have to do.

Only eight rebels. Surely he could hold them off, keep them from following. A musket fired—someone got too anxious— the ball whipping past as Fox ducked low over his horse's neck. The others fired in reaction, while he was still far enough away that the muskets' notorious inaccuracy kept them from hitting him. One ball grazed his horse's rump, sending it leaping forward with a squeal.

They wouldn't have time to reload before he was on them, even if they'd been Tibran warriors. But they weren't, weren't even proper Adaran soldiers. They'd never have fired early, if they were. Fox broke through their ranks, his trained warhorse kicking out, rearing, wreaking havoc, as he laid about him with the sword.

"Don't let them get away!" One of the rebels pointed back up the shallow slope behind Fox.

Fox *saw* Stone holding Aisse's hand as she scrambled over the edge. Stone's other arm held a wriggling bundle. A pair of rebels started toward them.

"Cowards!" Fox spurred his horse to go after them and it collapsed beneath him, blood pouring from its neck. He leaped free and charged on foot, slicing through the man who would have stopped him.

Stone passed the baby to Aisse and turned to meet the onrushing rebels. Pain blasted Fox's shoulder and he turned, thrust through the man behind him.

The seconds it took allowed the others to reach Stone. He fought well, holding his own with a flurry of blows Fox's *knowing* couldn't follow. Then he fell—tripped, Fox thought—and vanished with a shout over the edge of the cliff. A woman's scream joined the shout, then another. Then silence.

"No-o-o-o!" Fox tried to run, to reach the spot where his family had vanished so he could know what had happened, could join them in whatever it was, but his feet wouldn't move. Other pain joined the agony in his back. He stumbled forward a few paces and fell to his knees. The warm wet on his back—and his arm and there across his ribs—must be blood.

Clutching his sword in one hand, Fox crawled on hands and knees. They couldn't be dead. Not now. Not after all this. He had to know. First, before he died, he had to know.

But his circle of awareness shrank with the ebbing of his strength. He realized feet were in his way before he crashed into them and turned to crawl around them. A hand—related to the feet most likely—gave him a hard shove and Fox toppled over. He dug his fingers into the grass to haul himself forward and one of the feet stepped on his hand.

"Die, damn you," a rough voice growled.

"Stop." That voice was female. "Go find the ones that got away. The Naishan wants them alive."

*Why?* Fox had no chance to consider an answer as his strength trickled away with his blood to nothing.

# CHAPTER TWELVE

The distant scream coming in the middle of a practice session jolted Kallista hard, so hard that she almost lost her hold on the braided magic, almost let it backlash in a way that would've been worse than what Obed had caused. Her family was in trouble.

She grabbed for more magic, a mother's fear for her children giving her strength, making her rough. She scrabbled for the links, frantically counting them. Still five, since Joh's had not formed yet—two close, three so desperately far away. She shoved magic hard down those distant links.

"What is it? What's wrong?" Torchay kept his voice quiet, as if afraid to distract her.

"Trouble." Kallista didn't say more, didn't know enough to say.

Part of her flew with the magic, chivvying it along, dragging it when needful. Part of her knew the men had gathered close, supported her, lent her their strength.

At the last gasping end of the magic, she found them. She couldn't sense where they were or what was wrong, but they were alive. Hurt, afraid of some danger, but alive. Kallista *reached* back down that long endless strand for more magic from those close to her, but it took so much strength, so much time to travel so far, and too much of it was used just making the journey.

Fox was badly hurt, bleeding his life onto the rocks. Kallista shunted as much magic into his healing as she dared. Not enough, not nearly, but Aisse needed help and—

*Hide.* The need came strongly from both Stone and Aisse. Kallista twisted the driblet of magic remaining her into veiling. As the magic left her to do its task, it took her senses with it, leaving her in darkness.

She woke, jerking herself upright in terror. Before she could move again, Torchay was there, holding her, murmuring nonsense in her ear. Fear ate at her, but it was a moment more before she could remember why. *Links.* She reached inside, touched, named them. Torchay. Obed. *Stone. Aisse…Fox.*

All there. Though Fox seemed faint. Weak from his injuries?

"Dreams?" Torchay brushed her tangled hair from her face.

They were in the suite again, in one of the bedrooms. Kallista shook her head. "Reality is bad enough. I don't need dreams to make it worse. Where are the others?"

"In the parlor. Training." He didn't stop her from sliding off the bed, though his lips tightened in disapproval. He followed, catching her arm when her knees threatened to buckle. "Obed isn't much for sitting still when he's worried. What happened?"

Kallista shook her head. She only wanted to tell it once. She opened the door and the sounds of men wrestling stopped instantly. Obed and Joh, stripped to the waist, glistening with sweat, released each other and straightened, staring. Then Obed flew across the room, leaping the furniture in the way, to grab Kallista by the shoulders and peer into her eyes. "Praise be to the One," he whispered.

Joh arrived more slowly, but the relief in his face was just as evident.

"Now, will you tell us what happened?" Torchay ushered her to her favorite sofa.

"Trouble. I don't know what kind or where. Probably they were attacked, but I don't know who or what. They're all hurt, Fox seriously, and they needed to hide. I did what I could to help, but..." Kallista shuddered, burrowing her face into Torchay's shoulder, trying to hide from her worry.

"So. We knew you'd pulled magic, but not what it was for. We were afraid you'd found the demon."

Kallista shook her head, wiping her eyes on Torchay's tunic as she did. She would *not* cry. She looked up, hunting Joh, and held her hand out to him. He took it without hesitation, but his magic did not answer and she didn't have the strength to drag it out by main force.

"Rest," Obed said. "Eat. Build your strength. Later, you can try again."

"We should never have split up." Kallista raked fingers through her hair, combing out some of the tangles. "I knew better, when the Reinine suggested it, but she's the Reinine. She—"

"Too late to worry about 'should haves,'" Torchay said. "Deal with what is."

"Right." Kallista felt as if she'd been flattened by a dozen freight wagons, then trampled by their mule teams. Her whole body ached and she could barely find energy to lift her head, but she was so bloody tired of resting. She wanted— *needed* to *do*. To act. "Have they found who ordered it? Who sent the gold?"

"No word yet," Torchay said. "They're still looking, apparently."

"Damn." Kallista closed her eyes, but a pair of tears forced their way out anyway.

"Right, then." Torchay pulled her into his lap and stood with her in his arms. "Back to bed with you."

"Not alone. Don't want to be alone." Why couldn't she make

her mouth work? The words didn't want to shape themselves properly.

"No, not alone. You know we're always with you."

"Yes, but I want all of you with me. I want to feel your *skin*, not just your magic. All of you." She sensed more than saw the looks exchanged between the three men. She didn't know how they would manage what she asked, but she knew they would and was content.

Days passed. Kallista seemed to spend most of them in an exhausted fog, for whenever she could summon strength enough, she would grapple with the magic and send it hunting her distant iliasti. She would renew as much of the veiling around Aisse and Stone as she could, though the daily increasing distance between them made it more and more difficult. And she would do what she could to keep Fox healing.

He was separated from the others, she knew, but why or what it meant or how far apart they were, she couldn't tell. She fought the infection that made him feverish and struggled to seal the holes in his body that let it in, but he was so very far away….

With every day that passed however, the long-distance magic drained her less. The magic itself did not answer her call any better, but she had more strength to wrestle it into doing what she needed it to do. By Secondday of the next week, she was able to return to her physical training and resume her appearances in court. Viyelle had suggested that by merely mingling with the inhabitants of the palace she might allow them to see her as an ordinary naitan rather than building up frightening images in their minds of strange magic performed by someone too powerful to be human.

Kallista had her doubts about how effective such a thing would be. She was not in the least comfortable trying to make small talk with people whose primary interests seemed to be clothing, jewelry and salacious gossip, but it did no harm to attempt it. No harm to anything more than her patience, at any rate, of which the One had given her a less-than-generous portion. It also kept them moving about the palace in unpredictable patterns, to Torchay's satisfaction.

Kallista knew she ought to be using her magic to seek out the demon lurking in Arikon, but until Fox was healed enough that she no longer feared for his life, and until she was sure Stone and Aisse had brought the babies to safety, she did not have the magic to spare. It was entirely possible this trouble was some diabolical plot to divert her attention away from Arikon.

If so, it was working. Kallista didn't care. Her iliasti came first. Without them, she couldn't fight the demons anyway. She needed the magic they carried. But the Reinine did not appear willing to wait.

Fourthday evening, as ordered, Kallista took up a post in an obscure corner of the council room, accompanied by her bodyguards and her new-bound ilias. With so many of them crowded into a small space, it was difficult to avoid notice, but standing at attention staring off into space did much to encourage the councilors and the prinsipi to overlook them.

Weariness dragged at her, weighting her eyelids, bringing up yawns. She wanted to sleep for a week, but didn't dare. She had demons to hunt.

As General Uskenda rose to give her report on the status of the rebellion, Joh slid his hand onto Kallista's nape, making his magic available to her. She called it from all three sources and kicked it out to scour the room. No demon, but she did find a null-spell hovering near the ceiling.

Because it negated magic in its vicinity, Kallista had to call up more and more of Torchay's stubborn strength before she could overwhelm and demolish it. The spell would have faded over the next few days, but while it lasted, it would have crushed the Reinine's truth-saying magic.

Null-spells were difficult to construct, requiring considerable skill and magic. *West* magic.

Kallista knew she hadn't built it. Could Gweric be involved? He was a West naitan. Could he have more magic than he claimed? She could not see him willingly working with demons, but without realizing it…? Joh had been lied to. Why not Gweric?

Except the Reinine had been having trouble with her magic before Gweric moved into the palace. Kallista didn't think he had magic enough to build such a complicated spell elsewhere and float it into the palace. She doubted anyone could. Not even a demon.

Demons could not act in the physical world except through a mortal being, because they had no physical presence. But did that limitation include an inability to work magic? Demons existed in the same realm where magic was found.

All magic was a gift of the One. Didn't that mean a demon couldn't use it? Could a naitan be demon-possessed and work this kind of magic? It made Kallista's head hurt, trying to sort through things.

The meeting wore on, prinsipi demanding, councilors arguing, generals refusing. The Reinine sat and listened. Kallista watched and hid her yawns.

She leaned harder on her iliasti, hoping she would have energy enough to walk herself back to their suite. She worried about Fox—she never had checked on his healing earlier today—and about Stone, Aisse and the babies. Were they all safe? They were at least alive—that much she knew. But where?

Finally, with the clocks tolling past midnight, the Reinine rose. The prinsipi present weren't ready to stop talking, but when the Reinine departed, Kallista left with her. The prinsipi remained behind to complain to each other.

A thought struck her and she stumbled, Obed's hand on her elbow supporting her through it, hiding it. Did the Reinine have someone to report these complaints to her? Surely she did. Kallista did. Viyelle had unobtrusively attached herself to her mother-the-prinsipas's entourage to collect information for her new superior. Though a raw novice when it came to palace intrigue, even Kallista knew the importance of knowing all that was being said.

*Goddess,* no wonder she was so tired. The political battlefield was a dozen times more wearying than any fought across with sword and spear. Or musket. But she couldn't avoid it any longer. The demon had to be found. That meant Kallista had to wet her toes in political muck. Pray the One she didn't have to wade in too deep.

Fog had closed in. It drifted down from the mountain heights to twine around the tower roofs and creep through every opening. Kallista couldn't feel its cold, damp kiss, but there was no mistaking the grayed veil it threw over everything. Except her iliasti.

Torchay's hair glowed as bright a red as ever in the light of the lamp he insisted on leaving lit. Obed's gleamed no less black, nor did the rich brown of Joh's hair fade in the fog. Kallista frowned. There should be no fog in their room. The window was closed. Though spring was fading quickly into summer, nights were still too cool—and Torchay too wary—to leave windows open.

The fog glimmered, lighting from within, a pale blue glow that shifted purple, then to a violet-rose and Kallista understood. Her dreams had come home to her again.

Joh shifted, muttered. Kallista soothed him with a touch,

then pulled the dreamfog around and over her sleeping mates to hide them, protect them from anyone—anything else that might wander these planes. She stood, holding her purpose firm in her mind. Whatever the demon's intentions, she had her own places to be.

Swift as the thought, she arrowed across the dreamscape. Mountains and rivers flashed below her, visible through streamers of fog thinned by the speed of her passage. She found them high in a mountain pass, crowded into a shallow space hollowed out of the mountain's rocky side. Kallista's twins shared a bed, an empty packsaddle crate, as they had once shared a much smaller space.

She sang voicelessly to them, needing them in her arms, but unable even to touch Lorynda's dark curls or press her lips to Rozite's fair, peach-fuzzed head. Rozite pursed her tiny rosebud lips, suckling in her dreams. Kallista's heart burned, wept, and she knew she wept in truth where her body lay. She wanted her babies home.

"K'lista?" Aisse stirred, shivered, snuggled back against Stone who lay curled around her back.

"I'm here. Sleep." Kallista wiped her face with the back of a hand, wiping away nothing. "All is well."

"Fox?"

"He's hurt, but alive."

"Good. That's good. Aren't the girls getting big? They're growing so fast." Aisse smiled in her sleep. "Come soon. We miss you."

"We will. Be careful. Torchay's kin are coming to meet you. Be wary of anyone else."

"How will we know who they are? Who we can trust?"

Kallista couldn't help grinning. "By the hair. They're all red as foxes. Redder."

Then she was spinning over the landscape again. She didn't

know how much dreamtime she had, didn't know if the dream had its own demands, and she had another purpose before it ended.

The dream took her out of the mountains, through the Gap into the western edge of the plains before dropping her into a rough camp where the dreamfog held a dark, almost greasy quality. Fox lay sweating on a canvas travois that had obviously been unhitched from the horse that had dragged it all day and left to lie where it fell.

The sweat eased her worry a bit. Feverish men usually didn't sweat, so perhaps his fever had broken.

Kallista lowered herself beside him and brushed her hand over his forehead, though she felt nothing, wishing she could touch him in truth. His eyes flew open so abruptly, she jumped. A shiver crawled down her back, because she could swear he saw her. Those piercing brown eyes *saw* something.

He sat up, his movements stiff, never taking his eyes off her face. She waited while his hand rose, trembling slightly. He would not be able to touch her dreamself she knew, but she also knew he had to try.

The rough warmth of his callused hand slid across her cheek and she shuddered in reaction and in shock. How could she feel his touch?

"Kallista?" His voice was scarcely more than a breath. "*Is* it you? How can I see you?"

"You do?" Had her long-distance healing given back so much? Then Kallista saw his body lying on its pallet and understood. "You're dreaming," she said. "In dreams, we often regain things we have lost."

He sank back on his heels, his hand falling away in obvious disappointment. "Then it's not *you* I see, because you're not really here. Just some construct of my fevered mind."

"No." Kallista took his face between hers, urging him to

look at her. "This is *my* dream, Fox. One of those that shows what is, or what is to come. This is what is. I truly am here with you. You have stepped into my dream."

"Why?"

She leaned toward him, intending to kiss his forehead and found herself swept into his lap, his face pressed against hers. "Perhaps because we both need this. Perhaps to say goodbye."

*"Goodbye?"* He jerked back, his dark eyes crying alarm.

"No, no." She did no more than smile, trying to show her chagrin at her poor word choice in the face of his fears. "We are bound, Fox. The strength of that binding is all the more obvious because you're here in my dream. You see me. But—" She caught her lower lip between her teeth, trying to find words to explain something she had no explanation for.

"I don't think we will meet again like this, in our dreams," she said. "Not soon. I've been helping you as much as I can—healing you, hiding the others—"

"The others." Fox searched her face. "They escaped? They are alive?"

"Yes." She hugged him. "Yes, they are all safe and well and worried about you. I saw them before I came here."

"Praise be." He held her tight, racked by the occasional shudder.

Kallista turned to kiss his temple. "They are safe. You are—" She pushed him back until she could look him over, his dreamself a copy of the physical.

He looked haggard, not as thin or battered as when he had first come to them last summer after the battle when he'd almost died, but as if he'd been ill.

"You're no longer in danger of dying, I think."

"Likely, aye." He made a face intended to amuse. "Though if they keep feeding me that slop they eat, that may change."

She made an effort to smile as he wanted, but couldn't maintain it. "My magic is needed in Arikon. Unless something changes, this is our last dreamtime."

His gaze traveled over her, as if he memorized what he saw. Perhaps he did. "At least I have seen you this once."

Fox cradled her face between his hands. "I know you this way, the silk of your skin, the wine of your mouth. Now I know the blue of your eyes and the pale blush in your cheeks, and I am grateful for this gift."

Kallista shivered, held powerless by the poetry in his words. She accepted his kiss, drank him down, yearning for more even as it dissolved into the nothingness of ordinary dreaming. She whimpered, feeling the loss, and a hand stroked along her arm, offering comfort. She followed, needing more, nestling in to the bare male flesh in front of her.

The hesitation in his response told her who it was before his scent and the isolated fluff of hair on his chest—more than Torchay, less than Obed—identified him as Joh. She didn't want to push him beyond his willingness, but allowing him to hold back as Obed had done obviously wasn't the right way to go either. Would he object if she spent desire roused by another on him? She didn't know him well enough to guess.

They hadn't been bound together for two weeks yet, and only since Sixthday last had they persuaded him from his isolated cot—when the other half of their ilian was attacked. Time enough to learn, to bind him closer. Kallista brushed her nose against his collarbone and let her breath out as she relaxed into him. Time enough—if it didn't take too long.

Kallista told the others of her dream, all of them grateful for the good news and that no demons had awakened them all with her screams. She wondered if that meant the demon had left Arikon, especially since a pair of days passed with no sign of it or its handiwork, save for a tattered, fading null-spell in the Great Hall.

On Graceday, Arikon farspeakers received word that the troop sent to find Kallista's mates and children had reached Sumald. They found the battered inhabitants full of tales of invasion and terror, but no sign of any travelers. Kallista urged the Reinine to send the troop on to Korbin prinsipality. Once the children were safe, Fox could be located and rescued.

Two days later on Peaceday, the city was at rest, beginning to gather energy again for the bustle of Firstday. Kallista lounged on the long yellow sofa propped against Torchay sitting in the corner with her feet in Obed's lap. Joh sat on the floor on one side of the low serving table trying to teach Gweric to play queens-and-castles, while Viyelle hung over the boy's shoulder and watched.

"If you'd keep your hands off the pieces, he might be able to catch on to the rules of the game." Joh's voice penetrated Kallista's lethargy.

"I haven't touched his queens," Viyelle protested. "*Or* his castles."

"I don't think those were the pieces our Joh was referring to," Torchay said, a sly grin winking in his half-open eyes.

"Oh, you mean *that* game…" Viyelle bent closer over Gweric until her cheek nearly brushed his. "I think he already knows the rules."

"I hope so." Kallista didn't want the boy hurt. It had to be good for him to know a woman found him attractive despite his scars or…missing pieces. She just hoped he wouldn't read more into it than there was.

Thunder rumbled through the open window. Kallista pillowed her head on Torchay's shoulder and let her eyes drift shut. Cuddling inside while it rained was one of her favorite activities. "Someone ought to close the window so the rain doesn't get the Reinine's furniture wet, Viyelle."

"It's not raining."

"It will be soon." Kallista turned her face into Torchay's neck. She heard people moving around—Viyelle walking to the window, Joh standing.

"No, Major," Viyelle said. "The sky's perfectly clear. Not a cloud in it."

Kallista flicked her eyes open. "Then why do I hear thunder?"

Obed and Torchay were on their feet with her, striding to the window together. She leaned on the windowsill, stretched over it as far as she dared, listening, looking for any sign of what she might have heard.

"You heard it, didn't you?" She checked with the others. Most nodded. Viyelle shrugged.

A sharp crack sounded, loud and close by, followed by a receding rumble. Kallista's head jerked around and someone caught her belt to keep her from tumbling through the window as she leaned farther out. Smoke, or dust, rose from a palace tower not two hundred paces to her right, spilling out through a gaping hole in the stone wall, and a faint, familiar scent drifted to her on the breeze.

"Sweet Goddess, it's *gunpowder!*"

## CHAPTER THIRTEEN

So many hands pulled her back through the window, she flew, skidding when she hit the polished floor. "Boots. We need boots. And weapons. Joh, to me."

Riding the fine edge of panic, Kallista caught his forearm beneath his pushed-up sleeve and called magic, pulling more of it through links with her other mates. She knotted it clumsily together and threw it out, hunting the Reinine. Hunting demons. Pray the One she did not find them together.

Viyelle tossed Kallista her rapier, belting on her own sword. All the men were already armed. They always were, since the assassination attempt. Obed knelt, holding her soft-topped boots open and she stomped her feet into them. Torchay tucked her gloves into his belt. Kallista shifted her grip on Joh to hold his hand.

"Our tower is clear," she said, diverting a stream of magic to check. "No people, no magic."

With a nod, Torchay led the way out of the room as another distant rumble sounded in the city. Kallista shoved down her fears and tugged at the tail of her magic. They needed to find the Reinine.

The palace corridors and antechambers were as crowded as

ever, filled with courtiers who seemed more puzzled or curious than frightened. A few attempted to stop Kallista with questions, but a growl from one of the men backed them off. The magic thrummed, finding its goal.

The Reinine was not in the ruined tower, thank the One, but moving rapidly down and east, perhaps to some safe room Kallista didn't know of. She left the Reinine to the care of her bodyguards and ilian, and spread the magic wider, hunting the stink of demons.

"Get down!" Torchay bellowed, spinning to throw himself at Kallista. She smelled it, too.

The explosion followed so quickly it drowned out his warning, sent them all flying. It blasted a hole through the palace wall. Gentle spring sunshine slanted in through the floating dust, lighting the dazed faces of those crawling back to their feet. A woman screamed and sound bloomed again.

"Are you all right?" Kallista touched Obed, got his nod, lifted Torchay's head. He winced as she touched a swelling knot on the back of his skull but claimed no other hurts. Joh was already checking Viyelle and Gweric.

"Courier, get help." Kallista rolled to her feet, favoring the hip where she'd landed.

"Already coming." Viyelle pointed out the broken wall at the soldiers and healers swarming up over the rubble.

"All right then." Kallista tried to think past the ringing in her head to what she should do next.

Others could handle this chaos better. The Reinine was safe, or as safe as a double quarto of bodyguards could make her, so what was left to do was…demons. She needed to hunt demons.

She grabbed Joh's hand and scooped out more magic, binding it with that she called from Obed and Torchay. She needed what each of them had to give—Torchay to provide an immovable foundation, Joh to see what was there, and Obed to know the truth of what she saw. She took the time to build the necessary spell, wrestling the reluctant magic into exactly the shape she wanted.

"Gweric, can you see the magic?"

"I—yes. I see it." The boy limped up beside her.

"Help me watch. Help me find what we seek." Kallista adjusted her grip on Joh, wrapping her arm in his for support while maintaining the skin-to-skin contact. She drew Gweric close to her other side.

"We should get out of the way." Torchay eyed the rescue workers bustling past.

Kallista took a deep breath, coughing a little on the dust. When she let it out, she let the magic go, giving it a shove when it didn't go fast enough. It floated motionless a moment, then began to drift down the corridor, past the blast center, beyond the moaning wounded and silent dead, in the direction the Reinine had gone. Kallista tipped her head after it. "That way."

Periodic rumbles, the thunder of explosions, continued to echo through the city. Where had the rebels acquired so much gunpowder? How had they hidden it? How had they smuggled it in? Or had it been in Arikon all along? Urgency drove Kallista, but the magic wouldn't be driven.

It sauntered through the palace corridors as if it had all the time in the world. As if it wanted to challenge her, like a child that knew it had to obey, but would sulk and delay as long as possible before finally obeying. Or perhaps the demon was simply too good at hiding its tracks.

The magic led them down into the bowels of the palace, into places Kallista had never known existed and wouldn't have guessed at without being shown. They came to a narrow corridor with a heavy iron door, barred, locked and bolted, tucked just inside its branching.

Ferenday Reinas blocked access to the door, blocked their way when they neared it. "What are you doing here? Who told you the way?"

"No one. I'm following magic. Tracking demons." Kallista wished she didn't have time to talk, but she did. The magic moved that slowly.

Ferenday paled but hid any other reaction. "Demons came this way? This close?"

"So the magic says."

"I can see its tracks," Gweric said, pointing. "A smear in the air."

"Can you? Good." Kallista patted his hand. "A demon hound is much better than a witch hound. Or a spell. What do you see?"

"It's faint." Gweric's nostrils widened as he sniffed. "I don't think it was here recently. Or maybe it's—"

"We should go." Kallista bowed to the Reinine's ilias. "Before the magic gets too far ahead of us. May we pass?"

"The Reinine may trust you." Ferenday gave her a hard look. "But I do not."

"Of course you don't. You're a bodyguard. You're not supposed to trust anyone." She wanted her smile to be reassuring but feared it held too much cynicism. "She is my Reinine, too. My commander. I am sworn to protect her just as you are. Which means finding and destroying demons."

With a last suspicious glare, Ferenday stepped back into the shallow recess before the heavy door and let them pass. They had to hurry to catch up with the spell. It seemed to be picking up speed.

"Do you still see the demon's tracks?" Kallista asked.

"Yes."

"Still faint?"

Gweric nodded, his empty eyes focused on things only he could see.

So, if the spell was moving faster, it apparently wasn't because they were closing in on the demon. Kallista tightened her grip on the spell and the men to either side of her and kept going.

The magic led them through a twisting maze of hallways until they reached a door that blocked their way. The magic slithered through the cracks and beyond reach. The door was locked and they had no key, so Obed and Torchay put feet and shoulders to it, bursting it open.

They fell into a tangled ivy that had grown up, apparently for decades, over the opening. It took a few more moments to fight their way through to the kitchen garden beyond. Leaving the kitchen help, gardeners and refugees from the explosions staring openmouthed after them, Kallista and her party hurried to catch up with the demon-hunting magic.

It bustled along at a brisk pace now, requiring its followers to break into the occasional trot to keep up. They left the palace grounds through the south gate, plunging into the terrified chaos of the city. Kallista could see smoke rising from fires in every quadrant of Arikon. As they scurried after the tracking spell, another explosion rumbled to the west, leaving screams and weeping behind.

"We have to help them," Viyelle shouted. Kallista had almost forgotten she was with them.

"We are." Kallista kept moving, grim determination joined with urgent need. "Others can dig the victims out and heal them. No one else can stop it."

The magic led them south, faster and faster until they were racing down Arikon's steepening streets. Kallista let go of Gweric to run easier, but she clung tight to Joh's hand. She didn't dare lose that grip. She might lose the magic.

Sudden screams burst from a small square ahead of them. The magic danced with excitement, bubbling in a multitude of colors. They were right on top of the thing. They had to be.

"I see it!" Gweric slapped both hands over his nose. "Oh, saints, I *smell* it."

Kallista sniffed cautiously. Nothing. People scattered, running from the square, crashing into them in panic, breaking her hold on Joh. But it didn't matter now. She could see it, too.

The dark malevolence that was the demon glared hate at her from red glowing eyes as it crouched on the shoulders of a well-dressed woman. Then it leaped to perch atop a burly carter.

"Joh!" Kallista couldn't take her eyes from the demon, wasn't sure she dared, but she needed all her magic. All her iliasti.

"Here." He shoved through the crowd, bodily picking a man up and setting him aside when he didn't move fast enough. Joh stretched across the gap swarming with frightened people and caught her arm, using it to drag himself through the human river until he was braced against her back. He wrapped an arm around her waist to lock them together and slid his other hand onto the bare nape of her neck, leaving her arms free.

"Now," he said into her ear, "where do you need to go?"

"There." Kallista pointed at the demon, still glaring at her from atop the carter's head. It seemed smaller than the one she'd encountered before. No less dark, but somehow…thinner. Not quite as solid.

Torchay led the way, forcing a path into the square, though the crowd's panic seemed to be lessening. Then screams and shouts erupted again and the crowd surged. The demon laughed, seeming to dance on its perch. It skipped across the crowd, bouncing twice, three times before coming to rest on one of the fleeing people.

"Look!" Viyelle pointed up.

Kallista fought back her shout of horror. Like some diabolical vulture pulled from its home element and twisted to serve unnatural purposes, a small boat floated in midair.

Its sail raised, it tacked in the down-mountain wind. As she watched, a face appeared over the gunwale, an arm moved, and a fat ball of fire flew, smashing into the building behind them. Flames licked greedily at the dry wood. This wasn't a wealthy part of town, though it wasn't the poorest. Fire would spread quickly here, and with the city so crowded, hundreds—maybe thousands—would die.

The firethrower's face appeared again and, acting on pure instinct, Kallista called lightning. It hit some kind of protective wall around the little boat, crackling blue all around it without doing any damage. But it did stop the devil-naitan's fireball.

How could a naitan ally with demons? Couldn't he see what they were? Kallista threw lightning again, hoping to keep him distracted long enough to form a plan. The distraction didn't work this time. A fireball lanced down from the other side of the air-sailing boat to bloom on the far side of the square.

She drew magic, pulling hard from all three of her marked ones, then more from Torchay's bottomless well. The flying boat was not a natural magic. It had to be powered by the demon, therefore, if she destroyed the demon, the boat would fall.

As if sensing her intent, the demon skipped across the few people left in the square, heading for the boat. Kallista fought her magic, trying to shape the dark veil, the deadly magic she'd used before, but it was like trying to mould rocks rather than clay. She hurled it at the demon, hoping to bludgeon it with the rocklike magic. It squalled, hurt, but kept running.

"There are two of them!" Gweric cried, pointing.

Kallista squinted, folding aside her physical sight, and saw a shadow flow over the side of the boat, reaching toward the darkness on the ground. It flinched away, as if reluctant to accept the offered help. She sent more magic spearing toward it, shaping it into a point this time. The demon screamed as the magic pierced it. Kallista threw her hands wide, willing the magic to expand and rip it apart.

With an enraged, desperate shriek, the demon spun into a wisp of stinking darkness and leaped toward the descending shadow. Instantly, its substance was sucked into the other, leaving only a faint wail echoing in the square.

Joh shuddered against Kallista's back, tucking his face into her hair. "It's not destroyed, is it?"

"I fear not." Her legs trembled with weariness, but she couldn't rest. She needed more magic.

It came easier this time, as if now she'd got it moving, it would keep on. Kallista wove it tight, willing it into the shape of the veil, visualizing the demons she'd seen in the boat. Two more fireballs exploded while she struggled.

"It's moving," Viyelle said. "Do we follow?"

"Yes."

Joh moved his arm from her waist, wound it with hers and clasped her hand before releasing her neck. Viyelle led the way this time, Torchay and Obed guarding Kallista with naked blades. She let Joh guide her, keep her upright and moving. The magic required all her attention.

Finally, she thought it was ready. She took a deep breath and *pushed,* sending the dark veil glittering toward the flying boat. It smashed into the same barrier magic as her lightning and melted away.

"Damn it!" Kallista's temper evaporated and she threw bolt after bolt of lightning in an attempt to batter through the damned barrier. Until the devil-naitan threw lightning back at her, just missing, and setting the bakeshop behind her afire. It had collected her own lightning to use against her. Which wasn't possible. Except he had done it.

Cackling with glee, the demon danced atop its mount, high enough she could see it above the boat's sides. Then the boat leaned into a broad turn and sailed toward a new, fire-free sector of Arikon. All those who had fled in that direction turned and came back, running into the roaring flames.

"Goddess, *help them*." Viyelle fell to her knees, knocked down by the panicked citizens crashing into her.

"Come, Courier. We're not done yet." Torchay lifted her back to her feet.

They couldn't be done. Not while the demon and its pet naitan continued their attack. But Kallista had run out of things to try. She couldn't quit, but couldn't think what else she could do.

She stumbled. The street was uneven, rutted. Joh picked her up when she stumbled again, carrying her as they trailed behind the flying boat, weaving their way through narrow streets and tiny squares. "I can walk," she protested.

"You can stagger," Joh said. "Not at all the same thing."

"It's slowing," Viyelle shouted back to them, pushing through the throngs running away.

"Put me down." Kallista struggled to get free.

"You don't have to stand to call magic." Joh broke through into the clear, and apparently changed his mind, setting her on her feet beside Viyelle. He stationed himself behind her as before, an arm around her waist, other hand on her neck.

Kallista beckoned her other two close. "Maybe it will help if we touch, too."

Torchay nodded. He sheathed one of his swords and slid his hand around her wrist. Obed took her other, and Kallista called their magic. Three skeins braided together, incomplete—she knew that. Three wells of magic were too far away for her to reach. But there was more magic present, needing to be added, woven in to the whole.

Kallista closed her eyes to see it better, gather it in, find its source. It was elusive, dancing close only to slide away again, but Kallista recognized it. It was meant for her. She needed it, and the magic needed to belong. But where did it come from?

"*Viyelle*," Gweric whispered, voice soft and awestruck. "I can see her."

But Viyelle had no magic of her own. Unless she had been…

"Torchay, take Viyelle's hand."

"I want my sword in my hand."

"We're the only ones left. Only demons against us. You think your sword will stop the demons? Take her hand. *Now*." Kallista wasn't sure what would happen, wasn't sure she was right, but if she was…they needed that magic.

Grumbling, Torchay sheathed his second sword and caught Viyelle's hand in his. Magic rushed through him into Kallista and beyond, into Joh and Obed. Kallista sensed a faint twisting, uncomfortable, but nowhere near as jarring as when Joh or Obed had been bound. Viyelle was marked. She was one of them.

The magic whirled out, touched the distant trio briefly, faintly, then returned. Kallista caught it, gathering it for a task rather than turning it to pleasure. She considered trying the dark veil again, but feared wasting this new-marked, new-joined magic against the barrier. She only had a taste of magic from Stone, Fox and Aisse, but already she could feel the eagerness, the obedience, the loyalty in the magic. And something else. Something new.

The boat was protected by magic, but it rode the winds. The boat could not be protected from the thing it needed to direct it, to buoy it up. And what could protect something so vast as the wind? But could Kallista direct winds with her magic?

She could only try. She hadn't been able to heal or speak mind-to-mind either, until she tried and found she could.

Weaving in Viyelle's just-marked magic, Kallista looked at the sky and struggled to see the winds. After a moment, though she couldn't quite *see* anything, she sensed the currents, rather like currents in the rivers that ran through her childhood home, but with their own patterns. They churned, disturbed by the magic binding them to hold up the flying boat. If she could tug a bit just there...

Kallista *reached*, tugged. The boat shuddered and bucked against its cushion of air. She shoved *there* and the boat tipped, the yellow-clad naitan tumbling over the side. He screamed, catching hold of the gunwale to dangle in midair.

There were two in the boat, the fire-throwing naitan and a woman holding the lines and halyards to the sail. The demon sat on her shoulders. Had it skipped from one to the other? The thing was hard to watch.

The woman stretched a hand toward the man. He reached for it, straining to climb back into the slowly righting boat.

Kallista snipped one of the air bindings. Wind picked up, blowing the boat to the south. "Follow. Don't let go."

It wasn't easy to walk with Joh wrapped around her back. Torchay twined his arm with Viyelle's and drew her in until he held her the way Joh held Kallista. Somehow, though, they didn't stumble, didn't tangle their feet.

The firethrower was almost back in the boat, one leg hooked over the side to climb in. Kallista didn't want that. She wanted someone to question. *There.* Another binding. Broken free, the winds drove the boat lower, skimming it just above rooftops. She yanked at a current, brushing the man against a temple dome, and he lost all he had gained, dangling once more.

"We're nearing the city wall," Torchay said. "If that matters."

"I don't want them to escape." If she destroyed the demon's mounts, would she destroy the demon? Or would it simply skip to a new victim and possess another? If she destroyed the boat, would she destroy the protections?

Kallista grasped hold of the winds and yanked, shaking the boat. The firethrower lost his grip, plunging to the street not far from the city wall. The boat surged higher with the loss of its burden.

"Gweric, go!" Kallista ordered. "Don't let them kill him. The Reinine wants him alive for questioning. *Run*."

The boy darted ahead and Kallista turned her attention back to the flying boat and its evil passenger. She ripped away magic almost as fast as the windcaller laid it. Almost.

The boat lurched and faltered, twirled in one direction and another, but always, it kept moving toward the city walls, rising higher and higher until it scraped over the parapet. Soldiers atop the wall jumped at the boat, tried to catch it, stop it. The demon screamed, rushed at them, and they fell back, save for one who caught a trailing rope. The boat dragged him over the wall, but he hung on.

He fought his way up the rope, Kallista doing her best to hold the boat steady now. Obed dragged her, Joh carried her up the stairs to the top of the wall where she could see, Torchay hauling Viyelle behind them.

When she reached the top, Kallista saw the soldier climbing over the side into the boat. Tying magic to his ankle, she managed to get it through the barrier with the courageous man. She rolled the magic up over him, hoping it would shield him from the demon he couldn't see.

The boat tipped and wallowed as the windcaller drew her weapon and fought for her life. Even with the demon's help, Kallista knew the woman wouldn't last long. When she went down, the boat would, too. Kallista hadn't the skills to keep it afloat. And there were rebels in the valley below.

Kallista had her major's golds on her uniform now, along with the blue-striped silver of the Reinine's personal command. She pulled part of her attention from the magic and called to one of the soldiers. "Captain!"

The patrol commander atop the wall dashed forward and saluted, trying very hard not to look directly at Kallista. They had to look strange, she realized, holding each other as they were, moving as a group. The strangeness couldn't be helped.

"Send out a sortie," she ordered. "Any man brave enough to do what that one has doesn't deserve to wind up in the hands of the rebels. Pray the One he lives through the crash when the boat goes down. If he does, your men will bring him back."

"Yes, Major." The captain saluted, executed a perfect about-face and began shouting her orders.

Kallista turned all her attention back to the scene in the valley below. The boat shuddered. She bound a current back in and the shallow-keeled vessel hared off eastward, toward the road. A good thing or bad? She hauled on the magic, trying to slow it so the Reinine's soldiers could reach it first. The winds kicked. The boat jumped.

Then it plummeted downward. The soldier had killed the windcaller. Kallista fought to control the boat's descent, threw protection around the soldier to keep the demon off him, keep the crash from killing him. Adaran cavalry rode yelling out the city gate, not merely a single troop, but an entire regiment thundering down the road.

The boat slammed into the ground, breaking apart. The soldier still lived—she knew because her magic had an anchor. The demon shrieked. The sound drove spikes through her ears into her brain and blurred her vision with tears as she screamed. Kallista tightened her hold on the soldier, not willing to give him up. She sent magic lashing out at the demon, wanting only to silence it.

The distant sound of steel clashing on steel had her blinking her eyes clear. The cavalry surged around the boat, sweeping over the swarming rebels and driving them away. The demon's black smear rode atop one of those fleeing the valley.

Kallista gathered magic one more time, shaped the veil, named it, threw it hurriedly after the evil, but it dissipated into a glittering emptiness before it passed the broken boat. She needed *all* her magic to fight demons, and half of it was hundreds of leagues away.

The cavalry rode in pursuit of the routed rebels, leaving bodies scattered across the valley floor, but the battle was over. A few soldiers brought their brave and battered comrade back to the city.

Behind her, residents and soldiers fought fires with water buckets and whatever magic could help. Kallista studied the air currents again, half-afraid to act. If she did the wrong thing, she could make matters worse, or cause problems elsewhere in Adara. But if she tugged just a bit *there*...

She *reached* and found magic there already. Another wind-caller? No, more than that. Weather naitan, teacher at the North Academy. She recognized the touch. Kallista watched for a moment, until she understood what was being done. Then she carefully lent the strength of her magic, pushing and pulling at the air under the other naitan's direction.

Clouds built higher. Lightning flashed—Kallista caught it and directed it over the wall, down the cliffs into the rocks. She held the clouds, pulled more moisture from the warmer plains until the first fat drops of rain began to fall. The instructor released the winds and Kallista let the strands of magic slide between her fingers and back home.

She sagged against Joh and turned her face up into the rain, closing her eyes against the beat of the falling drops. The cool, clean wetness washed away the smoke and dust, and seemed to take the lingering taint of demon with it. Saints and all the sinners, she was tired.

"What—" Viyelle stepped away from Torchay and wiped the streaming water from her face. "What *was* that?"

Kallista opened one eye and looked at her. "What was which? The demon? Or the boat? Or—?"

"All of it." Viyelle shoved Torchay farther away. She looked as if she'd like to skewer him. "Who do you think you are, hauling me around like I was some—some sack of goods? I'm capable of walking, you know."

The wicked look in Torchay's eye did not bode well, but Kallista couldn't stop him before he made an elegant leg and swept into a deep bow. "Who am I? Only your ilias, dear Prinsipella."

## CHAPTER FOURTEEN

"What?" Viyelle's shout had heads turning all the way to the towers. "You're mad!"

"Torchay, stop it. Viyelle—" Kallista got no further before the younger woman turned and ran. "Viyelle, don't. Stop!"

She didn't reach the top of the stairs before she staggered and fell in a twitching convulsion. Kallista was already moving, but couldn't keep up with Viyelle's mad dash, tired as she was.

As she passed Torchay, she smacked him on the back of the head. "You're supposed to be the sensible one," she scolded. "Quit poking her sore spots."

"Sorry," he muttered, staying at her side. "Just wondering when the One plans to stop enlarging our ilian."

Kallista sighed. "When we have enough, I suppose. However many that is."

Viyelle was groaning to a seated position when they reached her. "What in seven bloody hells did you do to me?" She glared up at Kallista.

"Nothing that hasn't already been done to the rest of us at one time or another." Joh reached down to clasp her forearm and pull her to her feet.

Viyelle couldn't stifle more groans. She ached all over. As if every muscle in her entire body had been wrenched out of shape. Her mind felt worse.

Nothing made sense. The past half-hour—hour?—of memory whirled in a blinding cacophony of terror, flames, pity, smoke, confusion, noise and wild, ecstatic joy. She hurt, and she had never felt better in her life. She felt lost and directionless, and yet she knew exactly where she belonged and what her life's purpose was.

Viyelle looked at the major naitan waiting patiently for her to find her footing. Except the ground had shifted beneath Viyelle's feet and she didn't think it would ever be steady again.

"I have no magic," she said.

"No," the major agreed. "You are no naitan. You have no magic to use." She hunched her shoulders against the downpour. "Do you think we could get in out of the rain to discuss it?"

Viyelle balked. It was instinctive. Any time someone in authority made a suggestion, she automatically did the opposite. She was trying to grow out of it—becoming a courier had helped—but old habits lingered like old fish.

The rain had soaked through to her skin and was starting to get cold. The major's suggestion made good sense. Viyelle was trying to learn to be sensible as well. She nodded once, all she could manage, and gestured for the major to lead the way. Her red-haired bodyguard did.

At the foot of the stairs, they ducked into a tavern across the way that catered to the military trade. Viyelle didn't quite feel comfortable in the surroundings, but the others obviously did. She stifled the urge to be contrary and didn't insist they find somewhere else. Sensible. Mature. The "new" Viyelle.

They settled at a table near the hearth for the fire's warmth and the two in blacks went for something to help them warm from the inside. Major Varyl let Viyelle have the side nearest the fire, sitting facing her.

Viyelle wasn't sure she liked that. It felt too much like "discussions" she'd had with her various parents. Especially when the others took their seats. Only Joh—Joh Ailo, she corrected, giving him the polite honorific—sat on her side of the table, and even that felt threatening. Six parents could bring a lot of pressure to bear. Thank the One, only four pairs of eyes stared at her now.

"Do you understand what has happened today?" The major slid the mug of hot spiced rum punch across the battered table to her.

Viyelle wrapped her hands around the mug, savoring its warmth, and shrugged. She took a sip of the punch, then another, impressed. It was as good as any she'd had in the palace.

The major sighed. Viyelle knew sighs. She'd heard a lot of them in her time. She'd sighed not a few of her own.

"Courier," the major tried again. "Viyelle, you were marked by the One this afternoon. Godmarked, like the rest of us. Like the rest of *them,* at any rate."

Viyelle laughed, which snorted punch up her nose where it burned, choked her, made her cough. Joh Ailo pounded her back, making her cough more. When she could breathe, she laughed again, but it faded quickly. No one else was laughing.

"You're joking," she said, beginning to worry.

The major shook her head. "I'm afraid not. I used magic placed in you by the One to drive off that demon-spawned boat. You're one of us, marked and bound."

"I can't be. I'm not religious. I'm not— I'm—" Viyelle fell silent, cowed by the weight of all the solemn looks focused on her. "Am I?"

She touched the back of her neck, feeling for a mark like the others wore. She'd seen glimpses of the marks beneath queues over the last two weeks she'd been quartered in their suite. Viyelle startled when Joh Ailo touched her hand, moved it higher on her neck, nearer her hairline.

"Here," he said, voice gentle.

"I heard you," the dark one said. "In the streets. You called on the God to save them. You offered yourself."

"And the One took what you offered," Joh finished. "That's how it happens." He patted her shoulder and returned to his drink.

"Oh sweet holy Goddess." Viyelle could feel it, the raised, round mark. She remembered doing exactly what they said. "But I didn't think She would take me up on it. I'm no— I'm not—"

Obed Ailo smiled, so gently it made her stomach hurt. "You can be no greater sinner than I, who has committed a thousand thousands of dark deeds with these hands. But even my offer was accepted."

She slumped against the back of the chair, stunned. One at a time, she looked at them, hunted for truth in their eyes.

The sergeant nodded, his red, red hair loose and curling in Peaceday's relaxation, blue eyes quiet above his narrow, hooked nose. The Southroner continued to smile, eyes dark as night above the strange blue tattoos on his cheeks. The one-time lieutenant, one-time convict met her gaze a moment before his lips twisted into a crooked smile and he flipped his long braid back over his shoulder. They all believed it. Finally, Viyelle looked at the major's solemn face.

Ever since last year, Viyelle had wondered. What did this ordinary naitan—relegated to a military career by the violence of her magic—have that made her so special? She was handsome enough with her sable-brown hair, fair skin and lightning blue eyes, but the palace was filled with women far more handsome. She seemed intelligent enough, but Viyelle knew scholars more brilliant, and naitani with greater magic. What made *this* one different?

Now, she knew. Because Viyelle apparently possessed the same quality. It had nothing to do with beauty or talent or intelligence or even knowledge. It was simply that she was *willing*.

At the time Viyelle had made her outrageous offer however, she hadn't considered any of the consequences. She had been too focused on stopping the attacks.

She cleared her throat. "So. Does this mean we're getting married?"

The major looked stunned for a moment, then laughter transformed her face. They all smiled, and Viyelle's heart pounded faster. *These* would be her mates? And the Tibrans. She hadn't considered those benefits either, and it made her just a tiny bit dizzy.

"We already are married, in every sense but one," Major Varyl said. "But that one…could get complicated."

"Which sense is tha—? Oh." Viyelle took a big sip of her punch. It needed more rum in it. Lots more rum. "The technical, legal, documented sense."

"Exactly." The major leaned back in her chair, obviously thinking hard. "You are after all a prinsipella, whether or not you're in line to be prinsep, and we're…not. Obed's trading business is doing quite well, but that belongs to him, so—"

"*No.*" Obed interrupted through clenched teeth. "I have told you. Everything that was mine is now yours. It is *ours*. Belonging to all of us. Why do you never listen to me?"

"Why do you never talk sense?" Kallista retorted.

It sounded to Viyelle like an old argument. One she'd never heard because she'd been an outsider. It made her change in status sink in deeper, and she didn't know if she liked the feeling.

"Maybe if you made sense, I'd listen," Kallista went on. "I don't know how things are done where you come from, but in Adara, a person doesn't disappear when they marry. You are still yourself and whatever you owned before you joined an ilian is still yours afterward."

Obed's face showed no expression, but his mysterious dark eyes glittered with some suppressed emotion. Silence stretched.

Kallista ended it. "It belongs to Obed." She turned back to Viyelle. "Still, maybe the wealth will influence your parents. We can—"

The boom of Obed's fist hitting the table stopped conversation and sent punch sloshing over the rims of those cups that held more than Viyelle's. "You do not understand."

The intensity of his voice could have sustained a shout loud enough to be heard halfway down the valley, but he spoke only for the five of them.

"*I do not want it.* All of those *things,* all of that wealth—it is…tainted. Stained with my sins. If I give it to you, to all those Chosen by the One, then perhaps that will begin to atone for…" He trailed off, eyes lowering to the table as if he could not meet any gaze. "For the things I have done."

Kallista slid her hand over Obed's still-clenched fist as she exchanged quick glances with the other two men. "You're right," she said. "We didn't understand how you felt about it. I'm still not sure I do. You said— Does this have to do with— You were one of the holy sinners?"

"Yes." Obed turned his hand and closed it around Kallista's. "Forgive me. This is not my time." He looked up at Viyelle, the black heat of his eyes arrowing through her. "If the wealth I have accumulated will smooth your parents' way to accepting this union, it is yours to use."

Viyelle cleared her throat, feeling extremely uncomfortable. As if she'd just been given a glimpse of someone's unprotected soul—a glimpse she didn't particularly want. Intensity of emotion was something she craved. She felt things deeply. It made her feel more alive, more truly herself. But when other people seemed to feel emotions just as intensely as she did, it made her feel strange. As if she wasn't so unique after all.

"*Will* it help?" Kallista's question called Viyelle back from this discomfort and into another variety of it.

"Possibly. Probably. Maybe?" Viyelle rubbed her forehead, frowning at her mug. She looked at the bottom for a leak. She didn't remember emptying it. She stole Joh's mug and swallowed down a good bit.

"Truthfully, I don't know. I've spent the last several years avoiding any and all discussion of marriage. Without my own magic, I won't inherit and no one's come nosing about with any dynastic offers. I'm not about to set up housekeeping with any of my sedili, no matter what our parents seem to think. All my mothers are sedili—my birth mother and the prinsep are blood sisters. And they fight constantly with each other when they're not scolding me. I won't live that way."

She took another deep draft of Joh's punch. "And now, I won't have to."

Viyelle toasted the others with Joh's ex-mug only to have it stolen at the height of her toast by Torchay who winkled it magically out of her grip. He set it too far away for her to retrieve, unless she crawled over the table.

"What have you eaten today, prinsipella?" He reached across the table and lifted her eyelids to peer at her eyes. "You're well on your way to flying without wings."

"Nope. Not me. The boat flew. It had *things* in it. But I don't have things." She leaned an elbow on the table to speak in a conspiratorial whisper. "I have *magic* in me."

Kallista chuckled. "So you do, ilias. And it's good for keeping out demons."

"Is that what those things were?" Viyelle shuddered in a sudden chill. Her clothes were too damp, that was all.

"Yes. Unfortunately." Kallista stood. "Come. Let's take our

new ilias home and get some warm food inside her and dry clothes outside her. Then we can send word to the Reinine. I have a feeling we will need her on our side when it comes time to explain certain things to certain people."

Viyelle was shivering, steady and uncontrollable. Joh put an arm around her, making her colder at first with the press of wet clothes against her skin, then warming her with the heat of his body. "We should hurry. She's too cold."

They were almost to the tavern door when it opened and Gweric put his head in. "Here you are. The guards want to know what the Reinine wants to do with the rebel prisoner."

"Saints, I forgot." Kallista looked guilt-stricken for a moment before she summoned her military face. "Tell them to deliver the prisoner to General Uskenda. The Reinine will instruct the general as to her wishes."

"Yes, Major." Gweric nodded.

"We'll wait for you. I don't want you running around this city alone either."

The boy grinned. "No, Major." Then his face turned to Viyelle and his grin faded. Whatever he saw made him unhappy. He slammed out the door, nearly slamming Torchay's nose in it.

Oh, damn. Damn, damn, bloody damn. Now that Viyelle was ilias, her liaison with Gweric was over. Iliasti did not look for sex outside the ilian. Viyelle must have repeated some of her swearing out loud, because Kallista turned and raised a questioning eyebrow.

"Gweric knows what happened." Viyelle had known before she did it that seducing him could be complicated, not just because of his hidden scars that ran so deep.

He wasn't Adaran. Who knew what his expectations might be? Tibrans didn't join together into families. Or they hadn't, before the war. A Tibran male could demand sex from any woman he encountered and any child that resulted belonged to the caste she served.

That may have changed. Viyelle had heard rumors that the caste system in Tibre had collapsed with the death of all the Rulers. But Gweric had left Tibre before that happened. So why was he slamming doors?

Outside, the rain had slowed to a heavy drizzle. Viyelle hoped it meant the fires started by that rebel naitan had all gone out. If not, at least the rain would keep them from spreading.

"What, exactly, was your involvement with Gweric?" Kallista was asking.

Viyelle sighed. She had to pay attention, even if she didn't want to. "Sex, mostly. He's seventeen, he thinks. He might be sixteen, but probably not eighteen. You know what they're like at that age. Sex mad."

"Is that all?"

"I took him to the scent gardens in the perfumer's quarter, and to a few concerts—things I thought he could enjoy without sight. Did you know Munday Kayiss is magically talented? That's why he makes people weep with the sound of his viol. He plays with bow and with magic. Gweric said it was like watching light dance."

Kallista cast her a sharp look. "Should I ask if *your* heart is involved?"

"Of course not." Was it? Viyelle probed that tender organ. "He's a sweet boy. Very…enthusiastic. But he's seventeen. An easily distracted age."

"And you're what—twenty-eight?"

"Twenty-seven."

"Old enough to know better. Did it occur to you that he might find 'distractions' difficult to come by? Besides his scars, he's a naitan. A *West* naitan. That tends to…disturb people."

"I—no." Guilt washed over Viyelle, an unfamiliar and decidedly unwelcome feeling. She didn't like it at all, but these people—her new ilian—seemed to think her comfort was immaterial. She wanted more rum punch. "He'll be fine. He's a handsome boy. He'll fall in love with someone else next week."

Kallista gave her a disgusted look and walked on, collecting Gweric as they passed the guard patrol. Viyelle tried to approach him as they walked back to the palace, but he always saw her coming, always sidled away.

If he wouldn't even talk to her, how would she ever get rid of the nasty uncomfortable feeling? *Was* she in love with him? Was that why she felt so bad?

And they hadn't even broken the news to her parents yet. Viyelle dragged her feet. Things would only get worse.

The travois where Fox lay jarred into and out of yet another hole on the endless Adaran plain. He let his head wobble from side to side, pretending sleep. He was healed enough that he could ride a horse and riding would doubtless be a dozen times more comfortable than being jolted across the countryside like this. But Fox thought it better that these outlaws rebelling against Kallista's queen believed him more injured than he was.

If Kallista had not been sending magic to heal him, he *would* be more injured than he was. Or he would be dead.

That had not happened and would not, now. So until he knew more, knew where the rebels were taking him and what their purpose was, he would play invalid.

Pretending unconsciousness most of the day left Fox with time on his hands, more time than he needed or wanted. Some of it he spent testing his *knowing* sense, counting the rebels in the band, learning to identify them, keeping track of their shifting places in the group. Some of it he spent actually unconscious, dozing on his pallet-on-poles until it dropped him into another hole and jerked him awake again.

Most of the time, however, was spent remembering things. Like the sight of Kallista's face in his dream. Of the certain sense that yesterday afternoon their ilian had magically joined into a whole again.

It was faint, nothing like that powerful blast of magic that had dumped him on his backside in the snow weeks ago. But he had no doubt it had happened again. Despite the distance, Kallista had somehow called magic from him and bound it with the others to do…what?

What need could have been so urgent that she was driven to call magic over such a distance? She had warned him in her dream that her magic was needed in Arikon, but for what? Had he been able to give her what she needed? Had she done what she needed to do? Were they still safe and well in Arikon, or had the thing that drove her to such desperate measures won out?

Fox wished he knew.

He had to find out. Had to get free, which meant he had to regain his strength. He had rested enough. He needed to work his injuries, rebuild fading muscles. If the rebels did not reach their destination soon and clap him in a cell where he could exercise in secret, he would have to give up his pretending and begin his recovery under their eyes. He would give them another few days.

*I'm coming.* He gathered the thought up and threw it toward Kallista, at that shimmer inside where she touched him. *Maybe not today or tomorrow, but I am coming home.*

Kallista managed to put off the appointment with Sanda Torvyll, prinsipas of Shaluine, until Secondday, much to her relief.

She freely admitted her cowardice, to herself if to no one else.

If the woman's own daughter was wary, who was Kallista to ignore the warning? The extra time was granted primarily because of endless meetings all Firstday with the Reinine's advisors and generals about the terrifying attack. Meetings which Kallista, and perforce her ilian, were required to attend though not welcomed to speak, once she told what she knew.

The traitors who had set the gunpowder bombs in the palace and the city had not been identified, much less caught, nor was it known how the gunpowder had made its way into rebel hands. The yellow-clad fireball-throwing naitan had survived his fall with no more than broken limbs—both legs and an arm—but they had learned little from him that made sense.

The man told garbled tales of recently awakening magic, though he was approaching middle age. He talked of power surges and flame outs, magic that came and went without warning. He raved about slaying death. His interrogators more than half believed the man was mad, without discernment between reality and myth. Except he had never set foot past the gates of the South Academy. No magic had awakened in him before his military service, as almost always happened. And he seemed to have none now, no matter how hard he tried to summon fire or how loudly he screamed.

The North Academy instructors had recognized the body of the windcaller who had been directing the boat. The woman had had a very minor talent for stirring the air, no more than a cooling breeze. Certainly nowhere near the magic required to fly a boat.

Kallista passed a note to the Reinine, bodyguard to bodyguard for privacy, suggesting that the power might have come from the demons she'd seen in the boat. But Serysta Reinine did no more than read it, nod and tuck it away. What else could she do? Kallista was the only one equipped to deal with demons, and without her other iliasti, she was hobbled.

Kallista did take a moment when the last meeting ended to obtain a letter from the Reinine to the prinsep of Shaluine. What little was left of Firstday she had to use in an attempt to sort out the tangle her ilian had snarled itself in.

Viyelle had plunged right into her new life, all her qualms and reservations over her marking apparently wiped away by the notion of being ilias to their ilian. She snuggled into the big bed along with the rest of them on the first night, making a place for herself between Obed and Joh. When Obed got Torchay to trade places, moving to Kallista's far side from her, Viyelle didn't seem to notice. Or perhaps she simply didn't care which two men she slept between.

She did attempt to talk with Gweric, which made Kallista happy, though Gweric refused to talk to Viyelle, which didn't. Kallista finally had to corner him in the big parlor after his ghost-tutor's departure.

"Sit." She pointed him back into the chair he'd just vacated in an escape attempt.

He sat. If he'd had eyes, Kallista was certain they'd be glaring daggers at her. She could feel them as it was. "What's going on with you and Viyelle?"

"Nothing. Obviously. Can I go?"

"No." Kallista sat in the chair beside him rather than the one across the table. How did she come to be playing the part of Second Mother to a seventeen-year-old? "Something's bothering you. It's best to spit it out. The doors won't take much more abuse."

Gweric slumped lower in his chair, kicking the table leg. He turned sulking into a work of art.

Kallista swallowed her sigh. Guesswork was not her best skill, but his refusal to speak left her few options. "Look, I know it probably feels like you'll never have sex again, now Viyelle's become ilias, but—"

"You think *that's* what I care about?" He started to burst from his chair like the words bursting from his mouth, then wrestled control from his impulses. His passion carried in his voice, quieter than before. Not much quieter, but some.

"The sex was great. Fantastic. But I've done without before. It's not important. But why *her*?" Gweric reached out to touch some unseen thing in midair. "Why her and not *me*? The way the magic dances between all of you—it's so beautiful. It's so—"

He drew his hand back and fisted it in his lap with his other. If he could have, Kallista thought he would have wept with unhappiness. "Why can't I be part of it?" he whispered.

She took a deep breath and let it carefully out. This would be tougher to resolve than a mere lost lover. "It's not that simple, Gweric. The One doesn't mark us because we wish it. It's not a thing of pride, but surrender. Viyelle—and all of us—"

How to word this so it came out right? So it wouldn't condemn or make him feel as if he'd failed some test? "We offered ourselves to the One, to be used as She saw fit. And this was how She chose to use us."

"I did that. I swear I did. Just like Viyelle. Why didn't the One choose me?"

"Oh, Gweric, I don't know." Kallista reached across the gap between them and pulled him into a clumsy hug. "Who knows the mind of God? I certainly don't. Maybe it's because you're a naitan yourself. Or maybe it's because you're so young. It could be that it's just not your time yet."

She released him with a kiss to his forehead. "Obed told me that he dedicated himself to the One years and years ago, but he wasn't marked until last year. At the same time Fox and Stone and I were, we think, though he was hundreds of leagues away. Maybe there's something similar in your future.

"Though honestly—" She shook him gently by the shoulder. "I don't know why you would want such a thing. The One's demands of Her godmarked are...terrifying. And I think it might be rather nice to choose one's iliasti for oneself, rather than have them pop up from nowhere."

She probably shouldn't have said that. It made it sound as if she didn't want her mates, which wasn't true. She valued each one of them, loved most of them and probably would come to love the rest once she knew them better. Still, acquiring iliasti in such a *surprising* manner did tend to be a trifle...awkward. It was awkward trying to explain it to herself.

"Are you sorry?" Gweric seemed to have finished his sulking, for now at least.

"No." It was true, Kallista realized. She wouldn't wish any of it away. "I honestly don't think I've been happier—well, except for those moments of stark terror fighting demons, and except for not having my babies and our Tibrans with us now. If everyone was here—and the demons weren't—everything would be...well, not perfect. You don't get perfection this side of heaven. But as good as it gets. Better than I ever dreamed was possible. More than I ever thought I would have."

She clapped him on the shoulder and stood. "And I didn't get any of it until I was thirty-four. Be patient. You have lots of time." She started to depart, then turned back, just to be sure. "Make your peace with Viyelle, will you? And ease up on the doors and furniture. It doesn't belong to me."

Gweric blushed, grinned and bolted for the far end of the parlor where he grabbed the staff for the exercises Obed had set him. One problem solved.

"*Stop it.*" Across the parlor, near the sitting area, Obed threw Viyelle's hand from him and stalked away, into the big bedroom, leaving her staring gape-mouthed after him.

Kallista sighed. One problem solved, a thousand yet to go.

## CHAPTER FIFTEEN

Not sure how or where she needed to begin, Kallista headed for the sofas where the ilian had been gathered before her chat with Gweric, where Torchay, Joh and Viyelle lingered. Torchay caught her eye and waved her after Obed, indicating silently that he would handle this end of things. Thank the One.

Joh got Viyelle up to move them closer to the side room, within their magical boundary. Kallista didn't see where they landed. She was already in the room with Obed.

He stood in the center of the small open area with his back to the door, naked from the waist up, his tunic wadded in his hands. "I have failed you and forsworn my vows," he said in a voice choked with emotion.

Kallista's heart sank. Were they back to this again?

But he stopped there. His hands tightened on the tunic they held and his head fell back, eyes squeezed shut. With a half-stifled cry, he threw the tunic across the room. "Why does it have to be so hard?"

Her heart started beating again. She moved behind him and slid her arms around his waist, laying her cheek on the flat plane of his shoulder blade. He hadn't shut himself off from her.

Obed pulled her arms closer around himself, held them in

place. "I have tried," he said. "You know how hard I have tried, and I have been getting better. Haven't I? It is easier, now I know I have my own place in your heart."

Kallista smiled against the warm silk of his sun-browned skin. "Not in my bed?" She felt the rumble of his quiet chuckle.

"Yes, in your bed, too." His voice dropped softer than a whisper. "In your body."

Kallista shuddered, his words sliding into her through their link, borne by the weight of his passion. "Then—?" She had to force herself to speak.

Obed took a deep breath, but didn't let it go again. Finally, he let it trickle out between his teeth as he spoke. "I find that while I may be willing to share you, I am not so willing to share myself. I do not want anyone but you, and it…offends? It *disturbs* me to be touched in such a manner by another."

He looked over his shoulder at her, wry apology in his expression. "And while I know that I may choose to say no, I am reasonably certain that *that* was not the proper way to do it."

Kallista pressed a kiss to his bare shoulder and laid her cheek against it again. "Do they have iliani where you come from? Is that why this is so hard for you?"

"Of course that is the reason. You know that."

She wanted to smack him, but settled for turning him around to look him in the eye. "How could I know? You don't tell me anything. You don't talk, Obed. The first I knew that you were a virgin was after you weren't one anymore. I've lived with you for a year. I know you—who you truly are. I love you.

"But I don't know anything *about* you. Except that you were a dedicat champion and a holy sinner. But I don't know what those things are. Please, don't expect me to know. I don't. Tell me."

He kept his eyes cast down. Kallista bent her knees, lowering herself until she could catch his gaze. She held it, slowly straightening again. He followed, the exotic brown of his eyes never leaving hers. She sensed someone in the open doorway—Torchay by his link.

Obed didn't seem to notice, which was probably best. "In Daryath, where my home is, and in most of the lands south of the Mother Range—Mountains of the Wind, you call them—it is true that there are no iliani. One man marries one woman. He gives his children only to her, she bears only his."

Kallista smoothed her hand across his beard-stubbled cheek. "Poor Obed. It's been one shock after another, hasn't it? The twins must have been the biggest."

After the birth, the local prelate-clerk had been called in to read the girls' bloodlines for the official records. They'd all been a bit surprised to learn Kallista's babies had different fathers. It had happened the night their ilian had first been formed, when the magic and her own desires had driven Kallista to bed Stone and Torchay one after the other. Her contraceptive spell should have been working, but something—likely the magic—had negated it.

Rozite was fair like Stone, a tiny bundle of energy who already seemed determined not to miss anything happening around her. Lorynda was dark-haired and chubby, like Kallista's blood sisters had been, but she had Torchay's wide-set hooded eyes and seemed to have his patience. Kallista hoped it didn't mean she would also have his stubbornness. *Goddess*, she missed her babies.

Obed turned his face into her hand, kissed her palm, recalling her from her thoughts. "Once, perhaps," he said. "But I think I have had a greater."

"Mmm?" She wanted to stretch onto her toes, bring him down into a true kiss, but just now, letting him talk was more important.

"I thought it would be the same as before—the jealousy—but it's not. When you and Torchay go apart together, knowing why no longer disturbs me as it did. That was the greatest shock, I think. That I have learned to share."

"Have you now?" Torchay spoke, startling no one. Perhaps Obed had not been so distracted as she thought. Torchay sauntered over, set his hands on Kallista's hips and leaned in to kiss her cheek. "No more backlash?"

"I—" Obed frowned. "I cannot swear in complete certainty it will not happen again, but I do not believe so." He lowered his head as if to kiss her cheek where Torchay had, then turned and kissed her other.

Kallista didn't know whether she should squeeze from between the two of them and refuse to play this challenge of manhood they seemed to be caught in, or if she should stay and enjoy it, possibly turn it to her own purposes. She opted for distraction. "Viyelle?"

"Joh took her next door. Seems she's not feeling quite married without sex."

"She isn't quite married." Kallista leaned the top of her head against Torchay's shoulder to look up at him.

He shrugged, never taking his eyes from Obed's. "What the One binds together, and so on. The rest is technicality. *Have* you learned to share, ilias?"

Obed took a step back, spread his hands wide. "Take her. Enjoy her."

Torchay shook his head. "That's not sharing. That's giving up."

A rush of heat flooded her as Kallista understood Torchay's intent, hot enough, deep enough it made her sway and surged out through the links. Torchay's sudden catch of breath, the throb of his erection against her told her he felt it, as did the flare of Obed's nostrils, the tension on his expressionless face.

Kallista held her hand out to him. "Stay," she said. "Share."

Obed's hand rose toward hers, but still he hesitated.

"Can't you feel it?" Torchay leaned closer, stroked his cheek along Kallista's. "How much she wants this? Wants both of us? Don't you want to give her what she wants?"

*"Yes,"* Obed whispered. He shivered, then in one flash of motion, he locked together the pentivas cuffs he still wore. Kallista's heart began to thump faster, echoing through her whole body.

"I want to." He lifted his bound hands. "But I do not want to fail you. You promised—*you swore to me* that you would not let me fail. I beg you to keep that promise now."

Torchay, bless him, didn't say a word, didn't indicate in any way that he even heard what Obed said. It freed Kallista to take that necessary step and draw her Southron mate into a kiss.

A sweet touching of lips at first, Obed deepened the kiss, drank from her mouth with lips and tongue. Kallista fell headlong into passion—Obed's, Torchay's, her own—she didn't know which. All three, she realized.

She didn't call magic. Not now, not yet. She wanted this to be just them, pure mortal passion. And she wanted Obed's hands on her.

Fumbling only a little, she released the latch locking his cuffs together. Obed broke the kiss, his eyes a bit wild as he stared at her.

Kallista held both his hands in hers. "I promised," she said. "You know I won't let you fail. But I don't think we need this now, and I want—" She set his hands on her breasts. "Touch me."

Torchay was whipping Kallista's tunic over her head before Obed's surprise left him and he smiled. His hands covered her naked breasts, moving, sliding, adjusting, until her taut nipples popped into the gap between palm and thumb. He squeezed, gently. Kallista gasped. Obed's smile changed, filled with certain knowledge.

He shifted, kicking his trousers aside and when Torchay moved in close behind Kallista again, she understood that he and not some new magic had made all their clothes go away.

Kallista leaned back, turned her head and twisted her hand in a tangle of red curls to bring him in for a kiss. Torchay drove his tongue into her mouth at the same moment Obed licked a line of fire along her neck. Kallista's whole body went taut. Then as Obed's mouth closed over her nipple, she went limp. Only Torchay's arm around her held her upright.

His other hand caught her chin, adjusted her position, held her in place for his kiss. He kissed her as if that alone would give him all he wanted, as if nothing more was needed. It had Kallista opening her hand, cupping his head in a caress. But her other hand had other business.

It was tangled in hair just as silky, black as night rather than darkest red, subtle waves rather than wild curls. Obed kissed his way from one breast to the other, every kiss making her squirm.

"Call the magic," Torchay murmured in her ear.

"Why?" She struggled to identify the hurt, her body's needs fuzzing her mind. "Isn't this enough?" Wasn't *she* enough?

"Goddess, that's not—" He kissed her, hard, almost bruising, as if he was angry or upset. The kiss gentled suddenly, went sweet and tender. Obed pressed a kiss to her stomach, his hands cradling her hips. Kallista whimpered, wanting more. Everything.

"Of course this is enough." Torchay turned her suddenly, so she faced him. Obed brushed his lips across the beginning swell of her bottom. Torchay cupped her face in his hands, his eyes blazing with sincerity. "You're more than enough for any man. I only asked for the magic because— Just a little. Just enough to know what you're feeling, so we can know you like what we do."

Obed's hands slipped around her waist, into the gap between Kallista and Torchay, roving across her stomach. She shivered, set her hands over his and held them still. "Can't you tell without it?"

Leaving Obed's hands in place, Kallista slid hers across Torchay's shoulders and down his chest, needing to touch him.

"I can guess," he said. "I want to *know*. Please. Call magic, just enough that we can know."

Obed was rising to his feet, kissing his way up her spine.

"Is this what you want, Obed?" she asked.

"I want you." He brushed her hair from the nape of her neck and pressed a tingling kiss to her godmark. "In any way that pleases you."

Still holding her face between his hands, Torchay kissed her, long, sweet and lingering. "Call magic for us, Kallista. Call our magic."

Unable to resist his plea, both silent and spoken, Kallista *reached*. It required more magic to blend the senses than it did merely to arouse, but perhaps— Instead of pulling magic from the men, Kallista tried sending it the other way. She felt stretched thin, her senses so aware, the faintest whisper seemed a shout, the lightest touch an intimate stroking.

Torchay flicked his tongue over her nipple and she cried out. He gasped, then laughed with knowing delight. "Yes, exactly."

Obed kissed the sensitive spot behind her ear, his erection nestled in the cleft of her bottom. She arched her back, pushing her hips against him. Torchay directed Obed back onto the bed so he sat on the very edge. Kallista found herself lifted into the air and settled onto his lap. Another tick later, Obed was flat on his back, lodged deep inside her and Kallista was fighting for air.

Torchay stumbled, fell to his knees without any of his natural grace. "Saints." His naturally raspy voice sounded even rougher. He laughed. "Be careful what you ask for indeed."

"Sorry." Kallista started to draw the magic back.

"No, don't." He forced his way between their legs till he was close enough to wrap his arms around Kallista's waist and nuzzle her stomach. "Don't take it away. It's exactly what I wanted. I just didn't know—"

He licked his tongue over her nipple again, flat, wet and hot, then blew on it. The sudden chill drew her whole body tight. Obed groaned and thrust against her internal hold, which brought a moan leaking from Kallista's throat.

"Goddess, it feels so—" Torchay slid his lips along her skin, down her stomach, as if he barely had energy to talk and none to spare for making kisses. "So good. I don't know if I can bear it."

Obed's hands tightened on Kallista's hips, lifting her slightly as he pulled back, drawing himself out of her a little way. Then he lunged upward as he shoved her back down over him. Kallista's cry sounded deeper, wrong—until she realized it hadn't been her voice alone. Obed thrust into her once more and the shock of pleasure had her hands tightening in Torchay's hair as he lost his balance again. He would have collapsed to the floor save for her grip on his hair and his position braced between their legs.

"P'raps," he gasped, "you could dim the magic a trifle."

"If you cannot bear her pleasure," Obed growled, "perhaps you should leave her to those who can." His hips found a rhythm and he began to pound her with pleasure.

But she could still think—if barely—could still move her magic. It was uneven, because their magic was uneven. She shook her head, trying to concentrate on the bright flow of power between them as Obed tried to drive all concentration from her and Torchay shuddered in the grip of her building sensations.

He clung to her, face burrowed into the curve between her hip and thigh. Kallista's feet dangled outside Obed's legs, giving her little to brace herself against except her two men. She couldn't think, couldn't focus, but she could see the magic. Too much poured into Torchay where he knelt before her, too little into Obed where he lay beneath her.

She did the only thing she could think of with her mind so fogged. She leaned back. The physical action allowed her will to pull the magic back from Torchay. The power she diverted from him slid into Obed until it was balanced.

Obed cried out, his body shuddering beneath her. "You *promised.*"

Oh damn, she had. Kallista thrust a desperate fist into his magic and held on. "Then be still."

He obeyed. Torchay kissed the angle of her body where his face hid and slid a hand up her thigh until his fingers tangled in her triangle of black curls. He slipped one into the very top of her slick channel, found the spot that ached for attention and pressed down, gently, carefully at first, then firmer, harder until her climax swept out of nowhere.

It smashed into her, drove her hard onto Obed so that he joined her, spilling himself inside her. Kallista didn't notice that Torchay had regained his feet until Obed's hands fell away and Torchay rolled her from his body.

Kallista rolled again, scrambling higher on the bed, laughing. Until she saw Torchay's face, Torchay's eyes as he threw himself after her, sensed his half-crazed arousal through the link. She opened arms, legs, self, and he was on her, driving himself inside her as if deep enough meant he came out the other side.

She fed every sensation back into him until the wild rush of pleasure flooded her again. And again and again. Torchay shouted, a sound that was almost pain. It startled her into releasing a hold she didn't know she'd taken, and his magic rolled free. He shouted once more, a different sound. His body jerked and he poured into her, seed, self and magic.

Time passed before Kallista could hear again. She still

couldn't see, but she was fairly sure that was because her eyes were closed. Though she wasn't absolutely certain. Torchay had slid partially off her, as if he didn't want to weigh her down but could move no farther. One heavy leg still draped across both of hers and an arm sprawled across her stomach. He was swearing, quietly, creatively, incessantly. Obed wasn't moving at all.

She could feel him along her other side, his hair brushing against the side of her breast, his shoulder pressed into her waist, faceup, she thought. He was warm, which was a hopeful sign. Kallista reached to touch him, make sure he still lived, but her arm wouldn't work right.

It didn't want to move at all, and when she forced it, it jerked up and flopped onto Obed's shoulder. He didn't stir. Kallista worked her hand up over his face, covered his mouth and felt his breath slide out from his nose over her skin.

"Oh good," she mumbled. "You're both alive."

"Are you certain?" Obed's lips moved against her palm.

"Reasonably so, yes." She considered rolling over, considered moving her hand off Obed's mouth. Either seemed more work than she could manage, so she stayed where she was.

"Next time." Torchay seemed to speak with some effort. "Next time I ask you to call magic and you think it's a bad idea, don't pay me any mind, will you?"

"I didn't think it was a *bad* idea."

"But you didn't truly want to, did you?"

"No, not really."

"So next time, don't." His thumb drew circles on her stomach, the only motion—besides talking—he seemed able to accomplish.

"I didn't do it to punish you for asking." Kallista's alarm was vague and far away and too much effort would have been required to bring it closer.

"No, of course you didn't. I just didn't realize what I was asking." He took a deep breath, making his arm rise and fall across her middle.

"Perhaps it was the sharing." Obed turned his head, let it roll toward her so that now his lips brushed her side as he spoke. "Because there were three of us, the magic was stronger."

"Perhaps." Torchay paused. Kallista could almost hear him thinking and she checked the link for remaining driblets of magic, shooing them back where they belonged. Torchay shivered, brushed his lips over her temple. "Goddess, you were coming and coming and coming, and I was there, right on the edge, but I couldn't go over. I wanted to, *needed* to, but couldn't. Not till…I don't know…"

Kallista grimaced. She patted his arm. "That was my fault. Obed asked me to help him wait for me, and I didn't realize I had hold of your magic, too. Sorry."

"Actually…" Torchay was thinking again. She didn't need magic to know that much. "Actually, I think I rather liked it. I just—I didn't expect it, so I didn't know what was happening or why and—well, it is a bit alarming when your bits don't work the way you expect them to. The way they did before."

He snuggled in, using his leg over hers to pull her closer. "Maybe we should experiment. See what else the magic can do."

"I thought you said not to. That I should ignore you when you ask me to call magic."

"I did say that, didn't I?" He sighed.

Obed rolled his body into hers, his arm going across her hips just above Torchay's leg, his forehead resting against her side, almost cradled under her arm. "I think we should try it. I think we should know what the magic can do in every area."

Torchay sighed again, deeper. "You're probably right. If we live."

"Excuse me." Kallista poked a finger into Torchay's side, Obed's shoulder. "Don't I get a say in this decision?"

"Of course you do." Torchay poked her back. Not with a finger. "You're the only one who can actually call magic, if you'll remember. But I think Obed's right. We should know what the magic can do. What we do together as ilian could have more of an effect elsewhere besides just preventing backlash."

She gusted out a heavy sigh and stroked a hand down Obed's black waves. The other hand slid round Torchay's lean, muscled arm. "You're right, both of you."

"But." Torchay kissed her forehead and shoved himself up to sit. "I think perhaps we ought to hold off on any more 'sharing' for a while. Till we know how the magic behaves with just one of us at a time."

"Agreed." Obed sat up on her other side, his face as solemn as Torchay's.

Kallista looked from one to the other, dark head to bright, pale skin to brown, and couldn't keep from saying what she thought. "We'll have to study hard and learn quickly."

The men exchanged glances and broke out in simultaneous laughter, so male it made Kallista blush and gave her the energy to squirm out from between them.

Joh and Viyelle apparently got the rest of the tangle sorted, at least temporarily, for no more uncomfortable incidents unfolded the rest of that day or the next. It gave Kallista a sense of confidence as she strode through the palace corridors at Viyelle's side, the men ranged before and behind in bodyguard position on their way to meet their new ilias's parents.

Sanda Torvyll was still quartered in Winterhold. She'd been at court through the winter, and with all the citizenry pouring into Arikon and the Reinine's court, there hadn't been room for her to make the shift to Summerglen when the Reinine did. It made for a very long walk through the two enormous palaces.

The walk nibbled at Kallista's confidence. After all, this was a prinsipas they were off to visit. A prinsipas whose daughter they intended to marry. Had already married in every way but one. It wasn't as if she could prevent them taking Viyelle into their ilian. But family could make things very uncomfortable. Kallista had personal experience of that.

At least they looked good. She had allowed Obed to indulge his generous nature and gift them with clothing more fine than what many courtiers wore. She and Torchay were in dress uniform of course, but uniforms made of thick, nubbly raw silk, embroidered in lustrous silk thread with touches of gold. Her rank insignia were clipped on with gold pins shaped like lightning bolts and their queues were tied off with gold hair clips.

Joh's tunic was a shade brighter than Kallista's uniform, bringing out the intense blue of his eyes. The short sleeves and lower edge of the tunic were slashed in the current fashion, the slashes bound and ornamented with heavy silver embroidery, but the lining that showed through was black rather than some other fashionably bright color. He wore black trousers, so that he seemed almost uniformed as well, though the clip that fastened his long queue was silver.

Obed wore his hair loose over his silver-embroidered black Southron robe. Beneath it, he wore a plain blue tunic the same color as Joh's and black trousers. A tiny silver loop winked from his right earlobe. Kallista hadn't thought he would actually pierce his ear, but he had. She liked the way it looked.

Only Viyelle had no new finery to wear. She had clothing almost as fine but had elected not to wear it, explaining that she hoped the contrast would help reinforce the fact that the ilian had no need for money. Kallista hoped it would work.

They reached the corridor that passed the Shaluine suite and Kallista drew to a halt. "Are we ready?"

## CHAPTER SIXTEEN

Torchay adjusted the shoulders of Kallista's tunic so it sat more squarely. Joh flicked an invisible bit of lint from his slashing.

Viyelle fussed with the cords that held her half cape tied over one shoulder. "Are you sure we wouldn't rather just write a letter?" She tugged at the cords, feeling as if she was about to choke.

"Relax. It will be fine." Kallista smiled as Joh moved Viyelle's hands away from her cape ties.

"If you leave it alone, it won't choke you." He retied the cape, using her weapons harness to hold the cords in place, away from her neck.

"Let me do the talking, if you're too nervous," Kallista said.

"It's not that I'm nervous, exactly." Viyelle's hand drifted toward the cords and stopped when Joh cleared his throat. "I'm just afraid—no, I'm *certain* that it won't be very pleasant."

"We can handle unpleasantness." Kallista winked, a sly smile creeping out. "We've fought demons together, remember? What's a parent or two?"

When she put it that way… Viyelle considered, then turned to leave. "Let's go find another demon."

Kallista laughed and clapped Viyelle on the shoulder, turning her to face the other way. "Courage, ilias." She propelled her forward, walking with an arm draped over her shoulder. "I do understand. I think I'd rather fight demons than deal with my own birth parents. But between all of us, we ought to manage."

Viyelle wasn't so sure, but she let herself be maneuvered down the hallway in the midst of her new family. Obed knocked on the door. It opened, and a young woman in court clothes looked curiously out at them.

Viyelle's heart froze for a moment, then started beating at a rate that threatened to shake it loose from its moorings. "Oh, hell," she muttered.

Joh cleared his throat. He must have heard Viyelle's quiet curse. Torchay as well, for he stroked his hand down the back of her arm that was free of the cape. It did calm her, a bit.

Kallista made a leg and bowed, not too low. "Major Naitan Kallista Varyl to see Sanda Torvyll, Prinsipas of Shaluine. She is expecting us."

"Yes, of course."

The door opened wider and Kallista strode in. Viyelle tried to hang back, but Torchay's hand on her arm "encouraged" her through the door as he followed.

"Kendra." Viyelle was sure her smile looked as false as it felt when she turned to her sedil and embraced her. Or rather the air around her, as Kendra held herself that much apart. "I'm surprised to see you here. Did—"

"Really?" Kendra spoke in the cool, superior tone she'd adopted since her magic had risen when she'd been fifteen and Viyelle almost seventeen. It had risen late, and it wasn't powerful magic—she had a minor East talent for encouraging crops to maturity. But it was magic. Kendra had it. Viyelle had none at all. And Kendra never let her older sedil forget it.

"I was surprised *not* to see you when we arrived yesterday," Kendra said. "I was given to understand by Second Mother that you were quartered here, despite your…" Her eyes flicked contemptuously over Viyelle's courier's grays. "Duties."

She made it sound as if whatever duties Viyelle might have, they were unimportant, possibly immoral, and Viyelle wasn't carrying them out anyway. Kendra had always been able to do that, and it had always infuriated Viyelle. She managed to hold her temper this time.

"I've been quartered elsewhere the last two weeks, with my new assignment." Viyelle edged away from Kendra, nearer Kallista. She couldn't resist adding, "Orders of the Reinine, direct from her hand."

Mother came in then and Viyelle escaped her sister. From one torment to another, but she had her iliasti around her. She wasn't alone.

A knot in her gut loosened, one Viyelle hadn't realized had been tied until this moment. She didn't know yet just how awful this meeting would be—worse, with Kendra here. But also better, simply because she was not alone.

Then another side door opened and her insides tied themselves into six, a dozen new knots. Her second mother, Saminda Prinsep of Shaluine, and her father, Vanis Kevyr, Prinsipas, entered the cozy, overwarm sitting room.

"Oh bloody, bloody hells," Viyelle muttered.

"Courage, ilias." Torchay spoke even more quietly, but it did give her courage, as did Joh's slight nod. Obed's touch on her hand helped more. If the dark silent man could bring himself to touch her, maybe she really was one of them.

Kallista was already going into her court bow. With the entrance of the prinsep herself, she swept lower, the rest of the ilian following a moment behind. Viyelle bowed, too. She was ilias now, as well as daughter.

"Viyelle." Saminda held her arms out for an embrace. "We

had hoped your duties would not keep you from us. It is good to see you."

"It's good to see you, too, Mother Saminda." Viyelle hugged her tight. She did love her parents, even if they were too...parental. "Are things so bad in Shaluine that you had to leave?" She hugged her father, kissing his gray bearded cheek.

"No, no. But you know how your fathers worry. Your other three parents stayed behind to look after things, but they insisted we come here and bring the children."

Viyelle looked around, half-expecting to see her youngest sedili pop up from behind the furniture. But they were half-grown now, the youngest of them thirteen. Too "mature" for such childish antics.

Saminda laughed. "They're off to the temple for their schooling. Do you think we would keep them underfoot if we had somewhere to send them?"

Viyelle's birth mother broke into the family chitchat. "Major Varyl," Sanda said. "Your note requesting this meeting said that it involved a personal matter. I am not sure what matters of a personal nature *you* would have with *me*..."

Viyelle hid her wince at the not-so-subtle insult. She knew Kallista caught it—she was the straightforward sort herself, but she understood subtlety. Viyelle just hoped this was as bad as it would get. She stepped forward and introduced her parents to her iliasti.

Kallista inclined her head in a polite bow of acknowledgement, no more. "Prinsipas, Prinsep. Our ilian has come—" she seemed to sort through a large selection of phrasing, speaking slowly "—along with your daughter to inform you that she has agreed to join us as ilias."

"Impossible. Your request is denied." Sanda flicked her wrist, dismissing them, and turned as if to walk away.

"*Prinsipas.*" Kallista's voice rang with authority and Viyelle's mother stopped, looked back. Impressive, but then Viyelle had always been impressed by the major, even when she hadn't wanted to be.

"Prinsipas," Kallista said again. "You misunderstand. We are not requesting permission. We are informing you of what is already agreed. Of what *will* be."

"Don't be ridiculous. Viyelle is a prinsipella of Shaluine. You are all…nothing."

"Mother—" Viyelle's face flamed with humiliation.

Sanda flicked a hand to silence her, and to her disgrace, Viyelle complied. For a moment. "No, Mother. I am five years past twenty-two. You cannot forbid—"

Torchay touched Viyelle's hand, calming and stilling her as Kallista spoke. "We have the blessing of the Reinine. If need be, she will make it an order."

"Even the Reinine cannot order such a thing." Sanda's face changed color with her anger, alternating red and pale. "Viyelle is promised to Kendra's ilian."

"*No*, Mother."

Kendra smirked behind their parents, where they couldn't see her smug satisfaction at Viyelle's too obvious distress. Viyelle knew that Kendra would adore having her to torment.

"*No*," Viyelle said again. "I will never join Kendra's ilian. Ever. You cannot force me to it."

"*Di pentivas* oaths have lately come back into fashion." Sanda gave a significant look to the bands with their looped chains around Joh's ankles.

"Mother!" Shock raced through Viyelle, so deep and profound she would have fallen if Joh hadn't steadied her. He nodded at her faint smile of thanks.

"*Di pentivas* is for men," Kallista said. "And only for those taken in war or other specific situations. Not for our own daughters—or our sons—even if their choices displease us.

And the Reinine can indeed order it. You may not recall, but our ilian was formed last year on the Reinine's orders."

Saminda spoke for the first time since greeting Viyelle. "Why?"

Kallista pivoted a quarter turn on her heels to face the prinsep. "Because we have been marked by the One. Our ilian is godmarked, Saminda Prinsep. All of us. Including Viyelle. She is already bound to us by things greater than a temple ceremony. She literally cannot be separated from us."

"Preposterous." Sanda Prinsipas crossed her arms.

"Oh?" Viyelle had had enough. She shouldered her way past her mother, striding across the broad, windowless room toward Kendra. She felt the slight dizziness that warned her she was moving too far, and kept going, shoving through it, hurrying, rushing to reach her goal before they could stop her.

She heard one of the men, heard Kallista call her name, but it sounded faint and very far away, the last thing she knew before every muscle in her body wrenched itself apart. She screamed and lost herself in the pain.

"You little idiot." Joh held her in his arms, smiling his insults down at her.

Kallista stood above him, scowling. "That was foolish."

"Probably." Viyelle licked dry lips. Goddess, even her tongue hurt. "Did it work?"

She looked beyond Kallista, saw her parents' faces—her mother's scowl, her father's worry, Mother Saminda's frown. She patted Joh's arm and held her hand out to Obed for assistance in standing.

Viyelle faced her parents. "You cannot separate me from my ilian. You cannot choose my life for me. It is what it is."

"Naitan." Mother Saminda had clasped her hands together and was tapping her forefingers against her lips. "Your uniform indicates you are from Turysh prinsipality?"

Behind her back, Viyelle hooked her little fingers together

in a childish request for luck. One of her parents had moved from denial to asking questions. It was a beginning.

"Yes, Saminda Prinsep." Kallista moved to stand beside Viyelle. "My parents have been with Riverside Temple in the city of Turysh for many years now. My mother is a healer, specializing in accidental injuries. Torchay's family are Korbin prinsipality horse breeders, as are Joh's people in Filorne. Obed is a trader from south of the Mountains of the Wind. We also have three other iliasti who are escorting our daughters to safety."

"Saminda, you can't seriously be considering—" Mother Sanda broke in, but cut herself off when her sedil-ilias raised a hand.

"You realize," Mother Saminda said to Kallista, "that if our daughter insists on going against our wishes, she could well be cut off from *all* family funds."

Viyelle stiffened, understanding exactly what she meant. It wouldn't matter, except Grandmother Viyelle had settled that money on *her,* not on the family as a whole. It both hurt and infuriated her that Mother Saminda would threaten to take it away.

"We have more than enough to support our family," Kallista was saying. "Obed's business is a very profitable one. We do not—"

Viyelle interrupted before Kallista could give anything away. "But I haven't been supported by the family since I came of age, have I, Mother? I have my own funds. Mine and no one else's. And they will stay that way. I need nothing else."

Only the thinning of Mother Saminda's lips showed her reaction to being thwarted.

"What, exactly does this 'godmark' mean?" Father spoke to the group for the first time. "I have heard about it in old stories told by jongliers, but never thought it could be real."

Kallista's smile twisted. "Neither did we. The mark is literal. All of us are marked here." She touched the nape of her neck.

"But it could be anywhere. The last godstruck—Belandra of Arikon—and her iliasti were marked here." She indicated her upper right arm, where Torchay's rank was tattooed.

Viyelle wondered if his tattoo explained why the mark had moved to its new location. But then he had been the last of them marked before Joh, according to what they'd said.

"Belandra of Arikon is also more than merely a jonglier's song?" Father looked as if his curiosity might turn his favor.

"Yes." Kallista said nothing more, to Viyelle's relief. She didn't think her parents would soften if they knew Kallista spoke on occasion to a legend, a woman a thousand years dead. "The godmarked carry magic that I, as the godstruck naitan, can use."

Kendra's laugh was scathing. "Viyelle has no magic. She never has. She's never been anything but idle and useless."

"She has been a courier serving her Reinine with distinction." Kallista's voice cut cold and sharp, and warmed Viyelle through.

She *had* been idle and useless. Before. And restless and unhappy. Wanting without knowing what it was she wanted. Joining the courier service had helped. This was better. She had a place where she could be busy and useful, and perhaps even happy.

Kallista was still speaking. "I did not say Viyelle *had* magic, in the way that you mean. Magic she can use. I said she *carries* magic. She *is* magic. All of our iliasti are. She brings something to the whole that no one else can bring."

That sounded good. Viyelle couldn't help asking. "What?"

"She—" Kallista stopped in midspeech, her mouth open. She blinked a time or two and Viyelle wondered if she understood what had been asked.

"I mean—" Viyelle edged half a step closer "—what do I bring to the whole?"

"I knew that." Kallista smiled. "I just had to think how to

explain it. Originality will serve. Your magic brings a new way of looking at things. Different solutions to the problem.

"When we were fighting the demons in that flying boat, I tried everything I could think of, and couldn't get through the protective warding around the boat. When you were bound into the whole, I suddenly saw that I didn't have to attack the demons directly, or even the boat. I could disrupt the winds that carried the boat and we could defeat them that way."

Kallista's smile made Viyelle's stomach hurt, in a good way. It was pure approval. No backhanded criticism. No "you could have done better." Just approval.

"We could not have done it without you," Kallista said. "The whole city could well have gone up in flames."

"Wait." Mother Sanda broke through the warmth where Viyelle bathed. "Do you mean to tell me that *you* drove that— that abomination away? Do you expect us to believe it?"

"*We* did, yes. All of us together." Kallista shrugged. "Whether you believe it or not, that's your choice."

"I don't believe it," Kendra said. "Viyelle has no magic. She's a perfect null. Magic won't have anything to do with her."

"True once, perhaps," Kallista said. "But no longer."

"You were out? In the city?" Father's voice shuddered with horror. "During the fire attack? Are you mad? You could have been killed."

Viyelle reached past Joh to squeeze her father's hand. "I'm a courier, Father. It's not exactly a safe occupation, either. But at least now, if I'm killed, it serves a purpose. When I was running with the bravos, I could have been as easily killed in all that brawling and dueling. What purpose would that have served?"

"She's safer with us than anywhere else." Torchay spoke up for the first time, startling everyone. "Kallista can heal us better and faster than any East naitan I've known. I was spitted through with an arrow a pair of weeks ago, and I walked out of healer's hall before dinner that same day with no more than another pretty pink scar."

*"Viyelle has no magic,"* Kendra said for a third time. Viyelle was getting more than a bit tired of it.

So, apparently, was Kallista, for she rounded on the younger woman. "It is a pity your self-worth is more concerned with what your sedil *doesn't* have, rather than what you *do*. Can you see magic? See when someone else calls it? Uses it?"

"I can," Mother Saminda said. "My talent is with animals—training them to obedience—but I can see when magic is called."

"Then see." Kallista removed the glove from her left hand—her nondominant hand—and held it up, her eyes on Viyelle.

With a smile, Viyelle reached out to clasp it, but Kallista shook her head. "Give me your fingertips, ilias."

Not understanding exactly what was wanted, Viyelle let her hand hover in midair. Kallista laid her four fingertips gently against Viyelle's, holding her thumb back. "Because Viyelle was only marked on Peaceday last, the link between us has not yet fully formed. In three or four more weeks, we'll no longer have to touch to call magic, and she will be able to move farther away from me."

"Then why is marriage necessary?" Mother Sanda asked. No one paid her any attention.

Viyelle waited, not sure what would happen. Then something touched her. Inside, where no physical thing could reach. It strummed across her senses, drawing her taut with pleasure, and she gasped.

"Can you see it?" Kallista moved her fingers, opening a small gap between her and Viyelle. The tiny motion stroked Viyelle with pleasure again, so intense she had to bite back a moan.

"I see it." Mother Saminda nodded her head.

"What are you doing to Viyelle?" Father Vanis demanded.

"The magic feels good," Torchay said. "When she calls it. *Very* good."

"But that's—that's—" Mother Sanda sounded utterly scandalized.

"One of the reasons marriage is necessary." Kallista did something and the magic slid back the other way with as much of a delicious caress as it made when she called it out. Viyelle could almost feel it, as if it curled down inside her to sleep, like a cat in a cozy hideaway.

"We are already bound, Prinsipas." Kallista addressed herself to Viyelle's birth mother as she slid her glove back on. "The magic has bound us just as it bound the first ilian over two thousand years ago. Do you honestly think that Viyelle could live among us until our link is secure and then go back to the way she lived before? Join some other ilian?

"What other ilian would endure the fact that through the link I know where my godmarked are at all times, and often what they are feeling? Who would allow her to travel with us while we carry out our duties? And if they would allow it, why would she want to be part of an ilian that cared so little about her? Why would you force such a thing on her?

"*We* want her, Prinsipas. We value her." Kallista smiled, opened her hands to show herself harmless. "We care for her. But you should know this. I said that we did not come here seeking permission. We do not need you to allow this binding. It is done.

"We would like to have your blessing. Viyelle would value your approval. She is your daughter, after all. But if you cannot give it, so be it. It changes nothing.

"Viyelle belongs to the One, and the One has given her to us. She *is* ours." Kallista ended her impassioned speech—apparently unusual for her, for the men stared at her in something like amazement—and she looked from one to the other of Viyelle's parents.

Their expressions did not change. Father Vanis still looked worried. Mother Sanda still scowled. Mother Saminda appeared thoughtful. No one spoke.

"So be it, then." Kallista clasped Viyelle's hand still hovering forgotten in midair, and gestured for Obed to lead the way from the candlelit room.

"Wait." Mother Saminda's voice stopped their retreat. "You cannot blame us for our concern for our daughter, our eldest child."

Viyelle didn't think their concern was for her at all. Maybe Father's was. He did love her and want what was best for her, and he was insightful enough to know her joining an ilian with Kendra in it would be disastrous. But still, his ideas of "what was best" had little in common with her own.

Mother Sanda's concern was similar, except she was three times as stubborn and never could see what was before her eyes—that Kendra was a vindictive witch. Moreover, Mother *hated* to have her plans thwarted. Mother Saminda's concern was for the family as a whole first, and then for Shaluine. Sometimes in the opposite order. Viyelle and her sedili came in a poor third.

But Kallista didn't know that. She stopped. Waited.

"I have heard," Mother Saminda said, "that you dined privately with the Reinine not long ago."

"My ilian and I were privileged to join the Reinine and her ilian for dinner, yes." Kallista sounded cautious. Smart naitan. Clever major.

"With a daughter of Shaluine as ilias, I am sure you would be willing to speak a word into the Reinine's ear on Shaluine's behalf from time to time." Mother Saminda smiled around her forefingers pressed to her lips once more.

"Certainly, Prinsep." Kallista inclined her head. "Just as I would be happy to speak a word for Turysh and Korbin. And Filorne."

Viyelle caught the quick flash of anger in her second mother's eyes before she covered it. Filorne neighbored Shaluine to the north and east, and was a rival in many, many ways. Not least the personal rivalry between the two prinsipi.

"One of our iliasti is Southron and our absent three are sons and daughter of Tibre." Kallista smiled and raised a casual eyebrow. "Would you also have me speak for the South? For Tibre?"

"Viyelle, are you sure—" Father Vanis stopped when Kallista continued speaking, and because Viyelle ignored him. Though she did hear him say "Tibrans?" in a quiet, bewildered voice.

"I serve the Reinine, Saminda Prinsep," Kallista said. "And as she is ruler of *all* Adara, so do I serve all Adara. Shaluine is a part of that whole, but I am sure you know it is not the only part. I have family in Turysh, which is overrun by the rebels— and yet I am here, rather than there."

Mother Saminda shrugged, not at all repentant. "Do what you can, daughter."

Viyelle blinked, not sure Saminda meant her, or Kallista. Was this it? Had she given in?

"When will the temple ceremony be?" Mother Saminda asked, and Viyelle could scarcely rein in the urge to leap into the air and whoop with joy. She could not hold back her wide grin. *They had won.*

"'Minda!" Mother Sanda burst out.

"You heard her, Sanda. It's done. The Reinine has authorized it. We can only make the best of it." Saminda patted her sister's hand. "Besides, even you must admit that if you somehow forced Viyelle and Kendra into the same ilian—which I do not think you could do—but if you did, before the next Graceday passed, Kendra would have tormented Viyelle into committing murder. They do not bicker like we do, ilias. They draw blood with their quarreling."

Sanda scowled. "I still do not see why—"

"And that is why I am prinsep and you are prinsipas." Saminda smiled and hugged her sister to take the sting out of her words before turning back to Viyelle. "The ceremony?"

"I—that is—I don't—" Viyelle looked wildly at the others.

"We cannot hold the full, formal ceremony until we are all together again," Kallista said with another ingratiating miniature bow. "But a small bracelet ceremony in our quarters would certainly be appropriate. On—Graceday?" She looked her question at the others, who nodded.

"If your quarters are no larger than ours, they will not hold enough guests." Mother Saminda began to pace, making her usual grandiose plans. "Perhaps in the Fountain Courtyard. Or—the apple trees are coming into bloom, so—"

"*No,* Mother Saminda." Viyelle blocked her pacing path. "This will not be the full ceremony. Just an exchange of bracelets between the five of us to formalize things until Stone and Aisse and Fox are with us. I would like my family to be present, but I will not allow you to turn it into some political festival. If you try, we won't come. A small ceremony in our quarters. Your only option."

Her second mother let out a deep sigh. "That is all I have heard today. 'You have no say in the matter.' I would like to know just what I do still have a say in."

Viyelle shrugged, a smile teasing her lips. "Whether you wish to come."

"Of course I will come. We all will." Saminda pulled Viyelle into a hug.

"Speak for yourself," Mother Sanda muttered.

"Oh, give over, Sanda." Father Vanis came forward for a hug of his own. "You'll be there if I have to hobble you and drag you."

Viyelle thought that might be what it would take for both

Mother Sanda and Kendra to be present. Kendra's face, when Viyelle chanced to see her over Father's shoulder, was dark with envy, anger and a dozen other ugly things. Viyelle congratulated herself on her fortunate escape.

"On Graceday then. We will send word of the time." Kallista somehow, with the aid of Torchay's and Joh's excellent skills at moving people along, finally got them all out the door.

Graceday. Five days from now, Viyelle would officially be a married woman. She felt like one already.

## CHAPTER SEVENTEEN

The smells and the noise of the city impinged on Fox's awareness long before they entered its streets, possibly before the rebels could see it. He'd been aware of the city since the noon stop, and they'd traveled far since then. He didn't know how he would identify this city. He doubted anyone would actually tell him, and he wasn't sure his *knowing* would recognize any place he'd been before. And he hadn't been many places in Adara. Or in Tibre either, come to consider it.

As they traveled deeper into the city, Fox had to grip the poles on his travois tight in order to fight the urge to sit up and *look* around. He did not want to alert the rebels to his improving condition, nor did he need to raise his head to *know*.

He lay there, hands wrapped around the poles until he feared his knuckles whitened, and sent his *knowing* out as high and wide as he could. The shape and placement of the buildings seemed familiar. Even the smells seemed familiar—the city smell of bodies, beer, cooking and sewage laid over a permanent reek of old fish and ripe swamp. Or river.

The rebel band clattered into an open space where a bridge rose in a high curving arch. The masts of boats thronged along a riverbank, and Fox knew. They'd brought him to Turysh.

He knew Turysh better than any Adaran city. Better than any Tibran city, save Tsekrish where he'd grown to manhood. It was here he'd found Stone again after the horror of the battle at Ukiny. And here he had also found Kallista again, though until that day he'd never known they had found each other before.

After the battle with the demon in Tsekrish, Kallista had brought them all here, to the city of her birth, so her mother could heal the injury to his leg that had left him half-lamed after Ukiny. The healing had involved reopening the original wound, cutting away the knotted scar tissue that had formed, and stitching everything back together. Then came the slow painful process of knitting the muscle back together as should have been done to begin with.

Fox hadn't got out much those early days, but as the healing progressed, Mother Irysta had pushed him out of his sick bed to walk. At first, just as far as the privy, but as the days wore on, he was fairly certain that he walked every street in Turysh multiple times with one or more of his iliasti at his side for company. He knew Turysh. He could escape from Turysh.

The rebels took him not to the barracks as he expected, but to the city's central commercial district away from the dirt and smells and noise of the river docks, where the merchants who bought and sold what the river transported and the bankers who financed the buying had built their shiny new stone buildings. The streets seemed quieter, not as many people as he remembered from last fall. Had the rebels stopped the commerce in favor of their war, or were the people simply too afraid to continue with "business as usual"? Perhaps so many had fled the rebel takeover it left the city feeling empty. Or perhaps they were dead.

Fox let his knees buckle when the rebels jerked him to his feet outside the Mother Temple, still playing invalid. In truth, his strength was pitiful, but not so bad as he hoped they would believe. They dragged him through—the north entrance, he thought. He could orient himself fairly well to the compass directions by his knowing and they had come directly from the Taolind on the north without much turning. They entered the temple's high central sanctuary and Fox recoiled.

The stench in the place nearly had him retching on his own boots. It smelled like a days-old battlefield piled with unburied bodies that had been baking in summer's heat. Only worse.

Except his *knowing* found nothing in the echoing chamber but the usual benches against the wall and a knot of people—four or five individuals—standing in the center around a woman in a chair. No, not a chair. A throne.

Was this the rebel's queen?

Fox didn't have to pretend illness when the outlaws hauled him across the mosaic floor, the toes of his battered boots catching on the slight unevenness of the tiles. The pattern in the mosaic was the Compass Rose, symbol of the One and Her gifts of magic, or so Fox had been told. He'd never seen it for himself.

He dragged his feet, trying to visualize the symbol—the many-petaled red rose in the center, the arms of the compass reaching from it to the four directions: blue lightning for the North, green vine for the East, yellow flame for the South and black briar for the West. He called on the presence of the One here in this corrupted holy place, cried out to the warrior face of the One for strength in the battle to come. But still, he was only himself. And still they brought him remorselessly on, nearer to the horror in the center of the room.

Desperate, beyond terror, Fox shouted, a horrible hoarse bellow. The cry inside his head called Kallista's name. At some impossible distance, he sensed her answer. *Fox.*

Then some *thing*, some dark, awful presence flowed out from the woman on the throne. It touched him, a cold, piercing pain. Fox screamed. It swarmed over him, surrounding him with agony, probing, digging, prying at his soul as if it sought entry.

*Survive,* a voice in his head whispered to him. *You've done it before, when you lost your caste. You did what you had to. Can this be any worse?*

Memories flooded Fox of that time in the Tibran war camp when he'd been blind and casteless, without even the *knowing* Kallista had given him. Anyone's plaything. Anyone's victim. He'd locked those memories away, but now—he couldn't block them.

His body jerked with remembered pain and humiliation. The hands holding him lost their grip and he fell to his knees, curled into a ball and howled.

*Let us in, let us in,* the voice murmured, sweet and seductive, promising an end to the torture, promising only pleasure to come.

Almost, Fox surrendered. Until he felt that loathsome thing pluck at a part of himself that had never been touched in all those terrible casteless, ilian-less days. He recoiled. This thing, this *demon* didn't want just his body. It wanted him, *all* of him. Who he was. Who he loved.

Fox struggled, but couldn't throw it off. Then the demon found his link to Kallista.

It bit at the link, clawed it, trying to break it, to cut him off. Or to follow it, use it as a conduit to gain entry to Kallista and from her to the others.

He fled. Wrapping himself around the precious link, Fox hid deep inside himself. Beyond the place he had gone when Tibrans had abused his body, to a place where no one could find him and nothing could reach him.

His senses still worked, recording what he knew and heard for the time when he returned.

Above him, around him, people spoke. "He is too afraid." A woman's voice, one of those standing. "Too weak. Too many of them are weak."

"Not this one." Another woman, the one from the throne. "He is protected. Too many more of these damned Adarans are protected." Her voice rose as anger overtook her until her shriek of fury echoed around the high sanctuary ceiling and out the open clerestory windows.

"Oskina Reinine."

"Oskina Reinine."

Voices in chorus murmured the name as all those in the room abased themselves.

"Oh, get up," she muttered. "I'm not going to hurt you."

"Of course not." The man who spoke was one of the first to rise.

"Of course not. I need you. The cause needs you. We fight to slay death itself."

"*Yes*, Oskina Reinine." The chorused voices shook with fervor and even hidden away inside himself, Fox's body shuddered.

"Take it away." The man waved a hand. "Destroy it."

"No." Oskina stopped the outlaws who'd brought Fox before they did more than take a step. "Leave him. Leave us. Go find your regiment. Report in. If I have further orders for you, I will send them."

The outlaws bowed low. When they were gone and only four remained in the chamber, Oskina rounded on the man who had spoken. "Do not think to defy me, Ataroth, or to usurp me. You may have devoured our sedil and absorbed its essence into yours, but I am still ruler here."

There was a pause that Fox's senses could not interpret, but when the man spoke again, his voice and his posture cowered. "Yes, Ashbel. You rule. No one can stand against your power."

Ashbel-Oskina turned to the two others in the room.

They cringed. "You rule, Ashbel. You rule." Their voices—male and female—sounded in unison.

"But…" Ataroth began tentatively. "Why *not* destroy it? Will its destruction not bring you pleasure?"

"It does not seem wise." Ashbel-Oskina began to pace. "This one is important. I do not know how or why, but if we can break it open and take it for ours…" She sighed. "Besides, we cannot destroy every prisoner they deliver to us, no matter how much pleasure it brings."

"Why not?" the other woman whined.

"Because, my dear Untathel, destruction means dead, and we are supposed to be defeating death."

"But that's impossible."

"You and I both know that, but these idiotic mortals think it is possible, and if we leave too many dead in our wake—even enemy dead—they will begin to desert our cause. We are not strong enough yet that we can afford to lose them. When we have won, when we have slain the Destroyer, *then* we can do as we please."

"What do we do with this now? Leave it lying here?" Ataroth said.

"Of course not." Ashbel-Oskina kicked Fox in the back, hard enough his body grunted. "If we can turn this one to our cause… Have the healers tend it. We will speak with it later. Learn what it knows at the very least."

"Will it speak truth?" the second male spoke.

"We have truthsayers among our followers, Xibyth. Call them."

"But—" Though Xibyth seemed fearful of speaking further, after a long pause, he did. "The truthsayer's magic is blocked when we are present."

"Then we will give them the questions to ask, and one of these bodies will attend the questioning without a rider."

Ashbel-Oskina crossed to the eastern entrance and pulled a silken cord hanging there. "This one is important," she said. "If we cannot ride it, we will seduce it to our cause. And if we cannot seduce it, we will break it."

"Doesn't break mean dead, like destroy?" Untathel asked.

"No." Ashbel-Oskina smacked the other woman in the head. "It just means broken. Broken is not dead, but broken will serve, if the man will not."

"Kallista, *breathe*." Torchay shook her again, hoping to bring her back from wherever she'd gone. People were beginning to stare—he knew Kallista hated that—but if she did not take a breath soon, he would give them a true spectacle by breathing for her, mouth to mouth, here in the corridors of power.

They'd been *mingling*. Torchay's mouth would have twisted in sour amusement were he not so afraid for Kallista. The announcement of Viyelle Prinsipella's intention to join their ilian had brought a flurry of invitations to luncheons, nuncheons, parties and flings. They'd attended every one Viyelle said was important, and Torchay had to give her credit. She knew just which were the important occasions. When they weren't at some event or other, they *mingled* with the court in the galleries, courtyards, drawing rooms and corridors, seeing, listening and being seen.

Today, it had been a corridor, once the interminable meal with the Prinsep of Turysh had finally ended. Torchay had never known anyone more dull or self-important, and he had chosen the army as a career. Loitering in the corridor below the Reinine's tower, half-listening to gossip and watching for danger hadn't been any more entertaining.

Until, as the sun was sending long golden shafts of light through the western windows, Kallista had gasped and her eyes seemed to turn inward. Torchay had stepped closer, took her arm to support her in case it was needed. Several ticks passed before he had realized she was not breathing.

It had happened once before, Kallista forgetting to breathe, a year ago when her godmarked magic was new. But that had been at night, in a dream, not in broad daylight in a corridor crowded with courtiers while Kallista walked and talked and smiled among them. He would not panic. He could not.

"All right." Torchay met Obed's eyes and saw him chase away the same mortal fear that gripped himself. "We haven't time to get her back to our rooms. I need to breathe for her now."

Obed lifted her in his arms and went to one knee, preparing to lay her on the hallway floor when Kallista's eyes flew open and she dragged in a deep, gasping breath. She glanced up at Obed, then searched until she saw Torchay and her hand reached for him. Relief flooded Torchay as he took it and kissed it. Her other hand gripped Obed's as she struggled to find her own feet.

"Demons," she whispered.

"Here?" Torchay spoke as quietly as she, despite his alarm. Why didn't she call on their magic? Or had the demon struck from ambush?

Kallista shook her head. "Back to our rooms."

Her hand trembled even when he held it tighter. Something had gone very wrong. Torchay wanted to carry her to safety in his own arms, but her safety depended more on his being un-encumbered. He signaled to Joh who took her from Obed.

"I can walk," Kallista complained as they started off.

"Not fast enough." Torchay opened a path through the crowds, glad to know Obed guarded her back. He wanted her safe—or as safe as it was possible to be.

"Wedding nerves." Viyelle raised her voice to be heard. She smiled, pacified the curious, soothed the fearful. "She hasn't been sleeping well. I believe she now pays the price." She kept up with them, skillfully slipping away from the grasping hands and malicious comments, easing their way with her patter.

Torchay was grateful once more for the One's wisdom in marking a courier for them. He'd been skeptical at first—very well, resentful. Most iliani stopped at four or six. Though they could legally expand as far as twelve, the difficulties of successfully managing so many personalities and relationships made such large iliani rare outside the temples. And temple families tended to change members more frequently than any others. But eight was not such a large number, certainly better than unfortunate seven, and Viyelle had proved a good fit.

Besides, by taking Joh in hand, she lessened the pressure on Kallista. With Obed, and yes, Torchay himself, focused exclusively on Kallista, having Joh wanting her as well made things more difficult. Viyelle eased that tension. And thinking about her kept Torchay's mind from his urge to panic.

Joh crossed the open space in the parlor and set Kallista on the sofa while Obed bolted the door, then joined them.

"Demons, you said?" Torchay perched on the arm of the sofa, hovering. He couldn't help it.

"In Turysh." Kallista closed her eyes momentarily, before locking her gaze on his. "That's where the rebels have taken Fox. I got that much before I lost him."

"By lost, you mean…?" Torchay asked carefully. He wasn't sure he wanted to know, but Kallista needed to be sure.

"Not dead." She gripped Joh's hand tighter and reached over her shoulder for Obed's, her gaze holding on to Torchay. "The link is still there, so he's not dead, but it's faint. Choked off." She took a deep breath and held it for a few ticks before letting it out. "I think a demon was trying to take him over."

Torchay recoiled, memory slamming into him. A demon had got its claws into him, had come too damn close to possessing him. It still gave him nightmares, the ordinary sort.

Only accepting the God's mark had kept him from that fate, and only the addition of the magic given him in that moment had allowed Kallista to destroy that demon. They had survived. *He* had survived, but the horror stayed with him. "Did it succeed?"

The fear in Kallista's eyes echoed the horror in his own. She knew what such a thing meant. "I don't know," she whispered.

He held his arms out and Kallista nearly lunged into them, abandoning their iliasti on the sofa. As he cradled her in his lap, offering comfort no one else could, he saw a brief flash of the old jealousy in Obed's eyes before it melted into understanding.

"Fox is marked." Torchay found his own comfort in that thought even as he offered it to Kallista. "Marked more than a year. That will protect him."

"I hope so."

"Is there anything we can do?" Viyelle's question was about emotional assistance, Torchay was sure, but Kallista didn't take it that way.

Her trembling stopped and she lifted her head, thoughts obviously turning. She glanced up at Torchay, then straightened, looking at the others. "We can go get him out of their hands."

"What if a demon *has* possessed him?" Joh asked.

"Then we will dispossess it. Fox belongs to *us*." Kallista stood. Never had she looked more like an avenging instrument of the One. Chills shivered down Torchay's back as he rose to his feet behind her.

"Excuse me." Viyelle lifted a tentative hand for notice. "What about the ceremony on Graceday?"

Kallista pulled the other woman to her feet for a hug and a kiss on the cheek. "We need time to prepare for our trip. We won't leave till afterward."

Viyelle grinned crookedly. "We don't have to tell my mothers that our wedding trip is a rescue mission into the rebel stronghold."

"Exactly." Kallista laughed, though it sounded a bit off to Torchay. Still it was a laugh.

She turned to Joh. "We need you to organize our supplies. Decide what we'll need to take—quickest, quietest transport to Turysh, disguises, whatever we need—and work with Obed to procure it. Go through army channels. I don't want anyone wandering the city alone.

"Viyelle, you're in complete charge of the ceremony, and of your family and the rest of the court. We need to cut back some on the mingling so Joh and Obed can get their work done, but we'll keep to what's necessary."

"Your faint today will give us an excuse to be less in the public eye," Viyelle said.

"Good."

"And what will you and I be doing?" Torchay asked, crossing his arms.

"You'll need to give Joh and Obed a list of the medical supplies we'll need."

He'd expected that. He was no East magic healer, but he had the best nonmagical medical training available. All bodyguards did. And he'd taught Obed what he could during those few peaceful months in their mountain home, so that the next time he was gutted—which seemed to occur with alarming regularity—there would be another with medical training. "What about you?"

"I will be consulting with the Reinine and anyone else necessary to get permission to leave Arikon and orders to go to Turysh. Serysta Reinine said that General Uskenda wanted me—us—to spy things out in Turysh, so that should be no difficulty. It would be nice to have orders to rescue Fox, but they're not necessary."

"We *will* rescue Fox, won't we?" Viyelle said in a small voice.

Kallista's smile held more than a little of the wolf. "Orders or no, we will get Fox out of the demon's hands."

"For curiosity's sake," Torchay said, dream memories coming back to him, "just how many demons are we talking about?"

"Four."

"Four demons, all in one place." He frowned. The others did not look happy, either. "And there were how many in the boat?"

"Two. Well, one of them sort of…ate the other one. But there were two to begin with."

"And with the five of us, you were barely able to drive them out of the city, but not destroy them."

"One did eat the other, so there's just one left now."

"Did eating the other demon make the first one stronger?"

"Well…yes."

"And there are *four* demons in Turysh." Torchay fought back the familiar urge to strangle his naitan.

"Fox is there. His magic makes all the rest of it much easier to control."

"But you don't know if he's been possessed, do you?"

"No. But—"

Torchay stopped her with a raised hand. "You don't *know*. Just how do you think you will manage *four* demons?"

"We'll hide. The demon couldn't find us last year when we were veiled. If we can't fight them, we'll grab Fox and go, under the veil."

"You think it will be that easy?"

"Hells, no. But what else can we do? We can't leave Fox there."

Torchay sighed, unable to argue against the agony in her eyes. "Of course we can't. I simply wanted to be sure you'd thought through all the difficulties."

"If we haven't, we'll improvise." Kallista waved a dismissive hand.

"That's what I'm afraid of."

# CHAPTER EIGHTEEN

Graceday dawned clear, fair and warm, spring's promise nearly melted into summer. Kallista fidgeted, wanting the day over, wanting to be on the road for Turysh. But Viyelle deserved her time in the light and politics had to be considered.

They hadn't been able to keep the ceremony small and private, after all. Saminda Prinsep had gone to Serysta Reinine who thought holding the preliminary bracelet ceremony outdoors so the whole court could attend was a wonderful idea. Major Naitan Kallista Varyl, Special Attaché to the Reinine, could only smile, bow and acquiesce.

Viyelle had kept it as simple as possible, limiting attendants to one total and forbidding her second mother any beribboned doves or fish swimming in glass towers. The blooming apple trees had been finally deemed sufficient for decoration, though Kallista noted as she arrived with her iliasti at the courtyard's eastern entrance that the trees seemed to have blossomed with pale green and blue ribbon bows and festoons of netting. The guards providing security around the perimeter were hidden from sight or doubtless they'd be decorated within an inch of their lives as well.

"*Mother.*" Viyelle ground the word between her teeth.

Joh patted her arm. "It's not doves or fish."

"True." She took a deep breath and looked up at Kallista. "Ready?"

Kallista straightened her tunic, another of Obed's extravagances—a long civilian dress tunic in red brocade slit up the sides so her red hose showed. They all wore red of various shades this time, the color of the One's rose. Kallista rather liked the symbolism of unity. She also liked how splendid everyone looked in their finery.

Torchay's red came close to matching his hair, shading a bit toward orange. Viyelle's red leaned toward rose and Joh's was more of a wine-red, while Kallista and Obed wore bright, true red.

"We do look good, don't we?" She grinned at the others.

"Arikon will be stunned." Viyelle grinned back. "We look *magnificent.*"

With a brisk nod, Kallista led out, Viyelle half a step behind her. They took their places near the entrance, to keep Kallista sufficiently close to Joh. Because half the bonded ilian was absent, no prelate presided over this ceremony. It really should have been a small private affair, but no use moaning over it now.

In unison, Kallista and Viyelle turned to face the entrance, and the males of the ilian present emerged into afternoon sunlight. One by one, beginning with Kallista, they each presented Viyelle with a bracelet and made their vows. When Joh stepped back to his place after crossing the circle to Viyelle in defiance of his *di pentivas* chains, Viyelle took all the remaining bands at once from their attendant, her sedil Kendra.

Kallista smiled to herself. She'd never seen such a sour-faced attendant. She accepted the bracelet from Viyelle, received her kiss of promise, then watched as she made the same promise to the others, kneeling to slip on each anklet. As Viyelle strode back to her own place in the circle, Kallista took a deep breath. Time for the speech.

She could give orders to a regiment and discuss strategy with a crowd of generals, but speaking like this gave her the colly-wobbles. She could do it if she had to, but she would truly, honestly rather not. This was one of the "have to" occasions. As the oldest female in their ilian, that made her their speaker, even if she hadn't been ranking officer among their military members.

Viyelle stopped, turned to face inward, her face smiling and solemn both at once.

"We will repeat our vows when our ilian is whole again." Kallista used her parade ground voice, letting it carry through the grassy garden. "Thank you for sharing our joy. Now please join us in the Great Hall of Summerglen for celebration." Short and sweet. Just how she liked it.

They remained in place on the small flagstoned terrace, receiving the well-wishes of a horde of people while Kallista fought to keep her smile on her face. They needed to be away. But shouting at all these silly people wouldn't help, and if they lingered long enough under the falling petals of the apple trees, it would be ages before anyone noticed they hadn't appeared at the feasting and dancing.

Their packs and horses were waiting at the stables, including the remounts they'd brought from home. Anything not making the journey with them was packed in trunks ready for transport to storage rooms. Viyelle and Joh had even arranged for a place near the stables where their riding clothes waited for them to come change out of their finery. But first they had to be rid of all these people.

Finally, the crowds dwindled to a last, lingering few. Unfortunately, those few included Viyelle's family.

"A beautiful, beautiful ceremony." Saminda embraced her daughter, then looped her arm through Kallista's. "Come. Let us walk together to the Great Hall." She took a step, then halted, frowning, when Kallista remained in place.

"I am sorry, Saminda," Kallista said, gently disengaging her arm. "We are not coming to the celebration."

"*Not coming?* Don't be silly. You must come. The celebration is to honor you." She took Kallista's arm and tried to urge her along. Kallista sighed. She had hoped to avoid this.

"Think of the scandal," Viyelle's birth mother Sanda said. "It won't hurt to delay your wedding journey by a few chimes of the clock."

"Mother, you can look at my beautiful iliasti and say that delay won't hurt? We are in agony already." Viyelle's smile was wide and bright, laid over half-hidden worry. "Besides, this celebration is what *you* wanted, not of our—"

Kallista laid a hand on Viyelle's shoulder. They didn't need old family quarrels either. "Adara is torn by rebellion. We have orders from the Reinine. The sooner we ride, the sooner we return." She looked each of Viyelle's parents in the eye—thank the One her sulky sedil had already departed. "I am telling you because you are Viyelle's parents and have a right to know, and because you are prinsipi and know how to hold secrets. Do not share this with anyone, not even your own family members. To the rest of the court, we must be merely overeager to reach our home for some privacy."

"When will you return?" Saminda asked.

"When our task is accomplished." Kallista paused, considering. No, she wouldn't tell them any more, not about Fox or the planned journey to Korbin afterward to collect the rest of their ilian. Saminda might be as tight shut as a river mussel, but Kallista had her doubts about Sanda's judgment. Instead, she swept into a bow, collected her piece of an ilian with a gesture and hurried away to the stables.

They rode all the way to Turysh, rather than risking a boat. The river was bound to be heavily monitored, and the road from Arikon in the mountains to Boren on the river was held by rebels. The rebels didn't have enough manpower to patrol all the passes through the mountains or all the paths on the plains.

Kallista tried calling a veil as they left the city, but without her links to Joh and Viyelle fully formed and only two magics to use, she couldn't veil much. She couldn't hide any of them from physical sight, but she did manage to hammer together something she thought would hide them from demon sight. She didn't want any demons invading any dreams and she especially didn't want them to know they were on the move.

The magic was a struggle to maintain, however. She couldn't simply lock it in place and forget about it. Without the traits carried by her absent three, the veiling magic required frequent attention. A dozen times a day, she had to call more magic and beat it into the veil. She woke up several times at night, like one chilled from the dying of a fire, to throw more magic on and build it up again.

She didn't want demons to find them, but she didn't know if she had strength to keep even this partial veil up for the length of time it would take to reach Turysh.

A week and a half after leaving Arikon, they rode into Turysh and across the bridge into the city proper on the south bank of the Taolind. Obed rode pillion behind Kallista. The last few days, since Miel's spring had given way to the summer days of Katenda, one of the men had ridden with her to hold her in the saddle when her exhaustion became too great.

Obed had been chosen for the entry into the city in hopes that behind Kallista, the greasepaint used to disguise his facial tattoos would be less noticeable. Fingerless gloves hid the markings on his hands and turned-up collars hid those on everyone's neck.

The brown dye had flattened much of the curl in Torchay's hair, making him almost a stranger, though his high, hooked nose was impossible to disguise. He'd suggested cutting Joh's distinctive long queue, but the idea had been vetoed by Kallista and Viyelle, though strangely not by Joh. He wore a wide-brimmed Filornish drovers' hat with the braid tucked up beneath it.

They had considered cutting or dying Kallista's hair, but such a dark brown didn't take dye well and she'd spent so many years wearing a tight military queue they decided that leaving it loose would be enough to turn aside a casual glance. Anyone who knew Kallista would recognize her behind any of the simple disguises they could manage. Turysh was the city of her birth. She hadn't spent much of her adult life here, but her friends and family still knew her.

They hadn't bothered with a disguise for Viyelle. Medium height, medium build, medium brown hair and attractive-but-not-striking face, she had nothing distinctive to mark her like Obed's tattoos or the red of Torchay's hair. No one in Turysh knew her, and if someone had perchance seen her at court, no one would believe a prinsipella to be riding into town with a down-on-their-luck ilian.

Kallista rested against Obed and closed her eyes to better see the veil that was supposed to be hiding them from demon sight. The horse would follow Torchay's and he knew where they were going. The veil was thinning *there*. She felt Obed's shiver when she pulled more magic.

Was it just the usual magical caress, or did it drain them the way it did her? Did it matter now? They could all rest—she hoped—when they reached sanctuary.

Obed reached around her and took the reins from her limp fingers. "We are in the city," he murmured, his lips moving against the sensitive skin of her neck. "More things to startle our mount. More paths to go astray. If you will not attend, someone must."

"Thank you." She shoveled the new magic into the raveling gap and mashed it into place. Were her patches holding a bit longer? She wasn't sure, but it seemed so. Because she was getting better at it, or because they were closer to Fox? She wished she knew.

The horses slowed and came to a halt. Kallista opened her eyes. Torchay had stopped outside one of the inns near the docks that catered to river traffic. Not one of the better ones. Obed lowered Kallista into Joh's arms while Torchay went inside to haggle for rooms and stable space. They'd decided to play a droving family off the plains, cash poor but horse rich. The drovers who wandered Adara's plains with their herds and flocks would sooner sell a precious child than one of their prized horses. The story would explain the quality of their Southron mounts.

Kallista pushed away from Joh to stand on her own. "The innkeeper won't want to give us rooms if he thinks I'm sick. I can walk in under my own power."

Obed tossed the reins to a stable boy who was trying to avoid notice and took her arm. "If you stumble and fall, you will look more ill than if you lean on us out of weariness."

He had a point. Kallista gave in and leaned. Viyelle stumbled over the threshold. Kallista didn't think it was entirely acting for her benefit. They were all tired.

Torchay led them to the big room they'd taken on the third floor and Kallista managed to kick off her boots before she fell into the bed and slept. When she woke, it was dark. Joh lay tucked in next to her, but the glimmer of candlelight reflected in his eyes told her he didn't sleep. Obed and Viyelle sat at the table in the center of the room eating by the light of a single candle.

"Why aren't you eating with them?" She brushed back the hair that had fallen from Joh's queue.

"You sleep better when you're not alone." He propped his head on a hand to look down at her. "You're our naitan. We thought it better that you sleep as much as you could, and it was my turn to help you do so."

"Where's Torchay?" She took the hand Joh offered and sat up.

"Gone to meet with your sedili as we discussed. So they can tell us how things stand here before we begin our search for Fox and the Reinine's information. Remember?" Obed moved a chair out for her as she walked yawning to the table.

"Oh. Yes." She knew it, but she was too tired to recall.

Obed filled a bowl of stew for her, then another for Joh while Viyelle hacked off pieces of the pale brown loaf. "Eat," he said. "You need your strength."

"Why do I feel like a prize pig being fattened for the fair?" Kallista pulled the bowl closer and sniffed.

"I don't know. Why?" Obed squeezed her arm, playing farmer checking his fatstock. "Needs more meat on her." He ladled another dip of stew into her bowl, face bland while the others laughed.

"Don't smell it," Viyelle advised. "Just eat it. It tastes reasonably good, but it won't do to ask what kind of meat's in it. Not fish. Other than that…"

"Given some of the things I've eaten on campaign, I know better than to ask." She took a bite—reasonably good, as claimed. "I've never been able to cure myself of trying to *guess*, however."

Joh's bark of laughter made him choke and brought on a flurry of back pounding and water bringing. Crisis over, they had almost finished the meal when Torchay slipped through the door, followed by Kallista's sedil Kami.

She and her twin sister Karyl were Kallista's full sisters by blood through both parents, though twelve years younger.

Karyl had farspeaking magic and magicless Kami ran their business. The twins had married a pair of brother sedili last fall, after Kallista's ilian had returned from their adventures. They'd delayed the wedding for several days, in fact, so Kallista could reach Turysh and act as attendant for her sisters.

"Are Shaden and Deray over being mad at me?" Kallista asked when she had hugged her sister.

"If they're not, they should be." Kami hugged her again, then startled Obed by hugging him before turning to the others. "Who are these, then?"

Kallista cleared her throat, slightly embarrassed, though she had no reason for it. "New iliasti. Joh Suteny from Filorne and Viyelle Torvyll of Shaluine." Quickly she explained where Stone and Aisse had gone, to forestall the question.

Kami frowned. "You should have gone with them. Or at least not come here. Turysh is overrun with rebels. They claim to want only 'the people's welfare,' but Karyl says there's something off. Things going on we don't know about. The barracks are locked down, nobody going in or out except for rebel patrols.

"Karyl had to register at Mother Temple as a naitan. All the naitani in Turysh had to register, but… I've seen people watching her. These Barbs. There's almost always one or two in the street whenever one of us sticks our nose outside. They just watch…like they're afraid of North magic now, not just West. They aren't following us. Yet."

"Farspeaking was once affiliated with the West," Kallista said gently. "So was truthsaying. It's only been a few hundred years since they were shifted over to the North."

"That's ridiculous. Farspeaking's inanimate magic. Of course it's North."

Kallista shook her head. "Think about it, Kami. North magic has to do with inanimate *objects*. Things. Wind. Water. Earth. Metals. Lightning. Lightning is still a *thing*. It has a physical existence. Truthsaying and farspeaking exist only in the mind. They are *meta*physical mysteries. West magic. Ask Karyl if the North truly answers her when she turns to it. Ask her if she's ever spoken to the West. Ask her if it answers."

Kami had gone pale as Kallista spoke. She hated to frighten her little sister, but she wanted them safe. They couldn't trust in false information. "Those two magics, along with farseeing were shifted North because they are so useful. The Barbs' heresy was very strong back then, spreading even into the prelacy before the truth pushed it back. The four Academies decided together to make the shift in hopes of preserving some West magic. The more useful of the West magics.

"From what you've said, however, I fear the Barbs remember what everyone else has forgotten." Kallista took her sister's hand, hoping to comfort. "Warn Karyl and the others. *Be careful.*"

"Bloody hells." Kami sank down on the edge of a bed. "Seven bloody, bloody hells." She looked up at Kallista, hand tightening fiercely. "What about the rumors? The ones about all the military naitani being killed and their hands taken for trophies? Is it true?"

Kallista swallowed hard. She didn't want to share that horror with her baby sisters. But they weren't babies anymore. "Their hands were taken. I saw myself one who survived it. Many—most of them, I think—were killed. I do know that some soldier naitani survived, but how many, and whether the hands went for trophies? I don't know. Information has been hard to come by, even in Arikon. We simply do not yet know."

"*Goddess.*" Kami looked undone. "We have to get out. You have to help us get her out of here."

"I will and soon, sister, I promise. But we have things we must do first."

"What could you possibly have to do that is more important than saving Karyl from—"

Kallista pulled Kami out of the chair and into a hug, squeezing her tight, too tight to move. "Hush, little sister. Peace. We will keep her safe. But the Reinine has sent us here for another purpose."

"What?" Kami's tone was sullen, but she seemed to be listening now.

"To learn what these rebels are doing. To spy on the demons that direct them. To—"

Kami pushed out of Kallista's embrace to stare in horror at her again. *"Demons?"*

Kallista shrugged and nodded. "They're real, too, just like the stories of the godstruck."

"Dear Goddess in heaven. Next you will tell me the One has come down to walk among us."

"Not so far. But if it happens, I wouldn't be surprised." Kallista tried a smile and was relieved to see a faint, quavery one in return. "Have you seen Fox in town?"

"Fox?" Kami seemed bewildered by the abrupt change in topic. "No. Why would I? Didn't he go with Stone and Aisse? I thought he sired—"

"He did. He was with them when they ran into some trouble, and I think he's here now. Alone. In the rebels' hands."

"Are the others all right? Your babies?"

Kallista took a deep breath, trying to hold on to her calm, but it took Torchay's hand on her shoulder to succeed. "They're fine. Safe, the last time we heard."

Which had been three long weeks ago. Twenty-seven days. Surely trouble would have come to her through the links, as it had with Fox's demon encounter, and as it had when he'd been injured at his capture. She had to trust in that connection.

"I haven't seen him anywhere in town," Kami was saying. "But I haven't been looking. I can do that, go and look."

"No." Kallista shook her head. They had discussed plans on the road, but now she could scarcely recall what they were. She had to stuff her worry back in its box. "Don't change your regular activities. Look for him while you're going about your business, but nothing more. I don't want you in more danger than you already are."

"I'd invite you to stay with us, but considering our watchers, it probably isn't best." Kami's smile twisted.

"True. We don't want them watching us, too." Kallista winked.

Kami hugged her tight. "If you hear anything— If you need anything—"

"Actually—" Joh interrupted the farewell. "If you know of cheap lodgings somewhere—" He gave Kallista's scowl an innocent look. "An inn also has too many watchers. We need to move on as soon as we can. We discussed this."

"Yes, we did." Kallista rubbed her temples. "Is there anything else I've forgotten?"

"Communication." Joh didn't hesitate. "If you cannot use farspeaking with your sedil, then—"

"Farspeaking?" Kami caught Kallista's arm and pulled her around to face her again. "You don't have farspeaking magic."

Kallista's head throbbed harder. "Actually, I may. I used it in an emergency in Arikon, but haven't tried since." She smiled at Kami's incredulous expression. "This godstruck magic keeps surprising me. So warn Karyl. I don't want to surprise her. If I can manage to do it again."

Kami didn't respond, other than to eye her with suspicion.

"If it doesn't work—" Joh stepped into the silence. "We'll send one of our men, or send one of yours. It would be best if you sisters were not seen together."

"You might ask Karyl to try farspeaking to me first," Kallista suggested. "Maybe she can explain a bit about how it works."

Kami continued to stare. It made Kallista squirm. "Don't look at me as if I've suddenly grown another head. I'm still me."

"Maybe," Kami said. "But you're not just you anymore, either, are you?"

"Yes," Kallista insisted. "I am. Just me. Nothing more." She hauled her sister into another hug. "Give your iliasti our love. And be careful."

"I will. We will." Kami studied Kallista's face another long moment. "You be careful, too." She put up a hand when Torchay moved to the door ahead of her. "You don't have to walk me back."

"It's dangerous near the docks," he said. "I'll walk you."

"Allow me." Obed put on the wide-brimmed Filornish hat Joh had worn, shadowing the paint covering his tattoos. "In the dark, my imperfections do not show so clearly. And you have not yet eaten tonight."

Before any of them could think to argue, had they wanted to argue, Obed swept Kami out of the room.

A few days later, they moved into a room over a stable on the edge of a moderately prosperous part of Turysh where the craftsmen and rising clerks paid to have their horses cared for, or rented horses if they didn't care to own their own. The ilian's rent for both people and horses was free, with enough coin for meals and a bit over thrown in, in exchange for work. Work done primarily by a prinsipella, a former lieutenant and a major.

Torchay and Obed were needed to spy out the situation. Because Kallista could not be separated more than ten or so paces from Joh or Viyelle, they had to move as a unit. Skulking and spying were not group activities.

Neither were mucking out stalls, pitching hay and harnessing carriage horses, but they managed. Kallista had more trouble reining in her impatience than doing the work. On the journey, they had agreed that it would be best to learn the things commissioned by the Reinine and her generals first.

How many troops did the rebels have? How were they disposed? What was the mood of the city? How many "true believers" in the Order of the Barbed Rose and its heresy were in Turysh? What was their plan of attack? And on and on through the list of a thousand and one other things the generals wanted them to discover. This would give them time to locate Fox and the information necessary to formulate a rescue with some chance for success. But it was taking too damn long.

At least keeping them hidden from the demons had become easier. Kallista still had to shore up the veiling several times a day and night, but when she had linked with all of her iliasti in the inn's attic room, it had occurred to her that she didn't have to hide their physical existence from demon sight. She only had to hide the magic—a much simpler task—and make them all appear to be nothing more than ordinary drovers stopping for a time to work before heading out to the plains.

Even with the backbreaking stable work, which Joh and Viyelle tried to do in her place, Kallista was able to rebuild her strength, now that the magic was not draining her so. And as her strength grew, her patience dwindled.

Torchay and Obed had to have counted every soldier, every musket, every sword—hell, every *dagger* in Turysh. They had tracked the Master Barbs on their rounds of the city and marked their bolt holes. They had listened at doorways and beneath windows. They had peeked at maps and lists of provisions. And still they had not laid eyes on Fox.

The whole ilian had even gone to worship on Hopeday at the Mother Temple in hopes of finding Fox. The Barbs had booted the temple ilian out of their home and replaced them with their own people, leaders of the rebellion. Kallista could smell the lingering stink of demons in the central sanctuary, though apparently they'd been driven out, at least for the day, by the presence of true worshippers.

Was that why Fox wasn't there? Because a demon rode him?

Kallista whispered a little prayer, asking protection for him. He was close, perhaps elsewhere in the temple itself. She could sense his presence through the link, might even have been able to call his magic if the link had not been squeezed so tightly shut.

She had turned, taken a step, following the magic's lead. Joh stopped her with a hand on her arm. His raised eyebrow asked a question, but she couldn't answer it here.

Nor could she leave the worship to go poking around in the temple, especially with Joh and Viyelle trailing after her like so many ducklings behind their mother. So they stayed through the service and went back to their room afterward.

Torchay and Obed continued with their spying, focusing more on the area around the Mother Temple, without any results other than more numbers and more rumors, until Second-day rolled around again and a full week had passed. Kallista was ready to tear out her hair.

## CHAPTER NINETEEN

On Thirdday, almost halfway through Katenda, Viyelle was paying the tavern keeper's son for the supper he'd brought from his father's place of business around the corner while Kallista and Joh finished the evening feed. They seldom left the stable and never in company with Torchay or Obed to avoid being seen together. The confinement did not help Kallista's patience.

Torchay would return soon to trade spys' duties for bodyguards' with Obed. They refused to leave her without a guard, and though Joh's skills improved rapidly, he had not yet passed Torchay's standards. Obed was their night spy. Kallista wondered when one or the other of them would keel over from lack of sleep, but they didn't seem too bothered by it so far.

Viyelle waited with the supper basket by the ladder-stair to their room above. Obed rose from the mounded hay where he'd supposedly been napping—and perhaps he had. He awakened as instantly as Torchay. Kallista handed the grain scoop to Joh who tossed it in the bin and lowered the lid as they passed.

Halfway up the steep stairs, Kallista paused. Something felt…strange.

"Is something wrong?" Obed asked from below her. "Are you all right?"

"Yes." She knew that much. Kallista hurried the rest of the way up the stairs. Nothing was wrong. Just different.

It wasn't until she reached the top of the stairs that she knew what had changed. The link with Joh had formed.

She twined a finger—or whatever the magic-using equivalent was—around the tender new strand and drew on it, gently, slowly. Until Joh gasped with the slide of magic through him where he stood three paces away, inside their room. Nowhere near touching distance.

He turned, stared at her. Kallista smiled. She let the magic slip back into him, then eased it out again. His hand fumbled for the tabletop's support, and her smile went wicked.

Viyelle stared from one to the other of them. "What is it? What's happening?"

Obed moved Kallista away from the stair landing so he could pass. "She is playing with the magic."

Kallista plucked the cord that was Obed's link, staggering him with the pleasure. Staggering them both. "Don't complain, love, unless you want me to stop playing with yours." She sauntered into the room after him.

"I don't understand." Viyelle frowned. "Whose magic is she playing—"

"Mine," Joh interrupted her, taking the basket she held when she made no move to open it.

"But you're over here and she's—"

"The link has formed," Obed said. "Between Joh and Kallista. She can call his magic without touching. He can pass beyond yesterday's limit without collapse."

"Good." Torchay slid in through the window from the roof. "We've been waiting for that. We need someone who won't sweat off his disguise." He wiped away the brown droplets trickling down his forehead, leaving faint streaks of stain behind. The red of his hair was beginning to show through the brown.

Kallista plucked Torchay's magic hard, choking off his chuckle, then she released all three of them. They shared out the meal and sat down to eat. Breakfast and supper had been the only times lately when they were all together. They had tended to become planning sessions.

"Why do we need someone with a better disguise?" Kallista cut a bite off her slice of smoked pork and ate it.

"No disguise, actually," Torchay said with his mouth full. "Except maybe for tucking that oversized queue inside his shirt. Don't know why you won't let us cut it."

"Because. But I thought you and Obed have finished the Reinine's work."

"Mostly. There's a few bits more we could do, but what we have is enough."

"Well then?" Kallista glared at him. She wanted to flick a spark at him, but didn't want the conversation to degenerate. "I told you, I can follow the link to Fox."

"But if we don't have a plan, how will we get him out?"

"How did they all get us out of that Tibran prison? They didn't have a plan."

"Of a sort, we did," Obed said. "We also did not face demons. Nor were they prepared for us. And we knew where they had taken you before we went in."

Kallista slumped in her chair. "I need to do something. I feel useless." She sighed. "And we need to get the information you've gathered to the Reinine, in case something goes wrong."

"Call your sister," Torchay said. "Send her what we have and have her send it on to Arikon."

Karyl had *called* Kallista mind-to-mind that very first night. The conversation had disturbed Karyl so much they'd kept it short. Karyl should have been used to this sort of communication, but admittedly, a new farspeaker popping up at Kallista's age could be disturbing.

"I want it to go out overland as well," she said. "To be sure it reaches her."

"Of course." Torchay wolfed down the rest of his meal. "Just let me write down today's observations."

"Should I still go out tonight?" Obed watched them all, seeming idle, but Kallista could see the alertness behind the facade.

"To make contact with the boat master," Kallista said. The woman, like a number of others, still traded with royalist sectors of Adara. Their interest tended to be more in personal profit than in rulers or government, but this boat master had no fondness for the rebels. Kallista trusted her to get the papers into the hands of her contacts, if little further.

"Give me what you have." She took the stack of papers from Torchay, leaving him the last page for scribbling his additions. "I can start sending it to Karyl to relay on to Arikon."

"Can she do that?" Viyelle asked. "Talk to two at once?"

"Better than I can." Kallista called magic through her three local links. The addition of Joh's magic made the whole harder to move, not because his magic was more reluctant, but because it made it all somehow weightier. More.

It also snapped the connection with Karyl into place all the quicker, with an addition. She could see Karyl's dining room, see Kami and Deray clearing the dishes, as if she saw through Karyl's eyes.

*Wh-what are you doing, sister?* Karyl's mental voice sounded almost frightened.

*Speaking. Am I not doing it right? We discussed you sending the Reinine's farspeaker the information we collected, remember?*

*Yes, of course I remember, but*—Karyl paused for a steadying breath Kallista could somehow *hear* before *speaking* again. *I see your Torchay and your new iliasti with the remains of a meal on the table. Am—am I seeing through your eyes?*

Kallista turned to look at Obed near the window. *Now what do you see?*

*That staggeringly handsome dark ilias of yours.* Karyl paused. *Are you seeing through my eyes?*

*It's not all I see, but—as if I am looking through a small window, perhaps, yes. You're also finishing supper with your ilian.* Kallista rubbed her hands together with glee. *This will make the transfer of information very much easier.*

*It would, if I could pass the ability on to Fenetta in Arikon.*

*Maybe you can. Try.*

But the ability, rare and treasured among farspeakers, apparently stopped with Karyl. Kallista was left to stare for hours at page after page of information with Karyl's *voice* murmuring endlessly in her mind as she relayed the words to the far-distant Fenetta.

Obed had departed on his mission and returned again before Karyl read out the last page. *Fenetta says the Reinine orders your return to the capital as soon as possible.*

*Respect to the Reinine, but we will return as soon as we have gathered our ilian together again. We'll be of more service to her whole.* Kallista closed her burning eyes. *Karyl, be ready. You and yours need to get out of Turysh.*

*You have a plan?*

*Yes.* Kallista reasoned that it wasn't exactly a lie. They would have a plan sooner or later. *But be ready. There may be no time for plans when the time comes.*

*We will. Be careful.*

*We will.* Kallista cut the contact. It felt strange to be so alone inside her head again. Though she wasn't ever quite, completely alone. Not anymore.

She stroked along the fascinating new presence tucked in with the rest of the magic and felt Joh's shiver across her own skin. Had there been this fascination when the other links had formed? Would it be the same when Viyelle's link solidified?

Kallista couldn't find it in herself to care. Not at this moment, when Joh tugged at her like a fish on a hook. She tugged back, not sure which of them had hooked the other, and drew a strangled sound from him. She opened her eyes and saw him staring at her, an odd expression on his face combined of hope, disbelief and desire.

"Come, ilias," Torchay said.

In some distant corner of her awareness, Kallista knew he touched Obed's arm and tipped his head toward the larger of the two beds, the one near the window.

"No place for us there tonight." He gathered up Viyelle, turned her around and steered her away. Obed went with them, watching for a moment over his shoulder.

Kallista held her hand out to Joh. "Come, ilias." She deliberately repeated Torchay's words.

Joh had proved himself a hundred times over, doing whatever was needed when it was needed without argument or question. Or sulking or eye-rolling or smart-mouthed comments or picking a fight or— Goddess, she missed her Tibrans.

But Joh was Joh. It wasn't in his nature to argue or sulk. He tended to withdraw into himself, but it wasn't a sulking withdrawal. More like a protective gesture, almost as if he was afraid to want too much, to reach too far. It made Kallista want to give him whatever it was he wanted.

She crooked her fingers, beckoning, pulling on his magic as she did. Like a marionette, he came.

His braid hung forward over his shoulder. He'd spent the evening taking each page Kallista passed to him and copying it over in his small, neat hand using the code General Uskenda had given them. The code was based on the *Meditations of Orestes,* a book Joh knew well, and his writing was the neatest of any, so the job descended on him. Kallista could feel the ache in his back, the cramp in his hand—at a distance, not as if it were her own. She could also feel his rising desire.

"There is still another page to be copied and coded." He toyed with the quill in his hands, passed it from one to the other. "And all of it to be cleared away and hidden."

"The last page is trivia. You know it, as do I. And all of it is already hidden." She took the quill from him and set it on the table as he turned to look at the otherwise empty table top.

"When did—?" He looked back at her, bewildered.

"Our sergeant is very efficient. Just as our lieutenant is." Kallista picked up his heavy braid, running it through her hand till she reached the soft brush at the end.

"I'm not a lieuten—" He stopped when she put her fingers over his mouth.

"You're not a lieutenant in the Adaran army, true," she said. "But you're *our* lieutenant." She pulled free the tie that fastened his queue and loosened his hair, beginning at the bottom.

Joh cleared his throat. "Torchay is your second."

"Torchay is my bodyguard. And the father of my child. He is very important to me. But *you* are our lieutenant. Just as Viyelle is our courier and Obed is our merchant. You have your own place among us."

She turned him so she could reach the top of his braid, sliding her fingers through his hair to free it, stroking them along his head beneath. His rich brown hair fell to his waist when free of the queue, slightly crinkled from being braided when wet. She combed the shining mass with her fingers, spreading it out across his shoulders.

"And what is Stone? What is his role in this ilian?"

"I don't know. Our clown?" Kallista stepped close and put her arms around him from behind, hunting through the fall of hair to nuzzle his neck. "Do you really want to talk about the others now?"

She leaned into him, started them walking to the smaller bed, the one that stood empty most nights. Joh pulled her forward to his side and tucked her there against him.

"Truthfully? No, I do not." He paused beside the bed so long Kallista could almost feel him thinking through the link. She stroked her cheek over his hair, giving him the time he seemed to need.

"I suppose talking about the others is a way of learning what I want to know without having to ask," he said finally.

"Ask. You know you can ask me anything."

He turned to face her, brushed her unruly hair back off her forehead. "Why now? We have been bound for over a month. This could have happened at any time since then. It could wait another month. Or week, or year. Why now? What difference does this link make? Is it the link?"

Kallista sighed and sat on the edge of the bed, patting the mattress beside her. After a brief hesitation, Joh joined her. Kallista leaned into him and after another moment, he put his arm around her.

"You realize this requires thinking," Kallista said. "That's never been my best thing. It's one of *your* best things, but not mine. Are you sure you wouldn't rather just do sex?"

Joh almost choked on his chuckle. "Absolutely. Never think I'm willing to pass that up. But if I can have answers *and* sex, that's better."

He searched her face turned up to him for so long Kallista lost patience. She closed the tiny distance between them herself and kissed him. Immediately, his mouth opened and his tongue touched her lips, requesting entrance, demanding it. Delighted by the demand, Kallista opened to him, welcoming him in, following his retreat. They kissed, tongues dancing together in a simple, seductive pattern until Joh bore her down on the bed and began kissing his way down her neck.

"Greedy," Kallista teased, keeping her voice low, though it sounded as if those in the other bed weren't sleeping either. "No either-ors for you. You want both, don't you?"

"Don't *you*?" Joh raised onto an elbow to look down at her as his hand slipped under the hem of her tunic to find skin. A faint smile curved his lips, visible in the moonlight coming through the window. When had the lamps been blown out? Very efficient, their iliasti.

He seemed to be getting lost in his thinking again, so Kallista took action, stripping off his tunic and his trousers, pausing to admire him when his small clothes were gone. He smiled that calm little smile and let her look, lying on his back with his ankles crossed and one hand behind his head.

Or maybe he was still thinking. Her suspicions were confirmed when he spoke.

"You said thinking was one of my best things, but not yours." Joh caught her hand and pulled her down on top of him for a kiss that went on longer than he seemed to have intended.

"What if—" He paused, speaking with his mouth pressed to her forehead. "What if I help you sort it out?"

"Sort what out?" Kallista slid her hands across his chest, pausing to play in the puff of hair over his breastbone.

"Why now?" He tugged her tunic up but stopped halfway, apparently distracted by the feel of her back under his hands.

Kallista pushed herself up far enough to see his face. "Do you ever stop thinking?"

He flushed. She couldn't see it well in the moonlight, but she could feel his face burn, faintly, through the link. "Hardly ever," he admitted.

"I am trying to distract you." She rose to her knees to finish removing her tunic and chemise.

Joh helped, or tried to. "I know. Sorry. I've never been very distractible. I just—I want to know."

"Why now?" Kallista lay beside him again and rolled to her back to get her trousers and smalls off. Joh was more help this time.

"*Does* the link make the difference?"

She sighed. He was obviously not going to leave this alone, so she might as well answer his questions—even if she didn't quite know what the answers were. But she was not about to give up her campaign to distract him. She'd always enjoyed a challenge. She would even play fair and keep the magic out of it. As much as she could.

"Yes," she said. "It does."

"How?" He shivered when her fingers found his nipples and pinched. "Does it create a physical awareness, or is it just— what does it feel like?"

Now she paused, turning inward to test, to probe, to measure.

Joh's lips skimming across her shoulder distracted her, made her shiver and arch upward, begging for more. His hand settled warm and still on her stomach, over her navel. "Tell me," he murmured, his breath warming her ear.

"It's like—a tiny piece of you curled up safe inside me." Kallista's fingers dug into his shoulders, tangled in his hair as he kissed his way down the upper slope of her breasts. "So yes, there is a physical awareness. I can feel what you're feeling, in a way. And you're new, so I'm not used to it yet."

He pressed a kiss at the margin where her breast changed from white to pink. "Like a new toy at Year's End?"

She twisted, brushing her nipple against his cheek, wanting more. "Yes. But no. That's part of it, but—" She caught his head between her hands and tried to move it where she wanted him, but Joh wouldn't move.

He caught her wrists and pinned them to the bed,

continuing his leisurely exploration. Just who was distracting whom, here?

"What's the rest of it? A new toy and—what?" Finally, finally his mouth closed over her nipple.

Kallista's whole body reacted, jerking into a high arc, and she cried out. Her hands convulsed where he held them helpless, curling into claws that would have marked him had she been able to reach him.

"What?" He moved to her other breast and she cried out again, unable to keep from tweaking the magic inside her. Joh's gasp echoed from other throats.

"Mine," she said before she could think. "You're mine now." She struggled for control, to grasp one magic and leave the others to themselves.

"I always was." Joh released one wrist to smooth a hand down over her stomach.

She used the freedom to touch him, memorize the shape of his shoulder, play in his hair. "It's different now. You're part of me. Wherever you go, whatever you do, I'll know it. No matter how far you might run, I still have you with me. Here."

She set his hand on the lower reach of her stomach, just above the tangle of black hair where her skin showed a few pinkish marks left by her twins.

"Is this where we live?" Joh curled down to kiss her navel, to kiss the places his hand covered. "No wonder the magic feels like it does."

He made as if to move lower and Kallista stopped him. "Another time." She wrapped her hand around him. "I want you inside me."

Joh groaned and collapsed, pulling himself from her hold, his face pressed against her belly. "I'll never last."

"Yes you will." She caught a fistful of hair and lifted his head until he looked her in the eye. "I won't let you fail."

He shivered. "That's almost a frightening thought."

She wanted to shake him. Wanted much more. "Do you want this?"

"Do you?"

Patience stripped from her, Kallista took hold of him with both hands and magic. She brought him up over her, wrapped her legs around his waist, and when she felt the blunt head at her entrance, she lunged upward, impaling herself on him.

"Don't ask—stupid—questions." She gasped the words out between clenched teeth.

Joh seemed at last to be beyond thought. He froze motionless for a few ticks, then exploded into a near frenzy. The bed rocked, banging into the wall with the force of his thrusts. Kallista rose to meet him, her passion as fierce as his. Strange sounds emerged from his throat, others came from hers. She held tight to his magic as the sensation built. He touched her deep and deep and deep again. Her body seemed too small to hold all he made her feel, until she screamed with the pleasure he drove into her.

She lost her grip on the magic and he shouted. His body shook as he poured himself into her. His hair fell in a curtain to either side of her face, hiding them in a private world of their own, until he lowered himself carefully onto her. "I'll move in a bit."

"Don't bother." Kallista had strength enough to stroke her hands up and down his back. She needed to touch him more, know this body by heart. "I like you there. For a while longer, at least."

"Then I'll stay." He turned his head so his lips rested against her cheek. "For a while longer, at least."

"Did you learn what you wanted to know?" She found a scar, a long thin one slanting across his lower back. A riot in Kishkim, she thought he'd said.

"Yes."

"Really?" She pushed him back to see his face and he slid off to one side. "I thought I'd managed to distract you."

He smiled. "You did. Very well."

"But you got your answer anyway."

His smile went smug. Joh tucked her into his shoulder so she couldn't see him. Probably best. She didn't want to get mad over a silly thing like smugness. "Yes," he said. "I did."

"Well, what was it?" She didn't mind him knowing, but it was annoying not to know it herself.

"You're sure of me now." He kissed her forehead and left his mouth there, speaking against her skin. "I'd never have left you before, but now I'm part of you. I'm the same as the others, so you're sure."

Kallista frowned. She didn't think she liked his reasoning. It made her sound insecure. Needy.

Joh's arms tightened around her and he kissed her again on her forehead, then used his straight blade of a nose to brush her hair aside and kiss her temple. "And if you're sure of me," he murmured against her ear, "then I can be sure of you."

She wanted to pull back to look at him, but Joh kept his hold tight. She'd been treating him like some mechanical, wind-up thing, she realized. Because he was easier than the others, because he did what was needed without being asked and made no demands, she'd been able to ignore him. To pretend he didn't have his own needs or even emotions.

She couldn't do it anymore. He was inside her, part of her like the others, but still himself apart, like the others. She couldn't pretend anymore. She held six links inside her now, with one yet to be formed. Could she manage so many? How many more would there be? Was there a way to find out?

Kallista snuggled down into Joh's arms, wriggling her head across his shoulder until she found a comfortable place and went still. Sleep stole her thoughts a moment later.

* * *

Torchay took Joh out spying with him the very next morning. He showed him all the safe paths and the hidden ways back to their quarters, then took him to the trade sector around the Mother Temple. They returned well before dusk, tumbling down the steep stairs to the stables below their room, bringing Obed awake with sword in hand.

"Peace, ilias. It's only us." Torchay drank a dipper of water from the bucket hanging on its nail, then poured a dipperful over his head. Brown rivulets trickled down his neck as he passed the dipper to Joh, leaving his hair brighter.

"One day out and he's found our missing ilias," Torchay announced. He waited for Joh to finish drinking before pounding him on the back in celebration.

"You've found him? *Where?*" Kallista bounded over the sacks of grain she'd been stacking to throw herself at Joh. He caught her in midair and swung her around in a bear hug.

"Near the Mother Temple." Torchay looked around the stable, the horses standing hip slung in the rising heat, and led the way into a vacant stall. "You were right, Kallista. They were holding him there."

"I told you I could feel—"

"They weren't *holding* him." Joh watched her face as he said it, his words, his tone careful. "He was walking free. With the rebels, like one of them." He licked his lips, never moving his eyes from Kallista.

"You're sure it was Fox?" Kallista looked at Torchay. "Joh's never met him."

"I saw him myself. It was Fox." Torchay's face had become as careful as Joh's. "He did seem very comfortable with the rebels. They were loitering in the plaza on the south side of the Temple."

What weren't they telling her? She knew they held something back simply by the way they held themselves. "How comfortable?"

Torchay sighed. "Very. One of the women…" He trailed off, as if not sure how to phrase his meaning.

"He wore her like a cloak," Joh said.

"Yes." Torchay nodded. "That describes it. She acted as if he was her personal property. Her pet."

Kallista took a deep breath, but it wasn't needed to control her temper. Fox was hers—*theirs*—and anyone who pretended otherwise would pay. But her rightful anger was overridden by fear. What had they done to him? Why was his link closed off so tightly? Why couldn't she reach him when he was here in the same city?

"I have to see him." It was the only solution.

## CHAPTER TWENTY

"Kallista, *no*." That was Obed.

"We won't risk you," Torchay said at the same moment.

"That wasn't the plan." Joh still watched her, had never stopped. "You don't see him until we're ready to leave Turysh. Are we ready?"

"Maybe you could see him through your sister's eyes," Viyelle said. "Like you did last night."

Kallista was shaking her head already. "No, they know Karyl. They're already watching her. We don't want to make them any more suspicious."

"But would it work?" Viyelle insisted.

"I don't know. I've never been able to do that before. I don't know if I could see what needs seeing."

"Well, what is that? What is it you need to see?" Torchay sounded on the edge of his infinite patience.

"Demons. I need to see—" Kallista hugged herself. "He's been property before. When he lost his caste, they made him nothing, and he survived. He knows how to survive. Maybe that's all this is. Trying to survive by playing a part."

"But if it's not?" Torchay's voice gentled, offered sympathy.

"That's why I need to see him." Kallista held on to her composure with both hands. "I need to see if the demon succeeded. I know it tried to take him over. But I don't know anything more. I can't get through the link. It's there, but Fox—or something—has shut it down. I didn't know it was possible, for the link to keep me out. Belandra told me I couldn't close them off. But it is and I need to know why. For that, I need to see him."

"What if you could see through our eyes?" Joh spoke hesitantly, gesturing between the three men. "You can heal us. You can contact us across leagues of distance. Maybe you can farspeak through us as well, not just to other farspeakers."

"I haven't been able to *speak* to our other iliasti, except through dreams." Kallista was afraid to hope. But now that the idea had been broached, Torchay would never let her go see Fox unless they had tried—*really* tried—this method.

"They're much farther away," Joh said. "It should be easier, since we're closer."

"Try it," Torchay said.

How had she done it with Karyl? Kallista drew magic and realized that, if she could do it at all, it should be easier than with Karyl. Not only were all her iliasti in the same room with her, they were already connected to her. Viyelle reached out, offering her magic.

"No, Viyelle, don't touch me. I want to do it with their magic alone, because they're the ones I'll be seeing through." Kallista *reached*, asking the magic to *see*.

There was a long moment of confusion. Her vision blurred, then cleared. She was looking at the same stall in the same stable with the same people looking back at her. Then she realized that a faint shadow image overlaid the other.

She concentrated on the shadows, and slowly they solidified, overshadowing the other view. Still the same stall in the same stable, but now she was herself in the center of the field of view. Whose eyes did she look through?

Kallista struggled to refocus her vision, to pull other shadows up and over, and was looking through her own eyes again. She tried once more to pull up a third view, but apparently there were only two: hers and one other.

"I can see through one of you," she said, blinking as she switched again to the other sight. The change was getting smoother with practice, but was still an effort. "But you're all three standing so close together, I can't tell whose eyes they are."

Three heads turned, swinging as they looked at each other. The motion dizzied Kallista and she closed her eyes. It didn't block what she *saw*, and it helped with the dizziness.

"Joh," she said. "I can see Torchay and Obed, so it's Joh's eyes I see from." She paused. "That makes sense. Joh's magic has…vision. Clarity of understanding." She saw herself again as Joh turned to face her. Kallista grappled with the magic, slid back into her own sight and let the magic go.

"I thought Obed's magic had truth," Torchay said.

"Knowing what is true doesn't always help, if you don't understand it." She closed her eyes, pressing her fingers against them. The magic didn't affect them physically, but still they ached. "Did it affect your sight, Joh? Could you feel me there?"

He shook his head. "I could tell you were using magic, but nothing else. Should I go back to the plaza now?"

Kallista judged the light. Hours yet till sunset. The sooner they found Fox and she could know whether demons held him, the sooner they could get him out of that place and retrieve the rest of their ilian.

"If he is taken," Torchay spoke before she could. "What will you do?"

"Take him back." She glowered at her bodyguard. "Do you expect me to leave him in the power of that thing?"

"Did I say that?" He gave her scowl for scowl. "But they have likely left the square by now. We'll have to hunt and find him again. By the time we do—*if* we do—it could be late. I know you, Kallista. You may say 'I only want to see him,' but the instant you do, you'll want to act. And we're not ready."

"We could be ready," Obed said. "The horses are rested. Our supplies are replenished. We need only to put them together."

Torchay turned his scowl on Obed. "You're no' helping."

"If I stay here and just look through Joh's eyes, I won't be able to act. I'll be here." Kallista couldn't bear the thought of waiting longer to rescue him, but she would do it. She would try anyway.

Torchay's expression didn't change. She didn't expect it to. She knew him too well. Just as he knew her.

"I don't trust you to stay here unless I'm here to sit on you myself," he said.

"Fine. Stay. Go. Stand on your head. I don't care." Kallista shoved past Joh toward the stall door. She would not let them see her tears.

Torchay caught her, held her. "Don't get your hair on so tight. We'll work it out."

In the end, they did. Joh would go back to the temple square near dusk. Obed would follow as backup and guide, in case Joh got lost in the unfamiliar city or ran into other trouble. Torchay would stay behind to sit on Kallista, and help Viyelle with the evening feed while Kallista rode Joh's vision into the city center and veiled their magic from demonsight.

When Joh got back to the Mother Temple square, walking as quickly as he could without drawing notice, the tall, yellow-haired man was gone. If he'd retreated inside the temple or the temple house, Joh doubted he could be found. But the man Torchay had identified as Fox had the look of someone out for a good time. Joh had hopes.

He scanned the square. Turysh's Mother Temple was built on the same plan as all others, in a square four-petaled shape with wings extending in each of the cardinal directions and a high-roofed sanctuary in the center. At most temples, each wing was fronted by a plaza, but at this Mother Temple, the plazas spread to either side, each melting into the next, making a huge hollow square of pavement, with gardens filling in the spaces between wings.

The earlier population of young parents and small children mixed with merchants striding purposefully through or gathering in small close-bunched clusters had given way to gangs of boisterous young women on the stroll. Ordinarily they would meet up with swarms of equally young off-duty soldiers to flirt and show off. Joh knew the pattern, had once been one of those soldiers, but soldiers were thin on the ground tonight. The girls talked and laughed and indulged in mild horseplay, but it was obvious they just went through the motions. Joh didn't think they would linger long.

The temple's golden stone paled in the harsh, late-afternoon sunlight. The workday had ended for most, but the sun would linger. Probably longer than the young women on the hunt. One of them gave him a long, speculative look until she glanced down and saw the anklets. Joh was suddenly glad Kallista had removed the *di pentivas* chains. They were more noticeable than his long braid.

*What are you waiting for?* Kallista whispered in his mind.

Joh somehow managed not to jump out of his skin. *Suggestions,* he thought back at her, though he doubted she could hear. This was her magic, not his, even if he did carry it.

He turned away from the temple to scan the buildings around the south plaza. Here, where they'd seen Fox, temple housing spread across most of the south side. A few shops, selling scholarly things like ink, paper and books, and a few more sweet shops, all catering to the south-side school, finished off his surroundings.

*The taverns are to the east,* Kallista murmured, making him jump.

Would he ever get used to it, her voice in his head? He was beginning to think not. She'd been whispering to him since he left the stable and nothing had changed yet. He turned his back on the sun and walked through the square of garden—trees, flowers and grass—planted in the shelter of the temple's east and south wings.

One of the taverns sprawled along much of the eastside square, rising high in the center where it offered rooms for travelers with business either in the bustling trade center or with the local prinsep whose palace rose a short distance to the north. Though Turysh's prinsep had escaped to Arikon.

The tea shop and dining room on one end was filled with dignified, richly dressed customers visible through the multipaned glass windows. The boisterous clientele of the alehouse on the opposite end had already begun to spill out onto the plaza. Joh paused only a moment before heading toward the convivial company drinking at the tables lining the plaza's edge.

Kallista's Fox wasn't visible outside the alehouse. At one of the wide doors, opening the front of the building to the plaza, Joh glanced back and saw Obed with his drover's hat pulled low, the hip-length drover's cloak thrown back to expose his bare arms. He was watching. Joh had abandoned his drover's disguise for the night, though with his Filornish accent, he doubted it would matter.

*Are you never going inside?*

Joh hid his reaction to Kallista's whisper in his plunge through the door. The enormous windowless room—the better to cut down on glass replacement costs—thronged with people, but the bright gold of Fox's short-cropped hair caught Joh's eye instantly.

*His hair,* Kallista keened through his mind. *He cut his hair. Why?*

He had done it today, in the time since Joh had last seen him. Then, Fox's curls had tumbled to his shoulders. Now, it was shorter than Joh had seen on any man who could grow hair, cut so close on the sides that his scalp showed through, and no more than the length of a finger-joint on top. The longer hair still curled.

*Can you see what you need to?* Joh hoped she could hear him. He felt exposed standing near the door.

Though the late-day sun slanted in through the openings, it was dark farther inside. His eyes finally adjusted to the dim smoky light and he edged through the crowd in the general direction of the central bar.

*I can't tell.*

No startling this time. Maybe he *was* getting used to it.

*Can you get closer?* Was there an edge of desperation to her whisper? Joh hoped Torchay was holding her tight.

He paused at the bar for a pint. Why else would a lone man enter an alehouse? Then he began working his way across to the area where Fox sat, the same woman draped possessively over him. She was attractive—brown waves of hair falling past her shoulders, pale Adaran skin, full lips in a natural pout, generous curves. She didn't compare to Kallista, of course, but he could see how some would be caught by her.

The tavern was crowded, but not with the young soldiers the wandering girls were looking for. These men, slightly outnumbering the women present, were older. Harder. Many of them, both men and women, wore the brown, scarlet-lined cloaks of the middle levels of Barinirab. They made Joh nervous.

He sat at an empty spot at the end of the table where Fox's woman held court and took a long draft of his ale. She was the focus, not Fox. Her words garnered rapt attention. Her quips

brought on boisterous laughter. Her smiles reaped preening satisfaction at her approval. She had to be high—very high—in
the rebel organization. Joh took the opportunity to study Fox,
trying to see whatever Kallista sought.

"I know you."

The words floated past Joh as he drank again, until he realized that the table's occupants had gone silent and everyone was
looking at him.

Carefully, he swallowed, licked the foam from his upper lip
and set down the tankard. "Are you speaking to me?"

"Yeah." The burly Rejuvenate, hair cropped as short as Fox's,
stared fixedly at Joh. "But how do I know you?" A frown appeared and grew, sealing his eyebrows into a single unit. "You're
in the army."

"I was." Keep to the truth as much as possible. Fewer lies to
remember that way. "I'm not anymore."

"That's it." The man stabbed a finger at Joh. "You're that lieutenant, the one that blew up the palace last year. I want to shake
your hand."

He leaned across the intervening drinkers, extending his
meaty, callused hand. Joh took it, squeezed and released. All
the attention made him decidedly uncomfortable, especially
since he'd once been one of them. A Barb.

"Didn't they send you to Katreinet?"

"I got out." Joh took refuge in his ale again. *Kallista,* he
thought desperately. *Do you have what you need?* "Just over a
month ago."

"I thought you'd been sentenced to a life term." The woman
beside Fox spoke.

"I was." He shrugged. "They pulled a lot of the guards after
the assassinations. It was easy to get out."

The woman's smile made Joh's skin crawl. "The Night of Justice changed many things." She extended a hand, whether in-

tending him to shake it or kiss it, Joh couldn't tell. He gave it a brief squeeze.

"I am Oskina," she said. "And you are Joh Suteny, Hero of Truth."

He hid his wince. He was no hero—of truth or anything else. He certainly didn't deserve the title for nearly killing three who were now his iliasti, who meant more to him than anyone in this world. He looked again at Fox. "And who is this?"

"Jealous?" Oskina's leering flirtation made Joh nauseous. She ran her hand along Fox's bare arm, making a point of feeling his muscle. "He's my little pet. A casteless Tibran."

*Tibran.* Yes, he knew that. Fox was a Tibran name. Joh was too nervous to think properly. He'd never been much good at spying.

"The casteless ones are so delicious," Oskina purred. "They know what they're worth. They don't protest anything."

"I thought all Tibrans were casteless these days." Joh kept his voice mild and hopefully inoffensive.

She tipped her head, granting the truth of his words. "But this one is special. He's blind. He lost his caste before the Destruction."

Blind? *Why didn't you tell me?* He hurled the thought at Kallista, not expecting her to catch it.

*I forgot.* She did hear him. *Are you sure we didn't?*

Joh couldn't swear that she hadn't, so he ignored her question. *How could you forget a thing like blindness?*

*Because he doesn't act blind. He moves like one who can see. He can see, after a fashion.*

Fox reached tentatively for the tankard set in front of him, sliding his hand across the tabletop till he touched it, then fumbling for the handle. Just as he found it, one of the rebels snatched it from his grasp and moved it a small distance away, forcing him to grope for it again.

*He can?* Joh put all his skepticism in the thought, hiding his anger at the cruel game behind his own tankard.

Kallista's worry flooded down the link between them. *Something's wrong. He's not like that. Or he wasn't before.*

*Demons?*

*I don't know. I can't see.* The worry crescendoed into fear before it was cut off, sucked back through the link. *I can only see what you see.*

*And I can't see demons.* Joh watched as Fox found a tankard—his own, as it happened—and wrapped both hands around it. He pulled it back in front of himself, not bothering with the handle as he drank from it.

*I'm coming down there.* Determination rang through Kallista's thought.

*Don't.* He wanted to scream at her, to warn Torchay, and all he could do was sit and smile at the small woman running her hands over his ilias. *Please. Don't. It's under control. We're fine, as long as you don't turn up and create a scene.*

He could sense motion through the link. Scuffling? He felt the sensual pull of magic and tried to stop it, but feared a backlash. *Kallista, stop. You're not helping matters.*

*That's what Torchay says.* She sounded out of breath, even in his mind.

*Torchay is right. Listen to him.*

*Get out of there.* Major Varyl was giving orders now. *I've seen enough. We'll regroup and be ready tomorrow.*

More than ready to obey this command, Joh drained his tankard and stood.

"Ready for more?" Oskina looked up from her fondling and shoved her tankard toward him. "Good. Bring drinks all round."

Joh lifted it and gathered more mugs in both hands. It was needful to tread with light steps. "Gladly," he lied. "But then I must go. Others wait for me."

"Who?" Oskina pouted. It wasn't pretty. "You just left prison last month. Or have you found entertainment here already?"

"My ilian." That much was truth. Now he had to assemble a few lies to go with it. "My parents found it for me when I went home to Filorne." He shrugged. "Why not marry? They can hide me if the Reinine comes looking for me. They're waiting for me."

Anger flitted across Oskina's face. No, not anger. Rage. Dark, ugly rage. At his modest defiance? Then it was gone, her face as beautiful as before. "I don't want you to go. Stay. Send word to your ilian. Invite them to join us. I'd like to meet them."

A shudder crawled down Joh's spine. He didn't want his ilian anywhere near this woman. *Kallista?* He needed help. How could he avoid this?

"They're camped outside the city tonight." Joh scrambled for plausible excuses. "I doubt a messenger could find them— without myself along as escort, at any rate."

"Stay with us tonight. I insist." She would not allow any escape. Her attitude was as clear as it was implacable. She would give him no choice.

*Kallista, are you there?* Joh screamed it into silence, but she had left him. He had no way to communicate the situation to her. He bowed. "Thank you for the courtesy."

He could only hope she would honor the bands he wore round his ankles. If she decided against it, he was afraid to object. This Oskina would not take his resistance well, and he feared what she might do in reaction. He hefted the tankards in his hands and headed for the bar, trying to think past his panic.

Obed had worked his way inside, leaning his elbows on the bar, nursing a nearly full mug of ale. Joh squeezed in beside him and delivered his load to be filled.

"Kallista's left me," he murmured, watching the barkeep at his task.

"Then we should leave this place."

"I can't. That woman insists I stay, and she apparently has the power to make me do it."

Obed swore, long and fluently. Joh didn't understand the words, but the tone was clear. He would have liked to join in, but didn't know the barkeep's loyalties.

"Go back. Tell Kallista, quick as you can. I need her back." He needed to be able to communicate, but more, he needed her presence in the back of his mind. Kallista might be able to sense him at all times, but he was only aware of her when she drew magic and when she'd been riding his sight. Right now, as Obed drank up and departed, Joh felt very, very alone.

He gathered the mugs, heavier now they were filled. A barmaid took the extras and followed him back to the table. The woman Oskina made a place for him beside her and reluctantly, under the scowls of the displaced, Joh took it. The tankards were handed round and he drank, deeper when he felt Oskina's hand slide up his thigh.

It curved around to the inside and edged higher, when he broke. He couldn't do this, couldn't pretend with a woman who left him so cold. Who frightened him somehow. He stopped her hand. "Please, Aila. I am married."

"And this matters—why?" She refused to remove her hand, but didn't push it farther.

"I am a man who prefers to keep his vows. I know this is something the Order values, though I am only a lowly Renunciate."

"As an Ascendant, I can release you from your vows." She squeezed. Joh twitched.

*Not bloody likely.* He was master of his own vows. What he made, he kept, unless they were broken on the other side, as his Barinirab oath had been. There was no keeping faith with liars.

Joh drank deep to hide his discomfort, thinking. He had to slow down on the ale if he wanted to keep his wits clear.

"Flattered as I am by your attentions, Oskina Aila, I must confess that I prefer—" Goddess, was he mad?

She could have him killed. Could kill him herself, or worse, given where her hand was. And no one here would lift a finger to stop her. Would likely assist her. Especially if they knew the truth of who he was now and his purpose here.

"You prefer men?" She moved abruptly to grope his quiescent privates, startling—*terrifying*—Joh, then withdrew her hand. "Would you rather play with my pet than with me?" She pretended to pout—though Joh was not entirely sure it was all pretense. "Is that why you do not rise?"

Joh pushed his mug aside. He wanted to drink it so badly he didn't dare. "Aila," he began. "Great lady—"

"I had not heard that about you, Joh Suteny. That you are a lover of men."

Could this get him out of betraying his ilian with the awful woman? "As a male commissioned officer in the Adaran army, I had to be absolutely above reproach." He sought his way as he spoke. "Female officers are often accused of using the regular troops and conscripts as their private hunting preserve. Truth for many of them. I did not dare take the risk." There. Every word truth, but she could take it as she liked.

"Mmm." She continued to eye him speculatively. "It is true that I have not heard you are a lover of anyone, man or woman. Are you gelding then?"

She enjoyed taunting him, Joh knew. He could see it in her eyes, in the way she licked those red, pouting lips. He did not want to drive her to rage, but would placating her work any better?

"My ilian knows the truth of that, Aila." He would try to walk a middle road.

"And how many men to women does your ilian hold, Joh Suteny? Is it my pet you desire?"

"It is a man-heavy ilian, Great Lady." Possibilities had burst upon him. Opportunity he should have seen earlier, would have seen but for all the ale. Could he separate her from Fox this way? "And your pet is everything I desire in this place."

Again truth, though he probably should not have qualified the statement. Maybe she wouldn't pick up on the tiny insult.

"You would break your vows for him, but not for me?" Oskina pretended to pout again. This time the pretense seemed purer.

"Oskina Aila, what can I say?" Joh spread his hands and tried an inoffensive smile. Fox was ilias. They had spoken no vows to each other yet, but the bonds were still there. He would be keeping vows, not breaking them.

"Come. Sit there." She scooted toward him, making a tiny space on the other side. She pulled Fox into the space to leave the gap on the Tibran's far side. "I have not tried him with a man yet. It could be…interesting."

Suddenly nervous, Joh stood. She did not mean them to go so far here, did she? Joh was truly not a lover of men. Was he a good enough actor to pretend?

On the other hand, Fox *was* ilias, and although Joh preferred women—his own women in particular and by far—he had no personal aversion to showing affection for his ilias in a physical manner. Even if this ilias was a stranger to him. He did have an aversion to Oskina and to the lack of privacy.

Joh squeezed back in next to Fox. Those displaced earlier made smug displays of superiority at regaining their position nearer Oskina. He ignored them, as did she. Instead, she took Fox by the chin and turned him to face her. She kissed him openmouthed.

Fox did not passively allow the kiss as Joh thought he might, given his silent submission to everything that had occurred thus far. He kissed her back, lips, mouth, jaw working as if he would swallow her down. He didn't touch her. His hands lay idle in his lap. But he kissed her.

Oskina broke away, laughing, her eyes glittering with something Joh did not like. "Your turn," she said.

To kiss…? Joh let his lips curve in a smile, hoping it wasn't as ugly as it felt. "I generally prefer more privacy for such things."

Her face changed, went feral, vicious, lips pulling back from oddly sharp teeth. She looked somehow not quite human, and it made Joh lean away as she hissed. "I have given your preferences all the consideration I care to give. Kiss him. Kiss my pet. If he cannot please you, perhaps I will decide he no longer pleases me. Perhaps I will discard him."

*Discard*—what did that mean? Imprisonment? Death? Or merely casting him aside? Did she know more than it seemed? Did she know Joh would act sooner on a threat to Fox than himself? How?

*"Kiss him."* Oskina licked her lips, eager avidity in her expression. Did she want to see a kiss, or Joh's self-destruction? Did she care which? Joh rather thought not.

He took Fox by the chin as she had and turned him. He was a handsome man with his bright hair and sculptured features. Joh understood why Kallista valued him, apart from his magic. How would Fox react to this kiss? Joh wished he knew. For himself, it was the watchers that disturbed him most, one more than any.

Joh shifted his hand, covering the exposed mark on the back of the other man's neck to hold him in place, and leaned in. Just before their mouths touched, he breathed a word. "Ilias."

Fox jerked, whether in reaction to the word, or to the kiss, or to something unknown, Joh could not guess. He could only hold on and kiss.

It felt strange, yet strangely familiar. Not so different from kissing a woman, save for the faint scrape of beard stubble against his skin. Then something happened. Some kind of resonance between them, or a recognition of like to like—ilias to ilias. It wasn't Kallista's sweet call of magic, but it was... something.

It tightened Joh's hand on Fox's neck and sent his tongue thrusting into the mouth that opened to receive it. It had them fighting to drink each other down, to roll in that recognition, wallow in the resonance.

The tavern faded away. The only thing in the world was the mouth under his and the thing that sang between them.

Joh had no idea how much time passed while they kissed. Time had no meaning or existence, until Fox began to pull away. Joh held him tighter, clinging to the connection. Fox was struggling, not to pull back, but to continue the kiss. He struggled against the pull, against someone else pulling him.

There were others in the room. Others watching them. Others intruding on this moment of knowing, this—Joh didn't know what to call it, even what it was, but it was too important to share. He let Fox go, let that woman tug him away.

"I can see why you asked for privacy." Oskina watched his face so closely, Joh worried what it showed. "I would ask you to kiss me that way, but I fear you failing and that would wound my pride so severely I might do something I would regret."

His breathing was better. Not under control, but better. Joh risked speech. "I would leave you with no regrets, Aila."

Fox had his face turned toward Joh, for all the world as if he could see him. It was disturbing.

"I want to watch," Oskina said. "I want to watch you take him."

Joh recoiled. He hoped he hid it. The thought gagged him. Not so much the watching by itself—he'd watched his iliasti make love just as they had watched him, with Viyelle and

Kallista both, he was sure. Nor was it her choice of partner for him, not so much anymore. Maybe it was the magic that made the difference. Maybe it was only the bonds of ilian, but the thought of touching this man in such a way seemed at least possible. But not in front of this woman.

How could he turn her aside from her purpose?

Joh damned the ale he'd consumed. He needed to think, needed to find the right words, the ones that would change her mind.

Oskina laughed, sending a chill down Joh's spine. "I can see your busy mind whirring, but in which direction? You cannot tell me you do not want to taste such bounty."

She caught a fistful of Fox's short curls and tipped his face up, putting him on display. Then her eyes narrowed. "Nor do you want to deny me my pleasure."

*Think.* Joh tried. "Great Lady, it is not that I *wish* to deprive you of anything. But I have never been able to—to perform well with an audience."

Her eyes went to tiny slits. "You're married."

"Recently. After a lifetime of keeping such things hidden."

"You hide from your own ilian?"

Joh shrugged. Better not to answer. With luck, she would assume what he wished her to.

"I don't believe you."

He shrugged again. He no longer knew how to argue. Though he did know he did not want this Oskina watching him do anything. He wanted to be far, *far* away from her. And Fox with him.

She tossed off the last of her ale and slammed the tankard down on the table. "Drink up."

She set Joh's half-empty mug in front of him and put Fox's tankard to his mouth. He took it from her and drank, swallowing it all down at once. His throat stretched, working, and Joh realized he stared at that smooth, strong line. What was happening to him?

He finished off what was in his mug, regretting the necessity. He needed a clear head now, and he feared the need would only grow stronger.

## TWENTY-ONE

Kallista was curled limp over the table in their over-the-stable room while Torchay pressed his thumbs hard into her shoulder muscles. He wasn't as good as Obed at this Southron massage, but she ached so after a week of mucking stables that she didn't care. Of course, he'd only offered to stop her pacing while waiting for Obed and Joh to return.

She pressed her own thumbs into her eyes, trying gently to relieve the ache there. Seeing through another's vision for so long not only made her eyes ache, it made her dizzy and headachy. The pacing hadn't helped, but she'd been unable to keep still while waiting. Until Torchay's offer.

"Better?" He worked his way from her shoulders up her stiff neck.

"I will be when they get back."

A sliding clatter outside the window announced their approach. Kallista came instantly alert. She stood as Obed spilled through the opening.

"They've taken him," he said between gasping breaths.

"Who? Joh? *Who's* taken him?"

Obed sank down on the end of the bed, chest heaving. He'd

been running a while. The whole way back? "Call him. That woman would not let him go. They recognized him."

*"As marked?"* Alarm skittered through Kallista, crashing through her attempt to reconnect with Joh's vision.

"No." Obed shook his head, hair flying. "No, as—as the one who nearly killed you, I think. They were shaking his hand, patting his back."

"Good. Then surely they won't suspect." She prayed so. Quickly. While she checked that the veiling still held. It did.

Viyelle's hand slid cautiously over Kallista's elbow, offering comfort as well as magic. Or perhaps she sought comfort. Viyelle had been with Joh more than Kallista had. She touched the younger woman's hand in thanks for the magic. "It will be well." She offered them both reassurance.

Kallista drew, taking magic from all those close, and threw it out, seeking the other magic that was hers. It flew unerringly to Joh and latched on with a silent clang, as if *pentivas* bracelets had just locked down.

Her will shaped the magic and it slid inside Joh like fog through an open window, following the spaces where his magic lived. She hugged him to her, breathing kisses on his soul, and he shivered, physically.

*Kallista?*

"Are you cold? On such a lovely summer's night?" The melodious voice grated along Kallista's hearing.

*I'm here.* She stroked along his magic.

*What do I do?* Joh sounded more than half-panicked. He tasted faintly drunk. What was happening there? *Kallista, help me. Help us.*

Joh's panic bled into Kallista. She *reached* for his vision, needing to see, but could bring up no more than vague shadows and hints of movement. He was too afraid. That wasn't like Joh. What was going on?

*Joh.* She slapped at his magic to break him free of his fear. *Joh, relax. Let me in. I need to see.*

*You can't?* Horror edged the panic a moment, then he fought it back. *Maybe that's a good thing.*

*No, Joh. I need to see. Let go. Give yourself over to me.* Could he trust her so much? Heaven knew Kallista doubted her own ability to trust like that.

One more instant, he held himself together, then all at once he let go, falling into her magical embrace. She caught him, kissed him, slid his vision over hers as she kept him safe. *Mine,* she whispered to him. *Ours.*

Then she opened his eyes. She stood in a room she recognized as one of the ilian bedrooms in the Mother Temple's house. She'd been in it more times than she could count when she was growing up. Temple children tended to run tame at all the temple houses in the same city, and one of her best friends had been a child of the Mother Temple. It hadn't changed much, save for a fresh coat of purple paint on the walls and a white coverlet on the bed.

She noticed those things peripherally, because the center of Joh's vision was filled with Fox bending over as he stripped out of the last of his clothes and stood, naked.

Joh's line of sight drifted upward, toward Fox's face. Kallista didn't object. She drank in the sight of her long absent ilias. He looked so much better now, well-fed and muscular rather than the gaunt near-skeleton he'd been when he found them last year, despite his recent injury.

*Is he healed?* She couldn't help asking.

Joh immediately looked at the long red scar running down Fox's left leg.

"What do you think of my pet?" The woman's voice sounded distant—echoing and tinny.

*No,* Kallista murmured. *That one is old, from Ukiny.* But his thigh looked better than before, not hollowed out and misshapen as it had before the surgery. *There should be a more recent injury. On his back, I think.*

Joh moved, walking toward Fox. Kallista took a deep breath and laid her hands flat on the table. She'd suffered very little from seasickness last year on their ocean journeys, even pregnant as she was. But riding Joh's sight as he moved threatened to bring it on more than any ocean storm. She closed her own eyes to see through only his and pulled a bit more magic. That seemed to help.

Joh walked around Fox as if on morning inspection in the ranks. Likely the pretense helped him cope, for she sensed his panic retreating. There, a hollow scar at midback, no more than a finger's length and width, it bore the deep purple coloration of a still-healing wound. Another, smaller lay not far from it.

"What's this?" Joh touched it. Kallista tried to feel it with his fingers, merging deeper into him, but couldn't quite.

"Oh, he put up a fight, they said, when we took him." The Oskina woman moved into Joh's line-of-sight, and Kallista choked back a snarl. She was so deep inside Joh, she feared her rage would come out his mouth.

Oskina was short. Not as tiny as Aisse, but too short for her to look at Joh over Fox's tall shoulders. She trailed a hand along his waist as she walked around him. Kallista forced herself to back out of Joh, to ride only his vision.

"Do his scars ruin him for you?" the woman asked.

"No." Joh said nothing more.

*What happened to his hair?* Kallista would not complain if Fox's hair was the worst thing done to him in Turysh, but still, she couldn't help mourning his curls. *Did that woman shear him?*

"At court, the bravos wear their hair cropped short." Joh brushed his fingers along the shorn sides of Fox's head. "But not so short as this, virtually shaved. I've never seen anyone with hair cut like this. Is it a new style in Turysh? Something you prefer, Oskina Aila? Should I cut mine?"

*Don't you dare.*

Joh's amusement shivered around her, showing he teased. His panic had faded tremendously, if he could tease. Then they saw Oskina's scowl and the panic came rushing back. Kallista caught it, tried to ease it.

"He had curls," she said. "Wonderful golden curls. But when I took him with me to the tailor's this afternoon, he stole the scissors and cut them off before I could stop him. This was the best the barber could do with what was left."

*Oh, Fox.* What had the woman done that would drive him to such measures? Kallista wanted to kiss him, comfort him—Joh did it for her. He kissed Fox's temple, right at that shorn hairline.

"Kallista." Torchay touched her arm, distracted her. "What's happening? Can we do anything?"

In that distant room, Oskina was touching Joh. "Show yourself, Hero. Let us see how you are made." She loosened the lacings at the throat of his tunic.

*Kallista, help me!* Joh shouted through her mind. *Help us both.*

*I will.* She began to pull back, and he clutched at the magic.

*Don't leave me. Don't leave me alone with her. I don't think I can bear it. Not again. Not here. There is something…wrong.*

*Joh.* She twined the magic through him, making promises with it. *I must go, but only a little while. Only a little bit. I must, if I am to help you. Be strong, beloved.*

He jolted at the word, so she repeated it as she withdrew from him completely.

She tightened her hand over Viyelle's where it rested on her arm, calling more magic, calling out to her blood sister. *Karyl, it's time.*

*Time?*

*To leave. To contact those friends of yours that you pretend you don't know. I need a diversion.*

Karyl's "voice" came back filled with suspicion. *Why?*

*So I can get Fox and Joh out of the Mother Temple house. They have them both. We need a diversion to call this Oskina away.*

*Oskina? Herself?*

*Apparently.* She'd seen a report about her, Kallista remembered now. Torchay had a list of the reported rebel leaders. Oskina was at the top.

*How big a diversion?* Karyl asked.

*The bigger, the better. Can your friends explode something?*

*Possibly.*

*We'll meet across the river. North side of the North Temple.*

*We won't be there, sister.*

*Of course you will.*

*We've been talking about it, Kami and the boys and me. If I go, the loyalists in Turysh won't have a farspeaker. If I stay, they will.*

Kallista did not need this. She already had enough to worry about. *You cannot stay in that house. They'll be on you in two ticks.*

*We have a place. Our friends will look after us.* Karyl's voice took on sardonic amusement. *We only have to hide. It's not like we'll be taking on demons with our bare hands.* She paused. *Rid us of them, Kallista. We'll do the rest.*

*I'll do my best.* What else could she do? She only hoped her best was good enough. *Be very careful.*

*You, too.*

*Call me when the diversion is ready.*

*Yes.* And Karyl was gone.

Kallista blinked up at Torchay. "We ride tonight."

"I will ready the horses." Obed paused at the doorway and looked back. "Everything will be prepared when your plans are made. You have only to tell me who to kill."

Viyelle stared at the now-empty doorway a moment longer before taking her hand from Kallista's arm. "Is he always that bloodthirsty?"

Kallista didn't know, not for certain. She shrugged and looked at Torchay.

"I think so, yes," he said. "He's never seemed to have a problem with killing. Or with dying himself, though he's so close-mouthed, it's hard to know sometimes.

"All right," he went on, "here's the plan. We go in and get them out."

"Sophisticated plan, that." Kallista drew magic from Obed and Torchay and threw it out to Joh again. She'd promised only half a moment's absence, and it had been over two ticks.

"You have a better one?" Torchay set Viyelle to packing gear with a look and the flick of a finger.

"No. Sounds perfectly reasonable to me." Kallista locked the magics together and skated in on Joh's paths. "Though we probably want to avoid notice as long as possible. I know the house. That will help. And Karyl's arranging a diversion.

"Will you be able to ride, or do I ride with you?"

"We're not walking?" Kallista diverted her attention from Joh to look at Torchay.

"Only the last part. How distracted will you be?"

"I won't ride his vision unless I need to. Just listen in." *Joh,* she whispered in his mind.

*Goddess, Kallista, I can't do this. Not with* her *here.* His panic flooded her and she did her best to calm it.

*Shh. We're coming. Hold on the best you can. I'm with you. I won't leave you alone with her.*

"Distracted," Torchay said somewhere in the distance. "Right, then."

Kallista tried to help them pack while whispering reassurance to Joh. She didn't attempt to borrow his sight, didn't think he would let her. Was fairly sure she didn't want to see.

She wasn't much use at packing either, getting in the way and forgetting what she was doing. Torchay finally pushed her into a chair and told her to stay there. He passed the last of the packs out the door and over the loft edge to Obed, and came back to guide her down the steep stairs.

*Not long now. Hang on.* Kallista breathed the promise in Joh's mind and caught his flare of relief.

She tried again and again to reach Fox, to let him know they were coming, until she realized—later than she should have—that with each attempt, he locked himself tighter away. He might as well be hidden inside an iron-bound dungeon. Would she ever reach him again?

Torchay lifted her onto a horse and mounted behind her. They were in the street already? She needed to keep better track of her surroundings, but it was difficult with Joh's panic shuddering through her.

They were halfway there when Karyl whispered distantly to her. *Diversion time. Armory outside the barracks.*

"Ride!" Kallista spoke aloud. It felt strange. "Our diversion is beginning."

"You spoke only truth, didn't you?" Oskina's voice had Joh fighting his instinctive wince. "You *are* a shy one."

It would serve no purpose to tell her that her presence was enough to shrivel nearly anything, so he kept his jaw clamped tight and clung to Kallista's whisper in his mind. He tried for nonchalance, but knew Oskina could somehow smell the truth on him. He hated this.

He'd never been particularly modest, not like Obed whose discomfort at being merely shirtless was obvious. But nudity was one thing. Nakedness was another. Just now, he felt *naked*.

With all his bits and parts exposed and vulnerable to being snipped off. He had no doubt that Oskina was the sort who would snip at any provocation. Or whim.

A tremendous boom, louder than thunder, made the floor tremble. Joh grabbed hold of a bedpost, wondering if the whole building was coming down on top of them. He almost wished it would.

*Diversion,* Kallista whispered. *To get that woman away from you. We're coming.*

She'd said it already, but only now did Joh begin to think they would come before— He shuddered.

Oskina yanked the door open. "What is happening out there?"

"I—we don't know, Oskina Reinine," a guard in the corridor spoke.

The title he used shocked Joh to his bones. Their ambitions went so far? But if not, why rebel?

"Do you want me to go find out?" The guard sounded eager for the task. To get away from Oskina? Did she affect even her own people this way? Why? Did he truly want to know?

Oskina looked over her shoulder at Joh and Fox standing side by side nearer the bed than made Joh comfortable. Her scowl made it worse. "No," she said to the guard. "I'll do it myself. I am surrounded by incompetents."

Then she spoke to Joh. "Wait for me. I won't be long." And she slammed the door shut behind her.

He heard the lock click. His knees wanted to buckle in relief, but he had no time. *She's gone,* he warned Kallista, *but there are guards outside our door. Two, I think.*

*Good. Soon. We're in the plaza. I need to leave you if you're all right. I can't do this and fight.*

*Go.* He wanted to cling, but had to let her go. He needed her whole. She whispered a kiss across some part of him he couldn't name and was gone.

Joh scooped up the pile of clothing and sorted it, tossing Fox's trousers at him. "Get dressed. Kallista's coming for us."

He didn't know what triggered it, whether Oskina's absence or Kallista's name or the trousers hitting the other man in the chest. Joh had his own trousers halfway up when Fox attacked. He tackled him, knocking Joh to the ground. Fox fastened his hands around Joh's throat, an animal growl rumbling from his chest.

Joh fought back, breaking the hold on his neck and kicking off his trousers to fight unhampered. "*Fox, stop it.* I'm here to help!"

They rolled together across the floor, grappling for advantage. Fox had it. He fought to kill while Joh fought only to control. "Kallista sent me!"

Nothing seemed to get through. Fox fought like a feral thing, using teeth and nails along with fists and feet. He weighed more, had a longer reach, and was nearly as quick as Joh. He'd been trained as a warrior since he was a child of six. Too soon, Joh had all he could do just to stay out of the man's grasp.

*Was* he possessed? Did that explain his single-minded fury?

Joh leaped onto the bed and across it to escape being cornered. He jerked to a stop in midair, head snapping back as Fox caught his braid and yanked. He slammed down and bounced on the hard mattress. The braid made a fine handle. "Fox, *stop.* Kallista sent me. She's com—"

"*You lie.*" The tall blond man used the braid to jerk Joh up off the bed, and wrapped it around his throat. "You tried to kill her."

Once he would have let Fox kill him because of that. But no more. She needed him, needed his eyes at the very least. He had to live.

"I'm marked." Joh squeezed the words out past the thick cord around his throat. "*Marked,* Fox."

"You lie." But the pressure eased. A bit.

"Just look." Breathing was still a struggle, but he could do it. "She's coming. She sent me to find you."

The braid loosened, replaced with Fox's big hand positioned to crush his larynx in an instant if he moved the wrong way. Joh spread his hands away from his body, opened them. Fox waited until Joh went still, then moved the braid aside and looked.

A wet thumb scrubbed across the mark. "It doesn't rub off." Fox's voice sounded harsh.

"No. It's real. I'm marked."

"You tried to kill them, Kallista and Stone."

"And Obed. I didn't mean to. I didn't know it would explode. I thought it would heal her, cure her of the West magic. I was a fool, but I know better now." Joh talked fast, trying anything, everything to convince this man who literally held his life in his hands.

"I should kill you." The hand tightened and Joh froze even more motionless. "Tell me why I should not."

"Torchay will be disappointed you didn't let him do it."

A single bark of laughter escaped Fox. "He would." He opened his hand.

Joh collapsed onto the bed. It was the quickest way to get away from that grip. He rolled off and found his trousers where he'd kicked them. "Get dressed. They'll be here soon."

Obed called their attention to a small woman riding out with an escort of brown-cloaked Barbs as Kallista followed him on foot across the plaza. They'd left the horses tied in the southwest corner garden. No one would bother them, even with things so unsettled. The horses had drovers' harnesses, and everyone knew drovers did not look kindly upon anyone molesting their precious horses. Too many earless drovers testified to that fact. And too many earless corpses of the non-drover variety.

She had to look again at the woman before she saw the dark cloud of demon floating above her. First, rescue Fox, then with his magic, she could deal with the demon.

Kallista led them through the quiet kitchens and back hallways, empty of workers at this hour. Most of them had gone to see what had caused the noise. The taste of magic grew stronger as they climbed. She'd gone gloveless all week as part of her disguise, and now Kallista called her lightning. Her anger needed the outlet. She almost wished Oskina had stayed, so Kallista could deal her the punishment she deserved.

"Let us take the guards," Torchay murmured from behind her, his hair standing out in a halo round his face because of the electricity she'd raised. "Your lightning's too loud."

Thunder did ride with it. Kallista let the lightning disperse back into the air with a crackle of sparks. "Do it." She backed away from the corner of the corridor, making room for Torchay and Obed to move up side by side.

They looked at each other, dark eyes and blue. Torchay mouthed the count and as one, they stepped around the corner and let their blades fly.

Kallista was running before the bodies hit the floor. She shoved open the door, putting her shoulder to it when the lock stuck, and she stumbled in to find Joh pulling his tunic down over his head and Fox—

Fox stood half-dressed in the center of the room, tunic in his hands, head up, nostrils flaring as if he could smell her. "Kallista?" he said in a voice softer than whispers.

She flew across the room, needing to hold him, to be sure he was safe and whole. He caught her—he could do nothing else—but moved his hands down to his sides as she hugged him. "Fox." She took his face between her hands and kissed him. *"Fox."*

She'd lost all ability to say anything else. He was here, with her. Nothing else mattered.

"I hate to break up this lovely reunion," Torchay said from the doorway. "But we need to be out of here before Oskina and her demon come back."

Joh took two steps and retched into the chamber pot. "She has a pet demon?"

"Actually, I think the demon has a pet Oskina. Come." Kallista tugged Fox toward the door. What was wrong with him? "Fox, get dressed."

Then she saw Joh's face. He was bruised and swollen, his lower lip half again its normal size and still rising. His neck looked almost worse.

"What happened to you?" she demanded.

"Fox." Joh licked blood from his lip. "He took exception to my trying to blow you up."

"Man after my own heart." Torchay grinned. "Now let's *go.*" He held his hand out to Kallista, demand in his face.

But Fox still wasn't dressed. He would call attention to them if he paraded shirtless through Turysh, even in this weather. She took the tunic from him and put it over his head. "Get dressed. *Now.*"

He obeyed her insistent command, almost as if he'd reverted to his casteless obedience of a year ago. Kallista's heart twisted, but she couldn't worry about it now. She could however use it, and would. "Where's your Heldring blade?"

He pointed at a locked chest in the corner. No one else could use the blade, especially now it had been matched to him.

"Get it. Viyelle, help him." She used the time to look more carefully at Joh's injuries.

"I'll be fine." He pulled away when she would have kissed him.

"I'm sorry. I forgot your lip."

He touched it with his tongue. "So did I. But—don't kiss me

now. Not till I've at least rinsed my mouth after losing all that ale from my stomach. I disgust myself."

Kallista laughed and kissed an unbruised spot near his mouth, then turned at the clatter of the lock breaking and the trunk opening. "Ready?"

Fox buckled on his sword as he followed Viyelle to the door.

"Too late," Torchay said. "We've got company."

Not just company. Kallista recognized the death stink of demons.

"Viyelle!" She held her hand out and Viyelle slapped hers into it, locking their fingers tight. "Calling magic," Kallista warned even as she acted.

Four skeins of magic lurched forward, sluggish and reluctant. She wove them together, slapping and kicking when the magic wouldn't behave, until finally she persuaded it to work together. Four skeins, not five.

"Kallista, whatever you're doin', do it faster." Torchay stepped out into the hallway, twin swords in his hands. Obed followed, turning to put his back to the red-haired bodyguard.

The magic dragged like a sulky child put to a hated task, one it didn't want to even know how to do. It was taking far too long, and she wasn't sure it would do what she willed. "Fox, I need you."

He drew his sword, started for the doorway.

"No." Kallista caught his arm as he passed her. "I need your magic. I need *you.*"

He kept his head down, staring somewhere past her right elbow. Kallista was vaguely aware of Joh catching the sword Torchay appropriated from one of the fallen guards and taking up a post just inside the door. She could feel Viyelle fidgeting and knew she wanted to join them but would stay to feed her magic to Kallista. She could hear steel sliding along steel and knew her bodyguards fought so that she had time and space to do what was needed. And for that, she needed Fox's magic.

She cupped his face and lifted it. "Look at me. I know, I know, you can't *see,* but you can do *something.* Do it here. To me." She used her command voice, trained on battlefields. "You have to open to me, love. I need your magic, but you've shut it off from me."

He glanced at her and away again, his eyes wild, unseeing. Kallista stretched up to kiss him and he straightened, tall enough to keep her away unless he came down to meet her. She slapped at his chest, shook him. "Stop it. Whatever this is, just stop it. I *need* you, Fox. *Now.*"

This time, he let her pull him down, let her touch her lips to his, but she might as well have been kissing a child's clay doll. "Fox, *please.*"

She could feel the demon—demons?—tearing at the links she held to all of them, clawing through the protections their magic gave them. She wrapped more magic around them, screaming as she fought it into shape. When she looked back at Fox, he stared at her with his wild empty eyes.

"Please, love, *please.*"

He shook his head, anguish bleeding into his expression. "Don't."

"I have to, Fox. I have to stop the demons, have to destroy them. That's why we were given the magic. It's what we were made to do."

"Take it," he said. "Take the magic, but don't—don't call me that."

Call him what? Kallista frowned. "Fox, love—"

He winced, a visible, almost audible flinching away. *"Don't."*

Oh. Kallista almost let go, almost lifted her hand from his golden-skinned face, almost let herself feel hurt because he didn't want her love. Didn't want her. But that didn't seem right, even without the link to tell her truth.

"*Kallista.*" Obed's voice came harsh. He bled from half a dozen flesh wounds, but his face—oddly, frighteningly pale beneath his tattoos—spoke of worse wounding. Wounds of the soul. Torchay looked in similar state.

She drew more magic. In itself, that would energize them. She didn't understand it, but it worked. Then she buttressed the protections, hammering the magic into place. She had to do better than mere defense. They could not wall themselves inside the magic forever. Or even for much longer. She had to attack the demons directly, and for that, she needed Fox.

And he didn't want— No. She wouldn't believe that. "Fox, do you love me?"

"For the One's sake, Kallista," Torchay cried. "We don't have time for that now!"

"Do you?" She shook Fox, bringing his attention back from the fighting. "Do you even trust me?"

He blinked, then slowly, nodded.

Kallista reached gently down his link, drawing physically closer to him as she did. "I'm here, Fox." She pressed her body against him. "This is me, touching you."

She stroked along the link, pushing magic toward him, hoping it could get past the barriers he had built. "Trust me," she murmured. "I won't let the demon have you. Let me in, love."

He shuddered, staring down at her with eyes no less wild, no less anguished, no less blind. "What if it is already there?" he whispered. "What if it goes through the link to you and the others?"

"It isn't there. I promise it isn't. Fox, demons can only take someone who is empty, and you are so far from empty. Please, beloved, let me in."

"I betrayed you." His voice sounded as if something had broken inside it. "Betrayed you all."

"You *survived*. We would never blame you for that." Kallista held his face tight between her hands and stretched onto her toes to kiss him. *"Never."*

This time, finally, he dissolved into the kiss. He kissed her back, lips moving tentatively at first. His hand rose, wrapped itself in her hair. His mouth opened, and as it did, the barriers across his link melted away. Kallista thrust her tongue into his mouth and ground her hips against his hardness as she stormed inside him, sweeping the last of his resistance away.

He was clean, untouched by demon save where one had tried to force its way in. She found his shame and whispered over it, unable to wipe it away, but hoping she had eased it some. Then she caught hold of his magic and came roaring back out to do battle.

"Now," she said. "Go join the others."

Kallista caught up the other waiting magic and poured Fox's order into it. It was no less difficult to move than before, but when she shaped it, sending it here to protect, there to heal, it did exactly what she willed it to do.

She closed her eyes, closing out the physical. No doors, no walls, just magic. And demons.

# CHAPTER TWENTY-TWO

The demons fought as ferociously as the rebels they drove, without the physical barriers that confined their followers to the hallway. They tore the magic, ripping holes in it, reaching through to weaken their opponents, Kallista's marked mates.

Gathering the magic around her, drawing heavily on Torchay's boundless well of booming magical strength, Kallista sorted the darting wisps of demonstuff into their separate existences. There were two.

No, damn it, *three*. She could sense the third approaching from a distance and beyond it, a fourth. Kallista built the magic higher, stronger. Did she have enough? How much was enough? How had she destroyed the demon last year?

She'd named it. But she did not know these names. Did she?

"Untathel." The name came out of her mouth before Kallista knew she was speaking it, coming to her from the same unknown, unknowable source as the demon's name last year. "Ataroth. Xibyth. Ashbel."

The very air seemed to cringe. To shiver and tighten with each name she spoke. The crash and clang of fighting echoed around her in violent accompaniment. She molded the magic into shape, willing destruction and nothingness for the names she'd spoken. It was heavy, filled with the weight of endings, ponderous with power. Once more, she named the demons and *pushed* the magic hard, sending it forth.

The instant it left her, it flew. Springing out in a glittering dark veil, it blasted into the demons, leaving behind nothing. A pair of rebels collapsed as the veil rolled on. Torchay and Obed, then Fox and Joh charged into the rebels remaining. The veil brushed against the third demon as it fled the onslaught. The demon screamed.

*Ataroth,* Kallista murmured. She tried to feed more magic into the veil, but it was collapsing even as she tried. The demons—Ataroth and Ashbel—were too far away for the veil to reach. She'd damaged the one, Ataroth, but not destroyed it. The magic hadn't even touched Ashbel.

"Come." Viyelle urged her forward at Joh's beckoning. "They're falling back."

"I got two of them. Only *two.*" Kallista let them lead her along. "There are two left. Last summer, demon worshippers died all the way to Adara. Why won't they die now?"

"They did." Torchay paused while Fox *looked* around corners, then clattered down the stairs. "The worshippers did."

"Not many. And there are two demons left."

"Oskina was their leader," Fox said. "Maybe—"

"Let's get away from here first," Torchay interrupted. "*Then* we can sort out what happened."

"But there are demons left," Kallista protested.

"They'll be here when we come back." Torchay stopped at the kitchen doorway.

"Empty," Fox said before he could ask.

"And when we come back—" Torchay plunged through the swinging door "—our ilian will be whole. They won't escape us then."

He was right. They were stronger whole than they were apart. Kallista hurried in his wake, clinging to Viyelle's hand. Likely they looked like two timid females cowering behind the protection of their men, but she needed the contact to draw magic in a hurry. Who cared how it looked? At least she had Fox's magic back, with the order it carried.

Order, strength, truth… Kallista stumbled, and Joh caught her arm, steadying her, bearing her along across the vast plaza. Understanding, creativity…joy, loyalty. Will. Why had she not seen the pattern to the magic before?

"Kallista—" Torchay spoke over his shoulder, his eyes on a company mustering to the west. "Do you have enough magic left for hiding us?"

"Yes." She thought she did. She should have done it already. Would have, if not for the distraction. Fighting now. Escaping now. Thinking later.

Their magic veiled from the demons, Fox disguised with a quick drenching of Torchay's brown dye and Joh's braid tucked under his hat again, they rode across the arched bridge over the Taolind and out of Turysh. They struck out north across the plains, to travel through Shaluine and the northwest "ear" of Filorne toward the Empty Lands and Korbin beyond, on the very edge of Adara.

They were a day and a night out of Turysh before they stopped long enough to catch their collective breath. Their Southron remounts brought from home had all been claimed by the iliasti they'd added, so they had not traveled as far as Kallista had hoped, but far enough.

Star-studded black overhead, a wash of midnight blue still painted the night sky above the mountains to the west. Kallista leaned back against Obed, staring at the fire as Torchay and Viyelle cleaned up after their meal. Fox lay sprawled on the grass beyond the fire, his head on his saddle. Joh squatted near him as he fed in more fuel. Having one who'd grown up in a drover household made plains travel much more comfortable. He didn't mind handling the dried horse and bison droppings that provided the majority of their fires.

"Joh, why weren't you cavalry?" Viyelle asked out of nowhere. "If you're drover-born, you know horses like flies know dung. Why were you infantry and not cavalry?"

"I asked for cavalry when I was commissioned as an officer," Joh said. "But the cavalry commander wouldn't have a male officer. The infantry would."

"Ah." Viyelle dried the last spoon and handed it to Torchay for stowing.

"I know how many our ilian will ultimately hold." Kallista didn't realize she'd spoken aloud until she noticed everyone staring at her. Even Fox had risen onto his elbows to turn his face her way.

She hadn't intended to drop it on them out of nowhere like that, but now that she had… "There are eight of us," she said. "We need one more. Nine."

"Three threes." Obed's voice rumbled in his chest and vibrated through her. "The number of perfection completed."

"…Perfection completed." Torchay spoke in unison with Obed. "And how did you come to this remarkable conclusion?"

Kallista sighed and sat up straight, waving those on their feet to sit. "It was after the fight in Turysh, when we were leaving Mother Temple house. I was thinking how glad I was to have Fox back. And his magic." She touched him through the link, since he couldn't see her looking at him. "Because his magic brings order to the chaos. And I was thinking what each of you bring to the magic."

Her eyes shifted to Torchay. "Strength."

To Joh. "Understanding." Obed. "Truth." Viyelle. "Creativity."

She let her gaze sweep across them again. "Then I thought of those who are not with us—Stone and the joy he brings, Aisse and her loyalty. And I realized..." She paused for a breath and Joh filled the gap.

"The Nine Attributes of the One." His eyes were wide, voice hushed.

"The One has many more than nine attributes," Obed said.

"True, but in Adara, these nine are considered preeminent. Power, Wisdom, Truth, Joy, Faithfulness, Creativity, Order." She paused and pointed to herself. "Will, or Intent. The only one we do not have is Love."

"So you think..." Torchay couldn't seem to make himself finish.

"I think there is one more ilias to come to us, yes."

They stared at each other across the fire a moment. Even Fox's face turned from one to another of them.

"Actually," Torchay said when the silence stretched too long, "it's a bit of a relief to know there's only one more coming. I was beginning to worry we might be pushed to fifteen or twenty just to deal with these demons."

Kallista smiled and leaned her forehead on the point of his shoulder. "We might yet. But I think once we're all together, and our ninth ilias has joined us—"

"Whoever that is," Viyelle said under her breath.

"I think we'll be able to handle as many demons as dare to come against us." She straightened to take them all in her gaze again. "I've been thinking about that, too, about why we only destroyed two demons."

"Heaven help us," Torchay muttered. *"Thinking."*

"I know, I know." She poked him with her elbow. "Not one of my best things. But I *think*—well, we know that distance does matter with the dark veil. So the other two were simply too far away to reach—though I think I damaged one of them. Fewer people died, mostly I think because this is Adara, and worshiping something other that the One just isn't *done*. And we weren't all together. We're missing two. I think having all of us together, even at eight, adds some extra…"

Kallista paused to think her way through. "Some new *dimension*. It's more than simply four plus four, more than just eight separate magics tied together. It's a *whole*. It moves us beyond that level to something never seen before.

"Or at least not seen since Belandra of Arikon walked the earth with her ilian." She stopped talking, wondering how foolish she sounded. "I know I'm not making much sense, but—"

"You make perfect sense," Obed said. "At least, I think you do."

It took Kallista a moment to realize Obed had made a joke, and she laughed. "I call save on first watch."

"Not fair," Fox protested. "You knew I was going to call it as soon as you finished, so you didn't bother to finish. Just called saves. Completely out of turn."

"What are you complaining about?" Viyelle jumped in. "I've been standing watch all week while you lazed about resting in a nice empty jail cell."

He'd been in a cell part of the time. They ignored the time when he wasn't, in an attempt to help ease his hurt.

"Stand first watch with me," Kallista said.

"Obed, you and Joh take second." Torchay ended the teasing discussion, pairing a competent fighter with a brilliant one. "I'll stand third with Viyelle."

They also pretended that Obed wasn't uncomfortable around Viyelle, even while they accommodated it.

After their watch, Kallista took Fox into her arms and into her body, to be sure he knew to his bones, down to the magic hidden inside him, that he was as much one of them now as he had ever been. And because she'd missed him terribly.

Soon, or as soon as it was possible to cross the endless plains, they would all be together. And they would not separate like this ever again.

Stone tightened his grip on Aisse's hands as she began to close them. He'd been able to keep her from grinding the bones of his hands together—mostly…occasionally—by holding tighter, but nothing could stop the crushing pressure. Only her grip and the strain of effort in her body, on her face, showed what she endured.

She didn't scream. Refused to, brave as any warrior Stone had known. Braver. He didn't know any warrior who'd be willing to put himself through something like this. And Aisse was so tiny.

Her whispered litany quickened as her hands squeezed harder. Stone would almost rather she screamed, even if the black lacy stone paving of the Empty Lands was filled with outlaws after the gold they escorted. He couldn't bear seeing her in such pain. She was so small.

Her body relaxed slowly and her grip eased. Stone took the opportunity to look over his shoulder at Merinda, moaning near the cave's entrance. "Are you *sure* nothing's wrong?" he asked for the five-thousandth time.

"Yes." Merinda snarled back at him. "I'm sure. What do I have to do to get you to believe me?"

"Come over here and look at her, maybe?"

Merinda gagged and crawled a little farther away, nearer the entrance where soft rain washed the stones clean, but her stomach was empty. Had been empty the last several times. Stone sympathized. Truly, he did, but she had chosen the worst of all possible times to fall ill. Aisse was having her baby and Stone knew less than nothing about bringing life into the world.

Well, except for how to get it started. He did know about that. But anything more?

His knowledge was more in the death and destruction line. He did know that if any Tibran male had ever witnessed a birthing, there would be no more talk about "women's weakness."

Stone freed his hand and found the cool, wet rag Merinda had tossed him to wipe Aisse's face. Thank the One that the twins were asleep. They'd begun sleeping through the night not long after they'd run from Sumald. By dawn though—or so Merinda said—they'd have a third infant to cope with. He hoped she was right. The alternative didn't bear thinking.

"Truly, Stone." Merinda's voice startled him. "Everything is going well. First babies take time."

"Pray we have the time then."

Outlaws had been tracking them across this desolate territory. Though the rough black rock that covered most of these lands made tracking difficult, the terrain was so flat and the gnarled, stunted trees so few that any travelers could be seen for hundreds of miles. Fortunately, the porous rock was laced with caves. Stone had hidden them in this one, but he didn't know how secure it was.

Still, the high reaches of the Devil's Tooth Mountains grew closer every day. They would reach safety soon, pray the One. Stone wanted desperately to lay down his burden of worry and let someone else take it up. But right now, he was their only protection—the two babies; the small, fierce woman laboring so intently to bring another babe into his protection; and the healer who was scarcely less helpless, even when she wasn't puking up her guts. He was terrified of allowing one of them to be hurt in some way, of failing them the way he'd failed others before.

He was a good warrior. One of the best. But he had a tendency to take stupid chances. To act as if the bullets, the cannonballs could not touch him. They hadn't. But that didn't mean they wouldn't. Stone shuddered, thinking of some of the things he'd done. No more. He had family. People who depended on him to keep them safe because they could not do it themselves, as Fox could. So Stone would. No matter what.

If that meant hiding in a cave, he would hide. If it meant walking away from a challenge, he would walk away. If it meant fighting, even dying, then he would do that. Whatever he had to do, he would keep them safe.

Aisse grabbed his hand and squeezed, whispering her prayers. Stone held on tight, swallowing hard as he watched her body writhe. *Whatever he had to,* he reminded himself. Even this.

If she was brave enough to endure it, he had to be brave enough to help. But Goddess save them all, it was going to be a long, long, *long* night.

Kallista rode with her marked ones across the plains. A drover's clan they met on the border between Shaluine and Filorne agreed to sell them six good remounts for an exorbitant amount of Obed's cash and provide six additional remounts—mares to be returned next spring bred to their Southron stallions. They only agreed because Joh was somehow kin to one of the males in the matriarch's ilian. Two changes of horses each would allow them to ride harder, faster.

About a week out of Turysh, she woke from a dream of her own babies' birth certain that Aisse's child had arrived, but she had no more knowledge than that. A few days afterward, Viyelle's link solidified so that Kallista could draw magic without touching. They would be ready for the demons when next they saw them, but first they had to reach Korbin.

They rode relentlessly north, passing from the sweltering heat of the southern plains into the gentler summer of the north ranges. They veered west to skirt along the edges of the Okreti di Vos mountains so that they crossed the short, sharp Vilaree

River near its source, before it became the deep treacherous current that stormed across the north plains. They followed the foothills nearly to the coast before the mountains faded away and they entered the black desolation of the Empty Lands.

"What happened here?" Obed stared at the endless vista of black, ropy rock, crumbling here and there into gritty soil where wispy grasses and gnarled pines clung to life. "What could have made such a place?"

"Demons." Torchay pulled his horse to a halt and dismounted. "This is the last water we'll have for a while. We'll camp here tonight."

"Have you ever seen a volcano?" Kallista dismounted, wondering if the numbness in her backside would wear off some day. "There are islands in the Jeroan Sea with mountains that spew out fire from the earth's molten heart. This is what is left when the fire cools."

"Is it likely to happen again?" Viyelle didn't quite manage to conceal her alarm.

Kallista didn't quite conceal her chuckle, either. "It could, I suppose, but there have been no signs of it in, oh, thousands of years."

"But what is this place?" Obed said again.

"Legend has it that this is where the last battle of the Demon Wars took place," Kallista said.

Obed swore in his own language, under his breath.

"Are you so sure it's legend?" Torchay took Joh's horse so the plainsman could start the night's fire.

"No. Not anymore." Kallista called a trickle of magic to hide the fire's light. It also seemed to help the fire's starting, perhaps by blocking the wind.

"I don't know this story." Fox collected one of the grain bags they'd bought at the last village and began sharing it out to the horses. "Tell me. What happened here?"

"The wars had been raging for years," Kallista said. "First between the demons and the angels—fighting between pure spirit. Then the demons began attacking humans, those the angels were sworn to protect."

"What are angels?" Fox asked Torchay from the side of his mouth.

"Like demons, but good. Demons were once angels, before they rebelled, went bad," Torchay said.

"Where are the angels now? Did they all become demons?"

"Listen. It's in the story." Torchay turned away, back to his horse grooming.

"Soon," Kallista went on, "humans were involved in the wars, divided just as the spirits were divided. The war spread, threatening to consume the whole world, but gradually the forces of the One began to prevail. The demons were driven back. To this place."

Kallista paused to look around her, at the evening sun reflecting off the black volcanic rock in an iridescent glow. The empty desolation held a stark, eerie beauty of its own.

Torchay took up the tale. "It was green and beautiful here then. A wide valley perfect for raising—anything you cared to raise. Or for battle.

"Two armies gathered here, vast armies, spreading out until the entire valley was filled. The demon swarms and their followers were there." He waved an arm toward the north. "And the hosts of angels with their human allies held the south. Hundreds and hundreds of thousands of fighters."

"When the battle began," Kallista said, "it was bloody and hard-fought, but against the power of the One ruler of the universe, who can stand? The demon's armies suffered the flaws of those who fight only for themselves. When it began to look as if their side would lose the battle, many of them broke and ran.

"The demons were desperate. They knew they faced destruction, and fearing it, they broke open the earth and poured the fires from its heart across the valley." Kallista knelt to poke up the fire as Joh added fuel.

Torchay took the horse Obed had unsaddled and began brushing it. "The molten rock burned everything it touched, everything in the valley, living or dead, including the demons' own followers."

"Did the demons escape?" Fox asked.

"No." Obed spoke, startling them. "Angels caught hold of the demons and plunged through the cracks the demons had made, into the fires and beyond them to the hells the One created to hold them. The angels that remained merged with those humans who were able to bear it, creating saints—"

"Naitani," Kallista murmured, "from the old *naishar*—to serve."

Obed continued as if she had not spoken. "And together with the fighters who still lived, who were willing to kill to protect the innocent, they used the gifts of the angels to destroy the demons who survived."

"So angels became naitani?" Fox looked as confused as he sounded.

"No." Kallista smiled at him. Smiles could be heard as well as seen. "The angels gave up their lives—whatever kind of existence they had. But the essence of what they were became magic. The magic a naitan uses."

"Do you think…" Joh halted, looking uncertain. Kallista waited. He tended to need time rather than encouragement to speak his mind.

He came back into his eyes and cleared his throat. "Could our magic—the godmarked magic—perhaps be surviving angels?"

"Possessing us like the demons possess their creatures?" Fox sounded more outraged than anything.

"Well, not *exactly* like—" Joh began.

"I don't think so," Kallista said. "I don't *know*, but— For one thing, what are we? *God*struck. And what characterizes the magic? Qualities of the One. I think we carry the tiniest part of the One's own essence."

"Now that," Torchay said, hobbling the last of the horses and turning it out to graze on the sparse grass with the rest, "is a downright terrifying thought. Reassuring, but terrifying."

"So…" Viyelle put her set of currycombs back in the pack. "If the demons were destroyed at that battle, the one that made this place, why are we fighting demons now—what? Two thousand years later?"

Kallista blew out a puff of air, looking to the others for ideas, suggestions. "Because some of them weren't caught with the others? Or maybe they escaped from hell?"

"Either is possible, I suppose." Torchay slung an arm over Kallista's shoulders, squeezing into the tiny gap between her and Viyelle. "Does it really matter?"

"I suppose not." Viyelle shrugged. "But I've never been fond of cleaning up other people's messes."

"*Our* mess now." And they *would* clean it up, Kallista vowed. Once and for all.

"I can ride." Aisse wasn't at all certain of any such thing, but she didn't like the worry on Stone's face.

"It's only been a week since your child was born," Merinda snapped. She'd been irritated at one thing or another for days. Of course, anyone emptying her stomach on such a regular basis deserved to be cranky. "You have no business getting on a horse for at least another two weeks. Four would be better."

"But the outlaws—"

"We're safe enough here." Stone ducked back through the cave's entrance.

"With all these horses to feed? And a goat?" Aisse had seen

the sparseness of the grass. Nothing to stretch the grain they'd carried with them.

"We'll manage. Let them get ahead of us and we'll sneak out to follow." Stone squatted beside the barricade of pack saddles that kept the twins confined and off the unpadded cave floor. Rozite rolled to her back and gurgled at him. His returning smile made Aisse's heart ache.

Then panic speared through her at a shout from outside.

"Oi! Tibrans!"

Cursing, Stone drew his Heldring sword and strode to the entrance. Aisse clutched her sleeping child tight as she eased past the restless animals to the farthest reaches of the cave, near the tiny pool that provided their water. Merinda followed her, a twin under each arm.

"We know you're in there," the voice shouted. "Hard to hide in the Empty Lands, 'cause they're so empty."

"What do you want?" Stone crouched to see out the cave's opening.

"The gold o' course. The women. You. They said you were a pretty one."

"*Who* said?"

One of the horses moved aside and Aisse turned her head against the shaft of sunlight suddenly in her eyes. The high opening kept the cave from total darkness. She looked up at the irregular hole. It was in the top of the cave, but it stretched close to the side. Could she…?

"Watch Niona." Aisse laid her daughter on a pile of horse blankets, tucking the soft coverlet around her face. "Don't let anything happen to her."

"If the bandits get in, I can't—"

"Just don't let the horses step on her." Aisse didn't have time for Merinda's fretting.

The bandits were still talking to Stone. Who knew how long

he could stall them, or what they would do when they got tired of it? Or maybe the bandits were doing the stalling, keeping Stone occupied while *they* worked their way to the cave's high opening.

Aisse found what she needed in the packs and slung it over her shoulder before starting her climb. The rocks were rough, porous, and scraped her hands as she climbed using the many hand- and footholds provided by the ropy, twisted formations. Every few steps, she stopped to listen, but the shouting in and out of the cave covered any other sounds.

At the top, she clung to the rocks and listened again, head down to keep from being seen, in case there was someone to see. She eased her Heldring blade—a rapier like Kallista's but smaller—out of its scabbard and looked through the opening. Nothing was visible anywhere she could see, but she could hear a faint sound of falling gravel.

Aisse poked her head above ground. There. Someone was climbing up, another behind him, but still some distance away. She scrambled through the hole and thrust her hand into the bag over her shoulder, pulling out a fistful of coins.

"Hey! Bottom feeders!" She had their attention. The two climbers scurried faster. She could hear Stone's shouts echoing through the opening behind her. He wasn't happy.

"Is this what you want?" Aisse threw her arm out and golden coins fell in a wide glittering arc to bounce across the black rock, coming to rest in crevices and crannies all down the slope.

The outlaws stopped scrambling after her and started scrabbling for the gold. Those below, in front of the cave's entrance, started up the slope after the gold. Aisse threw another handful, and another and another, until she shook the bag empty. Gold winked all down the steep hillside like stars against the night sky.

Below, she saw Stone creep unnoticed from the cave, and adjusted her grip on her own sword. She was weak, completely out of any shape resembling a warrior's, but she would fight for her babies.

Stone dispatched two bandits before the others noticed him at their backs. He leaped high, catching one around the ankle that kicked at him, pulling her down on top of him as they both fell. The fight was over quickly and Stone rushed up the slope after the rest.

A distant shout had Aisse jerking around to see half a dozen riders pelting across the rock at a reckless pace and another lurching up from the dry gully where they'd hidden their approach. Aisse shouted a warning. The outlaws glanced at the riders and sped up their gold mining.

Stone didn't bother to look. "Go back inside!"

Aisse ignored him. She wouldn't be much help, but some help was better than none, even if—especially if—the outlaws' numbers were doubling.

How did these new outlaws ride so fast? Stone had held their group to a crawling pace for the horses' sake as well as hers. This rock weathered to a sharp grit or porous lace that abraded the horses' feet and sometimes cut them open. But these riders raced across the rough surface as if it were a grassy meadow, their mounts' hooves striking sparks.

An outlaw, pockets bulging with coins, cast another look at the oncoming riders before she broke and ran. Maybe the new group wasn't part of this one. Maybe they intended to steal from the thieves. Stone let her go, as he did the next few to abandon the gold hunt, slide down the hillside and race for their mounts. Two more remained, the two who had been climbing before Aisse threw away the first gold.

They still ranged across the slope, picking out each shining coin between glances at Aisse, at Stone, at the galloping riders. Did they mean to take over the cave and defend it? To take hostages, or just kill them all?

# CHAPTER TWENTY-THREE

Aisse eased away from the gaping hole. If she had to try to fight, she didn't want to worry about her footing.

Stone had almost reached the outlaws when one of them—younger, with only a thin fringe of brownish beard—threw himself sideways, on top of Stone. The outlaw slashed with a dagger. The close quarters and steep slope made it almost impossible for Stone to bring his sword to bear. Did he have a dagger? Aisse wanted to watch, to see him safe, but she couldn't take her focus off the other outlaw. The one closest to her.

He grinned, showing blackened teeth in a mouth surrounded by grizzled beard stubble, and changed his ascent to come directly at her. Aisse backed away, circling the opening in the ground, afraid to move too far away, though she feared stumbling and falling through. She couldn't let this outlaw past her. Not without a fight.

The riders thundered nearer, to the base of the conical hill and past it, chasing the outlaws fleeing on the backs of their tender-footed horses. Stone shouted, still wrestling with the young bandit.

The old one looked from the vanishing riders to Aisse and

chuckled. She adjusted the grip on her sword and flexed her knees, glancing back to check the position of the cave opening behind her. Maybe she could fall down and hamstring him as he ran by, or maybe—

He rushed her. Aisse stumbled and fell, not quite intentionally. She managed to get her sword up and edge-on as she rolled to the side, slicing him across the knees. He shouted, flying forward. His head struck the far side of the opening, jerking back at an impossible angle as the weight of his shoulders dragged him lower. He balanced there a moment, an unnatural stopper in the neck of the cave's bottle, then his muscles went utterly limp and he slid into the darkness below. The noise of horses frightened by bloody, scary things echoed up through the hole.

"Aisse!" Stone's shout caught her attention. He scrambled up the slope toward her, his face a mask of blood, the hill empty behind him.

"He's dead," she said. "But you're hurt!" She rolled to her knees—standing wasn't much easier this week than it had been last—and Stone was there lifting her up.

"It's a scratch. Are you hurt?" He swiped at the blood on his forehead, revealing a tiny cut. "Always bleed like a slaughtered pig from a cut there. You're sure? You're all right?"

"I fell, that's all. I'm fine."

"Thank the One." Weary, he rested his face on her shoulder, smearing blood on her already filthy smock. "You know that you are in big, enormous trouble for climbing up here and risking what you did. I'm going to beat you for it once we get to Korbin and I've rested up a bit."

"You can try." Aisse didn't bother hiding her smile. He couldn't see it from where he was. "I'll be rested up then, too."

"True."

She stroked his hair, still cottony soft even short as it was, and stared across the black wasteland at the fleeing outlaws and their relentless pursuers.

Aisse sighed. "Of course it all depends on whether we survive the next thirty ticks. The riders are coming back."

Stone straightened, turned, shaded his eyes to see. He sighed, too. "You'd think they'd be smarter. They ought to realize they've got no chance. Not with the Tiger Aila on our side."

He gave Aisse a quick, tight hug and kissed her cheek. "You stay and defend this opening. I've got to get back down below."

She watched him slide down the crumbly rock, blinking in shock. A Tibran warrior trusted *her* to help defend a position? Her legs quivered with exhaustion. Her back ached. Her hand barely had strength enough to hold the sword, much less swing it. But she would stand. She would hold. Stone depended on her.

The riders advanced at that uncanny speed. They seemed faceless under the dull gray metal hats they wore. The featureless shadows unnerved Aisse until they came near enough she could see that they wore hoods under the brimmed helmets with masks that covered their faces up to their eyes.

Stone stood his ground in front of the cave's lower entrance, looking rather frightening himself with blood coating his bare skin. The riders galloped up with a deafening clangor of hooves to halt a scant pace away.

Stone never flinched. "What do you want?"

The rider in front pulled off his helmet and hood, revealing garish orange hair and a beaked nose rivaling any hawk's. "Would you lot happen to be iliasti of an ugly rogue goes by the name of Torchay Omvir? We're kinsmen, and we've been hunting them for weeks."

Finally, finally the green of the mountains flowed down to mingle with the rusted black rock of the Empty Lands. Kallista could feel the links with her two absent marked ones grow stronger with every day, every league that passed, and it made her more and more anxious to cross those leagues that yet separated them. Gradually, the rocks jutting up from the grassy earth changed from harsh black volcanic extrusions to the gray or pink or green of granite as they pushed deeper into the mountains.

The Devil's Tooth range rose high and higher as the neck of land narrowed, connecting Adara's continent to the one of the Tibrans to the north. Few could live in the higher reaches of the mountains—trappers, a few goat herders, hermits of one sort or another. The wide southernmost valleys on the edge of the Empty Lands were filled with a hardy folk, many of whom raised the sturdy, surefooted horses that performed best in Adara's mountainous regions. Torchay's family lived very nearly in the center of the populated sector of Korbin prinsipality.

As they rode into the lands owned by the Omvir line, Torchay's kin and cousins came out to greet them. They rode companionably alongside for a league or two, sometimes more, sharing food, drink and news, most notably of recent arrivals. A man, two women, three babies and a hulking great bag of gold, not to mention a number of very fine horses, and a goat, had paraded through the valley not two weeks before, escorted by a number of Omvir kinsmen.

A whole troop of soldiers had also come all the way from Arikon to Trondholl on the coast and thence to Grassy Valley to chase out rebels, protect the locals and find Torchay's missing iliasti. All of Korbin had rarely seen so much excitement.

Kallista hadn't visited Torchay's home since they'd been up here on a bandit-suppression assignment six or seven years back, but she recognized the landmarks as they neared. Or perhaps she simply read Torchay's rising eagerness. Then a rider broke away to race ahead of the galloping throng coming toward them. Kallista kicked her weary mount into a canter.

Stone didn't slow as their horses neared. He leaned out and snatched her from the saddle, yanking her into his lap as he galloped on toward the others. She was laughing, alternating between hugging him and smacking him for his outrageous prank when he pulled to a halt beside Fox.

She swatted Stone's shoulder. "I don't know why I'm so glad to see you."

"I'm irresistible." He grinned at her and she hugged him again.

He dumped her in Obed's lap so abruptly, the dark man almost dropped her, and reached across the gap to haul Fox into a back-pounding hug, despite their horses' distress. "*You're here*. You're finally here."

He let go of Fox to scowl at Kallista. "What took you so bloody damn long?"

"We had to go collect Fox first." She'd have smacked him again, but he was out of reach and wisely, he stayed there. "So tell us about the baby."

"She is beautiful." Stone grinned. "Not as beautiful as Rozite, of course, but with Fox as a sire, she was behind from the start."

Their pace picked up as he told his own news, slowed only a bit by the arrival of Torchay's sedili. Kallista let them share news of the valley, delaying their own stories until they were all together.

They found Aisse and the babies ensconced in the great communal hall in the center of the clustered houses, used also for visiting guests. Kallista swooped down on her twins where they played on a pallet of furs, just in time to see Lorynda roll onto her stomach and poke her sister in the eye. They had grown so much, had learned so many new things, and Kallista hadn't been present to see it. She held them both in her arms, though Rozite squirmed and protested, covering them in tears and kisses while Torchay told their news.

He introduced their new marked ones. Stone didn't assault Joh. They'd been friends of a sort before the explosion. Aisse did, blacking his eye before Obed could pull her away.

Tales all told, Torchay's family had withdrawn, leaving their ilian alone together. Kallista sat snuggled against Stone, finally giving the twins up to Torchay for his turn at baby cuddling.

"Never again," she said. "We are not ever again separating like this, I don't care who suggests it."

"The babies can't go into battle," Aisse said, but mildly, as if merely curious.

"No, but they don't have to be so far away to be safe. We can protect them better if we're together. We can *hide* them better." Kallista looked around the shadow-filled room, suddenly realizing she hadn't seen someone. "Where is Merinda? Didn't she make it through all right?"

"She made it through just fine," Stone said. "Unless you count the stomach trouble she's suffered the last few weeks."

Kallista rolled her head down his arm to look him in the eye. "What sort of—?"

"I think she's pregnant." Aisse looked up from where she leaned against Fox admiring their month-old infant.

"What?" Kallista sat up straight. "How? No—I know that. But—when? *Why?*"

Fox and Stone exchanged red-faced looks. "*Is* she ilias? The same as the rest?" Stone asked. "We didn't know. Not for sure. And she kept *pushing*. So we…"

"We talked," Aisse said. "And I told them—*we agreed* they should, to turn her attention from the magic."

"Were we wrong?" Fox asked quietly.

"No." Kallista shook her head. "No, you weren't wrong. Merinda is ilias—but if she's pregnant, it's not temporary anymore. I should have explained it better. I should have known sending three Tibrans off—"

"Is it such a bad thing?" Torchay laid a restless Rozite on the pallet where she began playing with the tassels on Obed's boots. "You said we would be nine."

"I said I *thought* so."

"Merinda is not marked." Obed removed his boot to make it easier for Rozite to reach.

"Neither was I when we married," Torchay said. "Or Aisse." He held Lorynda on his shoulder, patting her to sleep.

Kallista sighed. "And there is the child. I suppose we ought to be certain there really is a child before we go any further. We have to hold a wedding anyway. Might as well marry three as two." She made a face and reached a hand toward Joh and Viyelle. "That sounded awful, as if I didn't want any of you. It's not true."

Joh blew her a kiss from beyond Obed. Viyelle reached across Stone and squeezed her hand. "We know. It's just confusing. Goddess knows, I'm confused."

"So." Kallista planted her hands on Stone's and Torchay's knees to either side and pushed herself to her feet. "I'll go have a little chat with Merinda, shall I?"

"Wait. I'll come with you." Torchay moved as if to hand Lorynda off to Obed.

"No, stay. Reacquaint yourself with your daughter."

"I'm still your bodyguard, Major."

"I will go." Obed passed Rozite to Joh and stamped his foot back into his boot as he stood. "I also serve as bodyguard."

"And ilias," Viyelle said. "You know, Major, it is more proper for two to pay respects, with this size ilian."

Kallista made a disgusted noise deep in her throat. "Why is it, if I'm a major, no one pays any attention to what I say?"

"Because you're *our* major." Stone grinned at her. "And we don't have to."

Torchay's grin appeared. "Can't deny truth, Major."

She couldn't smack all of them, not without it degenerating into a wrestling match. So she rolled her eyes, shook her head and walked out, Obed chuckling at her heels.

At the door she turned back. "Don't suppose any of you might know where I could find Merinda, do you?"

"In the temple, maybe," Aisse offered. "She's been spending a lot of time there. When she hasn't been puking."

The small temple sat on the highest spot in the village, its white-painted compass vane drawing the eye for leagues. The temple house across the lone plaza on the south was sized for a six-person ilian—more than this area would need.

Kallista climbed the winding path, wondering whether Merinda actually was the ninth intended for them. She was a naitan in her own right, unlike the other godmarked. Still, the One could use any who offered, and there was a child to be considered—if child there was.

Merinda sat on the east side of the central sanctuary on one of the benches provided for the elderly and infirm, leaning against the wall behind her as if weary beyond all bearing. She was thinner than Kallista remembered, no longer the plump cheerful midwife-healer who'd come from Arikon to their mountain home for the twins' birth and stayed. The journey to Korbin had obviously been hard on her. Perhaps too hard.

Obed laid a hand on Kallista's shoulder as she squared them, offering silent support. She stepped fully into the wood-floored sanctuary with its painted compass rose. "Merinda?"

The other woman startled, then jumped to her feet, pulling at the bracelets on her arm. "Here." She thrust them at Kallista. "Ilias no more. The need is ended."

Kallista took them, fearing Merinda would drop them on the floor if she didn't—her own bracelet given to her by Torchay at the first wedding, and Torchay's anklet from Stone. "There's no need for such haste." She spoke gently, as gently as an army officer could.

"There is also no need for delay." Merinda backed away. Would have run away if she dared, Kallista thought.

"Is there not?"

The healer's eyes rolled as she looked from Kallista to Obed and back. "No, of course not. No reason at all. The need is ended. We're all safe in Korbin."

No use hinting at meanings. Kallista asked it, point blank. "Merinda, are you pregnant?"

Her eyes got wider and she backed into the bench where she sat down with a thump. "What does it matter if I am or not?"

Goddess, this was a role for someone else, not a mannerless soldier, naitan or no. *Think of it as practice.* The girls would not be babies forever. "You know it matters, Merinda. The sire is one of our iliasti. We have a responsibility to this child. It is ours as well as yours. You're already ilias. We have only to formalize it."

"But I don't want to," she wailed, burying her face in her hands. "I thought it would be grand, living in your fine house, going to court, meeting with the Reinine. But it's *awful*. People *hate* you. People try to *kill* you. There are swords and blood and dead people everywhere you go. I hate it! I hate being afraid all the time."

*Dear Goddess, had she gotten pregnant deliberately?*

Kallista wanted to be angry, but she was too tired. Besides, she could understand wanting something and discovering when one had it that it wasn't at all what was expected. Merinda had been ilias when she took their warriors into her body. She hadn't done anything either illegal or immoral. Yet. Evading the consequences of what she had done would cross that line.

Kallista touched Obed's arm to ease the anger coming through the link. "It's too late now to change your mind, my dear."

"It's early on. The soul hasn't yet taken root."

"Is that truly what you want to do?" Kallista hid her shock. Healers rarely ended a pregnancy. Something about their East magic made it more difficult for them than for others.

"No." Merinda sounded miserable. "But I'm afraid. I'm tired of being afraid."

Kallista sat beside the younger woman and put an arm around her. "You don't have to be. We'll protect you. We kept you safe all the way up here."

"Safe?" Merinda jerked away to stare at Kallista in horror. "I've been caught in a blizzard, shoved rolling down a mountainside, hidden in cave after cave after cave afraid even to breathe lest someone hear me. I've eaten things I don't even want to know what they were. I'm bruised, battered, cut and scraped. There isn't one part of me that doesn't hurt even after two weeks' rest, and you call that safe?"

"Yes." Kallista held back her amusement. She knew Merinda wouldn't appreciate it. "You're here. You're alive. You may be bruised and battered, but you're not maimed. Your injuries won't even scar, not like Fox's. Comfort isn't the same as safety."

"You don't understand," Merinda wailed.

"I do. Believe me, I understand." Kallista stifled her sigh. Merinda wouldn't appreciate that either. "I think it's you who failed to understand a few things. You saw us at court. You didn't pay attention to the fact that most of us are soldiers. As soldiers, we *can* keep you safe. But as soldiers, our lives are not always comfortable. We have our duties. And one of those duties is to you and this child. *Our* child."

Now Kallista let her sigh out. Anger might have been preferable. It would have felt better anyway. "Marry us, Merinda. Formalize the relationship. Then, after the child comes and everything is in order, if you still feel the same way, you can sever the ties then. Your child is ours, too. Don't deny us that. Do the right thing."

Merinda swiped tears from her dripping cheeks. "I hate this. But I know you're right. I'll do it."

"Good." Kallista lifted Merinda from the bench as she stood. "Come with us. Meet the others—there will be three of you joining us in this wedding."

Merinda's expression soured, something Kallista hadn't thought possible. Did she expect a separate ceremony just for her? Goddess help them all. They had neither time nor aptitude for dealing with such moodiness. Obed had been bad enough.

Once more, Viyelle stood under the sky and the spreading branches of apple trees, though this time they were filled with tiny green fruit rather than pink and white blossoms. With her, spaced evenly around the compass rose created on the orchard floor by colored chalk stood all the members of the ilian she was about to join. Viyelle had always expected to marry, but she had never expected it to *matter*. Not like this.

Truth told, marriage had been a thing to dread, even had she been able to escape her mother's intentions. She had never expected this giddy anticipation, never thought she would feel more than tolerant resignation toward more than one or two of her iliasti. Instead—

She smoothed out a wrinkle in her deep rose-red wedding tunic, standing a fraction straighter as Kallista crossed the circle to take her hands. Bracelet already given, the naitan spoke the vows binding them together.

Viyelle liked Kallista. She admired and respected her, in some ways envied her, and in others—she was grateful she didn't have the major's problems. In many ways, Viyelle felt as if she were marrying someone out of the old legends, who wasn't quite mortal, who performed nine impossible tasks before breakfast every day. In truth, she was. More astonishing, Viyelle had herself somehow become one of those legendary beings.

Aisse slipped a bracelet onto Viyelle's right wrist, repeating the ancient words as Viyelle watched and listened. This woman she didn't know well, but given the stories Stone told of their ride north, Aisse matched the rest of them. Viyelle hoped yet again that she could live up to their standards.

Torchay came next, another she liked and respected. She found his reluctance to share with her the physical side of marriage frustrating, but had to respect it as well. He was so obviously deeply in love with Kallista.

Stone. Viyelle had been attracted to him from the first, had seen him as a tragic, romantic character from an old jonglier's song. Now as she began to know him a little, she understood what a silly idea that had been. Yet one thing remained. He was a man she could love, maybe more easily because of who he truly was.

Obed approached to say his vows, all dark mystery and brooding emotion. He seethed with it, the sort of man she would once have made a fool of herself over, the sort she had believed Stone to be. Thank heaven he focused all that moody attention on Kallista. Still, Viyelle couldn't help liking him.

Then Fox came, bringing his bracelet to slide on her left wrist with the four others chiming there. Stone's *brodir*. They were as close as sedili and each as beautiful, as golden as the other. But Fox held that tragic core Stone didn't have. He didn't brood or seethe, but it was there and it made Viyelle shiver. She could fall in love with this man, too.

After Fox, it was Joh's turn. Ordinarily it would have been Viyelle's turn and then Merinda's, as all three were binding themselves into the ilian today, but Joh and Viyelle were already bound by oath, bracelet and the marking of the One to at least a part of the ilian, ties more complete than the arrangement with Merinda. Joh had been marked and bound first, so he would go first.

Viyelle studied him as he took her hands and spoke his vows, his bracelet already on her wrist. He wore his hair loose today—Kallista's request—and it framed his serious face. He was reserved and thoughtful, quiet, kind—the sort of man she'd never noticed, much less thought about. But she liked him, too. And she loved his attentive, meticulous approach to sex.

Now it was Viyelle's turn to cross the smudged compass rose to each of the others, to say her vows and give her bands, those not already given. Seven times she repeated the words, kissed their lips. The ceremony seemed endless with so many swearing vows. The eighth time, she crossed the rose to Merinda, carrying the band provided from Obed's seemingly inexhaustible store. She'd brought her own bands for the iliasti she knew about: Stone, Fox and Aisse. Merinda had been a surprise to all of them.

Viyelle studied her as she slid the bracelet onto the other woman's outstretched wrist and spoke the words that would bind them together. Merinda wouldn't meet her eyes. Viyelle was willing to give the woman a chance, mostly because the others were. But would Merinda meet them halfway? Viyelle had to wonder. And worry.

For when Merinda took her turn, she spoke the vows so softly, no one could hear save for the one she vowed to, and then only with effort. And she never raised her eyes, not even when she shared the kiss.

Then it was done. They were ilian together, nine strong. Viyelle marveled that she should be a part of it, that they had welcomed her in. There was love here—real, wonderful, terrifying love—and it seemed possible that it might spill over onto her.

The most terrifying thought—could she live up to what they deserved? To who they were?

The prelate stepped forward again to speak. Briefly, thank heaven. She clasped Kallista's and Torchay's hands, signaling the rest of them to do the same. With nine, they scarcely had to move farther into the center to reach.

The prelate proclaimed them one. She placed Kallista's hand in Torchay's and backed out of the circle. Viyelle smiled. No, she grinned, something rare for her. Then the magic hit.

It flowed into her, a mountain stream rushing down the slope, picking up speed and power as it leaped from one to the next, from Fox to Viyelle to Stone and back to Kallista. Merinda cried out, would have pulled away but for Fox and Joh holding on tight. It was frightening, Viyelle thought, and it was glorious. Delight beyond any she'd ever known.

They were with her, riding the magic, all nine of them together, though Merinda felt faint, distant. She heard Stone laugh out loud, felt joyous tears sliding down her own cheeks, but mostly she danced in and around and through her iliasti, one and yet nine. Hers as she was theirs. Home.

Merinda wrenched herself away as she wrenched her hands from the men on either side of her. The magic shattered, snapping through each of them in a sharp and startling pain. They all cried out, the women's higher-pitched cries sounding above the men's deeper shouts. All of them except Merinda.

It *hurt*, though Viyelle couldn't point to the place where it did. She whimpered, cutting off the sound when she realized it. Fox turned to her, his back on Merinda, and folded her in his arms. They had all let go hands when Merinda broke the magic.

Stone joined them, sandwiching Viyelle between the *brodir's* embrace as they sought comfort. She could see the others past the Tibran's broad shoulders as they did the same. Kallista and Torchay lifted Obed from his knees where he'd fallen. Joh already cradled Aisse in his arms. Only Merinda stood alone.

# CHAPTER TWENTY-FOUR

Then Torchay's family recovered from their shock. They swarmed them, babbling their concern and rampant curiosity. The new-wed ilian was borne off to the great hall to recover—and to clear the orchard so the feasting tables could be set up and the food brought out. Kallista assured them that whatever had happened was no more than a mild peculiarity of the extremely peculiar magic they all shared, and the celebration should go on as planned. But they needed a moment alone.

As soon as Torchay's mothers were gone, Kallista rounded on Merinda. Torchay was already there, hand closing on her throat.

"Sergeant! Stand down." Kallista's order snapped through the room.

Torchay growled, his hand not moving from Merinda's throat. It did stop closing. Merinda's eyes were wide and terrified, rolling from side to side hunting escape or help.

"Sergeant Omvir!"

The whipcrack of her major's voice reached him and with another wordless sound, he released his victim and whirled away to be caught by Obed who didn't look any less violent.

Kallista sighed. Would things never get easier in this magic-riddled ilian of theirs? "She didn't know what would happen. We didn't warn them what would happen. How could she have expected it?"

"Viyelle nor Joh pulled away," Torchay argued. "They didn't cause it."

"They're marked. They knew what it was. And they know about backlash."

"Actually—" Viyelle raised a tentative hand. "I don't. What's backlash?"

"Nor I," Stone said, still cuddled around the prinsipella, Kallista couldn't tell whether for her comfort or his own.

She told them, succinctly, about backlash and its potential for harm. "Fortunately, as backlash goes this wasn't so bad. It just hurt. It didn't harm. Probably because Merinda isn't marked. Her only magic is her own. Nothing shared with us."

When Kallista looked at her, now and finally, Merinda stood glowering at them, sullen, defiant, angrily miserable. Kallista took a deep breath and let it out. No sighing, no matter how tiresome this got.

"If she has magic of her own," Obed said, "then she should know already about backlash."

"He's right." Kallista's anger came seeping back. "You should. You *do,* don't you."

To Kallista's surprise, tears overflowed Merinda's eyes. "I never meant to hurt anyone. I thought it would rebound into me. I didn't know what else to do. I was afraid. I—I—"

"Panicked?" Kallista managed to soften the sour edge of her voice. A bit. The younger woman did seem truly sorry.

"Yes." Merinda stared at her feet, her voice as soft as it had been in the ceremony. As if she didn't want anyone to hear her. "I'm sorry. It won't happen again."

"Since you're not marked, I doubt there'll be opportunity." Kallista smothered the rest of her anger. "But I will hold you to your word. You agreed to this binding. What happened in the orchard, at the end of the ceremony—*that* was the binding. Not the ceremony itself. The magic."

She frowned. If the magic was the binding, could Merinda's pulling away have harmed—? But when Joh and Viyelle had been marked, been bound, they'd been bound to all of them— even those far distant. Surely Merinda's action would have harmed only her own connection. That was bad enough, but— Kallista would make sure nothing else had been touched. Later.

*Was* Merinda the ninth intended for their ilian?

"I *am* sorry." Merinda addressed Torchay. "Truly. Can you forgive me?"

Perhaps she was. People made mistakes. It was part of what made them mortal beings. People could correct their mistakes, and refusing to allow it wouldn't help matters here. Kallista raised an eyebrow at their red-haired ilias.

Torchay put his scowls away. "The One commands us to forgive, and I was in the wrong myself. I overreacted. I apologize." He rubbed his hands over his face as if scrubbing away tension.

"I'll forgive you, if you forgive me." Merinda smiled and Kallista saw again the quality, the person Merinda could bring to their magic.

"Done." Torchay took the hand she offered and used it to draw her in for a kiss.

It seemed to disconcert her a bit, as if she hadn't intended to get so close to any of them. A little late for that now, given how very close she had to have been to get them into this situation. Kallista smiled, showing her teeth more than anything. This ilian was going to work if it killed them, and at this point, she didn't care which of them survived.

"I'm sure they're ready for us now," she said. "Let's go help everyone celebrate."

\* \* \*

They had much to celebrate. Three new iliasti, at last joined formally and legally to the whole. Three healthy daughters in their parents' arms again. Kallista never tired of holding them— her own twins or Aisse's Niona—and her girls had finally stopped looking at her like she was a strange creature dropped into their midst. The celebration—the feasting and dancing and drinking, tales, tears, laughter and games—lasted the rest of the day and well into the late hours of the summer's night.

The moon had already set when Torchay's two mothers laid claim to the babies and sent the new-bound ilian off to their oversized guest house. The door closed with a definite echoing *thunk-clank,* and there they all stood, staring awkwardly at each other.

Kallista let her gaze drift over the big empty room. The polished wood paneling of the building's interior walls gleamed in the lamplight. The tables and benches that normally lined the walls were all outside, under the apple trees. The movers had left the richly colored cushions and fur throws stacked on the couches pushed together to serve as beds or in big piles on the stone floor. The rugs that softened the stone had been taken up for summer. It was a comfortable place to stay, more comfortable than Noonday Suite in Summerglen Palace, because no one had to worry about breaking something priceless or getting bloodstains out of silk. And none of this musing was helping ease the current situation.

She drifted her gaze back to her iliasti who were mostly staring at her. Merinda seemed to find the floor utterly fascinating, and Viyelle was staring at Stone. Hadn't she got that fascination out of her system yet? Then again, once *in* a woman's system, Stone was difficult to dislodge again. Kallista ought to know.

"So…" She couldn't come up with anything else to say.

"I'll just—" Merinda waved her hand toward a pile of cushions and fabric at the far end of the room from the pushed-together couches. "I don't—I think it would be better if—I'd rather be alone." Her voice got softer and softer as she spoke until she was barely audible.

"You don't have to," Kallista said.

"I'd rather." Merinda edged backward until she seemed to feel no one would stop her, then she turned and scampered away.

Kallista let her go. She'd talked the woman into marrying them, but damned if she would talk her into sex if she didn't want it. She looked at her remaining iliasti. Now all of them were looking back. "Did someone die and promote me to command?"

Torchay chuckled. "You've always been in command, Major. Whether you wanted it or not."

She grimaced. "I never did. I don't want to think about it." She looped an arm around Aisse's neck, caught Joh by the wrist and started off. "Let's go to bed."

"Who?" Torchay stayed where he was.

"All of us. Together." She snagged his belt and tugged, then shoved at Obed to get him moving. "I want us together, touching no matter who is inside who, and I want to use magic. I want the magic binding us like it did at the ceremony this morning, but closer. Tighter."

"Go." Aisse used both hands to push Stone and Fox toward the couches. "I never had magic sex—" She stopped talking as her Adaran words tangled. "No, I had that. In the cave. But never had magic *and* sex. I want it. Now."

Kallista laughed, remembering the Aisse who had hated sex only a year ago. The small woman had her clothes off and folded neatly beside the bed, waiting, with an equally naked and eager Stone whose clothing had been tossed in the four directions, as the rest of them walked up.

This was new to Kallista, utterly different from any of their previous weddings—mostly because of her. She'd resisted the first one, when she and Torchay had joined Stone and Aisse. They'd all have slept alone that night if the magic hadn't broken her resistance to what she truly wanted. They'd slept alone for weeks afterward. Even after Obed joined them, they'd been separate. Alone. Her fault.

When Fox had married in, they were already on their way to Tibre and he'd been a wreck of a man—starving, lame, profoundly blind without the *knowing* the magic gave him later. She'd feared hurting him. And had still been fighting her feelings for the others.

Now everything had changed. She'd given up her fight and accepted the love she had for them. Even for Joh and Viyelle, though she scarcely knew them.

Once again, they stood and stared at each other, but these stares held admiration, awe. For they were all naked and they were all beautiful. At least the others were. Kallista had a strong urge to hide the little belly she hadn't been able to rid herself of since the babies.

"Shh." Torchay read her mood—he'd always been able to—and moved into her, setting his hand on her waist, brushing himself across her stomach as he curled down to kiss her. His flame-red curls teased her cheek.

Fox pressed himself against her back, between her buttocks, and stroked her hair aside to kiss her compass mark, his lips making it tingle. Stone kissed Viyelle, Aisse kissed Joh. Only Obed held back. Kallista stretched her hand out to him, wishing she could help him be more comfortable. As he took her hand and let her draw him in, she touched the links—all seven at once—and nearly drowned in the rush of sensation.

She kissed all of them at once, Stone's devouring mouth as well as Viyelle's mouth being devoured. She touched Fox's scar and toyed with the hair on Joh's chest, even as she knew the softness of her own breasts crushed against Torchay's hard planes. She knew, somehow, which sensations came from her own body, but willingly lost herself in the flood.

"Bed," someone said. "Before we fall."

"Before it starts." Someone else. Male.

"Dear Goddess, she hasn't started yet?" That was female.

Strong arms lifted Kallista, savoring the feel of her bare skin, arms that belonged to the man who toppled onto the bed with her. She could have named him if she wanted to make the effort, but she didn't want to.

She drew the magic in, wrapping the pleasure around her to bind herself together with them. She stirred it until the separate tastes of her iliasti could not be picked out from the magic and then she poured it back out along the links.

Aisse cried out, shivering with a tiny climax as the magic touched her. Kallista tightened her grip to keep the others from joining her. The touch of mouths on skin, skin beneath hands, hands moving everywhere, slowed her thoughts, but Kallista knew this wasn't how she wanted it, wasn't what she wanted the magic to do.

In the ceremony, it had begun with her, ended with her, but it wasn't—it didn't— She couldn't *think*. Kallista let go of the magic for a moment, let it slide back where it belonged and she understood what was wrong. She didn't want to call the magic to her and send it back out to them, bound only to her.

She wanted the magic to flow between all of them, not just Kallista to Obed, Kallista to Joh, but Obed to Joh, and Viyelle to Aisse, and Aisse to Joh and Fox and Stone and Torchay. She wanted a web of magic, not a starburst.

Could she do it? It was a thing that had so far happened only at a wedding, whether in a legal ceremony or not. She'd never tried it on her own, but she above all others knew that meant less than nothing.

She gathered up the strands of magic again, delighting in its eager, joyous response, in the gasps and groans of her iliasti as she slid it from them. Again, she blended it so the parts could not be picked out of the whole, and she poured it into the man closest to her. Torchay, she thought, when he shouted as the magic hit him.

She wrapped her legs around him, drawing him in, and took a breath. This was the new part. Kallista clutched the magic tight and tumbled out of Torchay into her next ilias— Fox. She took a moment to bind him into the magic and blundered on, into Viyelle who screamed as the magic hit her, not in pain.

This wasn't new, Kallista realized. She had done this before, but frantically, half-panicked in the overpowering surge of long-dormant magic. It was easier now she didn't have to rush. She wove Viyelle into the web and found Stone on Viyelle's other side. As she understood what she did, she began to do it faster, the magic changing from tiny trickle to tumbling stream.

Stone to Aisse down by their feet, and Aisse to Joh. Joh to Obed and from Obed back home again. Kallista spilled magic from one to the next, finding the channels connecting each of them to each of the others. She pushed the magic through until the glow of the shining web nearly blinded her. They were connected, bound by bodies and magic.

She felt them all, plunging inside her, against her, taking her in, urging her on. She poured more magic into the stream until it became a flood, a storm of magic beating against their fragile selves. Still she whipped it higher until one of them screamed and the storm broke over them because she could not hold it back any longer.

Someone poured his seed down her throat—but it wasn't her throat. Still it made her writhe and cry out, and they all writhed, all cried out, and that started it yet again and again. Climax crashed through them, each one triggering the others, endlessly, violently, ecstatically, until nothing was left and they lay tangled together, drained and filled to overflowing.

"Dear sweet Goddess in heaven." Many, many long, long moments later, Viyelle's voice floated up from somewhere in the middle of the sticky, sweaty pile, not in cursing, but in obvious supplication. "We won't last a week. The demons won't have to kill us. We'll do ourselves in."

"How can you talk?" Stone mumbled. "M'mouf won't work."

"You're talking now, aren't you?" Fox's careful enunciation betrayed his state.

"Shut up the lot of you," Torchay said. "I'm sleeping here."

"Not till you get off me, you're not." Kallista managed to poke him with a finger. The rest of her hand wouldn't move.

"Oh. Right." He slid to one side, squeezing in next to Fox.

"Is everyone still with us?" She could feel all the links lying silent, deep inside her, but nothing more.

"I'm not," Joh said from beyond Aisse. "I am definitely no longer among the living. Can't possibly be."

Aisse giggled, nothing more, but Kallista decided a giggle was enough of a sign she'd survived. That left—

"Obed?" With a sigh, she struggled to roll over and spoon herself against the broad back beside her. She kissed his shoulder. "Obed, it's all right."

"Yes." His voice sounded odd. Strained.

He jerked as if startled, and Kallista looked down their bodies to see Aisse stroking Obed's ankle. After a moment, Torchay reached across Kallista and laid his hand on Obed's arm, tentatively at first, as if afraid it might be thrown off. When it wasn't, Torchay relaxed, letting the weight of his hand settle in.

"Can I—?" Obed hesitated. "I want to move."

*Where?* What had gone wrong now?

"I want to sleep in the middle." He sat up, looked at Kallista with red-rimmed eyes. "I am ilias. I want in the middle."

Torchay swore. "You expect me to move? After that?"

"Don't move, if you cannot. I will." Obed crawled over Kallista, over Torchay and squirmed his way between him and Fox.

If Kallista had the energy, she would have been shocked. Obed was not in the least attracted to men. She'd sensed his emotions enough to know. So his move had nothing at all to do with sex and everything to do with…what?

She crawled over Torchay, rolling him toward the edge so she could fit next to Obed.

"Saints," Torchay grumbled. "Next thing you'll be shoving me on the floor."

"You know better." She accompanied her scold with a kiss. "Go to sleep."

"I'm *trying*." He turned his back with a grumpy bounce.

Kallista turned the other way and tucked herself into Obed's back once more. "What is it, love? What's wrong?"

"Nothing."

"Well then, what's right?" Exasperated, she had to struggle to keep her voice quiet.

Obed sighed and rolled onto his back, shoving a bit to fit his shoulders into the tight space. "You love me. I expected— *hoped* for that. But I never expected—I have always been on the outside. Always. Apart from family, not a part of one. Until now. I do not have just you. I have them, too. I am tired of living on the outside. I want to be in the middle."

Kallista kissed him. A kiss that was interrupted by Aisse crawling up to insert herself between them.

"He always was yours, but not mine," she announced. "Now I have him, too."

"Well, I'm not sleeping by myself down here." Joh shoved his way in between Kallista and Aisse so energetically that only Kallista's quick action kept Torchay off the floor.

He swore, long and creatively. "Are we through now? Everybody where they're by damn going to stay?"

After a chorus of agreement and a false snore from Stone, Torchay gave Kallista a hearty push, moving everyone over and Stone nearly to the floor on the far side.

"Now," Torchay grumbled as the laughter subsided and eyes closed. "Go to sleep. No more change-your-partner. Sleep. Or I'll be forced to take measures."

"Oh, no," Kallista muttered. "Not *measures*."

"Watch your mouth, woman. I know where you sleep."

On Thirdday after the wedding on Graceday last, as the midsummer month of Norenda was almost done, Kallista gathered up her household, babies and all, collected the troop of soldiers assigned to the valley, and rode for the western coast. They skirted the northern edge of the Empty Lands until they reached Korvell, where they took ship.

The sail south along the coast took just over a week, saving them endless days in the saddle and allowing Aisse to rest and recover further. In Sarit, a merchant's caravan attached themselves to their party for the trip into the Shieldbacks and Arikon. Kallista didn't object.

She was in no hurry to abandon the illusion that their ilian was anything out of the ordinary. Duty would still be there, no matter how swiftly or slowly they traveled. She wanted to indulge herself in family life just a little longer. But the illusion got harder and harder to maintain.

Only two days out of Sarit, the feeling of oppression, of being weighted down, became so strong, Kallista threw up a veiling, hiding their magic. With all of them together, it was nearly as effortless as breathing, especially since the oppressive atmosphere eased as soon as she did it. Joh surmised that the demons were either trying to keep naitani away from Arikon, or to weaken those already present. Kallista thought he was probably right, and the possibility that the demons could cast their power so wide increased her unease.

Nor was magic the only threat. The nights were filled with alarms that had the soldiers endlessly chasing from one end of the caravan to the other so that they rode the next day sagging from lack of sleep. Kallista finally ordered them to ignore any threats to mere property. They got a single night's sleep before the first merchant's throat was cut.

The rebels obviously couldn't match their force or they would have attacked openly, but the sneak attacks from darkness or under cover were taking too great a toll. The caravan was a week away from Sarit and almost that distance to Arikon when Kallista made her decision.

"We ride for the capital without stopping at night." She looked at the gathered merchants, the soldiers, at her family, trying to convey the seriousness of her words.

"If you merchants can't keep up, we will not wait for you. If you turn back, the rebels may leave you be—I think they only intend to stop travel to Arikon. But I do not know for certain."

"What if *you* cannot keep up?" one of the merchants demanded. "You're traveling with infants, with invalids."

"I am no invalid," Aisse protested.

"I think he meant Merinda," Fox murmured to soothe her. Merinda had suffered terribly from sea sickness and still had not recovered.

"We are ilian," Kallista said. "We will carry our own as needed. But we *must* reach Arikon. If you ride with us, then ride. Don't complain."

"When do we go?" another asked.

"Now."

The gathering burst into a flurry of activity that increased with Kallista's refusal to listen to arguments or pleas. The babies were fed, cleaned, placed in carriers. Packs were loaded, remounts collected, horses saddled, and within the hour, they were off.

At least four of the merchants joined them. Two more were still frantically harnessing their heavy wagons. Kallista walled off her heart as they left the stragglers behind. The merchants riding with them had abandoned wagons of their own, ranking lives more important than trade goods. The greedy might survive, if they turned back.

She summoned the veiling, both physical and magical, and threw it over the entire caravan. She hadn't intended to veil the merchants until it occurred to her that if the rebels could see the merchants, they could track her ilian with them.

That first day, while everyone was rested, they pushed the pace to a canter a time or two, stopping only as the babies needed tending. Fox took Merinda up with him early in the day, which meant switching horses more often, but they had plenty of the sturdy Korbin beasts. In the night, more of them shared mounts, one sleeping while the other held on. The babies rode in the pack carriers Stone had devised during the trip north, slumbering blissfully to the sway of the horses.

That first night, Kallista thought she heard screams and the sound of clashing steel, and worried about the merchants left behind. But when she spoke of it, Obed, riding with her, had heard nothing. She might have thought him lying to ease her conscience, but none of the others had heard anything either. She marked it down to guilty dreams while she dozed and let herself drift off again, secure in Obed's tattooed hands.

Between the magic and the relentless pace, they halved the time expected for traveling the remaining distance. It was early on the third and last Fifthday in Vendra, summer almost gone with the waning of the month, when they blundered into the rebels camped along the road just out of musket range of Arikon.

Everything began with Kallista. She should have expected the rebel presence, but she was stupid with exhaustion and she startled when the brown-cloaked rebel stood, appearing without warning from the brush where he'd been hidden. She lost her grip on the veiling, and the entire party flashed into view.

The sudden appearance of armed and mounted travelers surprised the rebels. They shouted. They let cocked crossbow bolts fly. Muskets went off. Horses reared. They bucked. Babies wailed. Men bellowed. Women screamed. Including Kallista, though her screams were supposed to be orders.

Soldiers were down, their saddles empty. Some were wounded, some fighting on foot. From the corner of her eye, Kallista saw Torchay's twin swords flash. Babies and Merinda were safe with Joh and Aisse at the front of the caravan. For now. Kallista didn't have time for more understanding. She needed to act.

She thought about calling magic and it was there, almost anticipating her call. She didn't want to kill the rebels. They were Adarans. What if they'd been deceived, like Joh? What if they could learn better? Could the magic *teach* them?

Quickly she shaped it, willing it both to stop and teach. She didn't know exactly what to have it teach them, but since the magic came from the One, she thought she could leave that up to the magic. "'Ware!"

## CHAPTER TWENTY-FIVE

The soldiers followed Torchay's example, flattening themselves in the saddle or on the ground. Kallista didn't think they needed to avoid the magic, but she didn't want them killing someone by accident when the magic stopped the rebels. The instant her people dropped, she let her magic fly.

Some of the rebels stopped motionless, as if frozen in place. Others fell. Still others stood as if stunned by a blow to the head, weapons falling from limp fingers. Obed stopped his saber's swing inches from a motionless rebel—he hadn't ducked at her warning, but he didn't kill the rebel, either.

"Leave them," she ordered. "Ride for the gate before any more of them show up."

"It's locked tight," one of the merchants cried.

"They'll open it for us." But would they know who was wanting in?

Aisse was already clattering down the winding road toward the Mountain Gate, Joh hard on her heels bearing Merinda and their third child with him. Kallista tossed her reins to Viyelle, nearest her. "Make sure my horse gets through the gate. I'm going to see if I can get word through that we're coming."

Viyelle tossed the reins back and slid from her own mount

to Kallista's, reaching around to gather them up again. "I'd rather make sure *you* get through the gate, and not just your horse. Call your sister."

Oh. That might be easier than broadcasting to anyone in Arikon that could hear. Kallista gathered magic and sent out the mind-to-mind call. A shout, since Karyl was who knew where on the Eastern Plains.

*Not so loud,* the younger woman protested. *What are you doing here? I thought you went to Korbin.*

*I did. No time to chat, dearest. I need you to call Fenetta in Arikon and tell her we're riding for the Mountain Gate with rebels hard on our heels, and to get it open* now.

"They're waking!" Stone shouted from the rear of the too-large caravan. "They're coming. With reinforcements."

*Now, Karyl. Now.* Kallista cut the connection and started to turn the horse, to go back and join the rearguard action, but Viyelle fought her for control of the reins. Joh had already slipped from the horse with Merinda and into Viyelle's empty saddle, shouting orders with the authority of a fifteen-year lieutenant.

"All troops to the rear!" He shouldered his new mount into Kallista's, lowering his voice to speak to her. "If you would en-sure the children's safety, Major?" He made it sound like a re-quest, but it wasn't.

He rode on shouting more orders, leaving Kallista to do as he advised. "Troops to the rear. Merchants next. Varyl ilian, take the lead. Guard formation, soldiers!"

"Ilian includes you, Lieutenant." Torchay blocked Joh's path. "She needs all of us for the magic."

Kallista leaned to the side to see around Viyelle. She could see Joh struggle with the urge to join the rear guard, but when Stone and Fox cantered up, he wheeled his mount and came with them, leaving the troop sergeant in command. Kallista and

Viyelle caught up with Merinda's slowing mount and Viyelle slid across to join the terrified healer.

"We will keep you safe, Merinda," Kallista said for the three-thousandth time. She'd never promised Merinda wouldn't be frightened—though if she trusted the promise of safety, what did she have to fear?

It didn't matter now. Kallista motioned Viyelle ahead and set her mount to dancing in the road as she forced it to wait the few minutes for their soldier iliasti to catch up.

The road leveled out as the land widened. They were able to pick up their pace, though not to a flat-out run, much as the twitching between Kallista's shoulders urged it. She kept herself between the babies and their pursuers. Their men kept themselves behind her.

*Karyl!* She threw the cry into the void.

*I've told her,* Karyl replied promptly. *They have to send runners to the gate.*

*Well, tell them to hurry.* Kallista wobbled in the saddle and righted herself.

*Are you all right?*

"Are you all right?" Fox's question echoed Karyl's, making Kallista's head feel hollow.

"Yes," she replied to both at once. *All safe—so far. We need that gate open.*

*I know. I'm hunting someone closer I can call.*

Kallista let go of the magic and tightened her hold on the reins, though turning her horse aside from the mass scramble down the road would be an impossibility now. Good that she had no desire to do so.

The city walls loomed ahead, the gates recessed so deep into the wall's thickness, they were hidden in shadow. Aisse vanished into the gloom, Viyelle and Merinda close behind. Moments later, merchants with their pack mules crowded into the protected area after Kallista and her ilian.

A shout filtered down through the murder holes overhead. "Who seeks entrance to Arikon?"

"Major Kallista Varyl, Special Attaché to Serysta Reinine, with my ilian," she shouted back.

"All those are your ilian?"

Kallista looked at the people packed in around her. "And four merchant caravans, and a troop of cavalry—the Fifth Tironde Regulars. You should have received word from the palace we were coming."

"Heard nothing. Need a password, or orders from inside."

She swore, then shouted, "I am Major Varyl. I order you—"

"How do we know you're the major? I take orders from no one but my superiors in Arikon."

She hadn't thought that one would work, but had to try it. Just how far was it from the palace to the gate?

Beyond the edge of the gate recess, where the soldiers had created a fence of bayonets, the rebels gathered, more of them every moment. As their numbers grew to more than double Kallista's entire force, so did their courage. Her people could hold them off for a time, but not much of it. They needed the gate open.

*Karyl, ask Fenetta for today's password.*

Moments later, Karyl came back with *Patience. The password is Patience.*

*Bless you.* Kallista shouted over the rising rumble from rebel throats, "The password is patience!"

"How do you know that?"

"My farspeaker asked yours. How do you think? Now let us in, dammit!" Her temper had frayed beyond mending. If she could have sent lightning up the murder hole to sting the idiot—who was admittedly only doing his job—she would have. But the stone in the walls would swallow it.

In reply, the gates banged, swayed, rumbled as the locks were opened. They swung outward, just wide enough for a single rider to pass through. Kallista pushed Aisse and her horse with the baby packs through first, then Viyelle with Merinda and Rozite. She let Torchay shove her inside next, and soon they were all gathered in the cobbled courtyard, the merchants crowding in behind them, as they dismounted and stretched aching muscles.

"Apologies, Major." The guard captain came striding up, looking a bit vague as to just whom she needed to address. Kallista was out of uniform. "The palace runner just now reached us. The city is pure chaos."

"No harm done, save perhaps to my temper." Kallista didn't salute, but smiled and offered her hand.

The captain clasped it briefly. "We'll have to keep the merchants here until they've been cleared and their baggage searched. We'll look after your troop as well, if you're willing."

"Good enough."

"The Reinine's compliments and will you report to her immediately."

"Very good, Captain. Carry on." Kallista nodded briskly to the captain's salute, turned to her ilian and sighed. "So. I need to go. Why don't the rest of you—yes, except for bodyguards, Torchay—follow at your own speed and get settled in. We're still in Daybright Tower, I assume. We can join you as soon as the Reinine finishes with us."

Aisse shook her head, disturbing the baby in her arms. "No. We stay together. You said it. We stay together from now on."

Kallista took a deep breath and let it out. "Your decision. But if you're coming, come." She hoisted herself back into the saddle, barely stifling a groan. Stone didn't bother to stifle his.

* * *

The Reinine's work chamber had soft chairs, steaming cups of cha and thick, meaty bread rolls. The council members frowned at the babies' presence, especially when the babies stayed and the council was dismissed. After introducing Merinda to the Reinine, Kallista held a daughter with one hand, a bread roll in the other and ate while she caught the Reinine up-to-date on everything that had happened since their departure. Then she held both daughters in her lap and listened to the Reinine's report on events in Arikon.

"So in all," Serysta Reinine concluded, "the rebels are more active in Arikon than we like, but it's nothing we cannot handle with the resources in the city."

"What about outside Arikon?" Kallista let Torchay take a sleepy Lorynda and hand her off to Fox. "Was the information we sent helpful?"

"Very much so. Unfortunately, it indicates that the rebels are planning a massive attack, and more recent information suggests that the attack will be against Arikon, and soon."

"So." Kallista took a deep breath, wondering if the skirmish on the road had been for show. No, she decided. Capturing all the godmarked in Adara would have been a devastating blow to the loyalists' cause. "Do you think it will make any difference, the rebels knowing we're all back in Arikon?"

"Who can say?" The Reinine dangled an enormous jewel on a heavy gold chain in front of Rozite and smiled when she stuffed it in her mouth.

"One more thing I have learned," she said. "It was High Steward Huryl who sent the gold for your iliasti to carry to Korbin. And it was Huryl who turned my comment that the children would be safer in Korbin into that most strongly worded suggestion."

"Huryl?" Kallista blinked. "But why? I know the man has

never liked me, but he's always been loyal to you and Adara. Hasn't he?"

"Always." Serysta Reinine sighed and leaned back in her chair. "Though I will be first to admit the man has flaws. He is ambitious and jealous, especially of his influence with me. Perhaps he thought with your ilian divided, you would not stay long in Arikon—which was true. Or perhaps—" She shook her head. "He has never been vicious before."

Her Reinas, the stocky, shaved-headed Keldrey, cleared his throat and Serysta waved a hand. "All right, yes, he has been ruthless, but never to this scale. Never a thing that put innocent lives at risk."

"Where is Huryl?" Kallista asked, suddenly realizing. "I saw him when we first arrived, back in Miel, but—have any of you seen him since?" She checked with the iliasti who had been with her in Arikon.

"I did a few times," Viyelle said. "Before I moved my quarters in with yours."

"Demons?" Torchay kept his voice quiet, but Kallista heard him. They all did.

"Surely not." The Reinine looked as if she didn't want to believe it, but did. "He has served so well and so long."

Kallista pinched off a tiny bit of magic and spun it into a demon hunter. "Best to know for sure. Ambition can make some temptations too great to resist."

She tossed the magic out. It circled the palace a time or two before winging out toward the city walls. Kallista quenched it. "My magic senses no demons in the palace, or even within Arikon, but…"

"But if there's no demon," Torchay said in his raspy voice, "why is he avoiding us?"

"Because he doesn't like us?" Kallista had no other answer.

"We are conducting a discreet investigation into his recent

activities—into all the orders sent under my seal—to be sure they are orders I actually gave," Serysta Reinine said. "So far, the only anomaly is the orders Courier Torvyll brought to you."

"Let us hope that continues to be true." Kallista bounced Rozite, beginning to fret, on her knee. "Thank you for allowing my whole family to accompany me here, but if there is more to be discussed, perhaps the children should be—"

"No, no. We are done." The Reinine stood.

Kallista tried to return the expensive necklace, but when Rozite set up a howl at being deprived of her shiny toy, the Reinine waved it away. "Keep it. Babies need their playthings."

"My Reinine, this is *not* a plaything." Kallista wiped the baby-fist-sized ruby on her tunic, realizing the Reinine might not want it fresh from Rozite's mouth.

"Your daughter thinks it is. Keep it." Serysta Reinine looked entirely too amused. "I'll send toys for the other two as well. They should not think I favor one over the other."

"*My Reinine*—" Kallista couldn't get anything else out. She set the necklace on a table and Rozite howled louder, twisting in Kallista's arms in a fierce effort to reach it. The Reinine handed the necklace back to the baby, whose screams turned instantly to sniffles.

"Now go." Serysta Reinine waved them toward the door. "Tend to your children. Find your demons and let me know tomorrow what you find. Go." She flipped her hands at them like a pie maker chasing away flies.

Kallista could only gather up her family and obey.

Gweric was delighted to see them again, though a bit sulky after his introduction to Merinda, until he realized that her magic was her own and didn't mesh with the others. He apparently had not liked living alone in the large suite, because he talked without stopping to anyone who would listen. The babies fascinated him, though he didn't seem quite to know how to react when they took notice of him in return. Kallista had to laugh at his bemused, confused expression when Rozite fell asleep on him in midchuckle.

But finally, they had everything, including babies, sorted and Kallista sent Gweric out with Joh and Fox to hunt up High Steward Huryl and see what their peculiar vision could see.

When they had been gone long enough to have made their way from the residential sectors of the palace to the administrative, Kallista settled back with her other iliasti and slid down Joh's link to peer out through his eyes. Alongside Fox and Gweric, he found Huryl in the throne room antechamber that served as his office, and they mingled with the petitioners and sycophants that filled it.

Huryl seemed to enjoy the supplication more than Kallista thought attractive, but he listened carefully to each one who spoke to him. She couldn't tell whether he favored any one over another.

*Closer. I can't see anything from here.*

Joh looked at his companions before responding. Fox gave his head a tiny shake—he'd seen nothing. Gweric had to be prodded to get his attention before he frowned and moved forward.

"Careful," Joh murmured. He held on to the hem of Gweric's tunic to slow him down. "We don't want him noticing us, and you're rather recognizable."

The boy nodded and edged behind a tall man in Tandayn brown and blue, searching the room with absent eyes. Joh eased up beside him, his own eyes on Fox's sightless watching.

*Pay attention to Huryl,* Kallista reminded him. She understood Joh's curiosity, but now wasn't the time. She didn't know what she thought she could see through Joh's eyes. Not the demon, but *something,* surely.

Like the way Huryl's face went stark white as he stared directly at her. At Joh. *Why?*

A moment passed. Others noticed Huryl's shocked expression and turned to look about the chamber, to see what had affected him so. His aide called his name and Huryl recovered himself enough to blink and look away, if not to regain his color.

He looked at his desk clock and cleared his throat. "I beg your pardons, prinsipi, aili. I have an engagement with the First Advisor." And with one last, near-panicked look over his shoulder at Joh, he vanished into the throne room in a flutter of multicolored pennants.

"What alarmed him?" Fox asked under cover of the babble that broke out the instant the throne room door closed.

"Don't know." Joh relayed Kallista's orders. "She wants us back in quarters soonest, before anyone gives you or Gweric stranger looks than they already are.

"Or go beyond looking," Fox agreed.

"What did you see?" Kallista asked before the door to their suite even closed. "Gweric?" Her hopes rode on him. She really hadn't expected the other two to have seen anything, though they might have.

The boy frowned, like he had in the antechamber. "I didn't see—or smell—anything. But…"

"What?" Kallista had to prompt him when it seemed he would take all day to decide how to finish.

"There's something wrong with him. Or about him. Or—" Gweric shrugged. "He's not right."

"But is it demons?"

Gweric shook his head. "I don't know. I don't—he's just not *right.*"

Kallista huffed a breath. "That doesn't help. I can't take 'just not right' to the Reinine and expect her to act."

"If he's not demon-ridden now," Fox said, "and I can't tell

whether he is or isn't—but I know he has been at some time in the past."

"How do you know?"

"How long in the past?" Torchay stepped into the conversation.

"I don't know how long ago—more than a day or two. Those I saw in Turysh, the ones who weren't regular mounts for the demons, looked..." Fox seemed haunted as he searched for words to describe what he'd sensed. "*Twisted,* I suppose. Deformed. They got better after a while. But the demon-ridden people, the regulars, looked only a little wrong. After the demons left them, they looked worst of all. He looks...wrong. Off."

"Wonderful," Torchay rasped. "So either he's demon-possessed *now* and the demon is hiding, or he's been possessed within the last few months or weeks, and we're just now learning about it. And if he's been possessed once, who's to say it can't happen again, any time?"

"How are we going to explain this to the Reinine?" Kallista set her hands on her hips, scowling at the floor as she tried out various beginnings. "How do we explain it so she *does* something about it?"

"What's this *we?*" Torchay's face held no emotion. "You're the major, Major."

He ducked away laughing, but she still caught him with a faint spark on his backside, which made him and everyone else laugh harder.

Except Joh. "What bothers me," he said, "is that Huryl fled after he saw *me.* Not Gweric, or Fox, but *me.* Why?"

"He doesn't know me," Fox said.

"True. But why would he know me?"

"You were rather notorious last summer." Torchay rubbed his hip where she'd stung him. "And this spring, when you joined us."

"The High Steward didn't come to the trial. He only ever saw me when I was on guard duty, when Stone was my prisoner, and High Steward Huryl is not one to notice any soldier with less rank than a red-fringe general. Why would he remember me?"

"That's true," Viyelle said. "When I was in my courier's grays, he never even looked at me. He had no idea I was the same Viyelle Prinsipella he drowned in flattery when I wore the Shaluine crest on my court clothes."

"Exactly." Joh appeared puzzled and grim. "It makes no sense. Things that make no sense need to be investigated until they are understood."

Kallista sighed. "Agreed." She looked from one to the other of her iliasti. "And, since I am the major, I suppose I had better go inform the Reinine of what we know and suspect."

"Just what is it we suspect?" Stone asked.

Kallista paused in her hunting of boots to reply. "That at the very least, High Steward Huryl has been demon-ridden at some time in the recent past and may possibly be at present. And he needs to be questioned."

"Will she believe you, or will she think you merely trying to repay Huryl for separating our ilian?" Obed said.

"I think she'll believe me." Kallista found her boots beneath a small nest of baby blankets and shoved her feet into them. "I hope she will. Fox, you come with me in case she wants to question you herself. And whoever else Torchay thinks needs to come."

Their departure was interrupted by the arrival of a brace of nursery servants with a note from the Reinine.

*"Accept the assistance,"* it said. *"You have said your entire ilian is required to deal with demons. This way, they can be. Sidris and Maritta come highly recommended and thoroughly vetted by my bodyguards."*

Grateful to the Reinine for tending to something Kallista

hadn't yet thought about, she still took a moment to spin a bit of magic out to sniff for demon taint. She found nothing, nor did Fox or Gweric. With a polite murmur, she left them in Aisse's hands to get settled in. Or perhaps Aisse was left in their hands. The outcome was still to be determined.

The Reinine did question Fox closely as to what he'd seen, but in the end, with the encouragement of her bodyguard iliasti, she agreed to have Huryl brought in for questioning.

Late that night, she sent word with the extra guards for their door that Huryl could not be found. This despite the fact that the palace grounds had been closed to the city—no one in or out—since the order for his questioning had gone out. The order was now changed for his arrest.

"I don't like this." Kallista frowned at the closed door to their suite. "This entire mess gives me a bad feeling."

"Major—" Joh walked beside her back to the seating area. "Kallista, I've been thinking."

"Oh?" Torchay's eyebrows flew up.

Kallista patted his arm. "Don't worry. He's actually good at it."

"Thank you, ilias." Joh bowed, eyes twinkling in his solemn face. "I have been thinking about Huryl's reaction to me, and about why anyone in Arikon might have cause to be alarmed by my presence."

"And have you reached any conclusions?" Torchay asked.

Kallista watched Joh's eyes go hard, his face lose all semblance of ease, and she dreaded his answer.

"One," he said. "There are many reasons for people here to hate me or to be suspicious of me. You most of all. But who would have cause to *fear* me—except for the one who gave me the gunpowder and lied about what it could do?"

"Huryl did that?" Kallista found it hard to believe.

"Why didn't you tell us before this?" Torchay took a step toward him, but allowed Kallista's hand on his arm to stop him.

"I didn't know. I still don't, not with any measure of certainty." Joh shifted as if he wanted to pace but wouldn't, and his hands closed into fists. "I never saw the Master Barb's face when we met, and he disguised his voice. But the height and the build match. It could be. It could explain his reaction. So could half a dozen other things."

Kallista sighed. "We have to send a message to the Reinine. She needs to know our suspicions."

"They are *my* suspicions," Joh said quietly.

"And now they are mine, too." She summoned a smile for him, feeling the weariness brought on by this thousand-chime day. She took the quill and paper Viyelle handed her and bent over the nearest table to write her message.

"I have a thought," Stone said as Obed returned from delivering the message to the guard at the door for conveying. "Let's hurry and go to sleep before anything else can happen."

"You think our sleeping will stop it happening?" Kallista let him push her in the direction of the double-sized bedroom.

"No, but if it's anything less than the invasion of Arikon, if we're asleep, maybe they won't wake us up." Stone herded more of their number toward the door, unlacing his tunic as he went.

"Excellent thought." Obed swept up the stragglers and snuffed the lamps and candles in the parlor before closing all nine of them in the bedroom.

This time, Merinda consented to join them in the enormous bed, on the outside edge, almost falling off it, but she did join them. It was a beginning, Kallista thought. She hoped they would have time to work their way through to the end.

The next day, after a breakfast that involved food throwing and fingers in eyes—without counting the babies' meal—after they cleaned themselves up again, Kallista gathered up her godmarked iliasti and Gweric, and trooped out to the city walls. They left Merinda behind to recover from the unexpected excitement. The guards at the door would keep them all safe, and Sidris, the male nursery servant, had bodyguard training.

Kallista's guarded optimism about Merinda was a bit more optimistic and less guarded after the way she'd finally let herself go and smeared honey in Stone's face in retaliation for the sausage in her hair. Kallista set her hopes aside as they climbed the rickety stairway to the walk atop the walls.

"What are we doing here?" Aisse pulled her sword from its scabbard for a few practice swings.

"Looking to see what we can see." Kallista thought for a moment before pulling magic. She reveled in the ease with which it came, its willingness to do whatever she asked of it. This time, she needed to see, not simply through Joh's eyes or Fox's *knowing*, but as if she were on her own flying boat. Only more. She needed to see what was hidden as well as that in the open.

"Watch," she said. "All of you, especially you Fox. And Joh and Obed. You see differently or more clearly than the rest of us. We need your watching. If you see rebels, do your best to count them. Gweric, look for any magic patterns or demons."

She released the magic, watched it rise and spread out until it seemed she saw everything beyond the city's eastern wall at once. After a moment, the vision ceased to overwhelm her and she realized it worked like ordinary sight. She could focus her attention on a particular spot and the rest would fade to her peripheral vision.

Slowly, methodically, she scanned the ridges, cliffs and gorges to the east of Arikon. Rebels gathered in the deep places, but no more than were already known. Still Kallista counted. She heard her iliasti counting, too. When they had finished looking, they moved to the south-facing wall, and on, until they had circled the city and searched out the forces arrayed against them.

The majority of the rebels were massed in the broad valley to Arikon's south. It would be difficult to fight their way to the south-facing gate and batter their way through the defenses, but the other gates were even more difficult to reach, given the terrain. The presence of demons among them was shockingly comforting.

She *knew* where they were. Ashbel to the south, Ataroth on the west, and a third demon on the east whose name Kallista had not yet been given. She had destroyed two, and one of these demons had eaten a third. But Joh had seen seven demons in his dream-vision. Where was the seventh?

Still riding Huryl? If so, why hadn't Gweric seen it?

# CHAPTER TWENTY-SIX

Kallista gathered more magic, weaving it this time into demon-hunting. Barring it from the three she'd already found, she turned it loose. With the sun lowering in the western sky, they trudged back to the palace while the magic quartered the city, seeming to find and lose a demon's trail a score of times. It circled and hovered as if confused, almost vibrating with indecision, until finally Kallista released it to go hunting beyond Arikon's walls. She didn't anticipate it finding anything new.

They found extra guards outside their suite beyond those Serysta Reinine had sent last evening. Inside Merinda was happily entertaining a quarto of young prinsipelli. Viyelle's younger sedili had come to visit with their own guards, apparently not for the first time, for Gweric greeted the eldest—a boy not far from leaving for his military service—with a nod and a flick of his fingers.

The two girls each held a twin on her hip and judging by the youngest boy's expression, had been cooing at them for some time. Viyelle introduced them, Mowbray and Tiray the boys, Dessa and Bella the girls. After some polite conversation, during which thirteen-year-old Tiray finished off the last of the pastries Merinda had served, Dessa asked about their trip.

Despite Kallista's attempts to emphasize the monotony of travel and the sheer awfulness of the demons, the youngsters hung on every word. Viyelle's embellishments didn't help. Now the gossip would spread like grassfire.

Three days later, on Peaceday afternoon, the prinsipelli were visiting again—roughhousing with Gweric while pretending to practice their hand-to-hand or playing with the babies—when Kallista and her iliasti returned to the room from their spying.

"I knew it." Viyelle hugged her youngest sedil despite Tiray's squirming attempts to escape. "You love me so much, you just couldn't stay away." She planted a smacking kiss on the boy's cheek, laughing as he wiped it off.

"More like we couldn't stand any more of Kendra," Dessa said. "And we knew you wouldn't be here. Not right away, any road."

Kallista burst out laughing and ruffled up Viyelle's hair as she passed her. "Truth hurts, eh, ilias?"

Dessa shrieked as Viyelle captured her in a gentle headlock and kissed her soundly on the ear, making the girl yell again.

"She hates that," Viyelle confided with a grin as she released her sedil. "Says it's too loud."

"And disgusting." Dessa swiped at her ear with a shoulder.

"Who ate all the spice buns?" Stone complained as he studied the picked-over remains of a generous pastry tray.

"Tiray," Bella said. "He eats everything, including the bones. Mother Saminda says he's growing. I've only seen him grow *out*." She spread her arms, as if holding up a vast belly.

Tiray protested, but refrained from retaliatory violence at a look and a raised finger from Viyelle.

Kallista took Lorynda from Mowbray and a plate from Torchay, holding it at arms length to keep little fingers out of it.

As she settled on the sofa and let Lorynda crawl out of her lap and pull up to stand, the rebellion seemed very far away. Here, in this moment, surrounded by family and friends, she could almost pretend that this was all there was. That the world outside didn't exist. That this was the center of the universe. It was the center of *her* universe.

The sudden shocking clangor of palace alarm bells startled them all. Bella dropped her plate and it broke. Rozite started to cry. Lorynda jumped, lost her balance and fell onto her mother's lap. Carefully, Kallista set her plate on the low serving table, lest she drop hers, too, secured her daughter and opened her mind to call the farspeaker she knew. *Fenetta, what's happening?*

*Attack.* The other woman sounded near panic. *Betrayal. They're in the palace!*

"What?" She spoke aloud and in her mind, then cut the connection with Fenetta. The woman didn't know any more, and panic was catching. Kallista snatched magic and sent it searching, as she should have done to begin with.

"What is it?" Joh was rebuckling the sword belt he'd just removed. Torchay already stood at the open doorway, conferring with the guards beyond, their own and the prinsipelli's.

"Rebels in the palace." Kallista pitched her voice loud enough for everyone to hear.

"How?" Stone caught the shield Fox tossed him. "We've been watching. How could they slip past?"

"Demons hiding them the way our magic can hide us, maybe." The idea terrified her.

Kallista's magic zeroed in on the open gate—gates. Two— no, three of them now as the third opened and rebel fighters swarmed through onto the palace grounds and into the buildings. The warren of doors and corridors gave them a thousand points of entry, a thousand ways through. She tried to stop them, touch their minds to frighten them, inhibit their advance, but they were too many and too far away.

"*Kallista.*" Torchay's voice penetrated her distant focus. "Major, what are your orders?"

Her gaze swept the room, all eyes looking to her, even her screaming daughters who reached for her comfort. Kallista shut down her rising terror, turned her fear for her family to determination. "We stop them," she said.

"Well, yes, of course." Stone stood by the door, hands on his hips. "But, exactly *how?*"

"The children can't stay here. The rebels will know this place is ours. Send them all with the guards to Viyelle's parents. The rebels are on the Summerglen side. They'll be safer in Winterhold with Torvylls."

The two oldest of Viyelle's sedili, Mowbray and Dessa, took the twins from those who held them. The servants appeared, one with Aisse's squalling Niona, the other with necessary baby gear.

"Merinda, you go with them." Kallista gave the healer a hug and pushed her toward the door. "You'll be safe. Gweric, you, too."

"I can fight," the boy protested. "I can see."

Kallista grabbed him by the tunic and hauled him close. "You can obey orders," she growled. "If you were in the army like Mowbray soon will be, you would obey orders. Obey now. I need you to help protect the babies. You have to see the way. Keep them from walking into trouble. Hear me? I *need* you for this." She let him go.

Gweric drew himself to his full height, tugging his tunic back into place. "Yes, Major. I will guide them."

"Lieutenant," Kallista called to Joh, summoning him. "Make sure the guard knows to follow Gweric. He can see the safe paths with his magic. You don't have to tell them it's of the West."

Joh saluted and left to do her bidding. The guard sergeants would listen to him as one of her godmarked iliasti, if not as an army officer. The children were ready, the burdens divided among all the noncombatants so no one was unduly laden.

"Go." Kallista motioned them on. "Be safe."

No time to kiss her babies. If she did, her control would shatter. But as she gathered magic, she let it embrace them, surround them, guards and all, with protection. Then, closing her eyes, she turned the magic toward demons.

There and there and over there. Kallista's magic flew straight and true. The demons were inside the city, but not yet inside the palace, spread far distant from each other so she couldn't take them all out at once. Evil they might be, but she didn't remember any claiming demons were stupid. They evidently could learn from their failures.

So could she. These were lesser demons than the foulness she had destroyed before, and her ilian had been only six strong then. They were together now, the eight of them bearing marks. If they were meant to be nine, the One would provide.

"South," she said. Ashbel was the strongest of the demons. They should attack it first while they were fresh. "The demons haven't reached the palace. We'll stop them before they do."

The palace corridors alternated between empty and echoing and crowded with bodies, depending on the corridor and the moment. At first, the bodies were fleeing courtiers and servants, but as Kallista and the others worked their way south, courtiers gave way to soldiers rushing to meet rebels or bearing their wounded comrades back for healing.

The soldiers parted to let them past. Many recognized them not just as a naitan going to fight, but as the godmarked, and the soldiers murmured blessings.

Kallista used magic to find her way around the fighting. They didn't need the delay. The rebels hadn't yet penetrated all the passages. She kept light contact with the presence of the other two demons to make sure one didn't suddenly surge ahead, get nearer the palace, but Ashbel was her target. The massed rebel soldiers pouring in through the city's broad south gate carried the demon along with their rapid advance.

The godmarked caught up with General Uskenda in the Southside Temple plaza, ordering her troops for a stand.

"How far?" Kallista startled the general when she spoke.

"Why didn't you see this coming?" Uskenda accepted a note from a runner.

"I'm a farseer, not a foreseer. They hid their actions from any sight I have. Besides, you knew it was coming. Didn't need a foreseer for that." Kallista watched the infantry fall into line, cavalry ranged behind them. "Begging your indulgence, but might you not stop them surer if your troops had protection?"

"First volley to shock them. Then behind barricades." Uskenda nodded at the carts to either side of the square loaded with stones and sandbags, ready to be pushed into position.

"How far?" Kallista asked again.

"You going after them single-handed?" Uskenda raised an eyebrow.

"After the demon that drives them, yes."

Uskenda shuddered, traced a compass over her mouth with her thumb and kissed it. "Don't tell me about demons. I don't want to know."

Another runner dashed up and signaled his news to the general as he doubled over gasping for breath.

"Two streets," Uskenda said. "First rebels are only two streets away on a front ten streets wide centered on the temple."

"Then we'll go eleven streets wide." Kallista saluted.

"Why didn't you just look for yourself?" the general asked.

"I'm saving the magic for when I really need it," Kallista

called over her shoulder as she followed Torchay west. She chuckled at the general's elaborate shudder.

They had to circle twelve streets wide to get around the spreading rebel front. The rebels' disciplined advance worried Kallista. She'd expected them to stop and loot, behave like a mob. Instead, they moved like an army.

The demon Ashbel was in the center of the approaching troops. Kallista peered around the edge of the recessed doorway where they'd hidden. The rebels didn't march ramrod straight, eyes front. They were wary, alert, one group watching while another advanced. Much like Kallista and her ilian had been moving.

Trying to get close to the demon through that kind of army without notice was more than she wanted to try. They were eight now, and Ashbel was less than Tchyrizel had been. Maybe she didn't need to be so close.

"Up." She pointed to the door and the house behind it.

Obed nodded and, with Fox, quietly forced the door. It was a merchant's house. The children huddled terrified in a second floor room while their parents stood on the stairway, swords in their trembling hands. Torchay touched finger to lips, asking for quiet as he glided up the stairs, Kallista just behind him.

"Loyal Adarans," she murmured. "I am Major Naitan Varyl. We have need of your roof."

"Take it," one of the three men responded. The two women nodded agreement.

Kallista pointed to Fox and Joh. "With me. Need your eyes. The rest of you stay here and guard."

"My eyes don't work," Fox said as he followed to the attic stair.

"Whatever it is that does work, that's what I need." Kallista let Torchay lead the way to the narrow dormer and open it. She hadn't ordered him along. He was always at her side. She couldn't order him away.

"Clear." He crawled through onto the steep slate roof and moved aside to let the others out.

Kallista set Joh to scan toward the north and deepened her link with him so she could slide into his vision at need. Then she rode her hunter magic east toward the demon. A smear of darkness over the center of the rebel advance, it seemed to coalesce into something thicker, darker, crouched above the shoulders of a woman in brilliant cloth-of-gold.

"D'you see it?" Torchay's attention roved deliberately from place to place, watching for danger.

"Yes." She took a deep breath, drawing magic as if inhaling it with the air. "Let's see if I can kill it from here."

Kallista shaped the magic, named it, and *pushed,* directing it toward Ashbel. No naitan before had been able to send the dark veil in a single direction, in the years before this magic had been lost. It had always spread in all directions like waves from a pebble dropped in still water. Until Kallista.

Pushing the veil like this gave it power and distance. But not enough. She could see it fade into a dark glitter before it ever reached the smear of demon presence.

She swore under her breath, mostly. "Too far. We have to be closer. At least four streets closer."

She plunged back through the window, almost falling on her face when her foot caught on the sill in her haste. Fox caught her by the back of her trousers and set her upright.

The crackling boom of a musket volley made her jump as it signaled the rebels' arrival at the temple square.

"Let's go. With luck, the battle on the plaza will distract them enough we can get as close as we need without too much trouble."

"How much is too much?" Torchay clattered down the stairs behind her.

"Stopping to fight." She handed a blue-and-silver ribbon token to the householders for repair authorization with her thanks as they left, warding the broken door with an aversion spell.

They dashed through the streets behind the rebels, following Kallista's hunter magic. She considered veiling them from sight, but decided against it. At this range, it was well-nigh useless, and as she'd told the general, she thought it better to conserve the magic.

Aisse was tiring. Fox fell back to help her and Kallista slowed the pace.

"No," Aisse gasped. "Run fast. I keep up."

"We have two more demons after this one. Don't spend all your strength now." Kallista rounded a corner and was hauled back by Torchay. They'd caught up with the fighting.

Kallista shut her eyes and tapped Fox's *knowing,* using it to see where her own vision couldn't. The square was pure chaos, hand-to-hand fighting where the rebels had torn apart the barricades, mixed with ragged volleys of musket and crossbow fire.

The Ashbel demon had spread itself thinner yet, filling its fighters with a violent frenzy that had them throwing themselves bare-handed at the barricade remnants. The thing was scarcely a double score of paces away, but those paces were filled with armed and vicious guards. Was this close enough to destroy it?

She drew magic and shaped it. As she hadn't yet learned how to make it curve around corners, Kallista stepped out into the street, her bodyguards at her side, and *pushed.* The magic rushed toward Ashbel, dropping a scattering of its guards, and struck. The demon screamed, its essence dissolving. Some, but not all.

Ashbel had spread itself so thin, the dark magic couldn't reach all of it. The demon shrieked again, pulling its far-flung bits in to coalesce deeper in the massed guards. The small woman in the golden dress collapsed bonelessly, silently on the cobbles.

"Oskina Reinine?" one of them said, before his head lifted and he turned to look directly at Kallista, his will coopted by the demon.

"They're coming," Torchay said. The rest of their eight stood with them as the berserker rebels charged.

Again, Kallista drew magic, strengthening her iliasti. The demon would be easier to kill, now it was condensed, if she could only get into range.

"Closer," she said. "I need to be closer."

"Ah," Obed said. Then with a deep-throated shout, he whirled his sword over his head and charged the oncoming rebels.

Her own terrified laughter in her ears, Kallista followed on his heels, shaping the magic as they ran. They plowed into the rebel line with a clash of steel on steel, cutting through them like a ship through storm waves, battered and wallowing, but still making headway.

Five paces, ten they advanced. The demon's new mount, a bearded man in a brown cloak, screamed at the troops until spittle flew from his mouth. A rebel loomed before her, then vanished as Torchay's twin swords crossed paths at his neck.

"Magic?" he gasped. "Demon? You are taking care of it, right?" He spun to ward off another threat, but Viyelle was already pulling back her bloodied sword.

Another few paces. Kallista packed the magic tighter. She'd been told gunpowder exploded more violently when tightly packed. Maybe magic would work the same way. One more step— She edged past Obed's elbow and *pushed*.

The magic sped, faster even than her enhanced senses could follow, slammed into the demon and burst into invisible fireworks. Ashbel didn't have time to scream. It simply vanished into nothingness, swept away by the magic's fire.

Obed grabbed her arm and yanked her back into the ilian's

center as Fox parried the thrust that would have skewered her. A swish of Obed's sword and the rebel died. The man the demon had been riding lay broken on the paving. Their leaders were down. The rebels would realize it soon and lay down their arms.

Or perhaps not. The fall of their leaders seemed to send the fighters into a greater frenzy. Why?

She grabbed a bleeding rebel and asked. Their leaders—the demons—had them convinced they would be slaughtered in retaliation for daring to rebel. Death in battle appealed more.

*Fenetta.* Kallista sent to the court farspeaker. *Tell the Reinine to offer the rebels their lives if they surrender. And bind the offer with a truthspell so they won't fear to accept it. The demons have them believing we're as bad as they are.*

*I can't tell the Reinine to do anything, Major.* Fenetta's shock and alarm came through clearly. *But I will inform her of your suggestion.*

*Do that.*

Kallista caught Joh's arm. "We're pulling back. Tell the others. We've still two more demons to kill."

It took more time than she liked to cut their way through to empty streets again. Before they were out of earshot, Uskenda had heralds with voice amplifying cones calling out the Reinine's offer of clemency. Kallista hoped it worked, at least here. She didn't expect it to have any effect on the rebel advances elsewhere in the city until the other demons were destroyed.

Death and danger stalked the corridors of power. Gweric began to fear he would never be able to lead the major's family through to safety. Every hallway he turned down screamed at him. It was just a matter of how loudly they screamed. This one—

He froze in place, putting a hand out to stop the others, and they waited. Even the babies kept silent. They waited more. Merinda shifted.

Gweric turned to *look* at her, and she went still again. He could tell how uneasy his empty eyes made her. He would have worn a cloth over them, but somehow it blocked his ability to *see*. And still they waited.

The Torvyll's guard sergeant whispered half a word before Gweric's hand on his mouth stopped it, just as a band of eight or nine rebels walked quietly through the intersecting cross-corridor twice a dozen paces away. An intersection where his charges would have been seen had they continued on their way.

They waited another little while, till Gweric's questing senses felt the danger ease down from screams to whimpers, and they moved on.

Just as they reached the intersecting walkway, the sound of quick-moving feet had the guards shoving the children back, raising swords to attack.

"Do you lead us to our deaths?" the sergeant snarled, snatching Gweric by the tunic and hauling him close to use as hostage.

Panicked, Gweric searched. *Had* he led them into danger? He could sense nothing deadly.

Then a small company much like theirs came into view. Bodyguards leaped forward, weapons on guard, pushing their charge behind them. Almost they came to blows, until Rozite squealed.

"Babies?" A woman's voice came from the center of the clustered bodyguards. "Rebel fighters won't have babies with them."

"It's us, Majesty." Gweric took the chance and called out. "Kallista Naitan's children and Shaluine's youngest prinsipelli."

Serysta Reinine pushed her way through her bodyguards. "What are you doing wandering the corridor, Gweric? You should be locked behind doors, safe."

The Torvyll's sergeant lowered his sword as if he'd never considered using it on Gweric.

"It wasn't safe in Daybright. The rebels know it's Kallista Naitan's quarters," Gweric said. The guards seemed happy to let him do the speaking, especially since the Reinine knew his name. "We're going to Shaluine's suite."

"You could come with us. My safe room is the most secure in the palace. And it's close enough you'll be out of these dangerous corridors all the sooner."

"My Reinine, we should go." The shaved-bald bodyguard almost twitched with impatience, and Gweric wondered if he could feel the danger building, too.

Maybe they *should* go with the Reinine. But the minute he thought it, alarm went screaming through him. "Thank you, my Reinine, but Major Varyl sent us to Shaluine. She'll be looking for us there."

"Don't be ridiculous." Merinda pushed her way through the guards. "The Reinine has invited us. Her room is closer and it's safer. We go there."

*"No."* Gweric caught her arm and pulled her back. "It's *not* safer. Death waits for us that way."

Serysta Reinine stiffened. "For all of us?"

Gweric questioned his magic, removing Kallista's family from the grouping. "Danger," he said. "But not necessarily death. Danger is everywhere now."

"And becoming greater the longer we delay," her bodyguard said. "Serysta, we *must* go." He took her arm and urged her on down the corridor.

"Wait," Merinda cried. "We're coming with you." She lifted the hem of her long tunic to hurry toward them.

"No, Merinda. The major said to go to Shaluine." Gweric had to leap to catch her.

She rounded on him. "I am ilias, not you. You're only a boy

who pretends to see things to make yourself important. But you're not. You're nobody."

"I am the one Kallista said to follow, not you. She told *me* to keep you safe." His anger flared, not at her insults—he'd had worse—but at her refusal to listen.

"Fine. You go where you want. *I* am going with the Reinine." She turned and ran after the retreating bodyguards. "My Reinine, *wait*."

"You going with 'em?" The sergeant spoke from behind Gweric.

"No, Sergeant." Gweric sighed. If Merinda wanted to get herself killed, he couldn't do anything about it. Maybe she would live. Some of them would.

"This way." He pointed across the intersection. "To Shaluine's chambers."

## CHAPTER TWENTY-SEVEN

Kallista had Joh "borrow" horses from a back garden stable to cross the city in better time. Aisse was grateful. Kallista sent back a sense of her own aches and gratitude, amusing them all.

This second demon—Keqwith was the name *given* Kallista—hadn't been in Turysh with the others. She got a vague impression of travel, that it had been in many places, probably stirring up support for the rebel cause. But it was here now, terrified and desperate to avoid becoming the next victim of the Destroyer.

Kallista smiled, not a pretty one. She rather liked the title the demons had given her.

The horses screamed and bolted the wrong direction, throwing their riders when they tried to turn them. Keqwith wasn't content to wait for them. It sent out its odorous magic to fend them off.

"Let them go." Kallista touched Joh's hand, urged him to open it and release the reins he held. "They're afraid of the demon."

"So am I," Stone said. "You don't see me tossing everyone on their heads."

"That's because the horses are smarter than you are." Fox dusted off his trousers and drew his sword.

"Smarter than you are, too, apparently." Stone helped Aisse to her feet.

"It's insanity, not lack of intelligence that afflicts me," Fox said.

"Anyone hurt?" Torchay asked. "Other than bruises?"

"We're all fine." Kallista started toward the sound of fighting, following the magic tagging Keqwith.

"That's because we all landed on our heads," Stone said. "Safest place to fall."

"*I* didn't land on my head." Viyelle made a show of rubbing her backside.

"Nor me." Aisse grinned up at the prinsipella. "We landed on extra padding."

"Do you need help tending your hurt?" Stone played at innocence. "I can kiss it and make it better."

Kallista let them play. They would be back in battle soon enough.

The demon attacked again five streets nearer, clawing at their links. Fox cried out at the rancid touch, panic flaring as he recoiled inside himself. Kallista raced down the link, leaping to join him before he could cut himself off from her again.

*Safe, Fox. It can't touch you. The mark protects you. The magic fills you. It can't get in. No room for it.* She whispered to him, curled up with him behind his defensive walls, maintaining only the thinnest thread of connection to her other six mates.

After a moment, he seemed to hear her. He didn't speak, but suddenly she was inside her own self, the links wide open and blazing with power. Keqwith threw talons at them to rend and tear, and flinched away as Kallista's magic lashed out.

She caught the talons, the tendrils of demonstuff, and yanked, stretching more of the demon's substance between her ilian and the person the demon rode. Winding it up like new spun yarn around a spindle, she called and shaped magic. This time, she didn't need to *push* it. With the demon in one insubstantial hand and magic in the other, she merely touched them together.

Keqwith seemed to blaze up, its shriek echoing through the mountains behind them. The magic ate it, leaving nothing behind, following the demonstuff like sparks along a gunpowder trail until all of it was gone.

"Two done," she said. "One left to kill."

"Then let us kill it and be done." Obed bowed and gestured Kallista into the lead.

"It's west," she said. "Back across the whole damn city this time. Joh, can you organize some horses again?"

He bowed and signaled for Viyelle to accompany him.

"You sure you want to risk horses?" Torchay slid his second sword into its lower sheath and locked it in.

"They didn't panic till we got close enough for the demon to reach them. We can't afford the time it will take to cover the distance afoot. We'll just leave them sooner this time."

They had to circle round the palace to get to the fighting on the western side of the city. It was afternoon, the sun halfway along its downward journey, and hot. Summer was waning, but even in the mountains, it had not yet given way to fall. Kallista wiped the sweat from her eyes and blinked away the sting. She needed no distractions.

The horses' hooves slipped on the round cobblestones if they tried to push them too fast, but even at a trot, they made better time than walking. They left the horses just two streets past the wide, avenue parks surrounding the palace. The rebels had advanced too far on this side for Kallista's comfort. If they linked up with those fighting inside the palace—

She shuddered. That would not happen. She would not allow it.

Summoning magic, she shaped it as they strode through the streets toward the battle sounds. Her iliasti drew their swords as the noise swelled, spacing themselves around her without having to speak a word. She drew more magic, sending her love to them, among them, recreating the web linking them all together.

This was the last demon. Ataroth, the weakest of the three, despite having eaten its sedil-demon during the aerial attack months and eons ago. It had spread itself thin, like Ashbel, Kallista saw when they reached the fighting at the barricaded Smith's Square. But the smeared shadow was smaller, thinner than that of the first demon they'd faced today. And with Ashbel, Kallista hadn't added the hunter-spell to the demon-killer magic as she had for Keqwith.

She'd done it instinctively, wanting the magic to destroy all the demon. Demons might learn with every encounter, but so did she.

Kallista was tired. Defeating two demons, not to mention quartering the maze of Arikon's streets, required a great deal of energy. One more demon and they could turn their attention to the palace. The guards and the Torvylls would keep the children safe until they could return and take over the job.

They waded into the edges of the battle, among the loyalist troops. The army was stretched thin across the three-front battle. Kallista compressed her magic, hammering in the hunter-spell, adding another bit that should stick like hot tar to demon essence.

"Down!" she shouted. She didn't know who or what this enhanced magic would affect.

Torchay and Obed dropped to a waist-high crouch. The troops beyond them fell on their faces, trained to respond instantly to the naitan-only command.

Kallista *threw* the magic. It blasted into the faint blurred edges of the demon, flaring up so brightly she had to turn away. All her iliasti did. Could they see it, too?

Squinting, she watched from the corner of her eye as the coruscating blaze flashed across the square and down most of the adjoining streets. When the brilliance died away, the demon was gone. As if it had never been.

The rebels still fought like madmen, but the colonel in command of this front began the shouted offers of clemency at once.

"That was almost too easy." Kallista stood panting in the center of the circle formed by her ilian. Not that she minded easy, but it made her fear what that seventh demon might be. She dredged up another tiny filament of magic and sent it to look, not sure whether to hope for or against finding something.

*"Easy?"* Stone sounded incredulous. "I'd like to know what you think is difficult."

"Last year," she said. "Tchyrizel, in Tsekrish. That was difficult."

"Oh. Well, yes. When you put it that way." He leaned wearily on Viyelle and after a brief, startled moment, she leaned back.

"Now what?" Joh paused, shook his head, straightened to attention. "What are your orders, Major?"

Kallista patted his cheek. "I liked the first question better. Back to the palace. Make sure the children are safe. Then—I suppose we join the cleanup." She started walking. The palace seemed a hundred leagues away, tired as she was.

"It'll take a while to root all the rebels out of that rabbit warren." Torchay fell in at her elbow. "You'd be more help using your magic to pinpoint their location than going after them yourself."

"Maybe so. It would require less walking. I've got magic out scouring for demon remnants, in case we missed something. I hope we have time to rest up before we have to fight again."

"I didn't realize you were still so out of shape after the twins," Torchay said, all seriousness. "We'll have to boost your workout schedule."

Kallista couldn't keep her horror from resonating through the wide-open links. "It's not the walking or even the fighting that tired me. It was working the magic *while* I was walking and fighting. I'm in perfectly good sha—"

She caught the glimmer of teasing and yanked his queue. "Not fair. I'm too tired to catch you at it."

The horses were still where they had left them, but it was so close to the palace, Kallista didn't see much sense in hauling herself atop one for such a short ride. She let Torchay push her onto the animal's back anyway. They left the borrowed mounts with the palace grooms. The tokens Joh left behind when he took them would tell the owners where to retrieve them.

They ran across a rebel patrol near where Summerglen and Winterhold abutted. Kallista stunned a pair of them with her lightning and the rest turned and ran. The corridors through Winterhold remained empty for the remaining distance.

Viyelle gave the family password that got them into the Torvyll chambers. Kallista forgot about the battle for a few moments.

"You had no trouble getting here?" Kallista asked Gweric once her twins were well hugged. Her eyes sought out the rest of the party.

"Other than having to backtrack a hundred times or so, no."

"Is Merinda feeling bad again?" She scanned the room, hunting their missing ilias in the crowded family grouping.

Gweric couldn't meet her eyes. His expression made Kallista's stomach knot up. "She isn't here," he said. "We met the Reinine and her guards. She went with them. The Reinine invited us."

"Why didn't you all go with them? I've seen her safe room. It's very…safe."

Gweric looked even more uneasy. "I didn't—it felt wrong, Naitan. Deadly."

Kallista's stomach knots tightened, then twisted. "Why did you let her go then?"

"I couldn't stop her," he whispered. "I tried. And it didn't feel so deadly if only she went. *Some* of them will live."

The knots exploded into full-blown alarm. "*Goddess.* Did you tell them this? *Which ones?*"

"I don't know. I couldn't see. I can't." His distress fed on hers, and Kallista tried to calm herself, to calm him. She checked her tiny hunter-spell. Nothing.

"It wasn't so dangerous if we came here," he said. "It was all death if we went with them. Wherever the Reinine went, some would die. But I don't know who."

Kallista kissed the baby in her arms—Lorynda—and handed her to Gweric. "Torchay, Joh—*ilian,* we go. The Reinine is in danger."

She kissed Rozite who was struggling to free herself from young Tiray, and cupped her hand over tiny Niona's head as she strode toward the door. She paused a moment while pulling off her gloves to speak to Viyelle's second mother.

"Saminda Prinsep." Kallista bowed her gratitude. "Thank you for your care of our children. The One's blessings be on you."

The prinsep bowed in return. "Thank you for your care of our children, ensuring they arrived here without incident. The One be with you." She paused. "Care well for our Reinine."

Kallista left the suite at a run, Torchay on one side of her, Obed on the other. Joh flanked Aisse immediately behind them, with Fox and Stone on either side of Viyelle bringing up the rear. Viyelle was a better swordswoman than Kallista, somewhat better than Joh due to her dueling experience. But she did not come up to either the warriors' or the bodyguards' level. Still as one of their better fighters, she took her place guarding their backs.

"Where are we going?" Torchay asked.

"The safe room. You saw it when we were following the demonscent, the day of the flying boat."

"I remember it." Obed surged ahead, taking point guard, leading the way through the deserted corridors of Winterhold Palace.

Evidence of fighting began to appear as they neared Summerglen—blood smeared on delicate wallpaper and pooled on fine parquetry flooring, an occasional body left crumpled and staring, waiting till the end of combat for removal. Kallista pushed the pace faster, past a walk, not quite to a run. Every dead body they passed added weight to Gweric's warning, until she felt she bore a waist-high boulder on her back.

In her room, the Reinine was hidden behind iron doors and reinforced walls. She was guarded by the best Adara had to offer. Kallista found no comfort in the knowledge. Joh had counted seven demons in his dream. She had destroyed only six.

And no one had yet found the least sign of High Steward Huryl.

Still, they knew about him, that he could not be trusted. Perhaps they didn't know enough to find him guilty at trial, but enough to suspect him. To keep him away. And if he ran from the chance of Joh recognizing him, surely he was too much the coward to do aught but run away now.

That seventh demon stuck in her gullet. Her little hunter was not enough.

Kallista reached for magic and winced. She ached, like she had an overused muscle rebelling against further strain. Except she could name no specific place that hurt. Nor could she coddle it, whatever it was.

"Wait." She stopped at the top of a back hall stairway leading down into the functional sectors of the palace. "Wait, I need to—"

Several steps down, Obed turned and looked up at her. She took a deep breath against the burn and caught his magic, lifting it gently out of him.

"You're too tired for this." Torchay gave her his strength, both physical and magical, holding her up.

"I can't be. We're not done." She bound his magic to Obed's and *reached* for Fox's order. Scant hours ago she'd done this at a run, weaving them all together at once. But one at a time, standing still, would work as well.

Stone's magic came, infusing the web with a shimmering eagerness. She *reached* for Viyelle, bound in Joh and Aisse and…no one. Their ninth should have been there.

She felt it, expected it, reached for it without thinking, and found nothing. Kallista needed her. There was a place in the magic waiting for her. They had managed with eight up to now, but after three demons, the strain of working without her showed. They needed their ninth.

Kallista knotted off the web and set it humming between them, connecting each of the eight of them to the others. Then she drew power. It burned as it coursed into her, leaving an ache along its path just under the pleasure it always brought.

Torchay caught a sharp breath. "What is that? What's wrong with it?"

She raised an eyebrow at him. "You feel something?"

"It feels good, like usual—but it hurts, too." He frowned at her, shifting his shoulders.

"Backlash?" Obed came up a few steps.

"No." Kallista shook her head, reassured him. "Do you feel it? The rest of you?"

Negative murmurs and headshakes answered her question. Torchay looked even more worried.

She patted his shoulder. "You've always been sensitive to my magic. That's all it is. I've just—strained a muscle. Used it too hard."

"I didn't know magic had muscles," Torchay said.

"Nor did I. And I don't dare baby it now." She bit her lip and found Joh's bright blue eyes. "I keep remembering that seventh demon, from your dreams."

"So." Obed pulled her attention back his way. "Let us go kill it."

Stone laughed. "Obed, ilias, I like the way you think. Let's do."

Kallista shaped and spilled out the magic she'd been holding, sending it to hunt the demon. She thought she knew where it would be—with the Reinine or on its way there—but she wanted to be certain.

"Which way?" Obed asked.

"The same. To the Reinine." She rolled her shoulders where the weight of the magic and the worry—the whole world—seemed to sit. "But not quite so fast. Just...fast enough."

Obed's eyes warmed, then he turned and flowed down the stairs. Torchay's hand on her arm kept Kallista from following. "Beauty leads," he teased as he went ahead of her.

"All right," Stone called from the back. "I think I've just been insulted."

"And you're only now catching it?" Fox's voice floated out.

Faint sounds of fighting echoed up from below, silencing them. Maintaining the web of magic was a bit of a strain, but it didn't burn like drawing more, so Kallista drew hard, piling up the magic ready to use. She didn't want anything distracting her when she needed her focus. Where was the blasted demon?

Did it even exist? The only knowledge they had came from a dream. Usually she dreamed true, but sometimes things changed from the dreams, and this one Joh had dreamed in her place. Could that have affected its truth?

The hunter magic checked in its outward flow. It searched and seemed to find nothing, but couldn't move on, dithering in confused circles. Outside the Reinine's safe room.

"Hurry." Kallista forced her weary limbs to move faster.

"You've found it?" Joh asked, just behind her.

"Maybe. Nothing definite, but…something."

The noise of battle grew steadily louder. Kallista stepped on Torchay's heels as he slowed.

"Fox, Stone, up here," he called.

"Fox, stay there," Kallista amended. "Stone and Viyelle in front. Fox, watch behind us. You can *see* farther. I don't want anyone catching us from behind."

Rearranged, Obed still in the lead with Stone and Viyelle just behind him, they reached the turning to the corridor leading past the Reinine's safe room. They crowded there close together. Kallista beckoned Fox closer. "How many?"

He went still, lips moving as he counted. "Eleven, twelve rebels in the hall. Another seven or eight inside—"

"They're *in* the room? Oh, Goddess—" Kallista let her military mind take over, blocking out all else as she'd been trained. "Hit them fast and hard. Watch for anything unusual—I still can't pinpoint the demon. We want inside quick. Now go."

Obed led the charge, a black and silver whirlwind slamming into the rebels. Stone and Viyelle dispatched what little got past him, leaving Torchay to stalk behind with a clean sword in each hand. Kallista's magic swept the corridor but found no shadow perched on any shoulder. She sent magic plunging inside the remaining rebels with ruthless efficiency, searching out any taint and scrubbing it clean. She found only demonstain, not the demon itself.

She turned into the recess in front of the safe room door and had to step over the black-clad bodyguard staring sightlessly at nothing. Blood still drained from a score of his wounds. The iron door stood open, as did the iron-bound oak behind it. Torchay hauled her back, pushed past to enter first.

Fox's voice rang out behind them. "More coming. At least ten, with more a few ticks behind them."

Aisse and Viyelle slipped through the iron door as Obed

pulled it to. His gaze locked onto Kallista's for a moment before it clanged shut and he took his place guarding it. Kallista wrapped protection around her ilian and sealed it before turning her attention to the room.

It was large, sized big enough to hold the entire Adaran government. Big enough to accommodate the battle now taking place.

Syr was down, the Reinine cradling him in her lap where she huddled in a corner. Her expression was peaceful, accepting, despite the tears that rolled down her face, a distinct contrast to the obvious terror of the woman cringing beside her. Merinda had come for safety and found blood and death.

Three rebels lay dead or moaning on the floor alongside two of the younger bodyguards. The Reinine's four remaining guards fought off twice their number, all of them bodyguard traitors, by their skills. Beyond them, on the far side of the room, stood High Steward Huryl Kovallyk.

"He had keys," the Reinine cried as two of the rebels turned to deal with the newcomers.

Fereday lunged, trying to take advantage of their distraction, and tripped on a corpse that—did it roll toward him? A rebel sword sliced through his neck and the Reinine screamed. Fereday fell, his head nearly severed.

No magic existing could heal such a wound, but—Kallista sent her magic questing toward Syr, trusting her iliasti to defend her from physical harm.

He was drained of blood from terrible wounds, almost to death, but maybe, if she sealed—

Demonstink came, rushing into the room as the seventh demon unfurled itself, flowing up and out of Huryl until its foulness filled the room. Kallista barely had time and magic to parry its attack and none for anything else.

Magic poured into her from her ilian's web. She ignored the

burn as she flung protection toward the Reinine and her ilian—
what remained of it. Two more rebels were down and the last
of the younger bodyguards. Leyja and Keldrey bled from multiple cuts and Torchay now bore a shallow slash along his left
arm. The wounds didn't seem to slow them much.

The demon ripped away the shielding around the Reinine
as if it were tissue paper. Kallista's scream echoed around the
room as she shaped and named her dark magic. "Khoriseth."

The scream continued—Merinda's scream following Kallista's. The healer scooted backward across the floor, away from
the Reinine, horror in her every line. Serysta Reinine clawed at
her throat, her face turning blue as she fought to breathe.

*"No."* Kallista *threw* her magic.

The demon shrieked as the magic hit it and blazed up. Then
Khoriseth flexed, or twisted, or—whatever it did, the magic
went out. Like a fire drenched in water.

*"Dear Goddess, help us,"* she whispered, horrified. How could
it do that? What would they do now? How could they defeat
this monster?

The Reinine thrashed in her corner, Syr sliding limply from
her lap. Kallista could see the demonstuff coiled thick and
black around her head and neck. Kallista drew, shaped and
threw more magic. The blackness thinned. Serysta took a shallow breath before Khoriseth flowed back thicker than before.

Bellowing, Keldrey threw himself at Huryl, fighting the defending rebels with a berserker rage.

Merinda edged farther back, whimpering. "No," she said. "I
won't. *I won't.*"

Kallista changed her magic's shape to claw at the demon, rip
it away from the Reinine. *Goddess,* it hurt. Every breath burned
through her lungs, every beat of her heart ached with the effort. She slumped against the wall, letting it hold her up as she
fought the demon for the life of her Reinine.

Save for Keldrey's attempt to reach Huryl, the fight had degenerated into a near standoff. Leyja swayed on her feet, her own blood dripping down the blades of her dagger swords as she held off two equally exhausted rebels. Kallista's iliasti stayed close, protecting her while she fought the demon.

Every time Kallista ripped the demon away, it returned before Serysta could catch more than a fleeting breath. Never enough. She was weakening, her body stilling, slowing. Dying.

Something had to change. It couldn't end like this. Not in stalemate. They needed their ninth.

"Merinda, *help us.*" Kallista threw magic toward her, willing her to catch it.

Merinda screamed, cowered away, hiding her head in her arms. *"I can't,"* she wailed. "Don't ask me!"

"Obed, I need you," Kallista shouted through the door, reinforcing her call with a tug on his magic.

Aisse darted back to open the iron door and admit him as the rebels launched fresh attacks, one against the Reinine's defender, one against Torchay and Kallista behind him. Viyelle bounced on her toes, her link taut with her need to take part. Kallista didn't know whether to encourage her or hold her back. Leyja needed the help, but Viyelle's skills were not up to a bodyguard opponent, even a wounded one.

Obed glided through the doorway and paused half an instant to take in the situation, then he threw himself at the rebels holding off Keldrey.

Khoriseth the demon shrieked and launched an attack directly at Kallista. At the last moment, it turned aside and wrapped itself around Aisse's head and neck.

"Coward!" Kallista screamed at it. "You don't dare attack me directly." She slashed at the demon, cutting it away from her ilias.

Khoriseth flowed to smother Viyelle, instead. *Why should I? Weaken you first. Take away your power. Then kill you.*

"You won't." If she could not destroy it all at once, maybe she could destroy it piece by piece. She sent strength to Viyelle and somehow breath as she called magic and named it.

Instead of throwing the dark veil at the demon, Kallista sent it through the link, through Viyelle and out. Viyelle shouted and the demon screamed as its suffocating blanket burned away from her face in a sudden flare of invisible incandescence.

It reached for Torchay. Kallista was there first, knocking it away with a burst of the dark fire, dissolving another bit of its substance. She slapped it away from Obed. Another bit gone.

Khoriseth's squeal of frustration rose to a wailing shriek as Keldrey's sword plunged through Huryl and came out his back. The demon tried to gather up the blood and shove it back in, until Keldrey split Huryl open.

"You can't heal, can you?" Pain tears welled in Kallista's eyes as she called more magic through the burning ache of weariness. "You're all about destruction, not mending, and now you can't mend your toy."

Khoriseth screamed its anger at her, hovering without anchor in the room. Kallista screamed against her own pain as magic poured into her. She shaped it, building it higher and higher yet. Anchorless, maybe it wouldn't be able to quench the magic this time, if she could only send enough against it. She whispered the demon's name, "Khoriseth," and let the magic go.

Once more the demon lit up, blinding her inner eye. It shrieked, whipping itself away from the blaze. Suddenly, it seemed to fold in on itself and vanish.

Khoriseth was gone. But was it destroyed?

# CHAPTER TWENTY-EIGHT

Kallista searched the room with all of her aching senses. So much demonstink had been left behind, it singed her nostrils, but she hadn't the energy to scrub it away. Especially if the demon was hidden, not destroyed.

Khoriseth had used deceit and treachery to achieve its goals, hiding its presence and its activities. It had been able to hide from her inside Huryl. But with Huryl dead, where could it have gone? Who could it have taken?

A keening wail captured Kallista's attention and she blinked away her inner sight. Wounded and bleeding, Leyja had dragged herself over to Serysta Reinine. The wail rose unnoticed from Leyja's throat as she checked for breath, listened for a heartbeat, tried to use her medic's skills.

Kallista whimpered as she sent magic wisping toward her Reinine. Goddess, it hurt. Torchay came and helped lower her to sit on the floor. Her magic touched the Ruler of all Adara and found no one there. Her own cry joined Leyja's.

"*No.*" Keldrey's hoarse shout seemed to drop him to his knees. "She can't be gone."

Leyja gathered her ilias into her arms and rocked back and forth, repeating Serysta's name. Viyelle walked over, stepping carefully across the bodies of the Reinine's other iliasti, then stood as if at a loss for what to do next. Her eyes met Kallista's, sharing her grief and confusion.

"There are injured," Obed said. "We need a healer."

Kallista looked to Merinda, who shook her head. "I have no skill in this sort of healing. I'll get help." She pushed to her feet and tiptoed for the door, trying to avoid stepping in blood.

"Wait." Kallista stretched her hand out, but Merinda side-stepped her touch. "There were rebels outside, too."

The iron door clanged as someone beat on it with metal, a sword hilt, likely. "Kallista!" Joh's voice came faintly past the barrier, half his words fading out. "What's ha—to—there?"

"I'll let them in."

"*Merinda*—" Kallista's protest had no effect. The healer was past her and opening the door.

Joh and Stone slid through, leaving the door slightly ajar, Fox just outside it.

"Dear sweet Goddess, what happened in here?" Joh whispered.

It looked like a slaughterhouse. Aisse had straightened Syr's body and closed his eyes, was just matching Ferenday's head to his neck again. Keldrey held Leyja in his arms as she held their ilias's body in hers. Ten more bodies lay strewn across the stone floor. Only Kallista did not bleed from any wound.

"The Reinine is dead." Kallista shuddered as the truth sank in. Saying it made it real, but they could not avoid it.

"And the demon? There *was* a demon?" Joh checked the rebel bodies, looking for wounded.

"Yes. Khoriseth. It was hiding inside Huryl." Kallista frowned. "I don't know how it could hide from me, but it did."

Obed shrugged. "You have destroyed it, so how does not matter."

Kallista could not keep her uncertainty off her face.

"You *did* destroy it, did you not?" Obed's voice held horror.

Torchay looked up from his attempts to tend the worst of Keldrey's and Leyja's wounds. "What's this?"

"I…don't know." Kallista scrubbed at burning, watery eyes with aching hands. "I *think*—bloody hells, I don't know whether I even think I killed it. I got part of it. I hurt it, I'm sure, but—"

"Why do you no' know?" Torchay demanded.

"Because I don't. It vanished. I can't find it. It might be destroyed, dissolved into nothing like the others, but it might be hiding again. This demon wasn't like the others. It could quench the magic."

She paused to fight back the grief and anger. "I wasn't strong enough, all right? I couldn't kill it all at once."

"There's only eight of us," Joh said. "Not nine."

"*Wait.*" Keldrey's hoarse voice sounded over the others. "You mean to tell me that—that *thing* got away? It killed our ilian and it *got away?*"

His rage flooded the room until Kallista could feel it. He crawled to his feet, staggered and fell, fighting his blood-loss weakness.

"I don't know, Keldrey Reinas." Kallista's throat choked with tears.

"She destroyed three demons before this one." Torchay moved to block him. "She's used so much magic doing it, it burns to call more, but she called it and used it, trying to destroy this one until she can't even stand. Who knows what harm she's done herself, fighting it?"

"It's not her I want." Keldrey kept crawling. "It's that damned demon."

"You can't touch it, Reinas," Kallista said wearily. "If you kill the one it rides, it simply moves to another. It takes magic to destroy it. More magic than I have, apparently." She paused. "I might have killed it."

"But you don't know," Keldrey persisted.

*"No more."* Leyja carefully laid the Reinine's body on the floor and closed the staring eyes. "I don't care what it takes. Whatever it is, I will do it. This cannot happen again. No more."

Leyja wiped tears from her soaked face. She turned to look at them—and her eyes rolled back in her head as she began to shudder.

Magic flowed into the room, new magic hunting a home. Kallista fought against board-stiff muscles to move. "Torchay help me. Aisse—Joh—someone, I have to reach her."

Keldrey swore, reversed his stagger back toward his still-living ilias. Obed and Joh picked Kallista up and carried her across the room to Leyja.

Kallista clasped the other woman's wrist and a flood of magic bowed her against her iliasti. It soothed the burning ache of exhaustion as it slid neatly into its place in the web of magic. The magic bound eight into nine and flared bright with completion, greater than any previous whole.

"Merinda. The demon's in Merinda." Kallista's voice felt larger, richer than before. "She refused the call of the One, and the demon took her."

"Then kill it," Keldrey growled.

"Yes." Kallista gathered the magic and sent it out, following the faint ilian bond that tied them to Merinda. She didn't deserve such a fate, no matter what her mistakes—and they were many. But she was theirs. They should have cared better for her.

The bond was severed, cut like a fishing line hooked in a tangle, but it didn't matter. Kallista knew where the demon was. The magic knew.

"Khoriseth!" she shouted, putting all the power of their nine behind it.

The magic crashed into Merinda, burrowing deep as it

sought the hidden demon. She staggered, fell, but Khoriseth drove her on. Kallista called more magic, sent it after the first, wishing she could simply feed in more power. Each spell was a discrete thing, complete in itself. The demon struggled, finally managed to quench the first burning, and the second hit it, searing more away.

But Merinda carried it stumbling farther and farther from her, from the magic. Soon it would be beyond her reach.

"Follow." She struggled to her feet. "We have to follow, stop her. Stop it."

Torchay picked her up, looking wildly around. "Bring Leyja, one of you. Tighten the bandage on her thigh and bring her."

"Hurry." Kallista dragged out more magic, fighting her own weakness.

The demon, half what it was at the beginning, struck back in furious desperation, catching her off guard. The magic burst and crashed through her in an uncontrollable backlash. She scrambled to hold it, to keep it from breaking through to her iliasti, screaming as the agony drove her into darkness.

Kallista woke to a sensation of floating, confused until she realized the bed was simply that soft. Bodies lay curled on either side of her. She recognized Stone instantly. How badly had he been hurt in the fighting?

She ached too much to want to think about calling magic, but the link could carry other things. With a bit of focus, she managed to isolate Stone's and read his condition—minor cuts and exhaustion.

A bit more focus and Kallista identified Leyja on her other side. Marked now, thrust into a new ilian before she'd had a chance to grieve for the death of the old, Leyja would not welcome Kallista's pity. So she wouldn't pity her. Sympathy was different.

Groaning, she levered herself up onto her elbows. Keldrey lay sleeping beyond Leyja, his myriad wounds bandaged. Keldrey had lost his ilian, too, without the…consolation? Penalty? He wasn't godmarked like Leyja, but they had been ilian together. It would be beyond cruel to toss him aside, force him to make his way alone. But Goddess, they already had nine in their ilian. Ten. So many.

So many, what was one more?

Kallista groaned the rest of the way up to sit with elbows propped on knees, face hidden in her hands. She didn't know what to do about the mess dropped in her lap.

"Awake now, are you?" Torchay pulled his usual trick, appearing out of nowhere. "Yes, we've all slept and had our scratches bandaged." He showed off a white-wrapped forearm. "Stone's still sleeping because he led the search for Merinda. We didn't find her. It's like she's vanished into the air. Like Huryl did."

Kallista dropped her head back into her hands. "Goddess, what a mess." She gave up hiding and crawled toward the foot of the bed, holding her hand out for assistance. "Let's talk somewhere else. I don't want to wake them."

"I doubt a full orchestra with trumpets and timpani could wake that lot." Torchay picked her up and set her on her feet before she could protest. "But there's others want to see you awake and whole."

Kallista was enveloped in hugs the instant she stepped through the door—hard, fierce ones from Obed and Fox, careful, gentle ones from Viyelle and Joh, and a careful, fierce hug from Aisse. Lorynda and Rozite pulled her hair.

"I'm fine." Kallista laughed, freeing her hair and setting the twins on the floor to continue their crawling. "Sore all over, but fine. We have a lot to discuss." She paused, looking around the parlor, obviously not Noonday Suite. "Where are we?"

The cozy room was decorated in shades of blue, lavender and silver, more luxuriously appointed than Noonday—a thing Kallista would not have thought possible.

"The rooms where the Reinine moved after the last explosions at the palace," Viyelle said. "They've already sent word out to the prelates and prinsipi—those not already in Arikon—to gather for selection, but until a new Reinine is chosen, Keldrey and Leyja are still Reinasti."

"Ah." Kallista started to nod, but her neck protested and her head throbbed, so she didn't. She sat, hoping the others would, too. Mostly, they did. "That's part of what we need to talk about. Leyja's marked. Keldrey isn't. I know our ilian's already nine strong—ten, with Leyja—but it doesn't seem right—"

"*Nine,*" Fox interrupted. "Nine with Leyja. Merinda betrayed us."

"The demon took her," Kallista said. "That wasn't her fault. It didn't ask her nicely, it just took her. The way Ashbel tried to take you."

Fox flinched at the low blow, making Kallista want to take it back, but how could she take back truth?

"Ashbel *didn't* take Fox. It was Merinda's fault she was vulnerable to being taken," Torchay said. "She wasn't marked."

"Neither were you when we took on Tchyrizel last year."

"But when it came down to it, I didn't refuse," Torchay retorted. "Merinda did. She turned her back on the mark and she turned her back on us."

"So just like that, she's out? No second chances, no forgiveness." Kallista held on to her temper, badly. "Why bother with choices then? Why should any of us have been given a choice if making the wrong one gets you kicked out in the cold? The demon took her. She didn't betray us."

"She betrayed us before we ever get to Korbin," Aisse said, her agitation stealing her grasp of Adaran. "She taked—took advantage because we were Tibran." She gestured between herself, Fox and the room where Stone still slept. "We didn't know the rules. She did. She wanted to be one of us, then she change her mind. That is betraying."

Kallista sighed, rubbing her aching temples. "You're right. Torchay's right. And so am I, dammit. Maybe I'm mad at her, too, but she's carrying our child and she deserved better from us than this. How will divorcing her solve anything? Especially since we don't even know where she is?"

"Goddess." Viyelle sank onto a delicately carved chair. "What a mess."

The others murmured agreement.

"And that's without taking Leyja or Keldrey into consideration." Kallista slumped lower on the blue-and-silver sofa. "My head hurts too much to even try thinking about it. Joh, *you* think about it for me."

He stammered a moment, then inclined his head in acquiescence. "If I might appoint assistance?"

"Certainly." She waved a generous hand. "All you like, as long as it isn't me. Did I hear someone mention food?"

"I didn't mention it," Aisse said. "But I have it brought."

"Had," Joh corrected gently. "You had it brought."

"I must have smelled it, and it spoke to me." Kallista rubbed her hands together before extending them to whoever might be willing to help her up. "While we eat, you can tell me what's happened in the palace since I passed out." Fox and Torchay reached her first because Obed had Rozite clinging to his leg where she'd pulled herself up.

Viyelle waited for Kallista to reach the dining table before speaking. "I already told you about the call for selection. Word is that the prinsep of Tironde and the prinsep of Turysh as well as Head Prelate Omunda here in Arikon are campaigning hard…"

It would take close to three weeks for all the absent selectors to reach Arikon, but none of the intervening time was wasted. Palace functionaries went into full attack mode, preparing for the coronation of…whoever. *Someone* would be crowned Reinine as soon as she or—wildly unlikely—he was selected. Judging by the flurry of activity, three weeks was scarcely enough time to prepare.

Kallista's ilian decided to leave the situation with Merinda alone, at least until they found her and dealt with the demon that had taken her. Their problem was that she truly seemed to have melted into the paving stones. No one had seen any trace of her, inside the city or out on the roads. Not that any could recall, that is.

Leyja had consented to marry into the ilian without argument. Without much reaction at all, truth be told. It worried Kallista, and she said as much when she and Torchay went to talk to Keldrey.

The stocky bodyguard was in one of the suite bedrooms, packing a trunk. The gear looked as if it would fit him, but he and Ferenday had been much of a size. The funeral for all three of their iliasti together had been two days before. He could be packing away his dead ilias's belongings, but somehow, Kallista didn't think so.

"I'll be out of your way by tomorrow," he said, confirming her surmise.

Kallista chose and discarded a dozen openings before giving up. She wasn't eloquent. She'd go with what she did best, plain speaking. "I'd rather you weren't," she said. "I'd—*we* would like you to stay."

"We want you to join us." Torchay's statement caught Keldrey's attention, stopped his activity.

"Join... What d'you mean, *join?*" Suspicion oozed from his every pore.

"Marry us," Kallista said.

"I ain't marked. You don't need me." He straightened, turned to face them, his hands curling into fists apparently without his notice.

"Actually, we do." Kallista rushed on, over his skeptical snort. "I'm worried about Leyja. She's too calm. Her whole world has turned over and she's scarcely blinked an eye."

"Leyja's like that. Practical. This mark thing happened. It's done, deal with it how you have to. No use moaning about it." He raised a hand to stop Kallista speaking. "And yeah, I know. Our ilian's dead. But Leyja's not gonna cry an' wail or make a big fuss, especially not where people can see her. She keeps to herself. We're all like that—we *were*. Reckon it's why we got on so well. We didn't have to say nothin' but we knew."

"That's exactly why we want you. Leyja's been jerked from one ilian into another without time to catch breath. I don't want her to lose the last bit of familiarity she has." Kallista willed him to understand, to agree. "What will you do, if you don't stay?"

Keldrey turned his back on her and started packing again. "I don't need your pity. Don't want it. Leyja don't need me. It was all Serysta. We all—it was about *her*, for all of us. I'm bodyguard. The army lost too many of us in this rebellion. They'll have a place for me."

"That's why I want you to stay," Torchay said. "We've got Tibran Warriors, and Obed's as fine a fighter as ever I've seen, but they're not bodyguard trained. We'll have Leyja, too, when she heals, but they're saying that knee could have trouble. We need you. Because you're *not* marked. The magic can be quite—distracting when she calls it."

"I can be bodyguard without being ilias." Keldrey's hands had gone still.

"You think they'll assign you to us?" Kallista edged closer. Not enough to make him uneasy. "I have a bodyguard. No naitan under the rank of general gets two. And if they conceded the need for more because of the marks, it wouldn't be you. It would be some youngster, like those we burned yesterday. You were the one who fought off those rebels and lived to talk about it. We want you. If you're ilias, we have you."

Keldrey gripped the sides of his trunk, leaning on it. After a long moment, he sighed. "I won't have your pity." He stabbed a finger toward the parlor. "And that convict ponce of yours better *never* correct my grammar if he don't want his head shoved up his arse."

Kallista laughed, dared to touch his arm, briefly. "He does it for Aisse because she wants him to. She wants to be Adaran, not Tibran, and that means speaking proper Adaran."

"Need help unpacking?" Torchay reached for the trunk, grinning.

Keldrey knocked him away. "I don't need help from you."

"Wedding's in two days, on Graceday afternoon," Kallista said. "Quiet. Here in the parlor—and we're keeping it that way because we're not telling Viyelle's parents till just before time. Her idea."

"Always suspected that one was sharper than she looked." He paused and looked at Kallista. "I'll tell Leyja, if you want. Better coming from me, I think."

She nodded. "If that's what you think."

"One thing," Torchay said, face solemn now. "This ilian is like your last in one way. It focuses on Kallista, but not exclusively. Leyja may have to…find comfort with one of the others. She can, I think, if she will."

Keldrey raised an eyebrow. "What about me?"

Kallista laughed, dared to kiss his cheek. "Ask me again on Graceday."

They did manage to keep the wedding quiet, though the ceremony itself wasn't with the twins babbling and Niona making her discomfort clear halfway through. Kallista didn't find the babies half so distracting as Saminda Prinsep's muttered complaining over lost opportunities.

That may have been why, beginning the day after the wedding, Saminda insisted on dragging them bodily into palace politics. She introduced Kallista to every prelate and prinsep in the city, starting conversations about diplomacy or trade—things Kallista knew little or nothing about—then abandoning her to carry on alone.

Stone took to hiding whenever he saw Viyelle's mothers approach. Aisse used her infant as an excuse to avoid unwanted socializing, and Kallista was half convinced Leyja used her healing injuries the same way. Kallista would have followed Stone's example, but—unfortunately—Saminda's arguments made sense.

Kallista would still be Adara's godstruck naitan, no matter who was selected Reinine. The demon Khoriseth had escaped with its hostage. It would have to be found and destroyed. And she had not forgotten the name screamed by the demon Tchyrizel in the Ruler's palace in Tsekrish a year ago. *Zughralithiss.*

The name alone filled her with horror.

Better that the new Reinine knew and understood what Kallista was capable of, and what was facing Adara.

So she dressed in the finery Obed brought her and ventured out into the corridors of power to somehow at the same time impress the selectors and allay their fears. Her iliasti came with her, most of them, most of the time. Torchay, Obed and Viyelle were always with her. Joh, Fox and Stone came much of the time. Keldrey would have also, had his injuries allowed it. They all appeared at the formal dinners.

The presence of her ilian seemed to soften many of the strained attitudes Kallista first encountered. The babies did more, during their outings in the gardens and courtyards. Kallista assumed it was difficult to fear a naitan's power when her nose was being pinched by an infant.

Finally, the last selectors arrived, the prinsep and prelates from far Dostu on the eastern coast just north of the Mountains of the Wind. Kallista sought them out on her own at the formal reception that evening, beating Saminda to it by only a few ticks. She'd introduced herself to new people so many times by now, it was no longer agony, and having her entire ilian with her eased the slight pain that remained. Goddess, she hated politics.

At the end of the reception, while the musicians put away their instruments—not that they'd been heard over the buzz of voices—the selectors were escorted by the entire crowd across the broad entry courtyard, out the palace gates and around the Mother Temple to its west entrance. Each selector was marked off a list held by the Mother Temple's own head prelate, and admitted one at a time.

Kallista had been a child, newly come to the North Academy in Arikon, the last time a Reinine had been selected. The Temple had been locked for a full week. The selectors had tottered out after nine days, rumpled and exhausted, with the word that Serysta Kallynder, a minor prelate from a minor prinsipality, had been selected to rule. All the other candidates had apparently been knocked out of contention by the bitter strife.

Given the circumstances, Kallista expected no less this time. Likely the decision would take longer, the fight would be more bitter.

So she was not prepared for the pounding at the door to their suite in the dark hours of the morning. Aisse, up with her baby, answered it.

"What in seven hells is it?" Keldrey headed out into the parlor to find out, and returned shortly. "They've made a decision. They've selected a new Reinine. Announcement in the Great Hall in half an hour, soon as they let 'em out."

"So quick?" Kallista kicked the blankets off and reached past Stone to shake Viyelle again.

"That's what they're sayin'. It's done." Keldrey pulled on his trousers and held Leyja's for her to step into. "Must've been on first ballot."

"They never select on first ballot," Viyelle mumbled, shoving her hand through her short hair. She always woke hard.

Kallista tossed a tunic at her. "They must have done it some time or other in the past. Where's my red tunic?"

"You're holding it." Stone yanked his trousers up and frowned at them. "Did I shrink?" Too long, the trousers crumpled over his feet.

"They're mine. These are yours." Torchay shoved another pair at him and took away the tunic Kallista held. "And this belongs to Fox. Yours is hanging in the wardrobe."

"Are we required to go?" Aisse stood in the bedroom doorway juggling Niona.

Kallista exchanged glances with the others before replying. "Not *required* exactly. But everyone always does. The whole city turns out. Everyone wants to know who the new Reinine is." She got her best red tunic out of the wardrobe and pulled it on. She didn't want to go in uniform tonight. "It's up to you, Aisse."

She considered a moment. "I go. Maritta can get Niona to sleep. That's what nursery workers are for."

Viyelle laughed. "You're learning."

Dressed at last, their ilian hurried through the corridors at

Leyja's best pace. Keldrey offered to carry her and laughed when she smacked him. Other courtiers straggled behind them. They weren't so very late. The Great Hall was only beginning to fill up.

The dais had been set up in the center of the room, the space behind it kept open for the selectors who were just starting to file in when Kallista and her ilian scrambled into a place near one of the white marble columns that marched up either side of the vast chamber.

Who had they chosen? Would Kallista be able to work with the new Reinine, or would she be one of the few skeptical of Kallista's unusual abilities? For the most part, the selectors looked satisfied, almost pleased with themselves, though there was the occasional solemn face. Those selectors didn't seem angry, though, or aggrieved, as if they'd lost a quarrel. More as if the moment were too important for anything less than solemnity. But Kallista didn't have a clue what it might mean.

"What do you think?" she murmured to her ilian.

They all looked at Viyelle, who shrugged. "No idea. Though I have never heard of them selecting so quickly."

Finally, all the selectors had crowded into the room. Kallista grabbed Aisse to keep her upright as they were jostled from behind. More people trying to cram through the doors rather than be relegated to the spillover in the corridor.

A tall staff topped with a golden compass rose began to make its way through the selectors toward the dais. Doubtless it was carried by Arikon's Head Prelate Omunda, but she couldn't be seen among the tight-packed bodies.

"Can she move any slower?" Stone whispered as the prelate climbed up the dais stairs.

"Pompous ass," Leyja muttered. "Always was."

Slowly, pushing the anticipation higher with every measured step, the head prelate moved to the center of the dais. She planted the staff and took a small scroll tied with silver ribbon from the sleeve of her heavily embroidered yellow robe.

"The selectors of Adara have met," Omunda intoned as a hush fell over the crowd. "Guided by the hand of the One, they have chosen a new Reinine to rule over Adara."

With a flourish, she held up the scroll. "That name is written here."

"Just get on with it." Joh spoke so quietly, Kallista heard him mostly through the link.

The head prelate handed her staff to an acolyte standing in front of the dais. She untied the ribbon and handed it to another, then slowly unrolled the parchment.

The entire waiting crowd seemed to hold its collective breath. Kallista knew she was.

"From this moment, until the One shall take her to glory, the Ruler of all Adara is and shall be Kallista Varyl of the city of Turysh in the prinsipality of Turysh, chosen and marked by the One as the first godstruck naitan in a thousand years. May she rule with wisdom, justice and mercy."

With the name buried in the middle of all those words, it took a moment for Kallista to realize just whose name was called. Then her knees crumpled and Torchay had to catch her. *"Breathe,"* he ordered.

One of the gathered prinsipi leaped onto the dais. "All hail, Kallista Reinine!"

The Great Hall echoed as the shout was repeated again and again. Hands pushed her, propelled all of them forward, toward the prelate and the dais. Voices spoke, jubilant, congratulating her. Faces appeared and disappeared, smiling, shouting, staring. Kallista clung tight to her links, to her ilian, too shocked to think clearly.

When they reached the dais, Kallista was lifted into the air by a thousand hands and deposited atop it. The prelate smiled, which startled Kallista—hadn't she been campaigning for the throne?—and embraced her, kissing both cheeks. Then she bowed and backed away.

Bewildered, Kallista stared at the Great Hall, at all the people cheering, shouting her name. Only not her name.

"Kallista Reinine!" they shouted. That wasn't her. She wasn't the Reinine.

She turned to the prelate, panic starting to hit. "There must be a mistake. I can't be the Reinine. I don't know anything about it." She held the scroll out. "Here. Take this."

Omunda closed her hands over Kallista's around the scroll. "No one is more qualified. Truly the One has spoken tonight, for not since Adara's beginnings has a Reinine been chosen by unanimous vote on the first ballot. You *are* our Reinine." She set her hands on Kallista's shoulders and turned her to face the crowd.

This couldn't be happening. She *hated* politics. She hated paperwork and being cooped up inside. She was a soldier. It was all she'd known up until this last year. She'd scarcely learned how to be an ilias. How could she learn to be Reinine?

She caught a strange gesture in the crowd and after a moment recognized Saminda Prinsep grinning like a madwoman, making a giant smile with both hands in front of her face. Hesitantly, Kallista smiled. The cheering swelled louder for a moment.

Where was— She followed the links and found her ilian crowded in front of the dais. Kallista held her hands out to them, beckoning them up beside her. Torchay jumped up first, taking his bodyguard's post just behind her left shoulder.

"You know I didn't sign up for this," he murmured in her ear.

"Neither did I. Where do I go to resign?" Kallista caught Joh's hand and pulled him up.

"I don't think they'll let you," Viyelle said, hauling Aisse onto the dais while Fox lifted Leyja.

"This is all your mother's fault." Kallista showed her teeth in an almost smile. "Remind me to throttle her later."

"Partly her fault, probably," Viyelle agreed. "Mostly, it's yours. You are who you are."

Kallista shot Viyelle a startled look, then expanded it as the rest of her ilian murmured agreement. The crowd's cheering changed, became a chant. "Speak! Speak! Speak!"

*Wonderful.* A Reinine had to make speeches, too. Kallista's stomach churned. "What do I do now?"

"I suggest you speak to them." Torchay didn't sound one jot sympathetic.

"Oh, Goddess." More as a delaying tactic than anything, Kallista made a leg and swept into a deep bow. The crowd's shout strengthened, then as she rose again, faded away.

Kallista cleared her throat. "I never wanted this."

Random cheers broke out across the room, and behind her she heard Omunda's quiet, "That's why you are the perfect one for the job."

She looked down at the scroll in her hand, her name written in careful script. She had to clear her throat again. "I don't know why the selectors would see fit to choose me. I don't know why the One chose me for the tasks I was given. I have never been anything more than a soldier, serving my homeland. And now, you have asked me to serve Adara in this manner, one that I do not deserve."

More shouts interrupted her, of "No!" and "You do!"

Kallista had to stare over their heads at the great doors in the far wall until the shouting died away again and she regained her composure.

"Since you have seen fit to ask this of me, all I can say is— with the help of the One God of us all, and with my ilian at my side—" She clasped the first hands she could find—Aisse and Joh—and held on tight. "I will do the very best that I can."

Kallista bowed again, her ilian bowing a breath behind her, and the crowd erupted into the greatest frenzy yet. Through the open windows of the Great Hall, she could hear shouts from the city beyond as heralds repeated her words from the palace walls.

"And you claim you can't make speeches," Torchay murmured as they straightened.

"I can't. Dear sweet Goddess in Heaven, Torchay, how are we going to do this?"

"*We? We* aren't the Reinine. *You* are." Torchay caught her when she would have bolted. "You've destroyed demons, Kallista. If you can do that, you can do anything."

"Ha!"

"We'll help you," Leyja said, easing closer. "We know the people here, who can be trusted, who can't. You are the Reinine, but you're not alone."

Kallista turned to face the sea of selectors behind them and bowed. "I almost think I'd rather face demons than twenty-seven prinsipi and all those prelates."

"Almost, so would I," Keldrey muttered as they followed her into the bow.

"Don't worry." Kallista forced a smile and waved to the crowds. "I fear you'll have your chance. We still have demons to hunt and destroy."

"And prinsipi to deal with before then," Viyelle said.

Kallista shuddered. "And may the One help us all."

\* \* \* \* \*

*Look for the Varyl ilian's next adventure—*
*available March 2007!*

# Pronunciation Guide:

Ailo, Aila: EYE-loe, EYE-lah
Aisse vo'Haav: Ah-EESS voe-HAHV
Arikon: AIR-ih-Kahn
Ashbel: ASH-bell
Ataroth: AT-ah-rahth
Boren: BORE-enn
Brodir: broh-DEER
Daryath: DAHR-ee-ahth
Dedicat: DEH-dee-kaht
Deray: deh-RAY
Di pentivas: dee pen-TEE-vahs
Domina: DOHM-nee-ah
Durissas: dur-ISS-ahss
Elliane: ell-ee-AHN
Fenetta: feh-NET-tah
Ferenday: FAIR-en-day
Filorne: fih-LORN
Gweric: GWAIR-ick
Heldring: HELL-dreeng
Huryl Kovallyk: HYUR-ill Koh-VAHL-ick
Huyis Uskenda: HOO-yis oos-KEN-da
Ilian, ilias: ILL-ee-an, ILL-ee-as
Iliasti: ill-ee-AHSS-tee

Irysta: ih-RIHS-tah
Joh Suteny: Joe su-TAY-nee
Jongliers: zhahng-LEERS
Kallista Varyl: Ka-LISS-ta VAIR-ill
Kami: KAM-ee
Karyl: KARE-ill
Katenda: kah-TEN-dah
Katreinet: ka-TRAIN-et
Keldrey: KELL-dray
Kendra: KEHN-drah
Keqwith: KECK-with
Khoriseth: KORE-ih-seth
Khralsh: KRAHLSH
Kishkim: KISH-kim
Korbin: KORE-bin
Leyja: LAY-ja
Lorynda: lore-INN-da
Maritta: mah-RITT-ah
Miel: mee-ELL
Miray: MEE-ray
Mowbray: MOE-bray
Naitan: Nye-TAHN
Niona: Nie-OWN-ah
Norenda: Nore-EN-dah
Obed im-Shakiri: OH-bed eem-shah-KEE-ree
Okreti di Vos: oh-KREH-tee dee VOHS
Omunda: oh-MOON-dah
Orestes: oh-RESS-teez
Oskina: oh-SKEEN-ah
Prinsep, prinsipi: PRIN-sep, prin-SIP-ee
Reinine: Rey-NEEN
Rozite: roe-ZEET
Saminda: sa-MIN-dah

Sanda: SAND-ah
Sarit: sah-REET
Sedil, sedili: SEH-dill, seh-DEE-lee
Serysta: se-RISS-ta
Shaden: SHAY-den
Shaluine: SHALL-you-een
Sidris: SIH-driss
Skola: SKOE-la
Sumald: soo-MAHLD
Syr: SEER
Taoling: TAH-oh-lind
Tchyrizel: CHIH-rih-zell
Terris: TAIR-riss
Tibre: TEE-breh
Tiray: TEE-ray
Tironde: tih-RAHND
Torchay Omvir: TOR-chay OHM-veer
Tsekrish: TSEH-krihsh
Turysh: TOOR-ish
Tylle: TILL-eh
Ukiny: oo-KEEN-ee
Untathel: OON-tah-thehl
Vanis Kevyr: VAN-iss KEH-veer
Veryas: VAIR-yahss
Vendra: VENN-drah
Vilaree: VILL-ah-ree
Viyelle Torvyll: vee-YELL TOR-vill
Xibyth: ZIH-bit
Zughralithiss: zoo-grah-LIH-thiss

# Glossary

*aila, ailo (aili)*—Sir or Madame, a title of respect in Adara

*brodir*—Tibran word with a meaning similar to "blood brother"

*dedicat*—Southron word indicating a person who has taken a special oath of dedication to the One

*di pentivas*—an ancient Adaran rite binding a man, usually a war prize or prisoner of some sort, into an ilian, without choice. Not presently practiced except in extreme circumstances

*durissas*—Adaran, a temporary agreement, rarely practiced except in rural, primitive sectors, in which additional persons are bound into an existing ilian during a crisis situation, to be dissolved when the crisis ends, unless otherwise agreed. Primarily intended for mutual protection, especially of children.

*ilian (iliani)*—four to twelve Adaran adults joined into a family unit—their version of marriage

*ilias (iliasti)*—spouse (spouses)

*jonglier*—a musician and/or story teller, an entertainer

*naitan (naitani)*—a person with a magical gift

*prelate*—a religious leader in Adara

*prinsep (prinsipi)*—the ruler (male or female) of one of the once independent governmental units now joined together to create Adara

*prinsipas (prinsipasti)*—the ilias of a prinsep
*prinsipella*—the offspring (male or female) of a prinsep
*prinsipality*—the "state" or "province" ruled by a prinsep
*Reinine*—the priestess-queen chosen by the collective Adaran prelates and prinsipi to rule Adara. A lifetime appointment, but not hereditary
*Reinas (reinasti)*—the ilias of the Reinine
*sedil (sedili)*—the relationship between children born into the same ilian. They may or may not have any blood relationship, but they are related in this manner
*selectors*—the fifty-seven prinsipi and prelates (the prinsep and head prelate of each of the twenty-seven prinsipalities, plus the head prelates of Arikon, Turysh and Ukiny) who gather upon the death of a Reinine to select the next Reinine
*skola*—a Southron place of learning, generally associated with the dedicats

GAIL DAYTON spent her younger years reading as many books as the library would let her check out (many thanks to the Houston Public Library System, which had no limits and would let her have ten books at once—as many as would fit in her bicycle basket), then changing the endings around to suit herself. Her favorites were the books with magic and adventure—the Red/Blue/Green Fairy Books, Andre Norton and Edgar Rice Burroughs among many, many others. Eventually she reached the point of making up her own stories and writing them down.

She currently lives in a very small town in the Texas Panhandle with her husband of many years, eagerly anticipating the soon-to-arrive empty nest. That ought to give her even more time to make up more stories.

If you enjoyed what you just read,
then we've got an offer you can't resist!

# Take 1 bestselling
# love story FREE!

# Plus get a FREE surprise gift!

## Clip this page and mail it to the Reader Service®

**IN U.S.A.**
3010 Walden Ave.
P.O. Box 1867
Buffalo, N.Y. 14240-1867

**IN CANADA**
P.O. Box 609
Fort Erie, Ontario
L2A 5X3

**YES!** Please send me one free LUNA™ novel and my free surprise gift. After receiving it, if I don't wish to receive any more, I can return the shipping statement marked cancel. If I don't cancel, I will receive one brand-new novel every month, before they're available in stores! In the U.S.A., bill me at the bargain price of $10.99 plus 50¢ shipping & handling per book and applicable sales tax, if any*. In Canada, bill me at the bargain price of $12.99 plus 50¢ shipping & handling per book and applicable taxes**. That's the complete price and a savings of 10% off the cover prices—what a great deal! I understand that accepting the free book and gift places me under no obligation ever to buy any books. I can always return a shipment and cancel at any time. Even if I never buy another book from LUNA, the free book and gift are mine to keep forever.

175 HDN D34K
375 HDN D34L

| | |
|---|---|
| Name | (PLEASE PRINT) |
| Address | Apt.# |
| City | State/Prov.      Zip/Postal Code |

### *Not valid to current LUNA™ subscribers.*

### *Want to try another series?*
### Call 1-800-873-8635 or visit <u>www.morefreebooks.com</u>.

\* Terms and prices subject to change without notice. Sales tax applicable in N.Y.
\*\* Canadian residents will be charged applicable provincial taxes and GST.
All orders subject to approval. Offer limited to one per household.
® and ™ are registered trademarks owned and used by the trademark owner and or its licensee.

LUNA04TR

©2004 Harlequin Enterprises Limited